GEARBREAKERS

GEARBREAKERS

ZOE HANA MIKUTA

FEIWEL AND FRIENDS

NEW YORK

A Feiwel and Friends Book
An imprint of Macmillan Publishing Group, LLC
120 Broadway, New York, NY 10271
fiercereads.com

Our books may be purchased in bulk for promotional, educational,
or business use. Please contact your local bookseller or the Macmillan
Corporate and Premium Sales Department at (800) 221-7945 ext. 5442 or
by email at MacmillanSpecialMarkets@macmillan.com.

Library of Congress Cataloging-in-Publication Data

Names: Mikuta, Zoe Hana, 2000- author.
Title: Gearbreakers / Zoe Hana Mikuta.
Description: First edition. | New York : Feiwel and Friends, 2021. |
    Audience: Ages 13-18. | Audience: Grades 10-12. | Summary: In an
    age of 100-foot-tall mechanical deities run by a tyrannical regime,
    two teenaged girls on opposite sides of a war discover they are fighting
    for a common purpose—and falling for each other.
Identifiers: LCCN 2020038685 | ISBN 9781250269508 (hardcover)
Subjects: CYAC: Science fiction. | War—Fiction. | Mecha
    (Vehicles)—Fiction. | Love—Fiction. | Lesbians—Fiction. | Youths'
    writings.
Classification: LCC PZ7.1.M5554 Ge 2021 | DDC [Fic]—dc23
LC record available at https://lccn.loc.gov/2020038685

ISBN 978-1-250-26950-8 (hardcover)
ISBN 978-1-250-84204-6 (special edition)

First edition, 2021
Book design by Mike Burroughs
Feiwel and Friends logo designed by Filomena Tuosto

Printed in the United States of America

10   9   8   7   6   5   4   3   2

To the reckless, lovestruck kids.
(The former may be lethal,
but the latter makes it worth it.)

CHAPTER ONE

SONA

It makes sense that, when the times were desperate enough, when the people were frenzied enough, at a certain point we went past praying to deities and started to build them instead.

I never truly appreciated that before.

Then my eyes open, and I choke at the sight of the bleeding heavens.

Even as I grapple for the edges of the bed, dry heaving over its side, even as the red sky burns above me, I understand. The logic of it all. The brutal, human need for greater beings.

Human.

I blink once, slowly, waiting for the rest of my thoughts to align.

They left those, at least.

I sit upright, bringing my hands around to inspect, noting how my fingertips still twitch at my command. They look like mine. All the calluses are still there, hard and smooth like river stones across my palms. I peel back my left thumb, searching for the thin, pale scar that marks its base, where again and again I would bury my nail to suffocate the quivering of my hands.

My hands will never tremble again, but not because I am absent of fear now. In that respect, they have not changed me at all.

There is no scar.

This, too, makes sense. Calluses have use. Scars have memories and not much else. Keep the soldier and discard her flaws, and make her a God.

I press the nail of my forefinger to where the scar should curl.

Coil inward, tighter, tighter, knuckle flashing white, wait patiently for the skin to give—

The small sliver splits open. A red drop rolls off my skin and breaks against the tile floor.

They did not take away my blood, but they did take my pain.

I will not get that back until I am synced with the Windup.

My Windup.

I look back up again to watch the red morning sky, still scattered with specks of aether and a pale moon that remains resiliently pinned despite the blush of the horizon.

If I opened my mouth, I could ask the ceiling to flicker to a star-choked cosmos, or an eternal thunderstorm, or any of a million other fantastical images. Only the best amenities for the Academy's top students.

I do not speak. Whatever I wish for will still be glazed with red, just like the walls, just like my limbs. I am terrified that my voice has changed. They could have altered it in any way they pleased, or taken it altogether. Just like they took my pain, my breath, my eye.

It does not matter—whatever projections splay across the ceiling, they are nothing more than a collection of mirages against cold concrete. Just pretty things suffocating hard truths.

I have long learned to be cautious of pretty things. Of beauty, of the grace of Gods formed from steel and wire . . .

It is all just warm skin hiding wires and bolts and the sharp edges of microchips.

Move. The thought flourishes, brittle with panic. *You need to move, or the fear will seal you here.*

I peer over the side of the bed. Slowly touch a toe against the ground, testing my weight, waiting for some seam to split the length of my leg, some part of me they forgot to seal up when they were finished bestowing the Mods.

I put my other foot to the ground and ease myself fully off the bed.

I do not unravel.

I do not even waver.

There is no longer a need for breath, and without the rise and fall of my chest, I feel so very still. My panic is a soundless, hollow thing.

The lights lining the mirror flicker on as I enter the bathroom. The tiles that encase the walls are pure black. Blue stone flecks the white marble sink. I know this. I know this, but as much as I cling to the memory of shades past, everything around me bleeds crimson.

Although . . . *bleeds* is not quite the right word for it.

I have made things bleed before; that red is always contained. It stains clothes and floorboards and lips, only things that *I* have permitted it to.

But this hue laps at my feet like ocean waves and corrupts the air I struggle to remember not to breathe, and it does not feel like victory.

This damn eye.

The left eye, to be exact. The distinction is important. One is artificial, one is not. One holds red and soaks the world through with it, and the other belongs to me.

It takes a while for me to drag my sight from the counter to the mirror, and when I do, Windup Pilot Two-One-Zero-One-Nine is there to catch my gaze. She wraps her fingers around my arms, parts my lips and folds my shoulders inward, and pulls a grating, splintering sound from my throat—part gasp, part ragged cry.

Right before the sound dies, it skips into a laugh.

What the hells have I done?

The Pilot moves her hands from her arms to her face, taking inventory of the features. Her father's strong jaw, the curls that bow against it. Her mother's soft nose and mouth, the fine, lovely shape of her eyes—but mine are larger, like they were drawn into place with an unhurried hand, or so she used to say.

They never dreamed that their daughter would hold so much more than bone and blood.

"My name . . ." The whisper comes at a crawl. "My name is Sona Steelcrest."

Their daughter is still here.

"My name is Sona Steelcrest. I am still human."

I am still here.

They could not carve me away completely, not without also removing the pieces that they wish to use. That they *need* to use.

How lucky I am, to be perfect now.

I pause, then place my palm over the left eye.

Color comes crashing back into place as the Mod disengages. Black spills against the tiles and brown pours into my hair and my eye. It is all so much better than the red that gleams beneath my hand, the red that they forced into me.

How lucky I am that when the Academy surgeons were sifting about—ripping away those pesky human imperfections—they did not burn their hands on every venomous thought that festers under my skin. That they did not think to look closer, where across each vein and bone, I have carved out the promise that in time, I will take them apart, too.

I pull my palm away slowly, leaving their eye closed, and stare at the half-blind girl staring back. She is wrought of bolts and wires and metal plates. She is wrought of bone and blood, and of rage.

"My name is Sona Steelcrest. I am still human." I take a breath, allow it to coil through me, to ignite me. "I am here to destroy them all."

CHAPTER TWO

SONA

There are seams, fissures in the skin, cutting a neat box into both of my forearms.

When I touch one and feel only me, I think to myself, *The panel is grafted with your own skin, your own nerves, and this is why you do not have to cry.*

Heat curling behind my eyes, I weigh one arm in my hand, switch, weigh the other. Feels the same. Feels fine. My teeth dig graves in my bottom lip.

A knock sounds at the door.

The room's mirage wavers before vanishing completely, depriving me of the false morning sky, and instead reveals the concrete-bound window that overlooks the vastness of Godolia. As the crown jewel, the Academy sits at the very center of the city, the epicenter of a tightly packed metropolis expanding fifty miles in each direction. Everything past the walls is considered the Badlands, dotted by resource villages and ravaged by wars past—and to the borders of this continent, the city-nation of Godolia owns it all.

From this far up, the only things I see are the other skyscrapers with enough height to best the ghostly fog, reaching up out of the mist like the lonely cypress trees of a marsh.

When the door slides open, I salute with a firm hand, forefinger steady on my brow, eyes dropped to the visitor's combat boots.

"At ease," Colonel Tether says evenly.

I now have permission to raise my sight, but I am still not permitted to look him in the eye. Students are never allowed to look the superiors in the eye.

I was unaware of this rule during my first week as a student of the Windup Academy, an instance that provoked this man's heel to seek purchase in my stomach, as well as my side when I had the audacity to drop to my knees. Twelve years old, gasping for air on the floor, it was not until I was done gagging that I realized how lucky I was. Lucky that I was hurt instead of discarded, tossed back out on the city streets from where they first plucked me, that when I was broken and starved they fed me. Lucky that when I was alone and lost, they gave me the chance to be worshipped, to be a divine thing.

Because they are merciful.

Godolia is a merciful place.

Tether steps closer. I do not move.

He must be able to see it—this throbbing disgust, the sick, overwhelming feeling of wrongness eating away at my every natural piece. How could he possibly miss it when it is all I can focus on, when it is all I can do to keep my feet sealed in place?

"Steelcrest," Tether murmurs low, "are you ready to become a Valkyrie?"

Despite myself, my heart skips a beat, and in the wake of it, a laugh nearly unfurls from my throat. We are small. We are mortal. And I am being asked if I am ready to become a God.

There is nothing else I could possibly say. "Yes, sir."

He turns on his heel and starts at a brisk walk, leading me

out of my bedroom and away from the residential wing, down a flight of stairs and onto the classrooms level. We pass the simulation domes, where children who span the ages of twelve to sixteen are encased inside luminescent glass barriers, arms outstretched toward the images flickering within their headsets. From behind their eyepieces, they see armies of autonomous mechas, helicopters rigged with submachine guns, and green tanks with cannons aimed at their heads. From within their domes, they shift their stances to evade, protect, and eliminate.

One dome we pass holds a girl, her hair tied back into twin tails that end just below her ears. She is barefoot and wears the Academy student uniform: black cargo pants and a gray shirt, dark in the places her perspiration has saturated the material. I do not know what virtual war she sees behind her eyepiece, but I know the moment she loses. Her guarding stance is weak, timid. Her sight flickers to the left behind the green-tinted glass, and she raises her arm, up, up, up—and hesitates.

Whatever is attacking her does not. Her defense breaks. Her small body is flung to the ground with an earsplitting cry, and her hands clutch at her ribs. She cannot be more than thirteen.

I keep walking.

The simulations told me I was damn good at this. At war.

They told the Academy I was ready to kill, to give me a mecha.

But those were simulations. Child's play, for any child feral enough.

We enter a glass elevator. Tether jabs one of the silver buttons with his thumb before tossing a sickly grin over his shoulder.

"You look nervous, Steelcrest."

"No, sir."

I listen for the small click that signifies the doors have sealed.

"I should remind you," he says, turning, head bending toward mine. "You do not have my permission to die during the test run."

I skim my thumb over my sleeve, over the thin gap carved into the skin there. "Or what?"

His grin freezes. "I've misheard you."

"You have not." I look up, sifting leisurely through his vulgar, stonelike features. Across the stubble of his chin, the curl of his mouth, the unfortunate poise of his nose. "If I die during the test run, without your blessing . . . what will you do?"

My gaze claws its way onto his.

I do not know what color his eyes are, and I do not care to.

There is no tech in his left iris, and it marks the absence of his ability. Perhaps a smidge of skill exists buried beneath the layers and layers of petty arrogance, but it could never measure up to the power that the Academy has implanted in my veins.

"You are out of *line*, Steelcrest," Tether growls.

"And you forget yourself, Tether," I say softly. "It would not be fun for you to hurt me anymore. Not when there is no pain to make me scream, correct?"

The elevator slips down into the haze, and the glowing infestation of my left socket becomes the only source of light amid the dark.

"Besides," I say to his shocked silence, "how much of me do you dare damage now?"

I am truly asking. He wants to break me into jagged little

9

pieces; I can tell by the twitch in his jaw, the way lines in the skin around his mouth go taut and pale. He can want all he likes.

He does not speak.

The elevator sinks beneath the smog, and the city bursts into view. Skyscrapers spiral upward into the haze, as if the shining beasts have the strength to support the heavens themselves. Every edge and crook is beaded with soft light, and from my tainted sight, it is as if everything is painted over in a glittering, crimson luminescence. It pours into the streets winding below, crooked and teeming with movement.

Strings of twinkling lights and paper lanterns are woven thick over the streets, sidewalks and roads alike congested by streams of people. Food vendor carts blast steam from underneath their painted plastic tarps. Skeletal girls teeter in pointed heels on street corners, wrapped in silks glazed with the streetlights, beckoning to the passersby who gawk with wide eyes.

It smells clean inside the elevator, like crisp linen and a tinge of bleach. I imagine the stench of sweat and dirty rainwater and car exhaust of the streets below. But I have not been outside in seven years. Perhaps things have changed.

Like me. Now, I do not know which smell I detest more. Inside or out, this whole city is suffocating.

These are the fortunate people, down below, even pressed together as they are, living under Godolia's protection rather than its gluttony. The only thing they had to do was happen to be born as one of its citizens, rather than one of the Badlands'. This has always been the way of the world: Some are born with luck, and the rest scramble to survive whatever the lucky ones might do with it.

The elevator enters the earth, plummeting down into complete darkness once again. Our descent slows, and my disgust thickens as the doors peel back.

We have arrived at the Windup hangar.

Where the mechas are assembled and garrisoned.

Where they rest after returning from the Badlands, and get the blood and carnage under their feet washed away and glossed over in an innocent, clean coat of paint.

Tether snatches my wrist, towing me along faster. His fingernails nip at my skin, but I ignore the dull prickling and allow my eyes to wander across the Windups that tower all around us, their gleaming metallic heads nearly touching the two-hundred-foot ceiling.

My lip curls. Their sheer size is a ludicrous; it is terrifying, and this is its purpose: to inspire and gorge on that very human feeling of smallness, of helplessness.

The mechas are given humanlike features, their iron skin molded meticulously to hold anger in their brows, lips taut in concentration, daggerlike eyes narrowed in their determination. When they are wound by a Pilot, their dimmed pupils will ignite into a smoldering crimson hue.

Once I begin the winding, once the wires the Academy forced through my bloodstream connect with the mecha's central power core, those eyes will be mine. The Valkyrie will be me, and I will be it, and I will move each part with the same ease with which I moved my fingertips.

The mechas stand divided by their respective units, polished head to toe, glittering sadistically beneath the industrial lights. To our left, the Berserker Windups, who possess more than enough artillery in their palms and their ribs to level a skyscraper. Next, the Paladins, reaching only eighty feet in overall height but serving more as battering rams than anything else, with a yard-thick layer of iron serving as skin. The Phoenix Windups shimmer with a red finish, even without this eye cloaking my view, signifying the flames they spit from the thermal cannons substituting for their right arms. Any creature that dares come close to their wound state will be met with near-instant second-degree burns.

"Steelcrest," Tether barks. We have stopped, and I go cold, all at once, sick with the urge to run from the feet of the deity before us. We are here too quickly. I cannot do this. I cannot possibly do this.

But I have to look. Because it is mine. Because it is going to be me.

I close my left eye, tilt my chin back and up, up, up— and *swear* that arrogant smirk across her ivory lips quirks a bit higher.

Greaves that shimmer gold guard her lithe shins, stretching close to five times my stature. Past that, a collection of black steel armor plates are bolted the length of her hips to her chest, breaking into clefts around her shoulders and spilling down her arms in an assemblage of ruthless, needlelike spikes, tinged by snowcap white. And far, far above, she looks outward with a ruby-speckled gaze that flickers dangerously beneath a furrowed brow. A knight's helmet, black and trimmed with gold, is etched with feathers. Her steel hands, clasped together as if in prayer, are encased within a pair of chrome-plated gloves, and between them, a black longsword rests between her palms. Iron outlines its blade, tip providing the barest kiss to the ground in front of us.

I am trapped in a wave of awe, disgust, and cold fear.

"Valkyrie," I whisper. "She is beautiful."

"That she is," chirps a voice, inches from my ear.

We were taught not to flinch; we were taught to strike. But when I turn, fist raised, a hand curls itself around my wrist—quick, startlingly quick—and a face is suddenly pressed close to mine. A red, glowing eye, bulging from its left socket, twitches over my stunned expression.

"Well! This is the first time I've almost been punched out by one of my Pilots," he says, a laugh lifting his words. My thumbnail hovers an inch away from his jaw, but he does not seem bothered by the near miss. "Before a proper introduction, anyway."

The young man releases me and places a hand on his hip. The other reaches back, fingertips curling to scratch at the nape of his neck. My sight catches on the clear rectangular indentation spiraling from his wrist to his elbow. My thumb unconsciously skims over the sleeve of my own forearm.

"They said you were young, but Gods," he murmurs. His other eye holds ice, blue as a clear noon sky. My gaze flicks over the rest of his features: white-blond hair, milky complexion with dimples like sinkholes, an attentive smile. I do not return it. "Name's Jonathan. Jonathan Lucindo. I'm your unit captain. You're Bellsona Steelcrest, correct?"

"Just Sona—"

"That's correct," Tether interjects at the same time. Lucindo glances over to the colonel like he just noticed the latter's presence, and his eyes tread downward, where Tether's grip still chokes my wrist.

"I asked *her*, Mister," Lucindo says, lips quirking on the common formality. The expression is gone as swiftly as it appeared, replaced by a chilling stare. "Do you think she's going to start swinging at you, too?"

Tether blinks. "Sir?"

Lucindo's grin is cheerful, but far from warm. "Let go of the Valkyrie."

A scoff trickles from Tether's lips as his fingers slither away from my wrist like maggots, each leaving behind a crescent-shaped imprint in the skin.

"Do not die and embarrass me, child," he spits.

I take a moment to imagine the mark my knuckles would leave across his cheekbone, the way I would bite down on the thrill of the fight I have never dared to chase. And I would win this one, too, like I have all the rest. But power comes from finishing fights, not starting them. So instead, my fist uncoils at my side. I smile and say, "I will damn well die when I please."

Tether stalks off, most likely to find a place to watch the winding, and behind me, Lucindo chuckles darkly. I turn to find the Valkyrie has offered his hand.

My bravado freezes in my chest. I stare at the panel set into his arm, the area where the Academy eased open his flesh and stole Gods know what from him. From both of us. Now he stands before me, blinking his eyes as if they both belong to him, pretending that the gesture he offers is full of only his blood and his bones, and not the wires that encircle them.

I square my shoulders and salute my new captain, an act he will consider to be derived out of respect rather than a resolution of my own fear. I need my full focus to survive the test run, and I will not be able to retain it if I clasp Jonathan Lucindo's hand and find it cold as the copper that runs through us both.

"Well, then, Just Sona," he says, retracting the handshake and flashing a smile. "Happy seventeenth birthday. Let's see what you've got, shall we?"

Despite this current infestation of Gods, the world used to be a truly Godless place.

Skyscrapers bloomed above the clouds as cities bulged with numbers they could not sustain, besieged by famine and diseases against which they had no shield. Fear and desperation flooded the streets like sewage, and like in ancient times, the human spectrum began to shift in one of two directions—toward gluttony and sin, as people sought pleasure to stall the pain, or toward piety, as people sought the Gods to save us all. The desperately righteous carved out a new theology, one that combined the deities of the dominant world religions into a single doctrine, and punished the people who had turned immoral with the proclamation of a twin hell eternity: one purgatory for the sins of the flesh, and one for the sins of the mind.

This religious fervor only exacerbated unsteady diplomatic relations between nations. As they panicked and prayed and found it was not enough, found they needed their deities here for them, to kill for them. They sculpted their new weapons of mass destruction in the image of the Gods, and called them the Windups.

It was a completely new kind of warfare—it is a completely new scale of destruction, when people find divinity in bloodshed.

Two and a half centuries ago, the world witnessed the beginning of the Springtide War, where the most powerful nations possessed the most powerful Windups, using their mechas to claim dominance over the planet's already sparse resources. The battles were hardly fought at all with human lives—until Godolia, ruthless in its determination, created the first generation of piloted Windups rather than the conventional autonomous systems.

It was a bit ironic, I suppose, that they utilized the human factor by ripping out some of the human parts. That was the purpose of creating the Academy: to find those with flawless reaction times, who had a knack for battle tactics, and, of course, those who possessed the raw instinct that no amount of gears and bolts and wires could replicate.

And so Godolia rose, pronouncing itself the capital of the world—what was left of it, at least, after the War, littered with felled idols and cut with ribbons of dead, dry earth. They tell us the Windups were meant to be a beacon of hope. They tell us it is as if the Gods themselves have descended to protect us all. They tell us to celebrate red skies and flesh rendered painless, for these mark our inhuman parts, our more than human parts.

Yet I have been biting back a scream since I woke up from the surgery. For me, and for everyone living outside Godolia's limits and under its thumb, what had been meant to end terror ended up thriving on it.

As Lucindo turns toward the Windup, I glimpse the insignia sewn across the back of his dark gray military jacket. It is the mark of the Valkyrie unit: a black sword, blade and handle edged with silver thread, stitched painstakingly into the image of the night sky.

The only things bigger than us are the heavens, and barely, our spines pressed fast against the stars.

He leads me to the base of my Valkyrie, where a door is etched into the metal of her boot.

"Look into there," he says, pointing at a small glass orb that juts out of the door. I lean in, but he shakes his head. "No, no. Open your left eye."

I hide my grimace and follow his command. The door slides open, revealing the inner workings of the Windup. A ladder spirals up the inside of her calf, and Lucindo begins to climb.

The mecha's innards brim with copper and silver wires that hiss with electricity, gears that whir together seamlessly, and valves that spew steam over the rungs of the ladder. As we near her chest area, I catch sight of a large box suspended in the same place a heart would rest: the Windup's central power core.

Once the chip they implanted at the base of my brain stem syncs to its network, the Valkyrie will be wound, and we will be one.

That, of course, assumes that my brain can survive the stress.

I pause on the ladder, noting the platform that branches off the core's box, coming to rest a few feet above my head.

"You coming or what?" Lucindo calls, ten rungs ahead.

"Why . . . why is there a platform?"

"What?"

I loosen my grip on the ladder to point. "Why is there need for a platform?"

He blinks. "For the guards to stand on."

"Guards?"

"Yeah, guards."

I keep my mouth closed for a few moments, before the curiosity pries it back open. "Why is there need for guards?"

"Gearbreakers, of course."

I blink. "Gearbreakers?"

Did you hear? A Berserker was taken out yesterday, outside of Auyhill.

A Paladin went out last week and never came back.

They found that lost Pilot at the bottom of the Hana River. Should we be worried about the Gearbreakers?

Worried? another would always say. *We'll be Gods.*

"They still don't teach about Gearbreakers up there?" Lucindo asks, turning back to look at me.

"I thought they were classmate gossip." A beat of silence passes. "I do not think I understand. They . . . they are—"

"Tiny? Yeah, but they're clever, I hate to admit it. Once they get inside, it only takes one of them to bring the whole mecha toppling down. A few snipped wires here, a cracked gear there, and . . ."

I glance over the edge of the platform, where the Valkyrie's leg extends a hundred feet downward, supported by iron beams and metal plates and ribbed gears, some as small as my pinkie finger, others as large as my torso, each feeding into another. One simple jam in the rotations, and the mecha is scrap metal.

This is why they did not teach about Gearbreakers in the Academy. It would be teaching us that their Gods are delicate.

"I suppose it's just proof that Godolia's the only truly civilized nation left." Lucindo sighs. "The Gearbreakers . . . they're all just barbarians."

Barbarians who can pluck apart deities.

We reach the head, a space expanding larger than my bedroom. Two long windows mark the Valkyrie's eyes, which glare proudly over the Windup hangar from behind the grated visor. Luminescent glass is set into the center of the floor, the same size and shape as the base of a simulation dome. From the ceiling above dangle a multitude of rubber-wrapped cables, and at the sight, a shriek begins to creep up my throat. I suppress it as Lucindo turns to me, offering me his hand again. This time, I take it.

He leads me over to the glass, which glows brighter once sensing our weight, and then to the very center of the cords. I can tell he is about to pull away, and my hand involuntarily tightens around his. Heat floods my cheeks. I wish they had taken away my ability to blush.

But Lucindo looks at me, eyes full of infinite understanding, smile almost reassuring. I drop his hand.

"Palms up, please," he says, voice suddenly soft.

I raise them, and he gently peels back my sleeves, fully revealing the panels running up my forearms. At his single press, they pop open, and I brace myself. To see blood and bone and arteries that bulge with each rapid heartbeat, threads of veins that glisten under the sudden light. To feel raw flesh growing cold against the air.

But there is nothing but a smooth, silver dish lying within each arm, lined on each side by a tidy row of small sockets.

Lucindo sees the shock on my face and chuckles. "I was expecting it to be disgusting, too," he says. "But they cleaned us up pretty nicely, huh?"

I wipe my features again, and nod at him to continue. He reaches up to grasp one of the cords, tugging it down to my forearm.

"You won't be synced until these are all attached," he murmurs, snapping a cord into one of the sockets with a small click. "And once you are, once the Valkyrie is wound, take it slow at first. It's almost like waking up in the morning."

My left arm is attached, six cords spilling into my skin,

like blood trickling from the radial vein. Nausea clenches at my stomach, and in the wake of it, I think of bolting. I think of wrapping the cords around his neck and *twisting* and my hands grabbing the ladder rungs before his body can hit the floor. I think of how many feet I can get before a bullet shatters the back of my skull.

I think of death, and how I think too much on it, and how little damage a corpse can inflict.

Lucindo moves to my right. "And you'll get the ability to feel pain back, too. It's like . . . it's a different kind of hurt, though. Like . . . ghost hurt, because in the back of your head you know it's not real, and you know that you can rip the cords out at any time and it'll be gone. I guess it's a little odd to think about it that way, like part of you doesn't exist. But you will get used to it."

I will get used to it.

His hand freezes, a cord pinched between his fingertips, hovering over the last empty socket. He glances up at me. Dull and glowing. Natural and unnatural.

"Do it," I say.

"I can't. Not if you're not ready. You need to be in the right mindset, or that little chip at the base of your head is going to fry you."

He waits as my silence seeps into the air.

"Okay, listen, Sona," he says, relaxing his grip a little. The cord leaves his hand to hang in the air. "You know why the Valkyries are the most elite unit of Windups? Why we're the most valued, why we handle only the most dangerous missions?"

"They . . . ," I start, stumbling to remember my lessons. "They are the quickest mechas ever created, because of their lightweight metal. They are the most carefully crafted of all the other units, so they nearly have the intricacy of the human body. Their hip, heel, and leg joints are set with detailed, tiny gears, so they can twist their stance, such as to perform a roundhouse, whereas other Windups can only walk or run. They can mirror any fighting style used by their Pilot with complete precision."

Lucindo shakes his head. "Incorrect, Sona."

"It is not."

"It most certainly is, in fact," he says, stepping closer. His eyes bore into mine. "You mean to say *I*. *I* am the quickest mecha ever created. *I* fight with complete precision. *I* am the strongest Windup. *I* am a Valkyrie. Say it, soldier."

I raise my chin. "I am a Valkyrie."

Lucindo flashes a grin and reaches for the last cord. I close my eyes, and the world ceases to be red, or colorful, or anything else.

The cord clicks into me.

A shock seizes my spine, a bolt of electricity that throws me to my knees and causes a cry to tear free from my throat. The jolt forces my eyes open, but I do not find the glass floor beneath my knees as I expected.

Rather, Colonel Tether's face is drawn wide with startled features.

The rubber of his boots screams across the floor as he staggers backward to escape the space between my gloved fingers, splayed flat against the ground. My other hand is wrapped around the grip of my sword, glinting wickedly in my peripheral vision.

I raise my head, noting the number of people who have gone still at the sight of me. Ignoring their stupor, I bring a hand up to my eyes, watching my fingertips twitch and the chrome gleam.

Oh.

I did not expect it to feel like this.

Like nothing new, nothing foreign at all.

It is just . . . *me.*

For the first time in a long time, I feel quite like myself again.

I rise to my full height, and their eyes follow me, gorging themselves on the God awakened. I take a step, and somewhere in the back of my consciousness, I know that I sense the glass floor shifting beneath my feet, the wires that grace my skin, and Lucindo's gaze boring into my back. I know about my second self, small as those gawking before me, but for right now, we are not one and the same. I am someone she could never be.

I am someone who could destroy Godolia.

The Windups were created to protect this nation.

I was created to protect this nation.

Godolia needed me, and so the Academy pulled me apart and put the Mods in the places where there was once breath and life and color and called it my evolution.

They said I should celebrate the day the sky bled.

I am celebrating. I am *reveling.*

Because they did not simply create another Pilot. Another soldier. Another protector.

They created nothing short of their own downfall.

"This feels good," I say, and I think she is smiling, that she is grinning ear to ear. "This feels really fucking good."

CHAPTER THREE

ERIS

Three Weeks Later

There's a lot of reasons to wake up kind of pissed.

You could blame it on the first thing you see every morning—a ceiling riddled with water damage, cracks splitting the cheap plaster into structurally questionable fragments. You could blame it on the fact that you're sweating from the dull heat produced by the fair-haired boy slumped underneath the covers next to you, or the fact that last night he took your shirt off and maybe some other choice articles of clothing, and at some point you'll have to go hunting for them.

Or maybe blame your driver, who's banging at the door with her little caffeine-fueled fists, screeching at you to get your ass out of bed because there's another two-hundred-foot-tall mecha on the loose and it's severely fucking up the world and it's your job to deal with it.

Blame anything and everything, because it hardly matters. Wake up pissed, wake up grinning—I still have to pull on my shoes and try not to die today.

"I'm awake, screw off!" I yell, and then the dust crowds my throat and I double over in a graceful coughing fit.

Seventeen-ish years ago, my parents named their second daughter after one of the many Gods of discord, destining that even as a chubby infant toddling around the renegade compound, I was synonymous with chaos.

Seventeen-ish years later, as I rub the sleep from my eyes with the heels of my hands, I think I can only manage one or two mediocre disasters before I have to take a nap.

I peel back the blanket, only one of my feet skimming the hardwood floor before Milo's hand catches my wrist. His eyes are still glazed with sleep, lips parted in a sloppy smile.

"You at least owe me five more minutes," he mumbles.

"Like hells I do," I snap, yanking my hand away. I stand, the cold from the floor immediately seeping up my legs, and for a moment I consider his offer. But then I mentally shake myself.

"Get out," I growl in the same harsh tone. "We have work."

He props himself up on his elbows, a crooked smile dimpling his right cheek. He watches me change into a pair of black overalls yanked from one of the piles of clothes heaped around the room. I narrow my eyes, scanning the floor.

"Looking for this?" he asks, producing my bra from underneath the sheets, strap dangling from a calloused fingertip. He already looked a little overly comfortable; now he looks far too smug.

I ease myself onto the edge of the bed, reclaiming my bra with one hand, and using the other to sweep the hair from his brow.

"Hey," I murmur, leaning in, lips brushing close to his. "I know it's early, babe, and I know we have a long day ahead of us." I smile wide. He feels it coming, but my fingers tangle in his hair before he can recoil, forcing his head back, making the whites eat up those pretty blue irises. "But when your crew captain says get out, it means you're getting out."

"Or what?" Milo taunts, though his own smile is nervous

24

now. "You going to carry me over the threshold like it's our wedding night, Eris?"

"You can carry yourself." I spot my shirt peeking out from beneath the blanket and release him to pull it on. "It's just the choice of whether your weight is on your feet or your hands, because I'll only let you keep one set."

He's up by the time I finish slipping my arms through the overall loops, taking the warmth with him as he stands to tug up his jeans. I drop to the floor and dig a hand underneath the bed, my fingers finding the familiar strap of my welding goggles.

"Your threats are better than coffee," he informs me.

I jerk the goggles on. "Designed to keep you up at night."

Milo pauses before the door, considering, and then turns around to plant a kiss on my lips. I let him, because although everything tastes likes cinders in the Hollows, he sometimes makes the ash a little sweet.

"Love you," he says, and I don't say it back. Not because it isn't true, necessarily; more because there's always a chance of him getting stepped on by a Windup and dying a horrible, excruciating death.

A bleeding heart doesn't really fit into this line of work. Not that I don't have one, or that I'm not viciously attached to each little idiot making up the crew—I'm just aware it's a problem. So I don't think about them dying too much, just like I don't think about loving all of them too much. Thinking about one always feeds the other, and then my heart feels like a sinkhole in my chest, and in all honesty, *screw that*.

I wait for the sound of the door shutting, and when it doesn't come, I say without turning, "You must be an absolute masochist if—"

"I'm not," comes another voice, thick with boredom.

I turn. Jenny stands in my doorway, leaning up against the frame, dark canvas jacket loose off one pale shoulder. Her own welding goggles perch on her crown, lenses as black as her eyes and her long hair, which crowds wildly around her shoulders whenever she's not fighting. A clipboard dangles from her fingers, Windup blueprints fluttering weakly.

I snatch the clipboard from her hand, singing, "You got suspended again."

Jenny says nothing, doesn't even look at me; just uncaps the pen from behind her ear and crosses something off her list, which is written across the length of her arm:

> ~~HARRY (DELIVER INTEL)~~
>
> ~~POPPY (DELIVER INTEL)~~
>
> ~~LITTLE BASTARD (DELIVER INTEL)~~
>
> REALIZE: I WON'T BE ON SUSPENSION IF I
>
> BREAK SUSPENSION (FIGHT ROBOTS)

Then she snatches my wrist, and, ignoring my shouts, scribbles wildly on the back of my hand:

> IF FOUND: BURY.

She resets the cap with her teeth and walks away, gaze rolling over her shoulder to call back in an uninterested breath, "Rot, little sister."

"Yeah, yeah." I shut the door and stand in front of the mirror, tucking flyaway strands of black hair into the strap of my goggles, then try to wipe the marker from my hand. It only smudges and stains my fingers.

Just above the front of my overalls, the black dots that scatter across my collarbone are blatant underneath the white shirt. One tiny, inked gear for each takedown.

Eighty-seven gears.

Eighty-seven mechas scraped from the skyline.

I know what makes the Windups tick, and each time I creep inside their limbs, I know precisely which pieces to pluck and shatter to make the entire atrocity collapse like a house of cards. Because as much as Godolia likes to preach otherwise, the line between their deities and scrap metal can be snipped away by simple human hate.

And the Bots—the Pilots who glow red and hold more wire in them than skin and bone, who gave up being human to destroy *my* people—they're no different. The Windups can't function without their movements, so when the gears don't provide enough destruction, they're my next target. They're even easier to dismantle than the mechas.

I grin at my reflection. I won't say I'm synonymous with chaos, not truly. If this world has taught me anything, it's that humans have no right playing pretend at being Gods.

But I am a Gearbreaker, and that comes pretty damn close.

Dust in their hair, fire in their cheeks, draped over our common room's worn, moth-eaten furniture like they were kicked into place, at too-fucking-early o'clock, every single kid of my crew is a sight for sore eyes. And—unfortunately—I wouldn't be doing my job right if I weren't constantly sore.

Nova, our driver, is settled on the splintering table, her tiny form balanced on her toes, legs tucked in her usual precarious perch. She's having popcorn for breakfast again, chucking the burnt pieces into the mousy fluff of Theo's hair. Neck lolled over the side of the fraying love seat, legs kicked over its puckering back, our marksman grumbles obscenities as he hunts for the wayward kernels.

On the couch, Arsen lies either dead or asleep, limp and facedown in Juniper's lap. June's face is turned, cheek to the back cushion, a faraway look in her brown eyes as she twists the demolitionist's curls around scarred, hazel fingertips. Behind them, Xander hovers near the single window that allows entrance to only a sorry amount of light, face pressed far too close to the filthy glass, breath spreading clouds that match the ones outside.

Milo sits neatly at the table, a paperback book clutched in his hand, his rifle leaned casually against his chair.

"Morning," I say.

Milo is the only one who lifts his eyes to me. I ignore him completely.

"Gearbreakers, I said, *good morning*."

Nova looks over with a shit-eating grin already snaking across her lips. "You didn't say *good*."

I stare back, unimpressed. She sticks her tongue between the gap separating her two front teeth, wiggles it around, then chucks the popcorn bag at Theo's head. Kernels stick to rug fibers and love seat stitches, and sputter and crack in the fireplace.

Theo lunges. "You can *wither*, you little—"

"Do *not*—" I start forward, trying to snatch for his shirt collar, missing by miles.

Nova shrieks, feet scraping against the tabletop before launching herself onto Juniper—which also means launching herself onto Arsen. He yelps awake just as Theo meets them, and then there's four of them on the couch, thrashing and shouting. Xander turns from the window, button nose blotted with dirt, and crawls over the back cushion and into the fray. Milo turns a page, completely unbothered and completely unhelpful.

I take hold of a nearby chair and send it crashing into the far wall.

When I turn back, they're detangled and sitting respectfully in the remaining seats.

"Good," I say, kicking away a detached chair leg before looking down at my clipboard. The pages hold the blueprints of a Phoenix Windup, charts of the allotted time during which we'll have access to it, and information about the Pilot. All the data comes from previously Gearbroken mechas, or from guards and Bots heavily persuaded to tell. The intel is then distributed throughout the Hollows—the Gearbreaker headquarters—by the higher-ups to the crews most suited for the task. And my crew, though they may not look it right now, is always suited.

Reckless kids for reckless jobs, you could say. Plus, they know it's always good to let us blow off a little steam. We find other ways to fill the time, of course. We read whatever we can get our hands on (though June is the only one who likes the romance novels), have movie nights (Nova is banned from making the popcorn because she's terrible at it), and do general fun, recreational activities (like last week, when we thought we were about to paint the walls because Xander thought it'd be a kick to throw an old pin from one of Arsen's grenades onto the table while we were eating dinner, or like yesterday, when Theo hung Nova out the window, and afterward, when we all had to stop her from ripping his face off).

But for us, nothing beats Gearbreaking. Call us adrenaline junkies. Hells, call us suicidal. We don't take this lightly. We're good at what we do, and we do it for the people who can't and who couldn't.

"The Phoenix is guarding a cargo train running from Pixeria—that small mining town a couple dozen miles south of here—up to Godolia," I say, rubbing at a spot of toothpaste at the top corner of the page. It was dropped there about ten minutes ago when I was brushing my teeth and leafing through the intel, piecing together today's deicide plan while trying to ignore what an absolute wreck our bathroom is. I'm making them scrub it when we get back. "As they could not meet their ridiculous coal quota this month, Pixeria has requested our assistance in assuring the train never makes it to the station, or else their numbers will be logged as insufficient and a Windup will be sent out to massacre them by next nightfall. You know the drill: We take out the Phoenix escort, stop the train, ransack its contents, and return it to the town."

"And take the blame," chirps Juniper, beaming brightly so her dimples show.

"Happily." It's a win-win situation—the town's population is spared, as the coal is marked as stolen rather than inadequate, and my crew keeps climbing the ranks of Godolia's watch list. "Nova, you'll coast us between the train and the Phoenix, preferably avoiding its footsteps, and Xander and I will carve an opening in the ankle and get us inside. Milo and Theo, artillery, as per usual. I don't want any of us getting shot again, so, you know, shoot first and all. Next—"

"I want to drive this time," Theo says.

I turn a page, studying the blueprints of the train. "Sure. Give Nova your gun."

"*Yes.* Give Nova your gun," Nova mimics.

"Never mind," Theo says.

"Once we're in, Juniper and Arsen will jump onto the second train car and place explosives along the link that connects the cargo to the engine room," I continue. "If there happens to be a conductor that gets in the way, take him out, but don't go looking for a fight. I'm serious, you two. Stop grinning at each other like that. Nova will be close, so jump back to the car once the bombs are set. You'll blow them remotely. Ideally by that time, Xander and I will be done with the Windup. We'll try to get out the same way we came, but if the mecha is already collapsing, we'll have to wing it. Keep an eye out, for us and for the rubble. Any questions?"

The room is silent. As before every mission, excitement has begun electrifying the still air. It energizes our souls. We live for nothing except to catch sight of that last glint of crimson in the eyes of the mechas before they flicker out from existence, to cause nothing but discord and disarray and yet still blink back the smoke from our sight at the end of it all, and recognize the sheer ludicrousness—no, the sheer *impossibility*—that we still possess breath in our lungs.

I take a moment to look over the lot of them once more. Just a bunch of kids splayed over crumbling furniture, in a crumbling world, helping it to crumble even more. Kids hurt by Godolia and the Windups in the past, who've had people stolen from them, who were thrown into absolute hell and *came back*, kicking and screaming and wanting, more than anything, to return the favor.

Yeah, we're small. Yeah, we're human. But we're also Gear-breakers, and we're here to dismantle the fuckers who thought we'd just sit back and take it.

I put a hand on my hip.

"Gear up, Gearbreakers. None of you have my permission to die today."

CHAPTER FOUR

ERIS

Nova revs the engine when the rest of us come out of the dorms, one arm dangling out the open window, the sleeve of her heat suit glistening with the sunlight that has managed to evade the tree foliage.

We all climb into the back of the pickup truck, Milo claiming a seat next to me. I kick my feet on top of his, and he watches as I adjust the strap of the black cryo gloves around my wrists. Tubes of blue fluid are stitched tight against the fabric, intricate as veins inside a hand. A small button lies on the side of my forefingers, awaiting a quick press to bring the gloves roaring to life. They're my most prized possessions, perfect for every scenario—especially when it involves a Phoenix.

Nova weaves though the Hollows compound, occasionally sticking her head out the window to scream at the streams of people who wander from one building to the next, teetering blueprints or tools or breakfast bars in their hands. Throughout the compound, worn concrete paths wind around the trunks of ancient oak trees, tall as the heavens but so heavy with autumn leaves that they seem to crouch over the earth. Jenny rigs up some mirage tech over the forest when the trees go bare, but through the winter, most of us can't help but hold our breath whenever a Godolia helicopter passes overhead.

We approach the gates, and beside the operator, a familiar

figure looms. His canvas jacket is as black as the iron spikes behind him, spine stiff as the silver-hooked cane he leans against. His gray hair is shorn close to the scalp—apparently a military style in the ancient days, but I think it just makes the veins snaking his head that much more visible—and there's a muscle ticking in his scarred cheek. Wrinkles crack the skin edging his eyes.

James Voxter, the first Gearbreaker.

I pinch the bridge of my nose. "Ah, shit."

It's been nearly sixty years since Voxter proved that humans could take down Windups from the inside, sixty years since the people of his resource village attempted to flee Godolia's reign. Most try to slip their servitude by escaping overseas, so his village headed for the coast.

A half day later, they sent the Berserkers.

As night fell over the scene of the massacre, Voxter learned a very important lesson: From the beginning of Godolia's supremacy, there had been such a degree of fear injected throughout the Badlands that the people would always choose fleeing over fighting back, and that this mindset existed because they viewed the mechas as invincible. They only needed someone to show them that this was far from the truth.

So sixteen-year-old Voxter goes out with a few explosives in his pocket, and he picks a fight. The Gearbreaker resistance begins, founded on the basis of sending a message to both Godolia and the people of the Badlands: *We can fight back*.

I stand up to hand the gate operator my clipboard, and the silver handle of Voxter's cane hooks over the lip of the trunk.

"Oi! Don't damage my car, Vox," Nova snaps.

Voxter ignores her, rolling his gray eyes up to me. He's mad. Again. "Shindanai—"

"Hang on," I say, twisting back. Behind me, Juniper is seated next to Arsen. Both of their hands are entangled in the wires spilling across their laps, heads bent, Arsen's brown curls threading into Juniper's green-dyed hair. Vials of colorful liquids are kept steady between their pressed knees. I snap my fingers at them. "I told you guys to quit messing with those."

Arsen picks his head up, black eyes wide and innocent. "Don't you want the train to blow?"

"No, I want *part* of it to blow."

"Oh," he murmurs, looking back down at the wires. "Oh yeah."

"You gonna let us out?" I ask the operator. "We do have a train to catch."

"Shindanai," Vox starts again. "What's this I hear about one of your crew members hanging another out the window yesterday?"

I shrug. "First I've heard of it."

At the same time, Juniper says, "We put a mattress down below her, sir."

This is actually true, but because Voxter knows we're on the fifth floor, he opens his mouth to start screaming at us.

"Jenny's breaking her suspension right now," I tell him as the gate splits open. His face turns a nice shade of purple, and Nova shoves her foot to the gas as soon as there's just enough room for the car to squeeze through. Then Voxter and the Hollows are growing smaller and smaller behind us, the splotch of his cheeks blending with the smear of fall leaves. I grin and give him a small wave before taking my seat.

After a half hour, the trees peel away and Nova's maneuvering the car through the rubble of decimated buildings and small valleys of Windup footprints that we all know double as graveyards, even though bones pressed to fine dust don't leave much of a mark. The landscape is evidence of battles from long ago, when people fighting against Godolia's reign looked up to see the mechas blocking out the sky, in place of the Gods they'd prayed for.

All of us were born enlisted in an already-lost war. But after the Gearbreaker resistance began, after everyone realized that we had the ability to dismantle deities, there was something new. Something that makes me grin rather than writhe with pain at every new tattoo that gets pricked across my collarbone. Something an awful lot like hope.

In the front seat, Nova leans over to the glove box and pops it open, digging around the stash of tapes before selecting one. She blows on it affectionately, gives the plastic side a kiss, and throws a wicked grin into the rearview mirror as she shoves it home.

The music spills out in thumping peals, and a happiness comes screaming into place, so warm and light that all I can do is tilt my head back against Milo's shoulder, feeling the rush of wind stinging my cheeks.

After a while, the land evens out and there's nothing but loose dust caking the earth. At the horizon's point, the world splits into two perfect halves: blue sky and brown dirt, holding nothing but a 175-foot mecha and a train car approaching from the east.

Theo whoops and slaps his hand on the side of the truck.

"Punch it, Nova!" he squeals, and the engine revs, wings of dust flying out beneath us. We streak across the desert, shrieking with glee at doing something so reckless, so important.

We careen beside the railway track, wheels momentarily skipping across the chrome bolts before Nova yanks the wheel right, hurtling us into the sprawling cast of the Windup's shadow. A shiver ripples up my spine, and I grin as we flip our masks on simultaneously, intercom piece crackling to life in my ear. Dirt thrown back from the Phoenix's pounding feet clinks against the plastic visors.

Fifty yards from the target. Thirty. Nova does something especially cruel to the engine, a pop of fire spitting from the exhaust pipe, a rush in my chest as the breath in my lungs is forced back, and then it's ten.

"Cavalry," Arsen yawns into his microphone as the black neck of a submachine gun sprouts from the roof of the last train car, the gunman's face shielded by a bulletproof riot helmet.

Nova slams on the brakes, sending us lurching for a hold, and mere feet from the hood of the truck, the ground puckers and splits with a spray of bullets. The rounds tear toward us in a rupturing line, and Nova, humming in our ears, spins the wheel right, shoves the gear into reverse once we've carved a full one-eighty, and, bullets scraping the dirt we were just over, flings us backward at a breakneck pace.

"Neck," I say.

"Yeah." Milo brings the rifle to his shoulder, taking a quarter second to line up his sights, and buries the shot in the gunman's throat.

He falls back, then off the train entirely. He hits the ground and then he's far behind us, last breath taken by the dust.

As we dart up between train and Phoenix, Nova easing us as close to its running feet as she can, I jab my thumbs onto the cryo gloves' buttons, tubes igniting with a luminous blue.

"I'm primed!" I yell, leaning toward the Phoenix, one hand outstretched. Its left foot is dropping in front of us, with a force that would crack my teeth if they weren't already braced together. As its step settles, I slash my touch against the ankle, the panels running along my glove's palm and fingers bursting with cold energy. The broiling metal begins to steam.

I pull back before the force of the Phoenix's step can pull me from the truck, and at the same moment, Nova says, "Hand!"

The sky disappears as a red-plated palm descends, reaching straight down to try to grab the car whole and chuck us into the desert.

"Brake!" Theo shrieks.

"Speed up!" Juniper cries.

"What did I tell you about backseat driving?" Nova screeches back.

"Nova, keep the speed!" Arsen digs around in his jacket and produces a small round orb, flinging it upward. It attaches itself to the descending palm, its tiny light letting out two meager flickers before exploding in a blinding flash.

"Sticky bomb," Juniper giggles, lifting a hand to bat away the shower of fragmented metal.

She and Arsen turn toward the tracks, and he flashes a thumbs-up over his shoulder. "Ready when you are, Cap!"

Their explosives are never pretty, but—between Juniper's borderline sadistic corrosives and Arsen's demolition skills—I have no doubt it'll blow. They always do. I make a slight gesture to Theo, and his firearm flips in his hands, sight locking on the area of the Windup's leg where my palm had rested for a half instant. Now, beneath the surface of the Windup's skin, the cryo serum injected by my glove twists its way through the iron, devouring every particle of warmth that dares be in its path.

The butt of Theo's rifle collides with the ankle, and the skin shatters like a pane of glass.

"It's charging up," Arsen shouts, noting the sudden whirring sound in the air.

"That's your problem, not mine. I'm first," I say, watching the leg swing away in the Windup's next step, steam trailing from its wound. On its opposite side, the air around the thermal cannon is shimmering, prickled with heat as it readies its attack. "You're second, Xander. June, Arsen, the train."

I don't wait for them to respond; I don't need to. The calf coasts back, and I'm flying from the pickup truck's edge into the opening, suspended in open air for a tenth of a second before entering the mecha.

By instinct and muscle memory alone, my hand seizes the ladder's rung before I can slam into the opposite side of the calf, and I deactivate the cryo gloves before they splinter the metal. I press my body close to the ladder as the Windup takes another step, the force of it sending my breath to the front of my throat. Then the leg swings back, providing me a brief glimpse of both my crew and Xander barreling over the ridge that divides us. He makes it past the broken edge and grabs an open rung before he can crash into me.

He takes off his visor and hood, gaze rolling up silently.

We climb.

Wires hang thick across the air once we reach the hips. We creep off the ladder and onto a support beam that spans the abdomen, and I put a hand on Xander's head to keep him low, eyes scanning for any movement above us.

"Go to the right hip," I breathe. "Wait for my signal, and then jam the leg gears." He turns to leave, and I grab his scrawny arm, tugging back my visor so I can look him in the eye. "Our intel says we've got two guards. Don't be stupid about it. Call for help if you need it. This thing is going to fall hard and it's going to fall fast. Don't wait up for me. If you see an escape, take it. That's an order."

The kid, retaining his infinite silence, nods again and retreats up the support beam, dipping under a curtain of wires before vanishing. I still remember the days when I wouldn't let him out of my sight, let alone leave him to wander through a mecha unaccompanied. Not particularly because I was afraid of him getting killed, but because one of my crew members dying when I had just been named captain would've been highly embarrassing.

Luckily, I've built up enough of a reputation that all of them know there's no point in dying anyway, since, if they did so without my permission, I'd march down to the twin hells and drag them back through the gates myself.

I tilt my head up, locating the revolving mechanism that controls the left leg, eyes sifting through nuts and bolts and gears, padded with wire arteries and clumps of electricity-bright artificial nerves. Why Godolia would want to construct the mechas so that their wound Pilots can feel pain is beyond me, but I'm not complaining. That just gives me more options.

The thing about deities, I've learned, is that they all have a weak spot. And on the off chance that they don't, I can always make one myself.

"Hey!" someone shouts. My head snaps up to find that two silhouettes have materialized far above, the sharp outlines of guns in their hands. Crude, unimaginative weapons.

"Catch me if you—" I sidestep as a bullet pings the metal of the mecha's stomach lining, inches from my left ear. "—can. So—" Another round; I snap my arms to my chest, heart rattling in its cavity as my heel momentarily dips into nothingness. Soon as I right myself: "—*rude*. Wire*fuckers*. I don't need this."

I slip away before the next barrage can start. Melting into the shadows, I pick my way through the patchwork of dark paths of whirling gears and shuddering wires.

I jump a gap and drop low, sight lifted to the darkness above. *Scurry along. This is my deity now.*

The instant their figures wander out of earshot, I leap onto a vertical support beam, grappling the giant bolts and using them as footholds to scale the Windup. The mecha's momentum sends my teeth chattering, though that may just be the shock of adrenaline. Either way, I clench my jaw to avoid snipping my tongue off as I climb. The hip mechanism whirs above, its giant lever jabbing the air as the Phoenix runs.

I reach a hand over the platform that supports the hip, an edge about six inches wide. Pulling myself up, I brace my feet against the landing, pressing my back against the support beam. Below me expands a straight hundred-foot drop, one that spirals clean through the leg to the bottom of the foot, where gravity would splinter my body into a million pieces.

I click the cryo gloves on and place them against one of the gears. Threads of frost expand from underneath my fingers, crawling across the metal and around the crooks of iron, and the gear slows in its hinges.

"Stop!"

At my left, a guard stands twenty feet away on a thin support beam, rifle aimed between my eyes. Retracting my hand, I raise the cryo gloves above my head.

"Hello," I say. "Where's your friend?"

"Take off the gloves, or I'll shoot."

I look at his face, which seems to still hold a significant amount of baby fat. Can't be much older than me.

"You better not miss."

"What?"

I gesture around the air. "Bullets will ricochet if you miss. You might want to step a bit closer. I'm defenseless, anyway. Just make it quick."

He hesitates for a moment, fingers twitching over the gun. Then, like a person who has been raised from birth to regard the Badlands people as idiotic barbarians, he begins to slowly approach. All there is to do now is drop my hand onto the beam, tilt my head to one side to avoid the first bullet, and—wow, a second one, too? Really?—then, once the frost has rooted, kick.

The beam shatters, and without its supporting bindings, the middle snaps underneath his weight, and then he's falling, form tearing through strands of wires that offer no assistance to his outstretched hands. Two seconds later, a splat.

I get it, I really do. Not everyone has the stomach to shoot a teenager in the head. But I'm not going to thank them for it; I'm not going to hesitate just because they do. I'm going to live with whatever I have to do because it means I get to live.

I roll my neck around and look back toward the turbine.

"Xander, now!" I call, preparing myself to smash a fist into the slowing gear.

Nothing happens.

The guard. *Where's your friend?*

I detach from the hip's edge, both hands wrapping around the support beam, and then I'm sliding, the frost grip of the gloves decelerating my fall. I drop onto the area where we separated and then under the curtain of wires. Directly above,

Xander teeters on the right hip mechanism's edge, back pressed against the beam to suspend his weight, just like I taught him to. His hand clutches both a crowbar and his other arm. Blood is trickling through his fingers in large teardrops, oozing through his grip to pool at my feet.

In front of me, a guard stands with a rifle leveled at his head.

Xander's gaze lists down to me, touching on my presence only for a split second before darting away.

"What did I say about getting shot?" I snap.

The guard's head turns, the silver speckles in his hair and beard shimmering despite the darkness strung around us. He's older, probably has been doing this for a while. He won't miss the second shot.

The reason he hasn't yet? He's taking his time.

And they call *us* barbaric.

Xander, meanwhile, looks back down at me. Kid hardly ever says anything, but I can always hear him, clear as day. In his silence, Xander says to me: *Go rot*.

I roll my eyes and raise my hands. "You can let him go," I inform the guard.

He smiles. It's almost fatherly, if you ignore the rifle in his hands, my crew member's blood speckling the tips of his combat boots. "You volunteering to take his place, Frostbringer?"

"Aw, you've heard of me."

"So I have," he says. "The child who came across some subpar tech a few years back and now thinks she can take on Godolia."

I shift my feet slightly as the Phoenix's movements take on a new, erratic gait. It's possible my crew is being chased in circles around the desert right now. It's more possible that Theo

43

is fighting Nova for the wheel again, and Milo is trying to kill them both, leaving the Pilot pursuing them both confused and disoriented. I wish I could say this was an intentional strategy, but mostly, they're just idiots. I also wish I could say I wasn't basing this off past events.

I lift one shoulder. "At least I aim high. What would it say about my self-esteem if I wanted to be something useless, like a . . . like a priest?" I consider. "Or a Windup guard."

"Didn't anyone ever tell you that playing the hero only delays the inevitable?" the guard muses, shifting the barrel away from Xander and toward me. I breathe a sigh of relief. "Any last words?"

"Yeah. Am I, like, really famous in Godolia?"

He grins crookedly. "Yes, you and your other Gearbreakers are quite the irritation. Have you ever tried to scrape a flattened mess of flesh off the underside of a Windup's boot? I've heard it's rather time-consuming."

"I would guess. But killing you isn't."

"I'd like to see you try, little girl."

I can't help but smile at that. "No you wouldn't."

I splay my fingers wide.

The veins of the glove burst blue, then white, and a writhing spark of light splinters from the palm's panels. Like a comet, the serum streaks across the air, its vicious luminescence a corrupt blight against the darkness of the mecha's innards. The beam collides with the guard's shoulder, and the light vanishes into its new host. Even as the shadows descend once more, I see a violent spasm skip along the tip of his finger: an attempt to pull the trigger. It's no use. The frost has already set in.

I wander over to him, observing the fear that glazes fresh across his eyes. I've seen the same expression time and time again, and when I was younger, I would sift through the agony-strained features for some hint of my own guilt. And, time and time again, I found not a smidge. It doesn't make me a bad person. It just means that no one serving Godolia deserves a single thread of my mercy.

"You see, the thing about 'subpar tech' is that it still hurts like a bitch," I murmur, putting my glove on his shoulder. Beneath my touch, the cryo serum coils through his veins, dissipating every existing particle of warmth. "But only at first. No need to worry, now. You won't feel this."

I squeeze, and he cracks apart underneath my fingertips, his last breath frozen in his lungs.

I look up at Xander. "What are you waiting for? A parade?"

The kid does something impressively offensive with his hands, flecks of blood wetting his black hair.

I dust guard bits from my palm onto my overalls, kick the rest over the side of the beam. "Yeah, yeah. Let's get going. We're late enough as it is."

CHAPTER FIVE

ERIS

I deactivate the gloves before Milo takes my hand and helps me out of the Windup. Xander's already standing on solid ground, looking a bit too pleased with himself as Juniper and Arsen fuss over his bullet wound, black smirches of ash smeared across both their faces. Below us, the Phoenix lies still, limbs splayed against the sand at awkward angles. Its head, both eyes cracked and dull, rests against its shoulder. The Pilot is still hidden inside, neck snapped from the shock of the landing, by the looks of it. Hopefully with a few large pieces of glass scattered through them for good measure.

I flip Milo's visor up and pull on his hood until he's low enough for me to kiss him. The barrel of his rifle, slung over his back, hovers close to my temple.

"Everyone's secure?" I ask, breaking away and turning. Over the curve of the Windup's thigh, Nova has thrown open a train car door, and emerges from it with a black lump in her hand.

"This is boring!" she declares, chucking the coal. It bounces harmlessly against the Phoenix's paint job. She plants her palms on the small of her back and tilts her head to look at us. "Oh good, you're alive."

Theo, who had been wandering across the Windup's corpse, slides down its boot and lands hard in front of her. Her nose twitches in the cloud of flourished sand.

"No thanks to your lunatic driving," he jeers, freckled face twisting into a smirk.

Nova puts her hand on his sternum and forces him back. "On the contrary, dipshit, my driving is superb. If you ever land an even shot in your life, *then* you can comment. I could do it better than you."

"Try it, then, princess," he snaps, taking his pistol from his holster and dangling it in front of her. She reaches for it, and he yanks his wrist up, so she knees him in the stomach, proceeding to grapple for his rifle when he doubles over.

"Rot!" she shrieks as he stands, her writhing form draped over his shoulder.

Even if we have a repeat arm-breaking/semiblinding incident again, I can drive and shoot just fine, so I leave them to fight and jump onto safe ground, where Juniper has finished tying a bandage around Xander's arm.

"You did good, kid," I say, receiving a rigid nod in return. "June, Arsen, did everything go smoothly with the train?"

"All good," they say simultaneously.

"Good. A cleanup crew should be here soon to pick up the cargo," I say, watching Nova run her hands through her hair, the coal on her palms streaking the blond strands black. Theo's kneeling on the ground, forehead to the sand—clearly Nova managed to escape his hold with a low blow. "Let's get out of here."

We all pile into the pickup truck, Nova in the driver's seat and the rest of us loaded into the back, Milo with his leg resting against mine again. Theo, recovering quickly, drums his fingers against the filthy side, humming as the engine turns over. Nearby, patches of the landscape glint with sand melted into fresh glass—evidence of the Phoenix's assault.

"Didn't have much trouble, right?" Milo asks.

I shrug. "Easy as always. You?"

The car jolts forward, makes a U-turn, and then suddenly stops short. From the front seat, Nova sucks in a breath, face completely colorless in the rearview mirror.

"Uh . . . guys?" she calls, and all of us look up.

"Oh shit," Theo curses.

Before us rests the Phoenix's head, glaring down at us with a single ignited eye.

"Theo, Milo," I shout, even as sudden fear sparks through me. They snap to attention. "See if you can get a shot on the Pilot. Nova, get us out of here."

The engine revs, and the car banks past the Windup's knee. We're about to make the bend of the waist when the mecha shifts to drag an arm—absent a hand—from beneath its broken form, wires bleeding out of the jagged metal. The arm collapses across our path, and Nova swerves to the side to avoid a full-on collision.

The Windup raises itself up on the broken wrist, heaving its other arm from behind its back. Someone to my left fires a shot, followed by someone to my right, and for a moment silence rips through my head, split by a feeble, hopeful voice—
We're okay.

Both irises splinter, bleeding glass. The perfect shots fill me with a swell of pride, before I realize that the mecha is still moving.

Its thermal cannon lands hard on the sand, quaking the ground beneath us, its opening wide enough to swallow the car whole.

The Pilot probably only has a few more seconds to live, but they just need to send out a single, last thought.

From within the void of the cannon, a small orange flame bursts to life.

"Oh *shit*," Theo screams.

The flame roars, and hot air gusts over our faces. Dust swirls around us.

"I'm not getting traction!" Nova shouts, and suddenly her door flings open and she's dropping next to the tires. "The wheels are buried!"

"Get the hells back in the car and get your visors on!" I yell, leaping to my feet. I summon my power back to my grasp with a simple press, allowing the cryo serum to flourish in its veins.

Above us, the barrel of the cannon gapes wide like a mouth, an orange tongue swirling angrily within its confines. It thinks us its next meal, swallowing up as many lives as it pleases, just as Godolia has for decades now.

I clasp my palms against each other, expelling the serum into my grip, and coil my hands into fists. Filaments of frost slip through the cracks of my fingers, its tendrils sparking across the air. My anger is not an entity that burns, like it does for so many others. But it is just as devastating.

Winter's got nothing on the Frostbringer.

From between my palms jolts a pillar of blue energy, streaking across the air like lightning spilling out of thunderheads. It twists gleefully unrestrained for a single moment before connecting with the Phoenix's flame, which accepts the serum in the same manner a balloon would a pin: bulging in a perfect swell around the point of impact and bursting apart.

Steam screams up the cannon, hitting me with such force that I lose my footing and fall against Milo.

For a few minutes, the air is opaque. I deactivate the gloves and rip off my visor.

"Everyone better be alive," I call, receiving only coughs in return.

Milo's familiar fingers find my palm and grip hard. I trace down his arm and onto his face, finding all the appropriate pieces to be intact.

"Eris," he says, "you're incredible, you know that?"

"Uh, yeah. I just took out a Phoenix blast."

"You're making it difficult for me to compliment you."

"You have to earn the right to do so, soldier."

A pause. Someone shifts around in the front seat.

"You guys making out?" Nova asks.

"Yeah, pervert," Milo says, even though he's let go of my hand.

I pat around to find Arsen and Juniper and Theo slumped against one another, all shaking with low chuckles.

"What are you laughing at?" I snap.

"I . . . ," Theo starts, taking a moment to draw in a breath. "I've never heard Nova freak before."

"You little punk!" she snarls. "If I could see you I'd kick your ass!"

I ignore them, still patting around.

"Xander? Say something. It can be quiet, if you want. I just have to know you're here, kid."

Everyone goes as silent as the steam that drapes between us. I feel myself go cold.

"Xander?" I say, voice suddenly amplified by panic. "Say something, anything, please. We just gotta know you're alive, okay?"

Silence. My heart stutters in my chest, stumbling to find its next beat.

"He's here!" Milo says, form nothing but a faint outline. I

crawl over to him and tentatively reach a hand out, fingertips gracing Xander's hollow cheek.

"Holy shit," I gasp, clutching his face. "X, why didn't you say anything?"

The kid remains still. I run my touch down his cheek, tracing over his jawline. His chin is listed toward the sky.

I look up, too. Far above us, the sun has been reduced to a single glowing dot, rays barely breaking through the mist. Pressed against the clouded sky is the silhouette of a massive eagle, large wings spread wide and pinned against the air.

Then it tips, and the feathers gleam with the luster of metal.

It's not a bird.

It's a delicate pattern of iron flakes, peeled away from the sharp brow of a knight's helmet. The sun disappears completely, and from behind the curve of a grated visor glow two red eclipses.

"Valkyrie," Xander breathes.

Something cuts across the air above us, dark as hells and easily twice the length of the truck, stealing the mist as it glides past. The Windup emerges into full view, iron-etched sword hovering above the ground in a steady hand, strands of silklike steam clinging to its black blade. It stares down at the earth, at the mortals who have the audacity to look back.

I draw a shaking breath and rise. I level my gaze at the Valkyrie's face, where inside, a Pilot stands with cords coiling through their bloodstream. Forgetting how small they truly are.

I step over the hood of the car and then onto the Phoenix's handless arm, my landing vibrating across the metal skin. Milo is already shaking his head when I look back down at the crew.

"Eris," he says softly, "don't."

"Gearbreakers," I say, but the word is mangled, fear clotting my throat and splintering my breath. "Gearbreakers, this is an order from your commanding officer. Milo is your acting captain now. Try to be as good as me, okay?"

"Eris—"

My name on his mouth, soft when it leaves his lips, it's . . . ridiculous. So ridiculous that warmth floods my cheeks, heat welling up heavy in my head.

"I . . . ," I murmur, voice cracking. *I want to go home.* I want to be in the common room, be buried in that dusty, disgusting furniture with the fireplace roaring and my family crowded around me, bickering like idiots, swallowing my threats like no one else could.

But there isn't time for it. There isn't time for me to be anything but cold.

"I am going to kill this fucking thing," I say, because hate is easy, and my hate is bigger thing than me. It makes me straighten my spine and the words slip jaggedly from my tongue, barbed instead of broken, and that's what they need to hear. "I don't need an audience for it. Nova, get them out of here."

A pause. I meet her green eyes from behind the filthy windshield, letting my glare burrow into hers. She nods once.

"You got it," she whispers, wrapping timid fingers around the wheel.

The tires churn the sand for a few moments before escaping their burial, and the car rolls back. The Windup breaks its amused, cocky stillness and swipes the sword through the air. Nova twists their path, and the iron point scratches against the paint job, nearly tipping them over, and cuts into the forearm of the Phoenix. I jump back, splaying the cryo gloves wide and sending a bolt of frost to seal the sword to the skin, if only for a few crucial moments.

Milo clings to the lip of the truck bed, face white as a sheet.

"Go!" I snarl, and then the dust is streaking behind them.

The Valkyrie turns with terrifying speed, faster than any other Windup, claws reaching for the truck. I raise my hands and land a blast to its left shoulder. It only staggers back a single footstep, but it's enough time for Nova to make it past the train.

And then they're gone, and they're safe, and that makes it easier to turn away.

Or to die, I think drily, facing the Valkyrie from its own shadow, *but, you know, semantics.*

I imagine the minuscule, weak person suspended inside the false form, drunk on their own distorted sense of power, the fantasy that they could be anything more than human.

"You want me?" I yell, clenching my hands.

The serum drips from between my fingertips, rolling across my skin as harmless teardrops. The frost knows better than to harm me.

"Try to get me."

CHAPTER SIX

SONA

The limb clatters to the floor, and I twist to cut through the neck.

Broken wires sparking in protest, the headless practice Auto drops to the ground. I wipe the gear oil from my blade with a fingertip and roll my shoulders back, sweat slicking my shirt to my spine.

"Next," I say to the room, and the mirror on the far wall splits open. Another Auto emerges from the dark gap, one hand gripping its sword. It bows, and I do not, an unpleasant feeling untucking in my stomach as the featureless face tips toward the floor, programming bleeding subservience. It straightens and lunges as the door behind me slides open.

"Damn, Steelcrest, you know these things are expensive, right?" calls a voice.

I tuck myself under the Auto's jab and slam my shoulder to its middle, taking a glance in the mirror as it stumbles back. Three Valkyries are stepping into the room, military jackets crisp.

"Good evening," I call. The Auto takes the opportunity to snatch my ankle, dragging me to the floor and planting one foot on my shoulder. I tilt my chin up to look at the Pilots—Victoria, Wendy, Linel—as the Auto raises its sword.

It drops to my neck, steel tip carving nothing but a cold

kiss to my skin before the Auto pauses, remembering it is not allowed to kill me. I knock its blade away and slide my own into its chest.

I heave it off me and stand, rubbing the oil from my cheek with my shoulder.

Separating me from the other Pilots are the remnants of the evening's activities: parts of training Autos scattered across the ground, gear fluid seeping into the floor mat, and the occasional hiss of severed wire. They pick their way gingerly over the mess, making their way toward me.

"Sweetie, this *eye patch*," Victoria gasps, red and green eyes splaying wide. She pokes a white finger at my temple, where the fabric stretches, torn from my bedsheets in the new hours of the day. "What's with it?"

I pull the cloth away from my face, shrugging as the world dips back into red. "Used to training with color, is all."

Wendy snorts, scrunching her sharp nose. "And bad depth perception, apparently."

I gesture vaguely around us. "Apparently."

Victoria laughs brightly and throws an arm around my shoulders, squeezing me to her side, and I let her, though I know the gesture is anything but friendly. A few weeks have passed since my test run, and not all the Valkyries have taken kindly to me. Most had to work their way up into the unit, and they dislike the notion that I am one of them despite being fresh out of the Academy.

I dislike how they think I am one of them at all.

"Ah, Bellsona," Victoria sighs, "you're an odd one."

"You are digging your nails into my side," I note, worrying at a spot of gear oil on my sleeve.

"You're not going to last very long if you can't take a little pain," Linel sings, and kicks a spare Auto head across the room. Wendy grapples two of the Autos by their necks and flings them to the side of the room, clearing a space.

I watch them, allowing Victoria to work bruises into my side that I cannot feel. *This is not pain.* Wendy takes my wrist and hauls me onto the cleaned mat, Linel's cloying laughs bouncing around the room. He grabs a sparring sword and tosses it to Victoria, who snatches it from the air and levels its tip toward me with an expert hand. *You cannot begin to imagine pain.*

"We are fighting?" I ask.

"Gold star for Bellsona," titters Victoria, taking her stance.

"Why?"

"Why?" She glances at Wendy and Linel, snickering from the sidelines.

"Yes, why? What is the reason?"

"Just want to see how the Academy's top student holds up," she says, though it sounds insincere.

"Are you lacking confidence?" I lean forward, and say in a hushed tone, "Do you need me to let you win?"

It was a joke; I thought it was funny, but none of them crack a smile. Victoria's smirk vanishes from her lips entirely.

"En garde," she growls.

I stare at her blade. The ring of my eye is the only clear reflection in the smoothed metal.

The Academy allows us to retain some strands of our humanity because with passion, we can ignore what makes us falter, branch past logical thought.

Usually, Victoria is an accomplished swordsman, light on her feet, fluid through her changing stances. But emotion makes her sloppy in her strikes, her expression smudged with anger.

A blunt deflection causes her to stumble, and before she can straighten, I bring my fist to her cheekbone.

When Victoria is sent out to massacre a place, she does so efficiently. She has no emotion toward the Badlands people, none of the rage she harbors now; she hardly thinks of them at all.

She drops to the mat with a gasp of frustration, cheeks burning redder, and only looks up when the tip of my blade is beneath her chin.

In this form, her death would be painless.

"Thanks for the fight, sweetie," I say, lowering the blade.

As soon as the threat is peeled away, Linel and Wendy step forward and grab both of my wrists, forcing the weapon away from my grasp. They twist my hands behind my back while Victoria composes herself and touches a fingertip to her chin. When she pulls back, blood has worked its way underneath the nail.

"Do you think"—she huffs, hand constricting around the sword—"that you're better than us? Just because you're younger, and take cheap shots?"

She motions to her cheekbone, which is sprouting what I imagine is a lovely deep violet. I glance at the two holding my arms.

"Forgive me. I fought unfairly," I say drily, and pause, realizing I forgot to eat dinner. "Do you know if the commissary is still open?"

"You know we can break your arms anytime we like, right?" snaps Linel.

I shrug as best I can. "It will not hurt."

Victoria opens her mouth to spit something venomous, but then from the hall comes the sound of approaching footsteps.

"Drop her," she orders, and they do.

I start wringing my hands, massaging feeling back into my fingertips, when Rose's freckled face appears in the doorway. Her Valkyrie jacket sits loose on her elbows instead of over her shoulders. Her name matches the ringlets that gather around her face, each curl deep red even when I do not have both eyes open, paired with the natural flush in her pale, dimpled cheeks.

"Holy shit, what happened to you?" Rose says, gawking at Victoria. She shakes her head. "Probably deserved it. Anyway, Jonathan's on his way back. He said over the comms that something . . . something happened while he was responding to a distress call. You guys better come check it out."

The rest of the Valkyrie unit is waiting for us in the Windup hangar, in front of the floor-to-ceiling hydraulic door set into the east wall. The door is peeled open, revealing the underground corridor that expands underneath Godolia, allowing mechas to enter and exit the Badlands without disturbing the city. From inside its concrete mouth we can hear thundering footsteps, vibrations shaking the ground beneath us.

Rose nudges a Pilot with his jacket slung over his shoulder. "Hey, Jole, any idea what's going on?"

He shakes his head, gaze leveled at the door. "No word on comms for ten minutes now."

Riley, the girl standing next to him, pinches Jole's arm. "Shut up for two seconds," she snaps. "The rest of ya, too! Shut it. Listen . . ."

She cocks her head to the side, a strip of hair coming loose from behind her ear and falling to rest against her dark brown cheek. The rest of the Valkyries go silent at her demand, making the approach of the Windup infinitely more apparent.

I know the sound of my own footsteps. These do not come anywhere close. Which means that something is broken within Lucindo's Windup.

"It's the legs," Riley announces, giving a sharp nod. "Jonathan's puttin' more weight on his left than his right."

Victoria laughs. "You know what mecha unit we're in, right?"

"I know what I hear, Vic," Riley mutters, and then points down the corridor. "Here he comes!"

Again, we all fall silent. The Windup rounds the corner, the distance reducing its figure to nothing but a thin sliver that wavers as it nears. Rose puts her hand above her brow, shielding her face from the harsh light of the fluorescent overheads, eyes pinching into a squint.

"What the . . . ," she murmurs. "Is that . . . *ice*?"

The Windup enters the light's reach. Or, rather, stumbles into it, the entire mecha listing to one side, favoring its left leg as Riley predicted. But the fluorescents could not glint so wickedly off her steel skin; the light scatters against jagged fissures of ice that entwine her. Fingers of frost claw the metal like a rot, nestled up against shrivels of puckered metal and the yawning trench that splits her right greave. The sword, attached magnetically between her shoulder blades, glistens with ice crystals that jut viciously from the black iron.

A sole ignited eye peers down at us from behind a fissured visor.

"He's about to collapse," Jole states, and, realizing his awe has dwindled his voice to a whisper, turns to the other Valkyries and cups his hands around his mouth. "He's about to collapse! Get back!"

Lucindo manages a single, pained step into the hangar before the right leg splits beneath his weight. The Valkyrie drops to her knees, catching herself on her palms before she can crush the Pilots who did not heed Jole's warning quickly enough.

The other hand reaches up, quivering fingers dipping between where the visor's grate has been cleaved away, and rips it free. A construction worker dives to the left as the metal bars clatter to the ground, splintering the concrete where they land. The mecha's hand slides down its forearm, signifying that inside, Lucindo is plucking back the cords that bind his nervous system to the Windup. The lone eye sputters out.

For a few seconds, everything is still. The Valkyrie crouches above us like a curious deity, observing our shock.

Then, the right iris bursts apart, and a moment later, Lucindo's body follows. He lands gracelessly but upright, hand extending to catch himself on a wrist bolt.

"She's still there," he croaks. The boyish impression I first had of him dissolves as he drags a knuckle over his left eye, attempting to remove his blood from the crevices. A humorless chuckle trickles from cracked lips, dark and brittle. "The Gearbreaker. My leg . . . I think . . ."

By now I have reached the base of the Valkyrie's hand, so when he drops I am there to catch him, Jole and Rose at my side. My fingers skim against his neck, feeling his pulse, and his eyes flicker open again.

"Hurts like a bitch . . . ," he murmurs, then shakes his head. "No . . . it *did* hurt. Not now." He nods toward the half-blind mecha above us. "Ghost hurt—remember what I told you, Sona?"

"Of course, sir," I say immediately, although my head is spinning. What could do this? Who could *possibly* do this?

I snap my gaze away from Lucindo's bloodied face toward someone who has emerged from a split in the Valkyrie's ankle, hopping over the jagged edge and onto the calf. Dark eyes sweep across the room, over the dozens of freshly made mechas that stand like statues around the hangar, and the crowd of Pilots glaring at her with glowing eyes.

The girl straightens, the gleam of the fluorescent lights glazing over her short-cropped hair.

"Ah," she says. "*Shit.*"

And then she takes off up the Valkyrie.

It is ridiculous.

I cannot look away.

I watch as a handful of Pilots leap onto the leg to pursue her, and I watch the corner of her lips tuck into a smirk.

And something strange happens—her hands twine with light, palms flaring with the delicate design of electricity, and then the light unspools, screaming away from her, clawing across the air and vanishing into the meat of a Pilot's shoulder. He lets out a startled cry, staggers backward until his foot hits open air and he falls to the ground—where his arm shatters into a million irregular pieces.

I cock my head to the side, pulling my sight away from the shrieking Pilot and onto the girl again. I close my left eye.

Raven floods into her hair, and an even darker color into her eyes, lithe and lovely and ignited now, an incredibly steady fury in her expression—I have never seen a scowl quite like hers in my life. It ripples from her brow and pulls her lips back from her teeth, cascading past her face to seal her hands into fists and envelop her shoulders in a rigid but proud stance.

And when I meet her gaze, the one that somehow seems to simmer more viciously than the artificial light forced into mine, I forget myself and draw a breath.

I am not sure if it is just the fact that she had the ability to obliterate a Valkyrie singlehandedly, or the audacity to attack a Pilot in front of twenty of his comrades with a smile pricking her lips, or that she is the first Gearbreaker I have ever laid eyes on and therefore represents every particle of destruction that I wish to embody—but she is the most beautiful girl I have ever seen.

Everyone in the Windup hangar has converged on the area at the sound of the commotion. Guards have appeared with rifles already cocked in their hands, aimed at the girl with ferocity stitched tight across her features. She raises her palms again, but this time, nothing sparks from her fingers except a pair of obscene gestures.

"Yeah? Fuck all of you!" she shouts. "Come get me!"

Next to me, Jole shakes his head. "She must know she can't get away."

Rose shrugs, smoothing a hand over Lucindo's hair, peeling strands out of the dried blood. "Gearbreakers. Think they can take on the world."

"Did you see what she did to me?" Lucindo coughs, jutting his chin upward. "All by herself. The distress call came in from a Phoenix, and by the time I got there, the mecha was already dead. Pilot, too. And there she was, waving at her crew to drive off, screaming up at me to *try* to get her. I thought she must be out of her mind, but then—"

The girl lets out a mangled shriek as one of the Pilots tackles her, landing a jab to her rib cage as they both go down. He manages to pin her wrist to the Valkyrie's calf, his hand rising to land another blow. She brings her knee to his stomach, unblinking in the spittle that hacks across her face, and rams her forehead against the bridge of his nose.

The moment the Pilot recoils, her palm presses flat beneath his chin, and his enraged shout winds down to a single note before disappearing altogether. Even from here, I can see the point where his eye flickers out, and an almost sweeter tone takes the girl's growl as she reaches the same conclusion. But before she can shove him away and leap to her feet, the butt of a guard's rifle falls against her temple, sending the dark eyes spinning back as she crumples. Her hand drops from the dead Pilot, coming to rest limply over the edge of the Windup.

Even in unconsciousness, the snarl stays pinned to her features.

"Who is she?" I whisper.

"A real pain in Godolia's ass, that's who," Lucindo murmurs, watching as the guard scoops the girl over his shoulder. "Took command of her own crew at fourteen years old but had been in the game for years before that. Supposedly she found a rare pair of cryo gloves, modified them so that they even have enough energy to sap the heat out of a Phoenix. The bounty on her head is staggering, but apparently fitting."

I shake my head, hiding the fact that my heart is in my throat.

"Yes, but what is her *name*?"

"Not sure. But they call her the Frostbringer," he says, and suddenly he is grinning. We all look down at him, bewildered.

He slaps Rose's attentive hand away, craning his neck to steal a last glimpse of the girl before she and the guard disappear into the stunned crowd. "We've got one, Valkyries. A Gearbreaker—and she's going to tell us everything."

CHAPTER SEVEN

ERIS

Wait, what—

I try to open my eyes. *Oh Gods.* Too bright. Blurry figures shiver around me. These stupid kids. I fell asleep on the couch again. Nova pokes at my ribs with a sharp fingernail; Arsen pinches my cheek viciously. I try to wave them away, but I don't think my hands move. Not feeling very good. Not even freaking close. Instinctively, I work my tongue against my teeth, counting to make sure each bone-dry tooth is in place. I can't remember how many I had in the first place.

Wait—

I blink in the sudden light, the situation dropping over me with excruciating clarity, and then get to work mulling over whether or not I'm ready to die. The answer, as always, is *not really*, which is *not really* helpful, so I do something that *is* helpful, instead—reach into the left socket of the person closest to me and rip their eye out.

A sharp, clean *pop* sounds. Its trailing wires are bloody—ugly, too, so I twist the cords around my fingers and pull. The strands snap, a single spark threading through the air from the broken copper. The pupil flickers out in my palm.

My limbs are forced back to the table. The one-eyed Pilot hovering above stares back, unimpressed, a fingertip reaching up to brush away the stream of blood trickling from the empty socket. Her other eye is green as the Hollows forest in mid-summer. I should've taken that one, too.

"Imbecilic Gearbreaker," the Pilot mutters, only slightly inconvenienced. She nods to her comrades, two other Pilots who hold my arms fast against the table. "I have to go get a new eye. Make sure she gets what she deserves."

"Of course," the boy to my right chirps briskly, even though the doors have already slid shut behind her. The Pilot on my left snickers.

"Of course," she mocks. His pasty cheeks flush pink. It's a strange sight; I didn't know that Bots could blush.

"What's the problem with that?" he snaps.

The girl snorts. "Come on, Linel. You might as well call her Queen Victoria and confess your undying love."

His brow furrows, cheeks coloring deeper. "Wendy, do all of us a favor and for *once* shut the hells up."

I take in as much of the room as I can while they bicker above me. The wall with the door is the only one not made of mirrors, most likely one-way. The only light source is a single fluorescent bulb that pulsates heat down on me, reflecting against the metal of the tabletop. A sheen of sweat breaks across my forehead, and there's coal dust in my mouth, I realize, from the train job. It seems like mere minutes ago.

"Give me my gloves," I growl, and they both stop their arguing to blink down at me. I've never paid this much attention to a Bot's face before. They look unnervingly human up close.

"What, these?" the boy says smoothly, lifting them up. They're clutched heedlessly tight in his hands, veins pinching. It feels like his grip is around my throat.

"Give them," I bark, and Wendy snorts a laugh.

"Or, what, you gonna go for our eyes, too?"

"Oh, I'm planning on it."

Another laugh from Wendy, but something darker is stitched around the edges, and she throws the boy a steady look. Then her hand shifts, and a metal clamp is clinking shut around my wrist. Before I can react, Linel does the same on the opposite side. I try to move, only to feel blood swelling in my fingertips, and the skin blushes purple from the pressure.

"Look at her, thrashing," the boy murmurs. He suddenly doesn't seem childish or embarrassed at all, the red flush gone from his cheeks. Now he's grinning, the expression sickly. "How the hells did she almost take down Lucindo?"

"*Almost*," I snort. "Tell that to the Valkyrie I left limp on your hangar floor."

"Uh-uh," Wendy tuts, when I try to slam my brow against her jaw. She puts her forearm across my neck and shoves my head into place, so when I gasp, I choke, and there's no air, just the feel of my lungs heaving, spasming. The eyeball slips from my fingers and leaves my palm slick, and I think to myself, with a rabid kind of desperation, *I do not want to die here.*

Wendy pulls back. While I sputter for air, Linel pinches my hand between his fingers.

"What does it say here?" he asks merrily, squinting at the smudged ink. "*If Found: Bury.*"

"That's from Starbreach, you assholes," I snarl, though Jenny would revel in the fact that I was using her alias as a threat. "And she's going to fuck up this whole place if you lay a finger on me."

"Doesn't look like it," says Wendy, long, dark hair slipping against my shoulder as her head tilts to read my hand, a thin smile sharpening her mouth. "And where would Starbreach be arrivin' from, exactly?"

I gather my spit and launch it at her cheek.

Across her face, the grin splits and deepens. My panic roots deeper. I want them both to look away, for those hideous eyes to burst in their skulls.

Wendy takes something out of her pocket—two small knives, set with glossy wooden handles, like they're part of a dining set. She hands one to Linel.

"Your people like gears, huh?" Wendy whispers, cocking her head. "How 'bout a couple more?"

My breath shudders in my chest, and for a fleeting moment of weakness and selfishness, I wish that the others were with me. Then the room would feel less cold, and I wouldn't be alone, soaking in the horror stories they tell all the little Gearbreakers about Godolia's vicious ways.

Linel takes my wrist. "You shouldn't have messed with the Valkyries, Frostbringer."

The blade's edge presses, slips beneath.

Stories no longer.

My scream scrapes up my throat; I choke it back, try to suffocate it in my chest, but once Wendy starts on her side, I can't keep it in.

Be brave, I beg myself, tears stinging my eyes, drowning out the room and the sight of the blades gliding, devouring, *please, for the love of Gods, be brave and get through this.*

"Something to say, Frostbringer?" Wendy coos, her voice far away.

Wirefuckers, I screech, but nothing comes out, nothing but another incomprehensible scream.

Shallow, superficial cuts, that's what I tell myself after they're done. But the fear is still rooted. This is only the beginning. This is what the rest of my life will be like, however short it may be.

Am I dead yet?

Blood trickles from my forearms, dripping to the ground in uneven intervals. My hands feel cold; it reminds me of the flush of my gloves, the sound of splintering metal.

No, you're not, so stop being dramatic.

The voice in my head sounds like Jenny.

I count the drops lost. I make mental notes. I attach a dark promise to each one.

I won't die from this.

I won't die from this, and that means I can make them pay for it.

CHAPTER EIGHT

SONA

"We are here to celebrate," Lucindo announces from the head of the table. The Spiders have reduced the cuts on his face to nothing but a few superficial pale marks, and stories below our feet, his Valkyrie is being plated with shiny new chrome, iron, and glass. All the Frostbringer's work, covered up as if it were nothing. "Yesterday's capture of a Gearbreaker, yes, but more importantly—"

Rose scoops a dollop of whipped cream from her plate, leans across me, and smears it against his forehead. The dining room bursts with riotous laughter from the Valkyries.

Lucindo brings a napkin to his face. "I am removing you from the unit, Rose."

"Can I finish my cake first?" she asks.

"No." And then Lucindo lunges for it; Rose snatches her plate and grabs the dessert whole in her hand, unhinges her jaw to deliver it home.

"So. Godsdamn. *Good*," she moans, crumbs clustered at the corners of her mouth.

I take a bite of my cake while they collect themselves, hold it on my tongue as long as I can. In the Academy, the students were hardly ever allowed sugar, except on Heavensday—the end-of-the-year celebration—but my childhood sweet tooth was never truly curbed. I blame my mother, with the kitchen smelling of freshly fried yakgwa whenever a birthday crept up and we had enough honey in the cabinet, the pastries pressed in the shape of small flowers with the bottom of a teacup.

Jole, at Rose's right, must see my elation, because he brings his plate over to mine and deposits his whipped cream onto my slice.

"As I was trying to say," Lucindo says, now back in his seat, cheeks flushed, "the true cause of celebration: Sona, our newest Valkyrie, successfully—and flawlessly, I might add—executed her very first mission today!"

He grins at me. I trace my gaze against his mouth, the creases pinching his eyes. The cake is cottony in my throat.

"To many more!" Rose cheers, raising her glass.

Around the dining table, every Pilot mirrors her. Victoria, sitting at the opposite end with Linel and Wendy, even tips her glass in my direction, albeit with a scowl. All eyes are on me, red irises searing, glancing off the silver of the cups.

"To many more!" they shout.

Today, I was a fantastic soldier.

Now, because of it, I want to cry, and just never stop crying. I want to choke on my cake. I have the strange, violent urge to swallow my fork, to feel the metal catch awkwardly in my throat, prongs snagging raw, pillowy flesh; I cannot hurt, but I can give myself something to claw at.

I do not cry. I cradle the heat behind my eyes until it dissipates. There is no quaking breath to fret over, to smooth back, not when there are tiny filters placed in the flesh of my throat to oxygenate my cells, leagues more efficient than my lungs.

The most vulnerable part of any piloted Windup is the Pilot itself. Back in the Springtide War, battles were often strategically set beside bodies of water, so that enemy autonomous mechas could drag Godolia Windups below the surface, cracking their eyes so the deities could only flail as their smaller selves, their Pilots, drowned blindly. In dry battles, Godolia's enemies would flood the terrain with poisonous gases, sending out their Windups with the sole purpose of grappling with Godolia mechas and then exploding, allowing for a breach. Pilots breathed, and so they fell. Godolia's creation of oxygenation tech was said to have turned the tide of war. Without breath, it did not matter if their bodies were thrown like rag dolls underwater, if their forms were shrouded with noxious fumes: As long as the Pilots stayed conscious and connected to their cords, they could fight. And they did. And they won.

And now, without the rise and fall of my chest, there is one less telltale sign of the panic.

"Tell us about it, Sona," Jole says a while later, when most of the Valkyries are thick with drink, including Rose; she hums as she rocks herself from side to side between us.

"Oh *yes!*" she exclaims, gripping my arm, eyes unfocused but shining. "Tell!"

"It was only an escort mission," I respond, resisting the urge to recoil from her touch. "Like all your first runs."

"Our first runs don't usually involve a brawl with Starbreach," says Lucindo, leaning back in his chair, that lazy, permanent smile hung on his lips.

When I speak, my words are soft. "She might still be alive."

Lucindo chuckles. "No need to be modest, Sona."

Under the table, my hands tighten around each other.

I am not being modest, because there is nothing to be modest about—there is no pride in what I have done today. Nothing but the lurch of nausea in my gut, twined by guilt.

"I went north." Rose is leaned up against Jole, Lucindo

attentively angled forward on his forearms. The other Valkyries stop chattering to listen in. I want to take a deep breath, but this would be a telltale; this would be pointless. The Mod barbed to my throat strings air across my vocal cords whenever I need to speak. "To a resource village, Franconia, just off the Hana River. I was to escort a hoverbarge of fresh water."

Which had seemed harmless enough.

Until the hoverbarge had cleared the river, deck stacked with steel barrels, and my vision flashed with a proximity warning.

I turned just in time to see a truck full of Gearbreakers driving headlong round the bend of the river—and a young woman, with twin dots of light as her fists, hair a voidlike black—before the barge exploded and threw me halfway across the river.

"There was not a drop of water on that barge," I say to the silence of the room. "Only gasoline."

Entwined in flame, the Valkyrie broke the water's surface.

Inside my own head, my other body slammed against the glass of my eyes. I awoke sharply when the cords snapped from my arms. The mecha was sinking, headfirst, and I thought to myself, *This would not be so bad.*

But the Gearbreakers, out on the shore—the Gearbreakers who knew I would not drown, that I could not drown, who would come for me to finish the job.

Do I want to die here? I looked into the press of deep water against the mecha's eyes, inches away from my fingertips. The cords strangling my arms, the lonely moan of the metal shell, the dark, hollow rupture in my chest—*Gods, no, I cannot die here, not when this is the last thing I will feel. I will not carry this with me, I will not—*

It was an especially magnificent kind of realization: I will die as this. I will never be rid of the Academy's touch, Godolia's vision. I will die as theirs.

It is out of my control.

Maybe it always was.

I looked through the Valkyrie's eyes and saw we had reached the bottom of the river. The water thrummed beneath my fingertips. Dark as dead night, down here. Quiet, for once.

And suddenly, the Frostbringer's eyes were resting on mine again, the furious, chilling gaze, as if she was the one on the offensive, as if this was *her* battlefield and I was the one intruding. The single glance promised destruction and promised hate, and without even realizing it, I had intertwined my own vow to her glare: I may die as theirs, but I will damn well take them with me.

But not if I perished here and now, at the bottom of a river, in the head of a mecha, with a Gearbreaker coming to snap my neck.

"I wound myself," I murmur. "I felt my feet on the shoreline, raised my head in time to see Starbreach's crew emptying from their car. She lifted her hands, and this . . . this light spilled from them, up over her face, over her team . . ."

And she was *glorious*. Wild grin, black hair alight, battle cries dancing from her tongue. She looked so . . . happy. When was the last time I was happy?

Can you see? One hundred and seventy feet of steel, iron, and wire, eyes aflame in my head, my features molded to hold only malice, to create only carnage. *Can you see I am not* this?

"And then . . ." Under my new Valkyrie jacket, my hand flattens against my ribs. "I was boiling."

I have not had pain in weeks, and I had started to miss it.

Then Starbreach was before me, and I did not remember anything past the cutting heat searing across my side.

"I still do not know what it was. What she did to me."

"No one does," says Lucindo wistfully, folding his hands behind his head. His gaze becomes unfocused, dreamy. "How does some dust-covered kid from the Badlands get so lucky to find a piece of magma tech like that?"

I take a moment to imagine breaking my plate over his head before continuing. "I pulled myself into the river." Water spilling over my head, a shock of cold against my cheeks. At my side, the scalded plating hissing and sputtering. "The pain was bearable by the time my knees hit the riverbed. I brought my palms together, twisting as I broke the surface, and sent water rushing onto the shoreline."

"And they drowned?" Jole asks excitedly, chin atop Rose's curls.

"They scattered." Bodies tossed by water across the bank, little ants squirming in a downpour. "Their driver was fighting against the rush, plucking up their crew with the wheels choking on river water."

"Wheels," Riley snorts across the table, cheeks flushed red from whatever is absent from her drained cup. "What a *joke*."

"They picked up all of them, curled up sopping wet in the back of the truck as I pulled myself from the river. Except for Starbreach, who had been thrown to one of the rocks jutting from the bank. The driver stopped around ten feet away; they were shouting at her, I think, and she shouted something back and did not move from her place." I do not say that she spit on my shadow the moment it cleaved over her head. "Her crew members ran from the car, then grabbed her up to haul her to safety."

As soon as Starbreach was in the truck, I rose to my full height, the rising sun at my back, my shadow so long it fell across the resource village dotting the opposite bank.

Go. Chins tilting back, expressions awash with the glow of my eyes, the Gearbreakers did not move. *Please, go.*

The engine revved. But this was not a retreat—it was a surge, and Starbreach's hands shook at her sides, and no shadow or light I could cast could compete with the glow that flooded her hands, and I was . . . scared.

Not just of her.

For her.

"Before she could raise her hands, I dropped mine." I smile around the lie weighing my tongue. "It was easy—to crush the car flat, tip the mess whole into the river. I only wish they had given more of a fight." I trace my finger in circles on the tabletop, feeling for splinters to catch myself on, finding none. "I wanted a chance to use that lovely sword."

Linel cackles. "That is *cold*, Steelcrest."

Victoria knocks the back of her fist roughly against Linel's shoulder and pushes herself from the table.

"Don't mind Vic," Rose calls after her, "she's just in shock from the story!"

"Nah," Jole says, rolling his eyes. "Someone could pluck the moon from the sky, and Vic wouldn't spare them a second glance."

"I'm bored," Victoria returns easily, but pauses on the threshold of the dining room.

The image is so odd, suddenly, with her framed in the doorway, the chandelier bathing the sugar-happy Valkyries in a soft glow, napkins and picked-clean plates strewn haphazardly around the large table. Rose's fingers on my sleeve, idle smile cutting her face. Jole's hand clapping amiably against my shoulders. There is something intimate about the scene. Comfortable, in a way that makes me fracture, just a little bit. *Family dinner*, Lucindo had said, when he came to collect me from my room.

When my teachers had announced that I had been accepted into the Windup Program, I smiled, shook their hands, and emptied my stomach as soon as I was alone in my room. It was from hate for them, hate for myself and the way my recklessness and childishness had forever bound me to this nation and the dream of its destruction, and hate of what I would become to achieve it.

And then I awoke from the surgery. I wound my Windup. For just a moment, a glittering, happy moment, I thought it was all worth it. That this was how I could avenge my parents. This was how I could avenge myself.

But I have been here for weeks. I have slept fitfully, clutched by nightmares, and awoken suffocating, swearing that Silvertwin coal dust was being stuffed down my throat. I have woken up nine years old again, crawling over torn hands and splintered knees in the village mines, peering upward where the ground had cracked apart above us all to reveal the speckled cosmos, and deities with crimson-eclipsed eyes glaring down from the heavens.

For weeks I have known I can do damage, lovely and shocking and horrible, and for weeks, I have known that I cannot do enough. I am just one girl. I have just one Windup. And I was so drunk on the mere *thought* of having power that I allowed myself to be made into this.

Now, I sit at a table with my enemies.

With my fucking *family*.

Victoria's gaze falls on me. The cheekbone I struck yesterday is as healthy as Lucindo's face. "But I'll admit, Bellsona," she says, "it is a truly unbelievable story."

If I had any breath, it would freeze under her stare. *She could not possibly know.* "Thank you."

She nods and takes her leave.

Lucindo rolls his eyes. "She's a regular angel, isn't she?"

"No," I murmur. "She is just a bitch."

Jole snickers and raises his glass to Rose's. "Cheers to that, Steelcrest."

"Steelcrest best watch her mouth," Wendy growls from across the table, Linel bristling like a shocked dog at her left.

Riley slaps her hand against her thigh. "Oh, we are so *very* overdue for a fight!"

Lucindo coughs, attempting to muster some authority. "Valkyries, we are celebrating, remember?"

"Aw, does the captain want to make a toast?" asks Rose, batting her eyes, chin perched on her fingers.

"Well, no—"

"I do not deserve a toast?" I ask.

It was only a joke, but Lucindo's cheeks go redder. He stumbles to his feet, hand knocking against his cup before he finds a grip on it. Raising it high, he stammers, "Oh, ah, of—of course! To our Sona's first mission, and her spectacular killing of Starbreach!"

I smile while they all raise their glasses, and take my first sip of the night. *To Starbreach.* The shocked, furious look on her face as her crew came up for air, goggles loose at her neck, tugged along by the pull of the river. Her truck sinking beneath her, far beneath the froth of the water—not crushed flat, merely dropped like a stone. From a reasonable, survivable height.

I will not be a killer. Not for as long as I can help it.

"And, of course, to the Frostbringer," Lucindo adds, a new expression touching his face. His ridiculous smile now feels anything but kind. He shrugs, the gesture almost shy, but his words are barbed. "May she crack."

"Has she?" I ask, once the cheering has died down.

"Ah, well, the Zeniths decided to give her a little time before the real interrogation starts." Lucindo sighs wistfully.

"Merciful."

"Don't worry, Cap," Wendy sings, ruffling the back of Linel's head. "We got a few jabs in for you, 'member? On behalf of the Valkyries."

Lucindo brightens a bit. "Officially, I have no knowledge of this. None of you do."

"She won't talk," Jole says bluntly. "Any Gearbreaker worth their salt isn't going to break."

"Cynic," Rose jeers.

"And if she does not break?" I ask. "What happens then?"

"Take a guess," Lucindo says.

"Execution?"

"Aw, you're such a *baby*," Rose coos, briefly pinching my cheek. "Nah. Ever heard of corruption?"

The word claws cold against my throat. "Of course. But it is not possible."

"Oh, it is possible," Lucindo assures me. "Just takes a while, you know, rewriting someone's head. Scrubbing out those memories, lining up new ones in their place, and then—ta-da—you have some brand-new loyalties."

Fucking Zeniths.

Of course the rulers of Godolia cannot help but turn a girl inside out when she refuses to slaughter her friends.

"Entire process is Godsdamn agonizing, though," Jole adds, taking a casual sip from his cup. "So I've heard. The shock alone kills most of them."

My fingers still against the tabletop. "Them?"

"Yeah," Lucindo says, and this time, when he smiles, it reaches his eyes. "Frostbringer's not our first Gearbreaker, you know."

"Anyways," Rose sighs, propping her chin on her fingers and looking over at me. She wavers as she does so; Jole puts a hand out from what seems like habit, steadying her. "Sooo, Sona, darling. How are you acclimating?"

It takes me a moment to absorb the abrupt topic change. "Acclimating?"

"Rose was freaked after the Mods surgery," Jole chimes in.

Without looking back, she launches a fist into his shoulder. "I cannot believe I ever told you that. But yeah, Sona, it's true. I mean, the panels, the whole light-jammed-into-our-sockets thing, a lot of Pilots 'freak' at first, as Jole so eloquently put it. So we're always here if you need to talk, 'kay?"

I stare at her. I almost want to start laughing outright. But there is something so sincere across her features, across Jole's, and when I raise my gaze to the rest of the Valkyries, I find they have all gone silent, nodding along.

Heat floods my face and I do not know why.

"All right," I manage. "Thank you."

A Pilot called Killian speaks up. "You really are extraordinary, Sona. Getting into the Valkyries right off the bat, at your age?"

"Most of us are transfers, promoted from the lower units," says Yosh, shrugging. "I'm from the Paladins. Linel and Killian, the Phoenixes. Vic, too. Riley and Wendy, the Berserkers, and Jole and Rose, the Phantoms."

Jole nudges his elbow against Rose's. "Yep. That's how we met."

I resist a cold shudder at the mention of the Phantoms: mechas with pure black metal skin, spring-fortified legs imbued with cutting-edge, shock-absorbing tech to make their steps utterly soundless. They work only at night, when their forms blend into the pitch-dark landscape, and will stand still as the horizon until the time to strike arrives. Then, their victims will look up and truly believe the night has been chipped away, fragments moving as their own entities. They will not realize what has arrived until it is too late.

In Silvertwin, most people never even had the chance to realize what was killing them.

It is a bad memory, one they do not know I possess, so I push it down, and when I look up, an awed smile is perched across my face. I am impressed by my peers. I am not terrified of my friends.

I am not terrified.

"So you have all piloted various Windups?"

Rose rolls her eyes. "Sure. But if I had the chance to be a Valkyrie from the very beginning, I would've, hands down."

"Did you always know you were going to be a Pilot?" Killian asks. "Or did your parents ship you off when you turned twelve?"

"Oh, nothing like that," I say. "I am an orphan."

"Nice going, Killian," Yosh mutters.

Thank you for your sympathy. It is because your nation slaughtered my family. I shrug. "It all turned out for the best, did it not? Being here, with all of you . . ."

Rose puts her hand in mine, squeezing as she threads our fingers together. I have the awful realization that despite these dark thoughts in my head, I am suddenly blushing under her careful attention.

"That's sweet of you," she says.

"Oh, Sona, you're nothing but a big softy, aren't you?" Jole teases.

Carefully, I detangle our fingers. "It is a shame, though, that I will never get to experience piloting another Windup."

"Why would you want to?" Lucindo teases, hands folding behind his head. "We're not scaring you off too quickly, are we?"

Rose laughs. "We're the elites, Sona, and I'm having the time of my life being one. We get the best floor, the best mechas, the best, most narcissistic spot in the Heavensday Parade . . ." She shakes out her jacket sleeves with a flourish. "The best fits."

"So you'd never transfer?" asks Jole, raising a brow.

"Please," she retorts. "Into what other unit? If they ever want to transfer me, they'll have to rip my corpse straight out of the Valkyrie."

Muttered agreements circle the table. Jole leans back in his chair, a smirk on his face, and interlaces his fingers behind his head.

"And if the rumors are true?"

"Jole," Lucindo murmurs, shaking his head.

Rose rolls her eyes again. "Oh please. You'll believe every bit of gossip that passes through the Academy. Gives you something to live for."

"What rumors?" I ask.

"They're nothing," she says smoothly, then shoves Jole's shoulder. "And shame on you for getting her hopes up!"

Jole ignores her, looking right over her head to meet my eyes. "See, Sona, there's been talk about a new model of mechas being introduced into the Windup Program. It's going to be even more elite than the Valkyries, and some of the Pilots are probably going to be hand chosen from our unit."

"So what?" snaps Rose. "Where are your loyalties, Jole?"

"Oh please," Jole coos, smile flickering. "Tell me you wouldn't trade a pretty blade for a pair of wings in a heartbeat."

I lurch forward. "A pair of *what*?"

"See, *that's* why the new unit's gonna be so elite. Freakin' wings, man. Pilots will be able to *fly*. Snatch drones, airplanes, missiles, and other nations' shit right out of the sky. And the *name*! Gods, they're going to be called *Archangels*. Is that not the most badass thing you've ever heard?"

The room breaks into excited chatters, every Pilot ecstatic at the possibility of a new brutal toy to play with.

"Look at her," Rose snaps. "She's shaking with excitement, you absolute idiot. Sona, it's just a rumor. Don't get your hopes up, kid. You have plenty of ability to wreak havoc in other ways, don't you worry about that."

I brace myself before she squeezes my shoulder kindheartedly, still scolding Jole. I want to break her fingers off one by one.

"It is just a rumor, anyway." I look to Lucindo with an easy smile across my lips. "It is not true. I will not worry myself over it."

A pause.

"You're being awful withdrawn, Jonathan," Jole notes.

The room goes quiet. The corner of Lucindo's mouth twitches, then he collects himself.

"I cannot confirm," he says, pouring the remainder of the wine into his cup. He takes a measured sip. Then his face breaks into a smirk. "Nor deny, I suppose."

Jole's mouth falls open. "Holy—"

"Shit," Rose gasps.

Archangels.

They cannot satisfy themselves with the mere earth, but now hope to steal the sky as well. As if Godolia's power is not so thickly strung throughout the air already that I cannot move. As if I am not already terrified enough whenever I dare to glance toward the heavens.

A sliver of pressure presses into my palms as my fingernails break skin. I glance down to see crimson seep onto my trousers.

How can I fight this?

How can *anyone* fight this?

I realize my sight is on the window. Outside, darkness envelops the clouds, and suddenly, I think of the Gearbreaker. The harsh glint of her midnight eyes, glaring back at me as she clutches lightning in her grasp, breathes out thunder in her snarl.

She stands, amid it all, furious and beautifully vindictive, and she does not flinch. She does not even waver.

Lovely thoughts.

My fingernails uproot from my palms. I flip them onto my trousers, pressing down, quelling the bleeding.

Lovely, destructive thoughts.

CHAPTER NINE

ERIS

Above me, the Berserker's titanium palms split into a garden of a hundred tiny valves.

OhmyGodsthisisdefinitelydefinitelywhereIamgoingtodie—

The air came alive with the hiss of gunfire.

Shit. Hands thrown over my head, bullets tearing the grass beside my flat form. Soil puckering, rupturing, particles flying into my ears and throat. *Shit shit shit*—

Jenny, my crew captain, wore her trademark expression as she wove between the mecha's footsteps—a sparkling grin, a fair competitor to the glint of the Berserker's skin. For only a single moment she hovered by my side, just enough time to yank me to my feet.

"No one in my crew dies on their bellies," she barked, grip tightening until I gave a convincing nod. "Good, then. You're coming inside with me."

A warning shout sounded from one of the crew members, and a blast shrieked across the field as a trench exploded open across the Berserker's shin.

And then the world was this: my sister, already stuffed to the brim with arrogance, standing with a straight spine, a hellish grin balanced by the cavalier tilt of her chin, and a deity kneeling before her.

My arm sheathed in her iron grip, Jenny sprinted forward.

She released me to launch herself onto the Windup's foot and spun back to hoist me up the rest of the way.

Her hand swept over my forehead, tugging my new welding goggles into place.

"Now you look like a real Gearbreaker," Jenny declared.

"I look like a dirt-covered ten-year-old," I snapped.

"You're ten already?"

"Oh my Gods, yes, and *die*."

"That's the spirit!" Dark eyes shining, her grin listed upward.

I followed her example, finding that the sun had disappeared, replaced by an ugly chrome head that glared down with crimson eyes.

"That's right, fucker!" she shouted up. "You're done for!"

"It heard you, Jen."

"That was the point," she stated, and then, as the Berserker reached for us, shoved me into the opening.

Instinct seized me. I snatched a ladder rung, and then I was climbing, a new kind of exhilaration controlling my actions. Below us, two of the mecha's fingers had followed us into the leg, wriggling, thick as tree trunks.

Jenny sent a wad of spit across its knuckle, dragged the back of her hand across her lips, and nodded at me to keep climbing.

I made it out of the thigh and into the hips, poking my head out the opening. And a guard's boot slammed into the bridge of my nose.

My grip broke, and then I was free-falling—utterly, unimaginatively devastated by the notion that my corpse would be without a single tattoo to speak of—

Until Jenny's hand caught my wrist.

Her gaze tore from mine to glare upward at the guard's

rifle, pointed down at us. With one hand on the ladder rung and the other tethering me, she had no way to reach her pistol.

But I could. My hand shot up, stealing it from her waistband, landing an even shot to the guard's collarbone. His finger stumbled against the trigger, and the bullet harmlessly cut the air next to my neck, pinging once off the mecha's writhing digits and ricocheting out the opening.

The guard teetered above, balanced on the edge for a single second before tipping, plummeting, hands brushing past my hood as he descended.

He cracked against the mecha's fingers, which twisted, pinching him between them before retracting.

"Your nose is broken," Jenny informed me once we were out of the leg, black eyes giving only a moment to my condition before wandering above. "But that was a nice shot, kid. I'll take my gun back now."

I wordlessly handed back her pistol, afraid that I might start bawling if I opened my mouth, then watched as she scaled one of the iron beams. Her bronze shears appeared in her palm, taking a coil of cords between the blades and handily snipping. The exposed copper shimmered as it dipped.

"Cuts like butter," Jenny sighed, peering down at me. "See, Eris? No reason to be intimidated by these things." She gestured around the air. "They are built to be feared, so once you stop fearing them, you're the one with the upper hand."

Her face lifted, and she pushed her goggles to her forehead to get a better look. Then her pistol rose, shot screaming through the air, and a guard fell from above, past me and into the leg chute.

Jenny continued her work, the wires sparking and dying around her, until the hum of electricity dulled and the gears decelerated before stopping altogether. Stillness took to the air, but despite that, something was still whirring—I could feel it in my fingertips, its kick in each tooth. My heart had never beat like this before.

I'd never *had* a heart like this before.

Jenny descended, landing soundlessly as a tabby cat, and nudged me with her shoulder.

"Don't go all shell-shocked on me now."

I didn't know what to say, how to put into simple words how much my nose hurt and how scared shitless I was and how all of it made me feel a little more than human, how I liked the sound of the bad things breaking by my hand and how *this was everything*—

All I said, in the least warbling tone I could manage, was, "What now?"

Jenny grinned again, looking upward, into the silence.

"Now we go for the Pilot."

Today, this is the story I choose to tell them as they pick at me. My first takedown.

Gritting it out through clenched teeth, between the growls, the escaped sobs, piece by fractured piece, exchanging true names for feared aliases, pain for some bright piece of memory, everything to me but useless to them.

I'm not even paying attention to you anymore, fuckers. I'm not even here.

"Where is the Gearbreaker compound, Frostbringer?"

Ice water, today.

Seems even the Bots have a sense of humor.

They pull me back from the metal bucket, arms pinned behind my back. I'm shivering so hard that they rattle along with me, and when I notice this, I get a fantastic, dumb spur of confidence—or maybe just desperation—and kick to my feet.

Throwing my weight to the left, I rip one arm free, and immediately crack my elbow against the guard's nose. He recoils—and I think, *that was a good idea*—then surges forward—*ah, you know, actually, maybe it wasn't*—

His knee hits me in a bad, soft spot in my gut while the other guard holds me steady.

She lets me drop to all fours when I start heaving. They watch me work my ration of a spoonful of water and gruel from my stomach onto the floor.

Oh my Gods, I think, with a dry, funny kind of thrill, *this is definitely where I'm going to die.*

"I feel better now," I say, dragging the back of my hand against my lips to wipe away the bile. "We can keep going."

CHAPTER TEN

SONA

The light is gray the next morning. Fingertips gentle against my left eye, I pad through the quiet halls of the Valkyrie floor, lost—again—in their sprawl. A curving corridor for the bedrooms and a library to the west; a pool, sauna, and steam room to the north; three lounges scattered throughout. Gray is rare this far up, even higher than the Academy floors. The clouds dislike how we reach, usually, and keep their distance.

There is a beautiful kitchen, too, countertop stacked with sugared breakfast pastries. Somewhere. *Where the hells—*

I turn the corner and run straight into Victoria.

Almost. Her hand extends a blink before, saving our heads from knocking together. Her eyes skip from the right side of my face to my left, where my fingertips hold down the lid. I lower them, conscious of her hand against my sleeve.

"Do you know where the kitchen is?" I ask.

Victoria snickers. "You've been here for weeks, sweetheart."

"That new eye is doing you wonders," I say.

Now her hand falls. She uses it to flick her pale hair over her shoulder and turns away.

"That," she huffs, corner of her mouth twitching, "was dangerously close to a compliment."

I follow her around a few corners until we reach the kitchen. Jole slumps at one of the countertop stools, dead asleep, the ridge of his cheekbone against Rose's elbow. On the counter-top beside a steaming cup of tea, her Valkyrie jacket is flipped inside out, exposing a large rip in the fabric of the pocket. In her hand is a needle strung with dark thread.

"Morning," she calls, eyes not lifting from her stitching. It is obvious she has never sewn anything in her life, judging by the way her thumb is bleeding from multiple pinpricks. Her hand jerks gracelessly, and the needle jabs again. The concentrated expression on her face does not so much as twitch.

I grab a pastry, heavy with glazed fruit. "Good morning."

"How was your run, Vic?" Rose asks.

"We don't have to talk," Victoria retorts, filling up a mug of coffee and exiting.

"Mmkay, bye-bye," Rose calls as I take the remaining seat beside her. "I think she's warming to you, Sona."

"No thank you," I say, taking a bite. I can see Jole's left pupil glowing underneath his copper-colored lid, only slightly, as if the skin there could blush.

"I think she's been stealing looks at you from the get-go, and it means something," Rose says. "Kiss and make up, already. And then kiss again."

"I am going to eat in my room."

"What, not your type?" Rose calls after me. "She might even qualify as your knight in shining armor, after today's run!"

I raise a brow and pause in the doorway, words muffled by bread and sugar. "Yes? And how is that, exactly?"

"She likes girls, you maybe—"

"The knight thing, Rose."

"Ah." She takes a sip of her tea. "Vic was sent out to clean up Franconia this morning."

The pastry dangling from my fingertips slips to the floor.

She does not notice. Her blood spots the countertop.

"What do you mean, 'clean up'?" I ask carefully.

"You know." She turns from her needlework, cheery grin lighting her face. Thumb tracing a slow line beneath her chin, ear to ear. "Spotless."

Sunup to sundown was spent beneath the soil. With no set of hands to spare on watching those too young to work, children were brought to the mines alongside their parents. Day after day, we reaped the earth, picked and pried at its shell until every soul was filthy with coal grime, powdered over the patches of skin that the lack of sunlight had rubbed pale.

Bone weary, dust caked, and near stripped down to nothing but bone and muscle, Silvertwin's people shuffled like ghosts from their homes to the mines and back again, forever tied to the earth to meet Godolia's staggering quotas. Sunlight was only seen in slivers, in the last look toward the horizon before the plummet—a sickle-shaped, marigold glow that sent the shadows spilling from the notched leaves of the ancient sycamores. Other than the fleeting dawns and dusks, Silvertwin saw only a sky shrouded in darkness.

Godolia knew this, because they had created this, created what our whole lives would be. And so they knew to send the Phantom, too.

The train held enough coal, iron, copper, and zinc to satisfy Godolia's gluttony for that month, but come one morning we found that it had failed to depart in the night. It was an autonomous transport—its railways strung between the neighboring towns, plundering their resources before looping back toward Godolia—and no one held the knowledge of how to fix the tech.

Ignorantly, we did not fear the potential consequences of the missed quota, as we knew that we were not at fault. We went along with business as usual, as if Godolia had a kind and understanding reputation. As if decades ago they had not forced those in the Badlands—the people who happened to live within the limits of nations that had lost the Springtide War—to form their resource villages.

They sent the Windups at twilight, when the exit tunnels would be choked with exhausted bodies shuffling toward the elevators.

We thought it was an earthquake.

And we panicked.

The frenzy of a thousand feet as people surged toward the exit. The clutch of fear shaking from them any notion of the nine-year-old girl caught underneath their steps, suffocating in the footprints.

At one point, my kneecap succumbed to their weight and snapped. My screams were heard only by the earth, which in return sent particles of filth clawing down my throat and wedging between my teeth.

Nearby, one of the birdcages had split open, wire frame crumpled like an eggshell. I could see the gleam of the canary's eyes, black and flickering around in its sockets, as if it had the good sense to be frightened, too. Then, a boot, and the sound of delicate bones breaking, resonating like kindling crackling in a warm hearth.

Somehow, I managed to roll to the side, back pressing against the packed dirt wall.

And then:

"Bellsona! Bellsona!"

My name, fractured. Choked on.

Lolling my sight upward, I saw that heavenly, unreachable pinprick of gray light that marked the exit. Saw a crack shoot across the ceiling, a fissure as large as my torso and as jagged as a serrated blade.

My name, skipping up the corridor, torn from my parents' lips.

"Bell—"

The earth caved in, dirt and coal burying my senses, hushing the screams of every person who had stumbled by me.

For a few dazed minutes, I thought that after everything we had taken from the earth, she had finally awoken to take something back.

But after my tears flushed the filth from my eyes, when I blinked and found myself staring at the cracks in the cavern ceiling, where the fresh night air was seeping through, I knew the truth. I saw its movement through the slivers, felt my breath freeze in my chest. This was not the earth's doing.

A Paladin, using its immense weight, had rooted itself over the hollowed-out ground, and simply took a few steps. A few effortless steps, and my entire world had split apart. The metal skin shone even with the absence of the sun, greaves creaking as it took a step away, disappearing from my sight.

Move.

Again, the ground quaked, and again, screams were snatched from the air as they were buried by black soil.

You need to move.

Broken leg trailing behind me, I heaved myself onto a slab of split earth. Adrenaline dwindled my life to small movements, my thoughts only of escape. Squeeze through the narrow slits. Ignore the pieces of fragmented stone that tear the skin. Ignore the bodies beneath. Ignore the broken fingernails, the taste of blood on the lips, the ring of their shrieks still nipping at the ears.

Climb, the panic ordered. My body obeyed, fear like a noose around my throat, tugging me toward the surface. This place would not be my tomb. I refused to die in my own grave.

I pulled myself over the edge and collapsed onto my back, sucking in the untainted air as the world spun. Grass against my shoulders. Aether blotted like cotton over my head. To my right, the sycamore forest, leaves chattering happily in the wind.

Oh. My fingers twitched against the cool earth. *I am dreaming*.

Suddenly I was pulled to my feet, the pain of my leg spewing black dots onto the starred heavens. I whirled to find a hand around my wrist, pulling me toward the tree line. Once we disappeared into the foliage, the person spun around and a palm was being pressed to my cheek.

"Are you hurt?" the man said breathlessly, and I faintly recognized him as the canary breeder. His pale eyes burned bright with tears. "*Bellsona*, are you hurt?"

My stomach rolled at the sound of my name. I slapped his hand away to double over and empty my stomach on the forest floor.

I am dreaming, I reminded myself afterward, straightening, and then, to remind him also, said, "Ajeossi. This is a dream."

He moved his hand to my shoulder and shook me until my teeth rattled.

I recoiled, screeching, and his palm clamped over my mouth.

Blood dripped from my fractured fingernails, my knee bent beneath me at an unnatural angle. Pain was a grounding thing; it made the moment solid, cauterized it into something real.

My lips moved against his fingers. "Where are my parents?"

I watched his eyes wander back toward the entrance of the mine, looking for a convincing lie. The mouth of the earth was coughing clouds of dust, and within it moved the barest hints of silhouettes: other survivors. He looked back at me, tried to smile.

"I will go search for your parents," he said, voice cracking. He swallowed hard, tried again. "I will go search for your parents, over by the mine. Stay here, all right? I will be only a moment."

Wordlessly, I watched his figure wobble toward the mouth, take a single step out of the tree line.

And then the night shed its skin.

The sky shifted, and suddenly the canary keeper was flying, legs kicking helplessly, scream curdling from his throat. A moment later his body shattered against the earth. He had no wings, but his arms spread flat like the canary's, the same red seeping out of parted, twitching lips.

The night took another step, and through the gaps in the trees I saw its hand reach into the mine's mouth to pluck out another form. Another scream, another round of bones crackling. This time the person twitched on the ground, limbs erupting at wrong angles, and the mecha took careful notice, turning back to complete its work.

Flat as the sycamore leaves, blotted with red. I doubled over, but with nothing left in my stomach, I could only dry heave over the lush ground.

And then I crawled.

Moss stained my tattered shirt, my fingers searching blindly for the crooks of shallow roots to pull myself a few more inches forward, a few more inches away from the Windups. I did not know where I was headed.

After what seemed like hours, my fingers felt the ground stop short. I hooked my hand over the drop, then my forearm, and felt only open air.

I did not know if what awaited me over the edge was a few yards' dip in the earth or a bottomless chasm. It took the last of my strength to push my body over the drop.

I was only weightless for a quarter of a second, and then my chest smashed against a hard, uneven surface. I did not have to wait for the pain to ebb to recognize my surroundings—I had grown up with the smell, the rough, chalky feeling of its remnants between my fingers. I had landed in one of the train cars, packed tight with our coal.

Some time later, voices I did not recognize awoke me, still curled up against the coal, skin black as singed flesh. The sun had begun to rise, and a brilliant blue sky snaked between the viridescent foliage like a river winding around crooked shores. I could not recall the last time I had seen a clear noonday.

The sight was excruciating. I turned away from its luster, closed my eyes once more.

Below, the Godolia technicians chattered about frayed wires and shot circuit boards.

I did not move, and I did not call out. Coal dust had caked my throat, and I could not speak.

The train began to move, and for the next few hours I watched the sky pan past overhead, dotted with small, puffy clouds that could never hold a candle to the complexity of the night sky. At one point a Windup appeared, jogging alongside the train, steel skin glistening like fresh dew. I waited for it to notice me, pluck me up, fling me to the horizon.

It did not once look down. Eventually it peeled away, and suddenly the sky became clouded, the heat of steam clinging to my cheeks. Above me, tall factory spires reached toward the heavens like the fingers of praying hands. We had arrived in Godolia.

When the train finally slowed to a stop, I did not wait for them to find me hidden atop the coal. Heaving myself upright and rolling, I missed the ladder completely, lay shocked against the gravel ground for a few moments before the earth stopped tilting. As best I could, I staggered quickly to the nearest alleyway. I am not sure what would have happened if someone had bothered to look in my direction and seen me, coal streaked and limping. Perhaps they would have asked for my name, and in my response, heard the Badlands accent twist my tongue.

For the next year, I wandered through the convoluted labyrinth of Godolia. Its streets, although contorted and confusing like the mines of Silvertwin, held not a particle of the cavern's effortless beauty, nor the comfort I used to find while snuggled into small spaces. The city was as filthy and false as the Windups—a pretty, shiny exterior with purely grotesque innards.

I learned to stay away from the eastern parts of town where the brothels were clustered, and taught myself to sleep sitting up, ready to wake and flee at a moment's notice. At night, prowlers with sharp tongues and sharper weapons would stalk the alleyways, searching for convenient children to snatch and sell to the highest bidder.

Naturally, I had to teach myself to fight as well.

It was especially difficult due to my leg, which under my

unskilled bindings had never quite healed properly. Hand-to-hand combat, the most common defense for those living on nothing but foraged trash scraps, would not be useful to me. I needed a skill that would allow me a safe distance from any assailants, and as I had no money to purchase a firearm, I took to carrying around a metal pole, which I had lifted from an abandoned construction site.

My fighting was not graceful, not with my gnarled leg, and it was not honorable. Whenever a slight noise in the night woke me, the sound of footfalls or something as innocent as a low laugh, I would hover by the nearest corner and wait for them to step into range. I did not hesitate long enough to see if the person intended to do me harm, and I could not risk to. If I did not swing with full force and break something within each person who dared to wake me, I could have been snagged and draped in a brothel's fake silks by daybreak. My only advantages were surprise and silence. In fact, I hardly said a word at all throughout that entire horrid year, and by the time the Academy officials found me, I had near forgotten how to say anything at all.

They were kind, at first.

Even fixed my leg, so it could take my weight as it should. Sealed away the scars that marred my fingertips, from when I pulled myself aboveground.

They wanted me healthy.

Usable.

By the time I find his room—this place is a fucking maze—my panic is about to slip its leash.

99

I might lose control right here and now, might start screaming, might start sobbing. Years and years of being cautious, of being stone, coming undone all at once.

My knuckles are too quick against the door, too many raps against the wood, but I cannot seem to stop. My other hand burrows in my pocket, twisting the cloth I keep there to cover my eye, coiling it around my fingers until my heartbeat screams beneath each nail.

I am going to unravel. This is going to unravel me.

"Lucindo," I shout, every letter sounding cracked. "Open the door. Open the Godsdamn door!"

When he does, I push past him into the room, tracing a small circle around the space for no reason other than my feet want to move. They want to *run*.

"Sona, what—" he says, my name split by a startled laugh, and suffocated just as quickly when he catches a look at my face. The wildness that cuts it.

I must look unhinged to him. Unlike myself. But this is the first time in years I have been myself in front of other people.

Scared.

"What happened in Franconia?" I whisper.

His hair is glistening wet, water dripping from his temples. A towel is slung around his neck, hands gripping its ends as he stares at me, bewildered. Behind him, the mirror hanging on the bathroom door is pale with steam.

"Same thing that happens to everyone who assists the Gearbreakers," he says, shrugging. "Eventually."

A shower.

He sent out a Valkyrie to slaughter a town, and then *he took a fucking shower.*

I take a step toward him. My nails burrow fresh cuts into my palms, squeezing into fists. I should have let Starbreach finish the job. I should have let her disintegrate me.

It probably took Victoria mere minutes. *Minutes*, to push my body count from zero to hundreds.

How many innocents has Lucindo claimed?

How many will he pin to me—little gifts, given with a smile, a pat on the back, an assurance of more to come?

I take another step. I am right under him, looking up, heart ticking in my throat.

I reach for his neck—

And loop my arms around it, cheek to his chin.

"Thank you," I whisper. The water on his jaw traces my cheek.

His arms close around my back. "It's nothing, Sona, truly."

Nothing.

I pull away, drag the tears from my eyes with the collar of my shirt.

"Let me do something in return, for the Valkyries," I murmur, voice thick. "Help, in some way."

Lucindo grins. "Yeah? How so?"

I meet his eyes, hold them for a long, heavy moment.

"Let me talk to the Gearbreaker."

He barks a laugh, taking a step back. "What?"

"I can get her to talk. To break." He starts to laugh again, and my hand falls onto his sleeve. "I am angry, Lucindo. At what they do. At what they think they can do, with no consequence. They think they can steal and kill and it will not matter and it *sickens* me." My fingernails curl, puckering the black fabric. "I will be kind. Gentle, you see—she expects violence, is primed for it, and I think . . . I think she will not expect the likes of me. I will coax the information out, bit by damning bit. And we will use it to destroy them all."

Lucindo is not laughing anymore, but he is grinning. I let him, let him revel in this cruelty he thinks is his. There is not one lie on my tongue. I watch those dimples sink like bullet holes into each cheek.

CHAPTER ELEVEN

ERIS

Unfortunately, at some point I wake up.

Inventory: Headache burrowed into each temple. So much salt on my cheeks that the skin feels like it's about to split apart. A slightly concerning tremor in my limbs that I can't pinpoint—hunger, thirst, or the loss of blood, or ... drumroll ... a thrilling mix of all three.

Mood: Shit.

I feel I can't be blamed for it.

Back at home, my crew would try to cheer me up with a game they affectionately called Let's Get Eris As Mad As Possible But Not So Mad She Kills One of Us. This has involved slathering glue on my coffee mug, stealing and ransoming my goggles, setting off the fire alarm—and then hollering and dancing like idiots on the couch cushions while the sprinklers soaked the carpet—and sending gushy, worshipping fan letters to Jenny in my name.

Little psychos.

Heat pricks at the corners of my eyes.

I'm really never going to see them again, am I?

Little.

Godsdamn.

Bastards.

I didn't even want them in the first place, not really.

Voxter turned his eyes from the office window, irises slate gray, the same color as the storm clouds blotting the skyline. I was thumbing through the stack of papers, looking over each bolded name, each sprawling, ridiculous disclaimer pinned underneath.

"Well?" he said gruffly.

"*Well*. I have some thoughts."

"I remind you that at your age, Shindanai, the Council has graced you with this opportunity—"

"Oh, I feel graced, all right." I began to draw some of the pages, six in all, and placed them in a neat row on the table that separated us. "Did Jen say I was a loose cannon? That's a bit hypocritical."

He sighed, sitting, starch-rigid canvas jacket crinkling around his shoulders. "Your sister supports your promotion."

"So this is . . . what? So all the Gearbreaker problem children can get blown up at the same time?"

He hesitated. I shifted the papers, lining their edges up neatly.

"Xander Yoon," I read aloud. "Eleven years old. Only been in the game a few months now, but his captain has asked—no, has *begged*—to have him transferred to another crew. Quite a charming kid, I see. Speaks only in violent threats when he bothers to speak at all. His crew's been sleeping with one eye open for weeks now. He'll be a great addition."

I slipped his file noisily back into the stack to stifle Voxter's response, moving on to the next paper.

"Arsen Theifson," I read aloud, tracing over his name.

"Thirteen years old, demolitionist. Seems to have a bit of trouble listening, accidentally blew a Windup's thigh before his crew could clear the blast zone, and—oh, *and* almost blinded them with the shrapnel? Bonus."

"Eris—"

"Juniper Drake," I continued. "Twelve years old. Chemist. Corrosives expert. One of her concoctions was so potent that it first burned through its vial, and then a hole through her crew's truck, while they were on a run, of course. Straight through the pistons and fuel line. Impressive."

"Miss Shindanai—"

"Nova Atlantiades, thirteen years old. Proficient in sharpshooting and hand-to-hand combat, like the rest, I'm assuming. But she prefers being behind the wheel, apparently likes running circles around Windups, till it got one of her crew nearly flung into a footstep. She seems like *fun*."

I didn't need to look up to know that Voxter's mouth was stretched taut. I moved on to the last two papers.

"Milo and Theo Vanguard, fourteen and thirteen, brothers. Gunslingers. Theo likes to shoot first and ask questions later—or to put it more simply, he's trigger-happy. Forgets to turn on his safety sometimes, and sometimes grazes his crew captain's ear with an accidental shot. I wonder how close he would've gotten if he was actually aiming." I looked over the papers again. "I don't see what this Milo kid did."

"Nothing," Voxter replied. "We thought it would be beneficial having someone your own age in your crew. That, and he has absolutely refused to leave his brother."

I carefully aligned all their papers again in an even stack, then shoved it across the table. "He sounds boring. And possessive."

James Voxter is ancient, in theory, but as far as I could tell, he looked about the same as he did when I was small: the hardness to his brow, the rippled burn scar enveloping his right cheek, the wrinkles around his eyes I'm sure wouldn't come out even if I took a hot iron to them.

"You wouldn't think this was so funny if you knew what we were up against nowadays, old man."

He's quiet for a moment, then he murmurs, "You sound just like your parents."

The anger rises first, then the irritation. "Ah. Did this work on Jenny, too?"

"She knew them for longer than you did. I didn't need to try so hard."

Now I go quiet, biting my lip, biting down on my words. But I can't get mad at him for telling the truth. "They loved the fight. Loved the adrenaline, like most of the lunatics running around here. They got sick off it. And they—"

"Got stepped on, I know," I snap, bristling. "It was an honorable death. A Gearbreaker death."

"Precisely my point, Eris. They didn't back down. They dug their heels in, and instead of running, they learned to function in the chaos. To turn it in their favor. Jenny has the same ability."

"Edgy shit."

He stood and shoved the stack of papers toward to me. "You have a lot to learn, and you can't do it alone. Not like you think you can."

"And why not?" I shot back.

He tapped the papers with a knuckle. "Because you need more to fight for."

My eyes treaded down. Across the top margin of the page, in bolded print: ERIS SHINDANAI'S GEARBREAKER CREW.

My crew. My artillery of loose cannons.

"Fine," I said, picking up the paper stack and holding it close to my chest. "But I'm not gonna like them."

In the one-way mirror, I watch my tongue slither between my teeth. The metallic taste of blood pricks the back of my throat.

I hope you lot are happy, I think to myself. *I'm doing this for you, and I'm not even going to get to brag about it.*

And then all of a sudden the door is open, and someone's hand is constricting around my mouth.

I retract my tongue and bite down on the intrusion instead. Their blood replaces mine across my taste buds. The grip doesn't budge.

I roll my gaze up. Above, two eyes stare back, one red and searing, the other a deep hazel. A chestnut curl unhooks from behind her ear as the silence beats forward.

"Hello," she says softly. "Would you mind releasing my hand?"

I clamp down harder.

The Bot blinks, and then, expressionless, tears her hand away.

I spit the flesh to the side as she pulls a long strip of cloth from her pocket and begins to bind her hand. The bandage immediately blooms red.

She walks around the room, fingertips tapping each mirrored wall. The glass shifts to an opaque black. This is a momentary relief—I think there's a lot of blood on my face and looking at myself accelerates the whole "you're going to die" chant in my head—until I realize what this might mean.

"This soundproofs the room," she says, and save for the Bot eye and the Pilot military jacket, she doesn't look like an executioner. Tall, with curly, dark brown hair gathered around her shoulders, fair skin with a spray of freckles on the little babyish curve of her nose. She peels back her bandage curiously when she notices it dripping, blinks when this makes it drip faster. "No cameras in here, either. They like a lack of witnesses. In some cases."

She has the proper Godolia accent, too silky in my ears—*s*'s soft and hissing and *k*'s neatly clipped, syllables handled with care.

There are calluses, hard and smooth, peppered generously across her knuckles. My eyes catch on her military jacket, one dark cuff slowly going darker with red. I never thought they'd make a teenager a member of the Valkyries. Never thought anyone her age could be ruthless enough.

"I hate you and I'm going to kill you," I say.

The Bot moves forward, and I release a low, rumbling growl through clenched teeth. If Godolia thinks the people from the Badlands are animals, then I'll be a rabid one.

But I can't help it—I flinch once she reaches my side.

The Bot leans over me, bandaged hand bracing on the table left of my face, her other hand trailing a soft fingertip across my hairline. She peels back the strands encrusted in the gash splitting my forehead, and I bite my lip as they snap free, resisting the urge to start trembling. *She's going to blind me.* The Bot's going to blind me, like I did to her friend, but I'll feel the pain in totality. I brace myself for the world to go dark.

"This was from taking down the Valkyrie?" she murmurs. "Is this all?"

"Don't touch me," I say, hating that my words don't crawl above a croak, hating my cowardice, my fear. I'm flat against the field again, shuddering along with the grass as the Berserker's bullets dimple the earth, waiting for someone to pull me back to my feet. But Jenny's not here. I'm going to die alone.

Her hand moves away from my face, and the heat of her fingertips hovers over my left forearm where the other Bot buried her knife tip. It's a mess of dried blood; you can't even see what it's supposed to be.

"Animals," she murmurs, thick brows furrowed.

"Wirefucker," I say to the ceiling. I just woke up and I'm already exhausted. Gearbreakers tend not to grow old most of the time, but right now, under the glare of the light bulb, I feel ancient. Like I could sleep for the whole year and still would wake up aching. I close my eyes. "You can go ahead and do whatever to me. I don't feel like talking today."

"I would like to change your mind," she says.

My thoughts are slow to churn up some snippy, violent response, and I'm already drifting away before they do.

And then the clamp around my right wrist clinks open.

I open my eyes as she reaches to unlatch the other restraint.

"My name," she says, a note of excitement quickening her voice, "is Sona Steelcrest. I . . . I believe we can help each other."

I sit up. Wait for the momentary spray of black dots across my vision to quell. Scrub my palms against my cheeks to gather myself. The pathetic, sloppy excuses for gears peek at me from both arms, outlined with stinging ache. Those dark promises I made bubble up: For every drop of blood they took from me, I'll take a thousand from them.

"You are an idiot, Sona Steelcrest," I say, and push off the table.

We hit the ground in a tangle of limbs. I send a fist toward her nose. She moves her chin, and my knuckles catch her hair—*soft*—and then the ground—*not soft*. I clench my teeth against the shock of pain and lurch my weight forward, free arm tucking underneath her chin. Her mouth opens wordlessly, eyes flickering over my face as I wait for those little muscles to give, one by one—Pilots can't suffocate, but they can still break.

Twisting, she swings her leg out from beneath me, knee driving into my stomach. She scrambles away as I falter back, keeping low, spine to the door.

We were originally trained to dismantle Windups, but once the Academy got wise and guards became a common parasite, we had to learn how to fight humans, too. Jenny was eighteen when I was assigned to her crew, eight years my senior, and still spared no second thought on knocking me flat on my ass. Repeatedly.

"You think Godolia's going to care you're a kid?" she would yell, watching me stumble up, then shoving me right to the floor again. "The Zeniths, the mechas, the Bots—they'll tear you apart and not lose a wink of sleep over it. *Get on your feet*." I would get up, and she would shove me back down. "You hit again and you hit fast and you hit hard. You're a Gearbreaker, Eris, and that means when your back's against a wall, you *go through the wall*."

"Frostbringer," the Bot hisses. She has only one eye open now. "Please, I need to talk to you."

I suck in a breath, hands clenching into fists. "Then talk."

I lunge. The Bot's spine collides with the door. I expect both of her eyes to spring open from the shock, but if anything, her left one pinches even tighter, creases rippling along her brow. I bury my fist in her ribs, once, twice. The third time, something shudders beneath the skin, the sensation undulating across my knuckles.

But her face doesn't even yield a twitch, palms still hovering, unmoving and complacent. *Feel something, anything, you damn Bot!* I land a hook to her cheekbone, and her legs wobble and collapse. She stutters back against the door, and I knee her in the stomach before twisting my hand around her shirt collar. My other fist stretches back to my ear, winding up a cross to the bridge of her nose, to hear another glorious crack.

The Bot locks her half gaze with mine, the flesh of her cheekbone already blooming dark and swelling, beginning to morph her eye into a crescent, and suddenly I hesitate. My fingers still wrapped inside her shirt fabric, my fist still raised, and I'm frozen. Jenny's voice is curling around in my ear: *Now we go for the Pilot.*

"You are spectacular, Frostbringer," the Bot croaks, hands finally lowering, going limp at her sides. The bandage comes fully loose and uncoils in a heap against the floor. "And . . . and beautiful. Even in red. But I prefer you like this, in this shading."

I bristle, eyes narrowing. Her chin is held high; I twist the fabric tighter around her neck.

"You're a riot." I laugh, but the sound is anything but light.

She shakes her head as best she can. "And you," she says, eye tracing up my face, "have a minuscule gash from destroying a *Valkyrie*. You—we can help each other."

I open my mouth, and her hand closes around my forearm. She's warmer than I thought a Pilot could be. Like there's nothing cold under the skin.

"You can help me *escape*," she whispers. "You can help me *destroy Godolia*."

A laugh spasms up my throat. "And you can rot, you f—"

Her fingernails burrow into my wrists with such sudden ferocity that I flinch. I can't tear my gaze away from the new expression that has appeared on her face. It's a look I recognize well, felt across my own features countless times, equal parts wild and panicked. Right now, unexplainably, the Bot is a wounded animal backed into a corner.

"What have they done to you, Frostbringer?" she murmurs. Her voice is soft now, but barbed. It strikes me as strange. And I realize why—where there was the Godolia lilt, now there's . . . something familiar. Something like home. What game is she playing? "There is an anger in you, Gearbreaker, a *glorious* anger. I saw it winding tight in your chest when you killed the mecha, and I see it driving you now, driving this . . . this hatred toward me. So I ask, what have they done to you? Did they kill your family, like they did mine? Did they turn you into something terrible, something powerful? Was it worth what they took away?"

Like they did mine? My fist falters, drops to my side.

And then—she draws a *breath*.

The thoughts collect back into their rightful line, that path toward the fight, toward my fist to her nose, to her teeth, to feel another glorious fracture. She's right—I am angry, so vividly angry, all the time, and you know what—it helps.

And then she leans closer, and there are words moving her lips. They don't make sense until they've left the air, silence falling between us. When they come into comprehension, they come in screaming.

And softly, too.

"How do you kill a God?"

I've always known the answer to this question. I say it aloud because everyone should know, too. "From the inside out."

She smiles. I ready myself.

Her hand drops from my wrist, dangling at her side. She's exposed, a million places for my fist to sink into suddenly left open and welcoming.

"Break me, then," the Bot murmurs, just before I move to, and the chill her words draw down my spine seals me in place. "If you are not going to help me escape, then take me apart. Make it stick. They left me in pieces just to sew them back together as many times as they pleased, and I *let them*, because I was so blind with the want for revenge, the want for power, that in the end, I was made into the very thing that ripped me from my home in the first place. They have not given me power; they gave me the ability to come undone. I . . . I never wanted to be a traitor. I just wanted to be like you, Gearbreaker."

From both eyes, tears dampen her lashes. A large drop rolls over her swelling cheekbone and plops onto the floor. She hurriedly wipes its trail away.

"I hate red and I hate my heartbeat and I hate *being* this. Their soldier. Their God. I must steal color back from an eye that paints the world vile, steal my thoughts back from the hum, that *damn hum*, because . . . because I refuse to end like this." Her voice is choked, nearly a whisper, and though she's crying, there's a fury pushing her words forward. And it is bottomless. "I will not die in a Windup. I will not die following their orders, and I will not die as their protector. I will die human or I will not die at all."

I stand still and quiet, mind stuttering, stunned by her

words. I stare at the tears I didn't know she could possess; at *her*, bleeding and swelling and crying, and in the back of my mind, Jenny's voice—*Go for the Pilot go for the Pilot go for the Pilot*.

"You need a way out. I need somewhere to run to." Her lone eye is fixed on me, hazel dropped to a dark brown with her head tilted down and away from the light, like overturned earth. "Do we help each other? Or do we die here, just two other insignificant Badlands girls to add to the rest?"

"I am *not* insignificant!"

"Neither am I," she spits. "So let's *show them*."

I recoil, fingers rising to tug through my hair. This is ludicrous. "You're not from the Badlands. You're just another poor kid who's been sucking on Godolia's tailpipe for the entirety of your life. I'm surprised you don't spew smoke every time you open your mouth. This is . . . another tactic. Some other form of interrogation, a sob story to get me soft—"

"Is it because of this?" Her left eye opens, a red eclipse gleaming back at me. There is a new hardness to her jaw, like she's trying to hold it steady. "Is this why you do not believe me?"

My laugh is dry. "It's not helping."

A small line appears between the Bot's brows. "And what about the prospect of an alternative?"

Her voice has changed, tucked back into that neat package of the Godolia accent. It's like the room's air has been replaced, heavier now, primed for a storm. My fear, momentarily suspended by the confusion, has fallen back into place. I'm suddenly very aware of the blood on her hands, the shine of her Valkyrie jacket under the light.

"Alternative?"

"They sent me as your last interrogator. If I fail, they will move to the corruption process." She searches my face when it's clear I don't intend to respond. "Do you have any other choice?"

Many choices. My knuckles bloom ruddy with bruises, but a few splotches of skin remain untainted. So much potential. So much destruction I could cause, so many ways to be feral. So many opportunities to make Jenny proud of me.

They'll tear you apart and not lose a wink of sleep over it.

"You're too good to be true," I murmur, and the thought scrapes me raw. I sink to the floor, fingers curling against the dirty tiles—I barely care how pathetic it looks. Juniper painted my nails black a few days ago, just like she's done dozens of times before, and the feeling of her small, scarred hand holding my palm is something that startles me now. A memory I don't want because it feels so viciously real and warm and safe, the old-paper smell of the common room mixed with the chemical tang of nail polish, the shriek of the kids brawling on the dusty rug—

It's all a joke. A delusion. I'm not going home. I'm never going home.

A pair of boots appear in front of my hands. My eyes trace up the long legs, to the jacket, to the face tilted down toward mine. It's hard to tell with the glow of her eye, but the features look as if they've softened.

"I am not good," she says.

I blink. She has two freckles on the left side of her nose, four on the right. There's salt dried against them. She's pretty, I realize, which is an odd thought, because I genuinely can't tell if she's about to start crying or hit me across the face.

And I think to myself—*Fuck it.*

"What did you say your name was again?"

A small, surprised pause follows before she says, "Sona. I prefer Sona. I do not believe I caught yours."

"I don't believe you're going to."

A smile flickers on her lips. "I suppose it is not relevant. I only need the Frostbringer, anyway."

CHAPTER TWELVE

SONA

My hand feels cold. The Gearbreaker must have bitten off more skin than I thought.

I close the door of the holding cell behind me, my arm already lifting to stop Lucindo's furious form from slipping past and ripping it off its hinges. The look on his face is quite pleasing, strikingly livid after taking a glance at my swollen face. He must care about me, like he does for all his other little Valkyries.

"No one lays a finger on my unit!" he roars, stopping his thrashing to face me with eyes blazing.

"I admit, she may have been a tad hostile."

His fingers tuck my hair behind my ear, and he leans closer to peer at the angry flesh of my cheekbone. I stand perfectly still, allowing him this prodding, hands folded carefully behind me.

"We offer her mercy, and she does this?" he hisses. "Where else—"

"I am alive, yes? She had the chance to kill me and did not take it. I would say this was a step in the right direction."

Something shifts over his expression at my words, and for a moment I believe his ridiculous sense of possessiveness is going to win out, and that he is about to tear past my outstretched arm and leave my only chance of revenge bleeding out against the tiled floor.

Then his shoulders lose their rigidness, and he takes a step back. Lucindo scratches the nape of his neck, brows furrowed. "I don't like it. These niceties. She doesn't deserve it."

She does not deserve any of this, I think to myself, but the dark expression on his face spurs panic in my chest. He is going to pull me from this, bar me from seeing her again. And I . . . I want to see her again.

"Tomorrow," I say, my voice miraculously steady, "I will do something worse. Something that scares her."

I match this with a smile, and he smiles back, because he finds me wicked, and he likes me in such a light.

"Can you trust me?" I ask him. I am genuinely curious. "Can you trust that I can do this?"

He shakes his head, throwing his hands up in defeat. "All right, all right. Of course I can. I only worry because it's my job to."

I take his hand, mostly to see what reaction it will provoke. "Thank you, Jonathan. It means the world to me."

He rolls his eyes, perhaps trying to distract from the new shade of red his cheeks have taken on.

My grin widens. Nothing but a fool stuffed with wires.

CHAPTER THIRTEEN

SONA

The next morning, as soon as I blacken the mirrors, her hand twists around my collar. She shoves my back to the glass, fist rising to shatter my nose.

It hesitates beside her jaw, and I meet her glare with my right eye, the left carefully shut. She herself has the most wonderful eyes—black as night air, rimmed by feathery lashes and heavy, dark circles.

"Well?" she demands after a few seconds of silence.

"What?" I say dumbly.

Her mouth twists. The fingers on my collar jostle a little.

"Oh. *Oh.*" My chin tilts down; she stands a good half foot shorter than me. "You want me to flinch?"

Her thumb skims along the skin of my neck. "Are you going to?"

"Are you going to hit me?"

"I'm undecided."

"Well, mull it over." I steal another glance at the circles ringing her eyes. "But do it sitting. You are wavering on your feet."

She sniffs and releases my shirt, the crimpled fabric relaxing under the absence of her grip. She hauls herself up on the table, crossing her arms. "Shockingly, it's hard to get any sleep around here."

Even so, she still has that same dangerous energy vibrating around her, a gleam in her glare, and still that lovely scowl slashing her lips, sending a strange twist through my rib cage.

"I have some things for you."

"My gloves?" she asks excitedly, pitching forward.

"Not yet." I hold out the damp rag I've been clutching, and rustle through my pocket for the other item.

She stares at the rag. "How generous," she says drily.

I shrug. "Truly, I do like the blood on your cheeks. And the soot."

She takes it and starts scrubbing at her jaw. "So," she says, "what's that?"

I move to the table, the vial in my fingers. I ease off the plastic cork and tip the round Spider capsule onto the tabletop. It rolls a few inches before meeting my fingers. When I press down, the Spider awakes, spiny limbs uncoiling from the metal abdomen. I tap its head to flip it upright, the razor pinpricks of its legs skittering across the smooth surface.

The Frostbringer recoils. "What the hells—"

"It's all right," I say, allowing the Spider to climb onto my palm. "Just a little pick-me-up."

"Is that why you're looking so bright and shiny today?" she snaps.

"Yes. Thank you for noticing."

I extend my hand, beckoning for hers. She does not move, so I close the distance and reach for her wrist, taking care with the broken flesh warping her forearm, and tip the Spider beside it. Glowing eyes scanning for the areas of interrupted flesh, it strings pale, fresh skin over the tattered portions from its spinnerets.

I take a deep breath. "Frostbringer—"

"When *am* I getting my gloves, by the way?" The Gearbreaker revolves her wrist around slowly, eyes darting over the new flesh.

I pluck the Spider away, placing it on her other forearm. "When we leave."

"Can't you just waltz in and grab them from wherever they keep the prisoner effects? That Valkyrie jacket must be a free ticket around here."

"It is. I am not getting them to you sooner than I need to."

The Spider finishes its work, and, tentatively, she pinches it between her fingers, transferring it to her cheek. Her eye winks shut as it climbs toward the gash in her hairline, and it bows its head over the laceration, weaving a thin pale thread across the cut. "And why not?"

"You are practically salivating. You would freeze me where I stood."

The Gearbreaker grins, a nervous, warbling expression that seems more like a grimace. "You don't trust me or something?"

"I trust your fear."

She pauses. The Spider, sensing no more broken flesh, stills on her crown. "I guess you're not as stupid as you look, then."

I take another breath, one hand wrapped to my side, ribs rising beneath my fingers. "Tomorrow night, I am going to tell my superiors that you will not break, and that they should collect you for the corruption process."

Her face is expressionless, fingertips patting the new skin on her knuckles. "I take it back."

I rub the bridge of my nose. "Frostbringer—"

She barks a laugh, slipping from the table, feet landing hard against the tiles. She begins to pace the room jaggedly, muttering under her breath. "I Godsdamn knew it ... has a screw loose ..."

I put myself in her path. She stops short, looking up with blazing eyes. "I have seen you fight," I say. "You are more than capable of doing this. This whole wing has no cameras so they can pick at you as they like; only the hall up to the elevators has surveillance. This cell stands at the hall adjoining it—when they come to collect you, you have until the turn to subdue them."

"Do I, now?"

"You pry back the vent that stands next to this room. The training gym is two levels down, and that is where we can rendezvous. And where I can give you the gloves. Then we will depart to the elevators, and from there, the Windup hangar." I study her face carefully. "We leave in my mecha. I have a run scheduled then."

"Brilliant. And if someone wanders in at, say, any other floor?"

"When I give you the cryo gloves I will also give you a jacket from one of the Windup units. As long you stay quiet, no one will be any the wiser."

"And the cameras?"

"I will ... put a patch over your left eye, and I think it would also be good if we pulled your collar up to your ears."

"You've got to be kidding me, Bot," she says in disbelief. "That's the plan? Stick me in a coat and hope that no one will recognize me?"

"You do your part, and stuff your fallen guards back into this room, no one will dare question whether you are anywhere you are not supposed to be," I respond, knowing the truth of my words. "Doing so would be questioning the Academy's authority, and no one in Godolia would dare do that."

"Except you."

"Except *us*. Just remember that for *no* reason should you open your mouth to talk. Your accent will identify you."

"I can do a Godolia accent," the Gearbreaker huffs.

"Yes?" I ask. "Go on, then."

"We are absolutely going to die and this plan has far too much uncertainty," she says, tongue glossing over each word. "Fantastic, right, Bot?"

"Passable," I say bluntly. "But you sound like a brothel madam, the way you exaggerate your *u*'s."

She rolls her eyes and moves past me, continuing her anxious circling. "And you sound like you're speaking to the president. All formal and articulate."

"There is no president of Godolia."

"The Zeniths. I don't care."

"My Godolia accent is perfect, Gearbreaker."

"Perfect, maybe," she muses. "Still sounds like you swallowed a slug."

Heat rushes into my cheeks.

"This is a shitty plan," she adds.

A beat of silence passes. "I am open to suggestions," I say, my throat dry.

"Holy hells—you *know* it's shitty!"

I whirl on her. "I know they will probably corrupt you in a few days regardless of what I tell them, and that is going to hurt a hells of a lot worse than if they shoot you while you are trying to run."

She is unfazed by the growl in my tone, just stares at me for a heavy moment. "You know it's shitty."

The Gearbreaker says it so flatly that I pause, and when I do, I realize how funny the whole thing is. Of course I do not know what I am doing. Of course this plan is in pieces, but I am, too, and maybe that makes it fit right. Maybe it just makes me an idiot twice over. My hands lift helplessly at my sides. "I know it's shitty."

Her nose wrinkles. She has a thin scar across her right eyebrow, only visible when freed from the lines of her scowl. For just a moment I see it flicker, before the relentless glare returns. She turns toward the blackened mirrors. I open my other eye so she can see it blaring at her reflection.

When I speak, my voice holds the bite of cold steel. "When I give you your gloves, Frostbringer, you will not turn them on me, because no matter how civil I am acting now, know that I am more than capable of holding my own in a fight. Even if it is against the likes of you."

Her reflection stands like a silhouette through smokestack smog. I cannot see the expression on her face. I take a step closer.

"If you stray from the plan, if you *leave* me here . . . ," I say, then pause, noticing the tremor in my voice.

My hands slip into my pockets, fingers twitching as they search for the nonexistent bandage. I forced myself not to make one this morning; I am too paranoid. The Academy could have taken those thoughts away easily, snipped them from our minds as we slept during the Mods surgery. But they didn't. They left our fear intact so that we could fear *them*.

But they underestimated my hate; rather, did not even think to consider the existence of it. Where they thought they instilled terror, they instead coaxed loathing, kindling to a starved fire.

I will not let them know my fear. But I will show them the flames.

"If you stray from the plan, I will pull the alarm myself," I hear myself say. "I will let them take you and do with you whatever they please. We leave here together, Frostbringer, or we die here together. It is your choice."

She turns, a cold smile pasted to her face. "I was starting to think you were some freak glitch in the Windup Program. Maybe I'm right. But either way, you're just as heartless as every other Bot out there."

I pluck the Spider from her crown and crush it between my fingers. "You should be counting on it." I wipe the fluid on my trousers. This is the part I have been dreading. "Now, come. I am supposed to try to . . . scare you, with a tour of the Windup hangar, so just . . . just know it will all be behind you soon. And—"

I stop short. The Frostbringer raises a brow. "Spit it out."

"And . . . try to not think worse of me." In my pocket, my forefinger curls into the crook of my thumb. There is so much heat in my face that it is a tangible weight. "Worse than you already do."

"I—oh," she says, surprise on her face that she quickly covers with another eye roll. "Please, Glitch. Does it look like I scare easy?"

CHAPTER FOURTEEN

ERIS

The night before I took control of my own crew, Jenny had crept into my room, presumably to kill me in my sleep.

"Get it over with," I mumbled, turning in my covers to escape the light of the hall.

She grappled my shoulder and forced me flat, midnight eyes twisted into crescents. She was leaned halfway on the bed, nose to nose, grin sprawled wide. I readied myself.

Then, Jenny smoothed a hand across my forehead, uncharacteristically soft.

"I'm dragging you," she said, and then we were up and running, my wrist held fast in her hand, down the stairwell and out into the cold night. We shot into the woods bordering the Hollows, dead leaves crunching underfoot, chilling mud seeping between my bare toes.

"Eris," she said when we stopped short, her without a thread of exhaustion from our sprint. I, on the other hand, was keeling over beside her. "All the great crews were led by Gearbreakers with names."

"No shit, Jenny," I gasped, and she slammed the heel of her hand into my temple. Lightly, though, only sending me stumbling a half step back.

"I mean aliases, you tiny bastard," she sighed. "You know,

Hookplunge, Pandora, Jumpscare, Artemassacre, Starbreach, all those legends."

I bobbed a nod. Those Gearbreakers' stories were encrypted in our history, their tales of valor and strength pounded into our ears like a war cry.

"Wait," I realized. "I don't think I've heard of Starbreach."

Grinning, she reached into her pockets and produced a pair of black gloves, coiled with what looked like orange wire. Nimbly, she pulled them into place.

Jenny turned toward the forest, fingers twitching at her sides. Shoulders pulled back to face the night, a stance that seemed to demand a round of applause, or a low bow of defeat.

A strange shock gripped me then, this feeling like a bolt of needles up my spine. As the cold fled from my cheeks, I thought to myself, *Something new is about to happen.*

Jenny's hands began to glow. Her shoulders lifted in a sigh, her black hair glinting in the moonlight.

"Oh hells," she said, raising her hands. "I am so fucking smart."

And nothing happened. After a moment Jenny dropped her hands to her sides, grin splitting wider, and I realized, excitement rolling out of me, *She's just absolutely shitfaced, isn't she?*

Then she tugged me to the side.

Before us, the tree swayed and gave in, branches cracking against the ground, dark smoke unspooling from the break. Veins of flame twisted through the trunk, the air around it fluctuating like it was trying to draw a breath.

She turned to me, glow fading from her hands, and after digging in her back pocket, pulled out another pair of gloves, this one twined with blue. She held them out to me, and a chill went through me that had nothing to do with the single-digit temperature.

"Oh no," I said.

Jenny leaned close, pushing the gloves into my hands. "Don't worry, don't worry. I've made it so the gloves are bound to our DNA. The serums recognize us. They won't hurt us. Why would they? Why would they *dare*? I'm their mother-freaking *God*. I—"

"You're drunk."

"I'm young, and a genius, and the world's ending all the time now, so you can shut up." She finished tightening them around my wrists. "I have made something exquisite."

I dropped my head to look at the gloves; her finger slipped under my chin, raising my gaze to meet hers. Her smile was gone, but its ghost still moved behind her eyes.

"Eris, I made you. From what's in your heart to what's in your head and everything in between. I truly and honestly feel sorry for the crew that's going to be stuck under your command."

"Jen—"

Her fingertip prodded my sternum, silencing me.

"I made you," she repeated, voice low, a hunting dog's growl. "I made you to be strong and I made you to be clever and I made you to be feared." Her hands slid from my shoulders, down my arms, and then her palms were cradling mine. "I made you so that every sorry son-of-a-bitch Pilot and Zenith and Windup that has the unfortunate luck of going head-to-head with you takes one look and feels as if their blood is freezing in their veins. I made these gloves, Eris. I created them to be tools, nothing more. It was *you* I created to be a weapon. And you will always be my greatest invention."

Her arms wrapped around me, cheek resting at the top of my head. My arms dangled at my sides, limp with shock. She hadn't hugged me since we were kids, maybe not even then. Her dark hair drifted into my face. She smelled like ash and moss dew and frost.

"I want you to be careful out there," she murmured, arms twitching around me, hesitant, unsure about the act of comforting. "Be fearless and terrifying and ridiculously reckless, as I know you are, but remember that you do not have my permission to die." Her hands shifted around my shoulders, and I felt her tug one of her gloves off. Her bare fingers threaded through my hair, timidly, tenderly.

"Give them hells, Eris. My little sister. My little Frostbringer."

Why do I reminisce about this emotional, sweet sibling moment? Because if this escape doesn't kill me, Jenny most definitely will.

At least the thought made the binds around my wrists, the small cluster of guards sent to surround me during Sona's little tour, and the army of mechas in my path seem a little less material, a little more of a joke. *You think this is scaring me, Glitch? This is my whole life.*

Large, slender eyes drawn low, half-red crescent burning beneath one lid, Sona guided our party between the mecha rows of the Windup hangar. We trailed past paint clouds marking fresh, vicious coats; skinless frames shot through with wire and workers; edges of steel boots made uneven with last runs, bumpy with bone. Her expression remained indifferent, almost bored throughout, as she repeated variations of *This is how we will slaughter your entire family* as we worked our way through. It was when we went before the Phantoms that I learned that her tell isn't in her face. It's in her hands.

She was bleeding. Fingernails burrowed straight through the skin of her palms, red licking into her cuticles. She barely glanced at them, just shoved them into the pockets of her Valkyrie jacket before turning and hesitating, realizing that I had seen.

It's in her hands, and in her eyes.

Imagine killing her, I begged myself. *Imagine wires spilling out of the open cuts, because this is how this ends, this is how this* has *to end*—

But something in her eyes—even the one provided by the Academy—was familiar. It was the same expression that infected my features during my first takedown, though I tried to suppress it. *She's wearing my fear.*

Now, even safely sealed in my cell, I can't get her out of my head.

I run a hand through my hair, carelessly tugging against the knots. I don't know what to make of the Bot. Glitch. Sona. It could all be an intricate lie—the plan, her tears, her story. We escape and I bring her right to the Hollows' doorstep, and she calls in her friends, who'll kill all of mine.

But I have no other choice.

I'll get no other chance.

I look at my reflection, pasted across each mirror whenever she's not here to darken them. I note the black circles under my eyes, so burrowed into my face it seems like they were carved there. Dried blood still sticks to my hairline and my collar, and the veins of my cheeks shine purple through the skin.

After the tour, when we were alone again in the cell, Sona went over the plan once more and then left me to get some sleep. I don't do that. Instead, I pace the room. I pick at the cold food they give me. I think of my crew and Jenny, at first only sifting through memories, but eventually beginning to imagine the future, too, after I escape.

My lips crack apart as I smile. Milo's going to lose it when I see him, grab me by the shoulders, lean in close—*Did they hurt you?* I'll swat away his grip and brush past him. *Did you really think I'd even let them get close? Don't insult me.*

I chase ridiculously simple and dull fantasies, everyday events that I didn't realize I missed, watching them pan out one after another across the tiled floor from my tabletop perch. Theo and Nova bickering, light slaps quickly turned into full-swing punches and bruised limbs. Xander and Juniper playing their brutally intense chess games, Arsen trotting around the briefing room, knocking over furniture and chattering loudly to grab their attention. Milo calm during it all, turning the worn pages of a paperback silently, eyes lifting from the words occasionally to touch on mine, a crooked smile, dimpled cheek.

I suffocate those thoughts as soon as they come. They have a near-dangerous quality to them—too comfortable, too real, and too much like a promise.

After hours of nothing—it must be daylight by now—I lie back on the table, knees up, and press my palms to my eyes until stars spark from the darkness. Jenny's voice has started ringing in my head again. What the hells am I supposed to do if Sona's telling the truth? Bring her to the Hollows, watch her get shot on sight as soon as they get a glimpse of her eye? Would I move to step in front of her, even if I truly believed her story?

At this point, killing her would be the easy path. For both of us.

Gods, she's quiet. I pull my hands from my face to see Glitch already getting to work on the mirrors, the one eye sliding shut as soon as she's finished.

"I'm bored," I say, sitting upright. I take to cracking my knuckles against the heels of my hands. I must've done it a hundred times today, and there's no longer any pops. "Nothing to do around here."

She blinks. "You are in prison, and your only complaint is that of boredom?"

"Of course that's not my only complaint. Want me to list them out for you?"

"Not particularly."

I hop down from the table. "Did you get my gloves?"

"Yes."

"And my goggles, too?"

"Why?" Glitch asks, tone even as always. "You look fine without them."

"What a high compliment. Are you always such a flirt?"

She cocks her head slightly, curls slipping off her shoulder. "I am trying to be more truthful."

"Are you joking?"

"No."

For some reason, that makes me bristle. "Why are you here?"

"This is the moment I realize that you are a lost cause, and afterward, I will go to my captain and tell him so." That makes all words momentarily depart from my head in a bolt of fear, and my silence allows her to clarify, "I have my run in a few hours, and I need to time it right, so we can rendezvous instead of you almost certainly dying during the corruption process."

"Thank you for that," I say faintly. "Can't we just both stand here in silence, then?"

"Do you not enjoy talking to me, Frostbringer?"

"I'm sure about as much as you like talking to me."

"I actually very much enjoy our talks."

"Is it my amazing personality?" The corners of her lips twitch. "I knew it. Who knew a Bot could be so perceptive?"

"It's not that," Glitch says, and suddenly, she moves a step closer.

My near feeling of ease snaps to shreds as fear, cold and rabid, steals my next heartbeat. Her finger treads along my shirt collar, other hand planted behind me on the table's edge, and I think, *This is it. You hopeful idiot. A girl with doe eyes spews a sob story, and you cling to it. You deserve this.*

But all Glitch does is tug down my shirt a few inches, revealing my collarbone and the eighty-seven gears in two inked rows down its length. It should be eighty-nine. Hungrily, her eyes skim over the tattoos.

"It is that, every time I see you . . . ," Glitch says, voice a soft, dangerous whisper. Sweat prickles at the nape of my neck. A new look has taken over her features—an eerily calm, resolved expression. Her thumb taps lightly on one of the gears, just once, touch as quick as my flinch. ". . . I see Godolia burning to the ground. I see ash and scrap metal peppering the crater where it once sat. I see its hideous mark scraped off every single map, its record split from history, its reputation not ruined, but obliterated. And I see every Zenith, every loyal Pilot, and every Windup dead along with it."

Glitch releases my shirt and tucks her hair behind both of her ears. Her eye is still locked on me, the other festering beneath the closed lid, as if trying to burn its way out to see my shocked expression.

"I see peace when I see you, Frostbringer," Sona says, grinning prettily.

I manage only a half step back before my spine meets the lip of the tabletop. I can still feel her touch on my collarbone, dancing across the gear.

"You—you sound . . . ," I stutter, grappling for the words. *Insane. Sadistic. Violent. Demonic.* I run a nervous hand through my hair. "Gods. You sound like a Gearbreaker."

For an instant, silence soaks the air between us, and I swear that both of our faces flush pink at the same time. I shouldn't have said it, but I can't take it back.

The look in her eyes—it's the same expression across my crew's features when a mecha crashes to its knees. A look of battle fervor, when you stand over your fallen enemy and feel how vividly your heartbeat pulsates in each vein, realizing how close you were to death but somehow, in the face of it all, you're still *here*, and you *won*.

"Do you remember the plan?" Glitch murmurs swiftly, scattering my thoughts. One of her hands is deep in her jacket pocket, and through the fabric her fingertips twitch.

I nod. "Yeah. I have until the end of this hallway to take out the guards. Once I drag them back here, I go into the vent, crawl until there's a split, and I take a . . . a . . ."

"A left," Glitch reminds me.

"Right. I mean, yes, I take a left," I say. "Straight until I get to the service shaft. Down the ladder, then crawl into the second opening I come to. Go until I get to the second split in the path, and that should lead to your training room."

"Third split, Frostbringer."

I shake my head. "Right. Third."

I consider for a moment, and then unhook my overall straps, taking the bottom of my shirt between my fingers and tearing away a strip.

"First left," I murmur, holding the fabric above my left wrist. "Third split."

I knot the cloth three times, then move to tie it. It's hard to do with one hand, and I fumble until Glitch's fingers suddenly take my wrist, nimbly securing the knot. Without thinking, I grab her sleeve before she can step back.

"Is it too tight?" she asks, and my throat constricts at her concerned expression. I release her jacket, shaking my head again.

"This . . . this is going to work, right?" I ask, hating the smallness of my voice, the clear urgent need for her agreement.

It doesn't come. "No. We are probably both going to die."

I laugh drily. "Good pep talk, Bot."

"Would you prefer I sugarcoat it?" she asks softly. "Listen, Gearbreaker—Frostbringer, whichever you prefer—I am not going to lie about the risks. I will not list them in their excessive quantity, or outline their particular cruelties, because you and I both know them intimately. But do you care about the consequences as much as you care about escaping? As much as you care about dying as your own person? If we do die, it will be with our weapons out, using our last breaths to spit on Godolia's name and taking as many of their pathetic sycophants down with us as we can. Our final words will be of fury and hatred and the *defiance* they believe to be extinct. So I ask you again, Frostbringer, would you prefer I sugarcoat it? Or would you like better to be reminded that no matter the outcome, we will not die as theirs?"

Oh Gods, that look she's giving me. I hide the sudden rise of my heartbeat by pulling my overall straps back onto my shoulders, taking a moment to thumb the bracelet Sona set around my wrist.

"I have a gift for you," she says, and removes something from her belt, laying it on the table. It's a knife with an ornate handle—the same type the Pilots used to carve my arms. For a moment, a flash of an image—Sona at a dining table, crowded by Valkyries. They're all cutting up their food with the same utensils, passing around the salt—

Then both of her eyes lift to me, one crimson, the other that dark, rich hazel. Both large, shaped like half-moons, and an oil-black lash shoved in every available space. The image sputters out of my head.

"What?" I snap, expecting another twisted pep talk. "What is it?"

"Just . . . you can trust me in full, if you would like," she murmurs. "Trust my fear like I trust yours, if it is easier."

"Easier for what?"

"Getting out. It does not have to be enemies on all sides." Another pause, and she shakes her head. "And after that . . ."

"What, we'll be friends?"

"We will be alive," she corrects me, and one of her hands brushes against her opposite forearm, where the panel rests beneath the jacket sleeve. It's a gesture so slight that I'm sure she doesn't realize she's doing it. "I suppose it is up to you whether I stay that way."

I know what she's getting at. She'll be wound, real body rendered helpless. With my gloves, I'll be anything but.

I look at the knife, glossy handle slick with light, blade hovering over the table's surface. There's us, reflected partially in the metal. An incomplete picture. There's none of her twitching fingers, her Mod eye, the Valkyrie jacket hugged around her shoulders. There's just this: a girl staring at me, carefully, a fragment of my dirty face, and a knife on the table.

"Glitch?"

"Yes?" she asks, not a flicker of doubt in responding to my ridiculous pet name.

"It's Eris," I say, hushing Jenny's voice in my head. I swallow hard. "My name is Eris."

A pause, and then a slight smile plays on her lips, one that, this time, doesn't leave my blood chilled.

"Eris," Sona repeats, trying out my name.

It's not soft, like the way Milo always says it, but she does say it carefully. Like turning it the wrong way could cut her tongue.

Then she says, "Eris, could you please hit me very hard across the face?"

CHAPTER FIFTEEN

SONA

0900 Hours

Her name is Eris.

I repeat it over and over in my head, as if I am afraid to lose the memory of the slight crack in her scowl, the eyes that for a slender moment rested on the one I loathe, but held the gaze as if it was not disgusting or unnatural.

I will not tell her name to Lucindo, nor will I dare utter it to anyone else until we are rid of this Godsforsaken city. Let Godolia know her only as a Gearbreaker or the Frostbringer. Let them know only the threat that rings in the mention, and let them demonize and damn the aliases. But the name Eris will not belong to them.

I find Lucindo in the Valkyrie common room. He takes one look at my face and scrambles to his feet, leaping over the back of the couch to grab my arm as I walk past, spinning me to face him.

"What—" he starts.

"I failed," I say bluntly, voice hard. My gaze is dropped to his boots. I am ashamed. I am not internally celebrating. "The Frostbringer, I tried . . . She will not—"

"Sona . . ." Now his other hand slips around my free arm, squeezing. *Do not touch me, you vile infestation.* "You did the best you could."

"I need a Spider," I mutter, pushing past him. The sprawling hallways are decorated with photographs and paintings, flowers pressed behind glass and mirrors with intricate frames. I catch a glimpse of the cut on my cheek as I pass one by; and also of Lucindo, dogging close behind. "I am fine, Lucindo."

"She'll be corrupted," he reassures me. "I'll send for them to get the process started immediately."

"She will die."

"You don't think she's strong enough to survive?"

I stop short and spin. "I think she, even after everything she has done, is just a reckless child. She talks like she is above all of this, but she is just another Badlands girl forgetting how small she truly is. My only hope is that corruption will shoot some sense into her before she dies."

Lucindo is suddenly smiling. "I was half-afraid you were going sweet on the Gearbreaker, Sona."

Good Gods. I would roll my eyes if I thought it would do him any good. We are talking about murdering a girl, and still he finds room to flirt with me. I do not care enough to tell him that one, boys have never been my interest, and two, I am planning to burn his nation to the ground. So instead I will be mean, and watch him gouge out some form of affection from it regardless. It is a predictable practice.

"I am about as sweet on her as you are on me," I respond, the yawn in my voice a simple taunt. But Lucindo is a simple boy, and his cheeks slip into a deeper hue. If I could see his colors, I believe he would be a collection of pastels—pale pink skin, cyan eye, milky hair.

"Which is to say what, exactly?" he manages.

"You could say nothing at all, so I can go get some training done in peace." I look briefly at his forearms, exposed by the rolled sleeves of his jacket, at the panel set into each one. I have thought about tearing out his silver dishes before, just as an experiment, a test run, to see how much blood he would lose. If he could survive that, then perhaps I could, too.

"Is that any way to speak to your unit captain, soldier?"

"Mm, and tell me, how would you prefer I speak to you, *Captain*?" I say, voice hushed, as I mull over these fantasies. "If you are looking for soft words, I would recommend the brothel district."

"You wound me greatly, Sona Steelcrest."

"I have not laid a finger on you, and do not plan to."

Lucindo smirks, hand rising to ruffle the back of his head, which is tilted over mine.

"You'll be okay for your run?"

"Of course."

"Good," he says, and hesitates. A cold dread suddenly wraps itself around my spine. "I, uh . . . I had to assign Victoria to accompany you today."

My mask slips. "What? Why? I am still on trial runs; it is just another escort mission. I do not need—"

"Gearbreakers were spotted late last night in the area you're being sent to." He shakes his head. "Sona—"

"And you know how I handled myself before!"

"I do, but . . ." He trails off, a guilty look snaking across his features.

"Do the Zeniths believe the Gearbreaker's words are twisting my thoughts? My loyalties?" I demand, mind reeling. "Is that what *you* think?"

"Of course I don't!"

"Then take her off my run!"

"It's not my call, Sona—"

I leave him in the hall, my feet finding my bedroom, hands finding my sheets. I seize its fraying edge, peel back yet another strip, and stuff it into my pocket. My canvas bag is tugged roughly over my shoulder before I leave the room, somehow reaching the elevator, then the right training room, barely keeping it together long enough to unlatch the zipper of the Valkyrie jacket. There is sweat slicking my neck, and the mirror makes the room too bright. *You need to get it together and—*

When I pull my hands from the sleeves, I pause, raising them to the light.

Am I shaking?

I skim my fingers over the knuckles of the opposite hand.

How could I not be shaking?

My heartbeat quickens, and so does the hum. My fingernails curl into my sides, seeking an invisible seam or a ridge separating my skin from the Spider's thread, to dip into and tear back. There is nothing—it is me, it is all me, humming, glowing, pretending to gasp for breath. I am not steadfast; I am not something rigid. I am a child who must kill today, and it makes me scared for myself.

I am so, so scared, and they will not even let me tremble.

"Give me an Auto," I grit through clenched teeth, forcing my grip around a sparring sword. Its weight and its handle and the way it sits snug against my palm are the most familiar things in the world, like giving an old friend a handshake. If I had any old friends.

The mirror that envelops the back wall splits down its middle, peeling back to reveal a slim corridor. Inside, a row of Autos spiral back into darkness. The frontmost one lifts its head.

My stance is weak, my reaction time atrocious. The finishing blow is heavy-handed, too much brute force and not enough control. Before I call for the next Auto, I rip the sheet fabric from my jacket pocket and tie it around my head—its length long enough to wrap around twice—knotting it behind my right ear. Color touches the world again, dark blue across the floor mat and a vicious silver into the blades of the sparring swords.

The second falls quicker, the third easier.

When the fourth charges, there is movement in the doorway that pulls my glance. *No.* Our blades crash, but I lose my footing, and I am on the floor with its knee swinging for my chest. It cannot kill me, but bludgeoning is well within its parameters.

Then Rose is there, shoving it back with her bare hands, jeering with a vibrant laugh, "Yeah, yeah, you can piss off, you old bag of bolts."

It revs back and swings; she ducks beneath its blade and plants an effortless roundhouse into its side, and, stealing a discarded Auto blade, makes a quick and neat line to sever head from neck.

She turns, curls crowding her face as she leans over me. In her other hand, held tenderly, skitters a Spider.

"Heard you needed this," Rose says, smile pinching her eyes. "Want a training partner?"

CHAPTER SIXTEEN

ERIS

0945 Hours

The knife goes in my shoe.

I realize this is a horrible idea only after the guards come and bind my wrists behind my back.

"Could you do it the other way?" I ask, because the worst thing they could respond with is *We're going to kill you*, which already feels implied. I'm answered with silence. "You could at least say something." The door is suddenly looking a lot like a gravestone. The hallway is laughably short, if I remember correctly. Sweat pricks at the back of my neck. "I'm not leaving until you say something!"

A guard with a shaved head shoves me toward the door and grunts, "Shut up."

"Say something else."

She shoves me again, harder, and I lose my footing, landing awkwardly on my shoulder without any hands to catch myself. I roll my cheek against the ground and sigh into the floor, because it looks like it's going to be that kind of day.

"Get up," another guard barks, grabbing the back of my shirt and lifting me to my knees. I flick my sight to the right, note that he's the one with the cuff keys, and then slam my forehead into his crotch.

"I didn't enjoy that either," I say as he doubles over, before the third guard brings his fist to my temple. My vision slurs—*does that even make sense, I'm not sure*—and he wraps his hand in my collar and lifts me clean off my feet.

"Don't," Shaved Head warns as my toes scrape against the ground. "She's going to be corrupted, and it's going to hurt a hells of a lot worse than whatever you're about to do."

"You could try," I say, and then spit on Third's cheek. His grip clenches momentarily, face darkening, but then, with remarkable composure, his fingers loosen from the fabric.

"You know, Starbreach had a mouth like yours," he growls, hand coiled around my arm, hauling me toward the door. "Didn't work out so well for her, either."

My entire body goes cold.

"What?" I murmur as we enter the hall.

Key Guard wraps a hand in my hair and pulls, my head bent back below his. "Crushed flat and drowned, her and the whole crew."

"Guess making that kid a Valkyrie was the right move." Shaved Head laughs. "I heard she stained the shores red."

"No," I breathe. Glitch wouldn't—she said—Sona said—*no*. Jenny.

Jenny, *dead*. It doesn't fit. Doesn't suit her.

Please no.

We are forty paces from the end of the hall. Third and Key have my arms; Shaved Head is a step in front of us.

"Aw, the little Gearbreaker is tearing up," coos Third, and I turn and spit on his cheek again.

He recoils. I lift my leg and drive my heel into the side of Key's knee.

He crumples with a shriek, hand slipping from my arm,

and I lunge my weight to bring my knee into the bridge of his nose. His head snaps back, limbs going limp.

"Get up, you idiot," Shaved Head shouts, while Third yanks me back with a growl. He opens his mouth to say something, and I spit on his face a third time. Never gets old.

He shoves me away with one hand still clutching onto me, so he can have enough room to strike me with the other. I drop to the floor—and to the guard on the floor—the blow sailing over my head, fingers grasping behind me, against fabric, fabric, belt, metal, and by the time he pulls me up, the keys are flipping into my palm. The first one doesn't click—note: cell door—and before I can try the next, his knuckles crack against my mouth. I feel the moment my lip splits open, and that must act as some sort of karmic payment, because the next key on the ring fits properly, and the cuffs drop from my wrists.

My fingers catch them before they fall. I twine my knuckles in their chain and swing a hook into the guard's ribs, then his stomach, uppercut into his jaw. He groans, grappling for the gun at his side, and at the same time, Shaved Head lunges for me, a baton materialized in her hand. It glances inches from my neck, a hum emitting in my ear, the taste of metal sparking on my tongue—electrified, really?—and I drive my foot to crush Third's hand into the wall. Shaved Head's boot finds my side; I drop to my knees with a groan, curl three fingers around the loop of one cuff, and send the other snapping across Third's brow. Eyes rolling, he falters against the wall and goes still.

Shaved Head descends on me, knee pinning my shoulder to the floor, baton arcing to collide with my crown. I flinch, so it only skims my temple, pain threading the point of contact in a violent, barbed web, and—I realize I can't see.

My eyes are seized shut. I can't move, fingers splayed taut

at my side, toes stiff in my shoes. Panic grabs me, throttles me. *This is it. I failed, I'm going to d—*

"Godsdamn it," Shaved Head mutters, toe digging into my side. A slight shuffling, and hands are sliding under my arms, lifting my dead weight from the ground.

She thinks I'm unconscious.

She's dragging me. My heels scrape against the floor, rubber squeaking against the tiles. How many paces to the end of the hall again? How far have we gone?

Move, damn it.

But I feel nothing of myself save for the tears on my cheeks.

My sister is dead.

She's dead, and Sona killed her. Sona, who waits for me two floors below my feet, who took my wrist like it meant something to her, like I could mean something to her.

She has to pay for it.

My fingers twitch at my sides.

She's going to pay for it.

I twist, the guard's hands slipping from me, roll once, stomach to back and then onto my feet.

With the knife in my hand.

Shaved Head's mouth forms a tiny O, and the blade finds flesh.

It goes easily, for a few inches, and then it hits something tougher. I pull until it gives, and the guard falls to the floor.

Still a little numb and a lot disoriented, I drag the guards one by one back into my cell and lock the door. Then I turn. The hallway is covered in blood. Streaked across the tiles. Speckled faintly on the walls, generously over my hands, the doorknob smeared red. Half-heartedly, I wipe it away with my sleeve. Can't do much about the state of everything else, but that's nothing new.

I peel back the vent grate and pull myself inside, crawling until the first split. The fabric around my left wrist; I turn left. The service shaft yawns darkly, a million-story drop, or only just around a hundred, but my body won't know much of a difference if I fall. I grip the ladder, descend past one opening, slip into the next. Crawl. Three knots; third split.

Sweat flattens my shirt to my spine. My hands pad against the metal, blotting red in ghostly outlines. Up ahead, the quick, ringing clash of swords shivers through the vent.

It'll happen once I'm safely away from this Godsforsaken city, before she can unwind and realize what's happening. Another gear for me; one less Pilot to kill off more of my family. Win-freaking-win.

I reach the end of the vent, and peer into a space littered with mechanical body parts. Sona traces the room in a slow circle, blade in hand, dark curls tied back, cloth wrapped around her head.

I follow the clean, practiced flick of Sona's blade before I realize there's someone else in the room.

As if the panic could speak, as if my hands weren't clasped around my mouth, the other Pilot turns.

And looks me straight in the eye.

CHAPTER SEVENTEEN

SONA

1000 Hours

"I had heard you use an eye patch," Rose chatters as she grabs a sparring sword. The Spider whirs against my cheek, set there by her hand. "Vic was bitching about it, but, hey, it's obviously a system that works for you."

"I . . ." *Need you to leave. Please, for the love of Gods, go.* "I usually train alone."

Unwillingly, my eye drifts toward the small grate bolted into the room's corner. Eris should be in the vents by now, making her way toward me. She expects to find me alone. Will she flee if she sees two Pilots instead of one?

Unless she has fled already, despite her lack of gloves, or took a wrong turn down a hallway and ran into a thousand other Pilots. Unless she is already dead, and this whole plan was shot from the start, and it was childish and ignorant to believe that I would *ever escape here.*

"Where's the fun in that?" Rose asks, punting aside lopped Auto limbs to take her stance.

"Rose," I strain, plucking the Spider away. My knuckles are white around the grip of the sword. "I would prefer to be alone."

"I heard that Vic is going on your run with you. It's a low blow, really, but none of the Valkyries think that of you. Think that Gearbreaker got in your head, that is. I certainly don't, I just think—I think you're just about the loveliest person, Sona." She pauses to beam at me, angling the sword thoughtfully in her hand. "Well, maybe Vic thinks something worse, but that's only her working out the more complicated feelings she has toward you. You'll have to forgive her."

"Victoria—" I stop short, shake my head. I cannot be talking about this now; she just needs to *go*. I need to be rude, even cruel, get her to leave quicker. It does not matter; I am not going to ever see her again, anyway.

But it is *Rose*. Sweet, cheery, caring Rose.

And she is already charging.

It is all I can do to get my blade up in time. It locks against hers, and then we are nose to nose. I can count the freckles on her cheeks. She is still grinning.

"Oh, you are *good*," she sings as we trace around the room, up and over broken bot parts, shoes sucking against the spilled gear oil. She chatters as she fights, hums during the spaces in between, light on her feet and practiced in her strikes, second in skill only to Lucindo in our unit. Rose brings her sword to my neck thrice, each time bubbling a bright laugh before pulling away to reset her stance. She does not want to hurt me. She wants to teach.

Lump forming in my throat, I force my gaze to her face as we start up again. Not at her right eye, the deep, warm brown, but at the left, smoldering red. I hate that color. I hate Godolia. I hate the Pilots, all the ones who have happily stitched their skin with wire for the chance to become the Academy's puppets. I hate her.

I need to.

I swing. Rose parries with a grin, and says, "Oh, I wanted to ask you—"

She goes very still.

It seems to happen slowly, her head snapping upward, enough of a lapse for the horror to fill up all the empty space and take root.

"I think . . . ," she murmurs. Her gaze is lifted toward the grate. "I think I saw someone in the vent."

"You are trying to distract me," I say smoothly, ice in my veins, allowing my eyes to touch on the grate for a moment. Eris is not there, but she may have been, just a moment before seeing the unknown person and ducking away. But nothing escapes Rose.

"No!" she presses, taking a step forward. "I saw someone; give me a second . . ."

I watch her reach the wall, rising to the tops of her toes, height just barely enough to see over the grate's edge. A small gasp falls from her lips.

My feet move.

"It's the Gearbreaker! Sona, get—"

Rose turns to face me again, and I run my blade across the width of her neck.

The skin splits open too easily, the act too seamless, too silent. Her hands go up to clutch the wound, and blood trickles over her lithe fingers and rolls in large teardrops down her sleeves. She stumbles forward, and I can clearly see her lips moving to form my name, a tone that would be soaked through with shock if the blood were not there to silence it.

I do not move, thinking she will collapse before she can reach me, or thinking that I too will break if I try to run, but either way suddenly she is too close, and she is too helpless, and her stubbornness and strength are too incomprehensible as she releases her neck to grapple onto the collar of my shirt, and it is all *too much*. I can feel her warmth spilling against me as she pulls herself closer to keep on her feet, and without thinking, I shove her backward with everything I can manage.

Rose twitches against the ground, blood pooling from her neck, red spreading from beneath her form like a canary's wings. Her lips are somehow still moving, my name still across them. *Help me, Sona. Why, Sona?*

"Just die already," I say softly—a wish, a plea.

And then, as if she was simply waiting for my permission, the red pool stops expanding. Her eye flickers out, glow dulling until it becomes nearly colorless, and yet, her gaze still clings to me.

"Come out, Frostbringer," I call. There is a blatant tremor to my voice. Pathetic, sympathetic. "We do not have any time to waste."

Nothing happens at first, and for a moment, I am afraid that she bolted. But then a hand emerges from the darkness, pressing against the bars of the grate. Her arms tuck around her head, rolling as she lands, on both feet before me in the next second.

She brushes her hair back from her face with one blood-streaked hand. She has a split lip, both cheeks flushed pink. "Who—"

I shake my head. It does not matter, because it cannot matter.

From the canvas bag, I remove a stolen Berserker jacket with Eris's effects wrapped up inside. I hold it out to her.

"You're shaking," she tells me.

"I am not," I say, shoving the jacket at her. I retract my hands, stare over each digit. Somehow, impossibly, she is right.

My hands are trembling. "That's . . . that's not supposed to happen anymore."

Eris slips on the jacket. It fits loose around her frame, but will suffice nonetheless. She tugs the welding goggles over her head, leaving them to perch on her hairline, and then pulls on the gloves. A sigh falls from her lips once they are secure—an expression of near bliss, of finally being back in the comforting grasp of familiarity.

I drop my blade to the floor.

"I told you," Eris says, and something passes over her face that I do not catch. "You're a glitch."

CHAPTER EIGHTEEN

ERIS

1025 Hours

I don't think Sona realized that she flinched when I hit the floor. I don't think she's aware of the look on her face now, the tremble to her lip, the slight fracture in the measured poise. Her shirt is slick down its front, the green material dyed a startling black, the blood only showing its true color on her right wrist and fingers and across the silver blade. Her curls swell around the strip of fabric wrapped around her hair, baby hairs stuck to the thin sheen of sweat on her brow.

All at once, I'm realizing how young she is, how young we both are. Just two girls, scared absolutely shitless, with hands painted red before midday.

"Was that your first kill?" I ask, securing my gloves—*oh*, my wonderful gloves—around my wrists and tugging on the soft, leather-rimmed goggles. The Berserker jacket is something unfortunate, but it's the best cover as the most common Windup unit.

I wait for her to lie. To nod her head, to say easily, *I have never killed before and this is why you can trust me.* But instead, she lifts her eye to mine, and there is no triumph there, no steel, just a look so steady and sad and raw it twists something in me.

"No," Sona says. "I have killed so many people."

"Oh," I say, because there is no other possible follow-up to that.

She doesn't move for a few seconds, staring at the dead Pilot. Then in a single, fluid motion, she pulls her bloodied shirt up and over her head. I stare, then realize that's the opposite of what I should do, and avert my eyes as she runs her tongue over her fingers, using her spit to wipe away the red dots scattered across her collarbone. Once clean, she zips her Valkyrie jacket up to her throat.

"We need to go," she says, dropping the shirt to the floor. "I put the medical patch in your pocket."

"This is not going to work," I say, even as I seal the patch over my eye. I yank away the strands of my hair that stick underneath the tape.

Sona calmly unwraps the bandage from around her head, winding it into a ball before storing it.

"As you have said before," she says, turning toward the door. "Come."

I ball my hands into fists, feeling how the veins of the cryo gloves stretch taut over the surface, and bury them deep into my pockets. Somehow, in hiding their power, I feel a bit of my unease dissipate.

I follow Sona out of the training room and down the hallway, then wait as she presses the elevator button. Her expression is so resolved that I wonder if one of the Mods included plating her facial structure with steel.

When the doors open, she doesn't even blink before stepping over the threshold, as if it were possible that she didn't also feel a jolt of panic at the five other Pilots standing inside the elevator.

"Are you coming?" Sona asks. "There is more than enough room."

She blends in *so seamlessly* with them. Oh, *ha*, and you know why she does—you absolute freaking *idiot*—it might be because she *is* one of them. That might help, good Gods, what the hells am I *doing here*—

Where the hells else can I go?

And then, too soon, I am standing next to her, and too soon the elevator doors are closing, their quiet click like the final nail in a coffin. Oh Gods, I'm *breathing*. The oversized jacket might be enough to cover the quick rise and fall of my chest, but the others must be able to hear the rapid cannon of my heartbeat. Jenny's voice rings in my ears: *Go for the Pilot go for the Pilot go*—

Sona's hand slips over my forearm, a gesture so soft and quick that I nearly miss it. But even from underneath the jacket sleeve, I can feel her warmth, the purpose beneath it. It's a reassurance, a comfort that couldn't possibly come from someone like her. And yet, I find the ability to draw a full, slow breath.

You still have to kill her.

The elevator stops, opening up to what looks like a cafeteria. Long rows of tables sprawl beneath a wall of windows, gray light filtering over the bustling space. Everywhere there are Windup jackets, Pilots with glowing eyes, pinched with laughter. Hands gripped around pieces of bread, panels scraping their forearms. Someone at the table nearest to us flashes a grin into their mug. It suddenly smells like coffee and cinnamon toast, startlingly soft compared to the bleachy air of the elevator.

Everyone but us exits the elevator. Even in the empty space, we stay silent, as if words will break the thin aura of pure dumb luck wound around us.

When the elevator stops again, she exits at a brisk pace. I suppress my urge to shudder as I silently trail her through the Windup hangar. It is a quite literal Gearbreaker hell. The sheer number of bright and shiny Windups—with their expanses of undented and unscathed skin and the eyes that I feel smoldering above my head—causes a dark thought to begin to throb, the same one that lies hidden inside every person who calls the Hollows their home: No matter how many mechas we dismantle, no matter how many tattoos we get inked across our skin, there will always be more Windups.

Thirty paces ahead of me, she stops at the base of one of the Valkyries. *Her* Valkyrie. Sona leans toward the side of its golden boot, offering her left eye as the key. When the door slides open, she turns back to look at me, hand raised to gesture. Then it freezes, and her gaze slips to the left.

I get the message immediately. I turn right, slipping between two other mechas, and glance back over my shoulder. The Pilot who was approaching behind me passes by a few feet away, pale golden hair fluttering with each of her hard steps. She marches straight up to Sona, who opens her mouth in greeting before the Pilot shoves her back against the mecha.

Heart rabbiting in my chest, I force my steps to even out, and I approach as close as I dare. Hugging the Berserker jacket closer around my form, I stop to hover behind the ankle of the Valkyrie neighboring Sona's.

"—blood *everywhere*," the Pilot hisses, finger drilling into Glitch's chest. Glitch looks on, face impassive, save for the vicious glaze to her eyes. "Where the hells is the Gearbreaker, Bellsona?"

High cheekbones, statuesque height, porcelain skin, one jade iris to best the Hollows' oak trees in high summer. I stumble for the Pilot's name. *Victoria.*

I plucked out her eye, and now she's bright and shiny and ready to bite Sona's head off.

Shit.

"And why would I know this?" Sona murmurs, eyes dropped to Victoria's hand gripping her sleeve.

"You jumped at the chance to interrogate the Frostbringer, and now she leaves a bloodbath behind just in time for your run? I don't think so." A cold laugh twists her words, and the sureness of them chills me. Yep, she got it. One hundred percent. "You are playing *pretend*, sweetheart. Have been since the Academy spit you into this unit, crowned on your high fucking horse. You hesitate, and I see it. You probably didn't even kill Starbreach. You don't have the guts."

A new expression takes over Sona's face, a look that I've felt across my own features a hundred times just today: the gripping urge to hit something. I expect it to quell in a second, for that incredible control to grind it down into dust. Instead, she unfurls. She straightens her spine and snatches Victoria's arm, pulling, shortening the distance between them.

"And *you* are a jealous child," Glitch sneers in Victoria's face, a cruel smirk crinkling her left eye. "It is so pathetic to watch, and so very irritating. I do not kiss the ground you walk on, so I must want to destroy you and everything you stand for, is that it? Make no mistake, Victoria. I am a damn good Pilot, and a hells of a swordsman, and I could do so much to you. But I do not. I do not bow or kneel or flinch, and you hate it, but you should take comfort. I do not hate you. I think nothing of you at all."

Victoria, to her credit, meets this absolutely decimating speech with a flare of her own. "You don't flinch for me, fine. You don't care for me, even better. But when they shower you with praise, when they cheer to your stories, when they pull you close—that is when you writhe, sweetheart. The only reason you don't recoil from me is because I'm the only one here who does not adore you."

"Does it look like I am one to recoil?" Glitch snarls.

It's that moment when they both realize how close they are.

Glitch blinks. When Victoria brings her mouth to hers, she blinks again.

Then her eyes lie closed, those long, dark lashes dusting her cheeks. At her side, her hand flicks toward the door.

Right before I duck into the Windup, Victoria brings her hand to Sona's cheek.

I climb, the thumping of my heart attempting to propel me from the ladder rungs.

You probably didn't even kill Starbreach.

Could it be true?

Can I risk it?

It's eerie being alone in the mecha's head. Whenever I've had the occasion to in the past, the room would've already succumbed to, well, me, pieces of it chipped or shattered or frostbitten. And amid it all, the Pilot, bloodied and bruised, still thrashing around in their false body or already limp and tangled up in their wires.

Glitch emerges from the climb a few minutes later, and I can't stop the words.

"You took your time."

She tucks her hair behind her ears as she brushes past me. "You are the one who left a mess all over the detention hallway."

"You gave me the knife," I shoot back, stripping away the medical patch and dropping it to the floor. "What did you think I'd do with it?"

Glitch steps onto the rounded area of blue Pilot glass, its glow sending shadows of her eyelashes spilling up her brow.

"Victoria is accompanying me on the run."

My hands slip from my pockets. "Hells. What are you—"

"What I have to." Her voice is hard. "Whatever I have to."

She presses her thumb to her forearm, and the panel pops outward, revealing a smooth metallic divot where there should be blood and bone and vein. As I fixate on the sight, I feel her glance at my expression before turning away.

One by one, she clicks the cords into place, a small jolt rocking her shoulders at each new addition. The wires spill down her arms, looping in the air before spiraling back upward toward their tethering mechanism, which I know shifts and swivels with the Pilot's movements so they won't get intertwined with one another, or with her as she fights.

Sona hesitates at the last cord, fingers rolling it lightly between her fingers.

"As soon as we leave the city limits," she says, "you will climb down and take out the guards. They should be arriving in a few minutes—three of them. They will not suspect you coming from above."

I nod. I figured as much.

Sona runs her thumb over the nub of the cord, staring

down at it. "Would you mind being careful? I will be able to feel it now."

"Why . . ." I trail off, unsure of myself. Her voice is thin ice, but it is nothing like anger. More like shame. "Why did the Academy make it so the Pilots can feel pain? While they're wound?"

It's a ridiculous question. Godolia is cruel for the sake of cruelty.

Sona shrugs. "Take your pick. To keep us motivated, perhaps. A testament to the technological superiority of Godolia."

"And what do you believe?"

She smiles wryly. It's a mask; I'm finding most of her smiles are.

"It's just a big joke to them," she murmurs, still staring down at the unhooked cord. "Take away our pain, stuff us with wires, tell us to rejoice in our evolution. Give back our ability to hurt whenever we feel a sliver of true power. Make it so that even when we are akin to deities, we still have flaws that can be exploited. The Zeniths have all the Pilots wandering around like barn chickens, thinking that just because can still take a step, it must mean that we are still alive, while in reality, they cut off our heads ages ago."

"What do you mean?"

She taps the nub of the cord on the edge of the silver dish. "They like us scared."

I smirk. "What's life without a little fear?"

"I just—" Her voice breaks. It's so sudden that the smile slips from my lips, but Glitch doesn't see it, back turning to me, silver stars scattered across her jacket. Head held high but shoulders stiffening, waiting for the hit. "I just want to be able to breathe."

Her curls are ignited by the light filtering from the Valkyrie's eyes, fluorescent beams stained red. It's when her gaze lists over her shoulder that I realize it's gone quiet. Not in the room, but in my head. My thoughts slow and lie still, save for one:

I don't want to kill you.

CHAPTER NINETEEN

SONA

Victoria is steady next to me, shoulder to steel shoulder on the frozen path stretched beneath our greaves. Billowing wind cuts the snow in icy sheets, and through it, the red of Victoria's eyes sears behind the visor.

Below the curve of the hill sprawls Winterward Lake. Seventy miles north of Godolia, the jagged line of the Iolite Peaks rises behind the forest and collection of lights and wood houses that stud the rim of the lake—a testament to the town's confidence that the surface of the water will remain ever-frozen, as it has been for decades. The hoverbarge can be seen from here, too: a large, perfectly square vehicle stacked high with massive iron crates. But even so, it is likely that each of the crates is packed to the point of bursting, with stacks of timber, drums of briskberries, large slabs of sugar, and solid blocks of ice that will be melted into clean, purified water, a rarity in Godolia.

"Godsdamn it," Victoria mutters, comms planting her voice right at my ear, as if she is standing inches away. "What's taking so long?"

Anyone looking on would believe that we are exact duplicates of each other, 180 feet of mecha, twin killing machines. Difference is, inside my ribs, my heart thuds like a caged owl. They must be able to hear its beat all the way back at the Academy.

"You could just enjoy the view," I say, feeling my real lips move against each other. It is an odd sensation—the sound of my voice resonating inside my own head, the roll of the words as they curl off my tongue, but at the same time, I know that the Valkyrie's mouth was not designed to be functional. Two bodies, two sets of everything that contradict each other in every piece and crook, save the mind that connects them.

Though that feels as if it is split, too.

This is not my body. These are not my hands, absent of scars, steel that bends with a mere thought. My skin does not ignore the cold; my head does not kiss the sky.

But it feels like it does.

And it feels *good*.

"Finally," Victoria snaps—the hoverbarge has begun to glow beneath its hull, tech awakening to lift it from the ice. Despite its immense weight, it takes off at a nimble pace, smoothly gliding about ten feet over the ice as it makes its way across Winterward. I hope that Eris is not teetering precariously on one of my support beams as Victoria and I turn, heading down the slope toward the thin canal where the barge will meet us.

"It's Jole's birthday next week."

"Oh?"

"Rose is going to ask you for help baking some ridiculous, elaborate cake. I said no, because I don't want to, and she said she would find you instead because you're all *lovely* and *nice*. Her words."

My heart rushes to my ears. My silence is a tell.

"What, sweetheart, no retort?"

The wet sputter of Rose attempting her last words. The soft thud of her body meeting the mat. "I—"

Something snags across my ankle, and the frostbitten earth rushes up to meet me.

Instinctively, I tuck my head, my sword going flat on the ground for half an instant as I roll, and in the next I have brought my leg around in an arc, drawing a half circle in the snow to spin back and bring myself upright, facing the path from which we descended. Inside my head, the other body's right knee is pressed against the cold glass floor, left leg still jutted outward from the swoop of the arc, fingertips of one hand perched on the ground to steady myself while the other reaches back for the hilt of my sword.

Over the path, a steady line of thick steel cord stretches twenty feet above the ground, ends fastened to two briskwood trunks standing opposite each other across the clearing.

Wind moans against the metal shell, icicles beading the grate of my visor. I clear them away. My stomach quakes. *Gods, Eris, please have been holding on to something.*

"Trip wire," Victoria growls. She rises to her feet, blade already in hand, dark and sharp against the soft snow billowing around us. Her eyes glisten wickedly behind her visor. "Gearbreakers."

Her head snaps to the right, and in the next moment a burst of gunfire rings from the tree line, the peace of the snow-blanketed landscape ripped to shreds by the shriek of bullets. Victoria has already thrown her arm over her eyes, the shots pinging off and ricocheting toward the ground. The frozen path splinters into a sky of tiny jagged stars.

Without hesitation, Victoria shifts seamlessly to a fighting stance, and she slashes the sword low through the air.

For a few seconds, the snow reclaims Winterward's silence, interrupted only by Victoria's low growl. Then, the briskwood trees let out a soft sigh, nearly a yawn, before succumbing. Save for approximately ten feet of their trunks, the trees list to the side, their snow coverings misting the forest in a thick cloud and cloaking their impact.

From within the veil rise the startled shouts of the Gearbreakers.

"I found you," Victoria sings.

Her tone draws her expression vividly—teeth bared in a slick, sharp grin, eyes alight, blond brows arched in her excitement. She paws through the grounded foliage, hand sifting through the cloud. After a pause, she retracts, and their shrieks ring out, louder than her voice in my head, louder than my heartbeat. A pickup truck is pressed between her fingers, driver strapped in the front seat, five other Gearbreakers in the open bed, faces lifted toward hers.

They have stopped screaming.

The sound is replaced by Victoria's howl, so shrill and piercing it feels like it scrapes ribbons against the curve of my skull. Her sword falls into the snowbank lining the path, right hand flying up to her shoulder, fingers clenching against the needled pauldron.

"What is this?" she rasps in my ear. "What—"

She cries out again, dropping to one knee. The metal bubbles between her fingers. She pulls her hand back; a thin coat of black sludge sticks to her palm.

In the truck bed, a Gearbreaker has risen to her feet. A grin perches on her face, radiant as the snow around us. The veins of her hands are ignited.

Victoria tips her palm to the side. A hundred-foot drop. I do not watch the Gearbreakers hit the ground; I cannot, because Victoria is rising, looking back toward me. Even now, in this form, the sight of the Valkyrie breathes panic through my blood.

Her voice sounds with a dry, unhappy laugh. "You didn't kill Starbreach."

Movement beside the path. The car hit the bank, deep with powdered snow. From within, a glow sparks, and grows.

"Neither did you."

Victoria moves for the Gearbreakers, and I move for her.

Unlike Rose, she does not take her cut silently. As my blade enters her side, her scream is so loud in my head it is a physical, thorny weight. I force the sword deeper as we both slam against the path, her metal skin wrinkling into jagged clefts.

But no matter how piercing her shrieks are, she will not die by pain alone. I reach for her visor, for the small Pilot hidden inside.

Victoria brings her knee up beneath me, foot extending into my abdomen and forcing me back. I struggle to my feet, her sharp, animalistic snarl sounding again, and I snap my head upright to see her pulling my sword out of her ribs.

"What the hells did you do?" she roars, clutching the blade tight in her hand. My glance over to the snowbank where her sword rests is quick, but she catches it, stepping in front of the path. "Oh, you've let that Frostbringer get all twisted up in your head. You were weak, and I knew it, and you—you—you will *burn* for this, Bellsona!"

My hands curl at my sides. "Better than dying for *them*."

I turn as she jabs, and the tip of my sword slices a clean, shallow line against my shoulder blades. A stinging pain erupts—sweet, *real* pain—and I duck underneath her next swipe and lunge past for the snowbank. She spins quickly to follow, but her sword is already in my hand, and the next slash collides with mine, freeing a metal-on-metal screech as our blades lock in a stalemate. Our faces are so close that even if our voice comms were not connected, I could still hear her discordant threats.

"You can't beat me," she hisses, blade pushing closer. The ice ignores my plea for traction.

"I have before."

She barks a laugh. "I was going easy on you."

I nearly scoff; mercy is not in her nature. "Why?"

"Why do you *think*, Sona?"

I feel myself losing footing at the same time I hear the note of hurt in her voice, so jarring from the likes of her. I push the thoughts away and my weight forward, slamming my forehead against hers. As she stumbles back, I reach out and dip my fingers between the bars of her visor. I toss it to the side, swiping to cleave her chest. She deflects the blow, vaulting backward, then doubles her swing back. I parry. The metal screeches again.

"They will never accept you as you are," Victoria seethes, pivoting and sending me careening past her toward the frozen canal. I raise my blade as I turn, fending off her next thrust. It forces me back another step, and the slick of the ice threatens to rob me of my footing. "You'll never be one of them."

She feigns an attack, and when I move to block it, her sword darts across my thigh, making short work of the armor bolted over it. I drop to one knee, barely catching her next strike. Her blade slides close to mine, our hilts meeting.

"You could've been so much," she spits, eyes so close their luminescence causes tears to leap into mine. "A legend. A deity. You could've had a family."

I snap my gaze away and stand, aiming a push kick to her pelvis that releases the gridlock.

I *had* a family.

I will not find another.

Her swings become erratic and heavy, one after another, so relentless I cannot throw an attack between my parries. She forces me backward down the slope, her assault occupying me so that I do not realize we have reached the canal until my boot steps onto its sleek, frozen shore.

I slip. My open hand spirals back to catch myself, the other rising, far too slow to deflect her next jab. Her blade slashes through my wrist, and my sword clatters against the ice, my amputated hand coiled around its hilt.

The pain is not real, it's not real—a scream tears from my throat. Victoria levels her blade at my neck. She leans close, towering as I kneel before her, remaining hand stuck behind me. I imagine the Valkyrie's proud expression matches hers perfectly, down to the shadow of a grin.

"Do as you wish, Bellsona," she coos, cocking her head to the side. "Damn Godolia, the Academy, whoever or whatever else you please. But those Mods that are so intricately, beautifully intertwined inside you—those are everlasting. You are forever bound to be a Pilot, and even in death, Godolia will still reside inside you. You will never not be theirs."

I can hear her grin as much as I can hear her truth, and the terror of it forces the words from my lips.

"Get out of my head!" I scream, with more of my true rage and hurt than I ever thought I would show to another Pilot. "*Get out of my head!*"

"En garde, Bellsona," Victoria sings.

Blade still pressed beneath my chin, her hand reaches for my visor, easily tearing it free. Then her finger enters my eye, and across my real cheeks I feel the whisper of shattered glass.

That does not hurt.

Everything else does.

Victoria digs for me, fingers twitching against the rim of my socket, both physically and mentally inside my head. Her jagged laugh is a noose around my throat.

I take my last breath.

Cold swirls into my chest.

Victoria screams, her hand jerking back, and through the eye she did not gouge I see that frost has sprouted over her finger-tips. It grows like a vine, a rot, threads of ice shooting up to her gloves, then over her wrist. In shock, she flexes her palm, and a deep crack splits it. She screams again.

"What is this?" she cries, stumbling back, blade falling from my neck. I stumble backward as soon as the threat lifts, and my real body thuds against something solid.

"Deities," Eris growls. "I leave you for one damn minute."

CHAPTER TWENTY

ERIS

The guards had clearly never been in the wonderful, terrifying hamster wheel that is a rolling mecha. But I don't have time to admire all their splattered, broken bits painting the inside of the Valkyrie, because somewhere above me, Glitch is screaming.

All I can think as I climb is *I'm scared I'm scared I'm scared.*

"Get out of my head!" She's bleeding. She's begging. In the hollow of the head, it's not one scream; it splits off and echoes and forms something worse. "*Get out of my head!*"

The mecha is leaning, the floor tilting under our feet. There are metal fingers taller than me writhing inside the room. I don't care about any of it; I *can't*. She's on her knees, blood on her cheeks, dripping from a dozen places. Her tears well in large drops, flushed crimson by the time they reach her jaw. There's glass in her curls.

Another splintering scream. The kind that'll be living in the back of my head until the day I die.

I crush my power in my hands and send it loose. Just as the frost threads begin to weave across the metal, the hand retracts, allowing a pure white light to pour in.

Glitch jerks to her feet, stumbling backward. I deactivate the gloves, hands landing on her shoulders. Catching her.

"Deities," I growl. "I leave you for one damn minute."

She's shaking under my grip, and it's not from the cold. Ice-strained wind hisses from the fragmented window.

"I lost my sword," she manages weakly.

I nearly roll my eyes. "Hold still, then. Give me an even shot."

I release her and step off the glass platform, thumbs on the gloves' triggers. The serum roars to life, blue light rushing up my arms.

The other Valkyrie's longsword stays clutched in an unbroken grip, despite her crumbling left hand. A smile twitches across my lips. She thinks she can beat me. That she can beat *us*.

I press my fists together, the serum bubbling between the cracks of my fingers.

The Valkyrie moves, one foot carving in an arc across the ice, sword lifting for a heavy-handed, downward blow, and the serum bolts from my grasp. It screams from the broken eye, across the frozen air, and finds home in the crook of her shoulder.

The frost splits the metal in jagged stars. The sword falls from her grip, clattering against the ice. The mecha falters.

When I breathe, it blooms from me. *Is that it? Did I actually survive this?*

Then, to my left, something like a growl. The wind picks up.

I look just in time to see Glitch break into a sprint, glass floor spinning beneath her rapid steps. The sudden momentum nearly throws me to my knees. In a half instant we're next to the other Valkyrie, and Glitch's head dips down, sending the floor angling beneath my feet. Her hand grapples open air. Outside, her Valkyrie's metal-plated palm reaches for the mecha, seizing the nape of its neck.

Another feral growl falls from her lips. Glitch snaps her arm forward, bringing the Windup's head straight through the ice.

The massive limbs spasm awkwardly against the ground, scraping up frost that the wind greedily takes. Glitch doesn't yield. Her hand doesn't shake.

Pilots can't drown, but they can still freeze.

The mecha stops thrashing.

My heart does not.

Glitch rises to her feet, and then stands so perfectly still, shoulders drawn back, one hand lifted slightly at her side. Tears fill her eyes, but not much else. I watch her take a breath.

Quiet, again.

I'm not built for quiet. Not built to be soft. I can't be.

I reach for her. My hands are ignited.

Now we go for the Pilot.

Her hands slide around my shoulders. She pulls me close.

She can't see me. How—

"Thank you," Glitch murmurs, words thick with tears.

I am frozen. My hands hover inches away from her skin; she must be able to feel the cold crackling across them. Her arms tighten around me, chin to the top of my head. She's warm. Despite the bolts and wires in her veins. Despite the snowflakes. When she breathes, her ribs move against mine. "Thank you, Eris."

My hands drop to my sides.

She shivers. And then she's screaming again.

"My leg—" she starts, and her knee buckles. Without thinking, I deactivate the gloves and catch her under her arms, one limp again, the other scratching blindly for the right cables. She binds them all in a tight fist and tugs sharply, jolting against me. Another cry sounds, and my chest tightens.

"Eris . . . the left cords . . . please," she begs.

I bob a nod she can't see, my hand trailing down her forearm and intertwining my fingers around the cables. I yank harshly, popping them free, desperateness leaving no room for gentleness.

I look up to see the blank glaze evaporating from her eyes, tear-swollen with the red roots of veins crawling against the glossy whites.

"Are you all right?" she croaks.

"Shit, did I do that right?" I say at the same time, dropping the cords.

And that's when it rushes in. We're out. We're *safe*. I'm laughing suddenly, and she's staring at me like I lost it, and maybe I deserve to after all this shit. I grin, happiness shooing away whatever particle of good judgment I have left, and I press my palms against her cheeks, flushed wondrously pink under the blood.

"You are insane," I conclude, nodding sharply. "Definitely a Glitch."

There's a moment when I think I feel a smidge of heat spark under my touch, before she shoves my hands away.

"We should leave before the Windup collapses."

"Collapses?"

She turns and points rigidly out of the broken eye. "Do you know her, by chance?"

Below us, where the ice graces the tree line, a group of people are walking toward us. They're led by a girl with night-dark hair, a rippling orange glow bursting from her fingers. A

ferocious grin perches on her lips, brilliant and lively in contrast to the ambiguity of her eyes, hidden behind the black
glass of her welding goggles. Of course, I'm not close enough
to see that detail, but I don't need to be. I would recognize the
unnerving presence anywhere.

She's alive.

Of course she is.

"Ah, shit," I murmur. "I'm in so much trouble."

We're both glazed with a sheen of sweat by the time we make
it out of the Windup. Glitch's curls are pasted against her
cheeks, and I see her fingers move to unzip her jacket, flittering
for a moment before dropping back to her sides. Her shirt is
back in Godolia, still soaked through with that other Pilot's
blood.

She stops short and glances back. About thirty feet away,
the gold of her Valkyrie's right greave is dripping down in swollen droplets, leaking from the molten-rimmed crater set just
below her knee. It's no wonder she buckled. Jenny's serum
should burn itself out soon, but not before the entire Windup
collapses under its weakened stance. We need to clear the ice
before the force of it sends us underwater.

"Are you okay?" I ask, watching as Glitch drops her stare
to her palms, where angry red blisters have sprouted across the
calluses. My gloves protected me from the broiling heat that
Jenny's serum shot through the entire structure, but Glitch
clung to the ladder rungs unprotected.

She shrugs. "Not like it hurts." She's bound the fabric
around her eye again.

I get a clear view of the moment when Jenny recognizes me. Her mouth unhinges slightly, and her footsteps stop. Her crew—the people I grew up with, who I could name by their voices alone—follow her example.

"Eris?" Nolan gasps, the barrel of his gun dipping toward the ice as he stops, blue eyes going wide. "We thought you were dead!"

"Knew it." Gwen nods and turns toward Zamaya, bouncing on her toes. The two guns in her hip holsters jostle along with her. "Seung, my candy, if you will?"

Seung takes a toffee rolled in wax paper out of his pocket and deposits it into Gwen's waiting palm. Of course they took bets on me. No reason to stop gambling just because I might be dead.

My gaze carefully trains on Jenny, on the rigid shoulders that might as well be screaming her next intention, at the dark eyes I know flicker behind her goggles, to me and to the Pilot on my left and back to me, over and over and over.

My feet move instinctively. I put myself between Jenny and Glitch, and the moment I do, the hairs on the back of my neck prickle. Like they do before a storm breaks out. Before a fight starts.

"Hey, Jen," I say, trying my hand at a smile. She peels it off my face with an abrupt scowl. During a takedown, Jenny will keep her grin stitched on even when—no, *especially* when—she's feeling particularly murderous. So naturally, when she frowns, I feel my heart skip a beat.

"Step away from the Bot, Eris," she says tightly.

"Jen, I will explain everything to you, I *promise*. She wasn't just my escape; I was hers, too. She's not like other Pilots. She's from the Badlands. She's like us."

For a moment, I think my words get to her. Jenny reaches up and pushes her goggles free.

"Oh, Eris," she says softly. The veins in her gloves burst alive with the magma serum. "What the hells did they do to you?"

"Jenny—"

I barely register the moment she breaks into a sprint, and when I do, she has already flung me against the ice, and her hand is rising toward Glitch's head. I swipe a leg across her ankles, sending her spiraling backward, but she scarcely touches the ground before she's back on her feet, rounding on me. I snatch her wrists with both hands, tugging her close, forcing her to meet my eyes. My fingers are against her ignited palms, but it doesn't hurt me, just like my serum can't hurt her. She designed our gloves to recognize us and each other, because she's crazy smart. Which means she's absolutely creative enough to find other ways to hurt me.

"I know—I *know*—it sounds crazy, but just listen to me!"

Her eyes flash black fire, head whipping toward Glitch, who has staggered a few feet backward.

"You put her head through the blender, didn't you?" Jenny spits. Her hands twist free, shoving me back to the ice. "You'll thank me later, Eris."

"I'm not corrupted!" I scream, scrambling to my feet, forcing myself in front of her again.

"We'll fix you," Jenny growls, and for a shocked moment I swear I hear a sob in her voice. Her attention slips past my shoulder. "Grab her."

Two sets of hands clamp down on my arms, hauling me backward. Something clicks in me, and I drop my gaze to the reflective gloss of the ice. Nolan's on my right—I smash my foot on top of his first—and after he yelps and releases, I twist, driving my elbow into Seung's ribs.

"Jenny, just let me—!"

"Stop." The voice is resolved yet hushed. Zamaya, Jenny's second in command. Demolitions expert.

I turn to find her twenty feet away, bow notched with a steel-tipped arrow—the special, explosive kind that Jenny made just for her. Zamaya swallows hard. She has two gear tattoos on her cheeks that disappear into her dimples when she smiles. But she isn't smiling now. "Eris, babe . . . please."

Nolan and Seung grab on to my arms again, pinning me tight. Zamaya shifts her aim, past me and past Jenny, onto Glitch.

Her uncovered eye skips off the tip of the arrow and lands on me. "I should not move, correct?"

"Correct, Bot," Jenny answers. She takes a step forward and snatches both of my wrists, holding them close to her face. Her eyes are narrow, thumb brushing against my forearm. "This isn't your skin."

I blink. She's touching the area the Spider healed, after Wendy and Linel had their fun. "There's no possible way you can tell that."

"They healed you?" she murmurs. "They healed you. So you could, what, infiltrate the Hollows? Take us down from the inside? Godolia loves the poetic, huh?"

Every part of me recoils at the idea, and I open my mouth to tell her this, but then see the tears in her eyes, glazed over each dark iris, and the words catch in my throat.

"Look at me." I flip my hands so that they clasp hers, and I pull her close. "Jenny, look at me, I'm not corrupted!"

"Then why would they heal you?" she shouts. "Why would they let you go?"

"They didn't do either. They . . . they *hurt* me, Jen." My voice breaks, and I didn't expect it to, and worse, now my bottom lip is trembling. I hate seeming weak in front of her. "They did— they did a lot, okay? But she healed me. We escaped together. *She* saved me."

Jenny snarls and snaps her hands away, turning back toward Glitch. Her gloves, clenched at her sides, ignite orange.

"*We'll* save you," she whispers. "We'll undo what they did."

Jenny begins to walk toward Glitch, and Glitch, despite her unnerving calm, takes a step back. Panic rising, I look from Nolan to Seung.

"Let go of me!"

Seung shakes his head. "We're not trying to hurt you, Eris. We're just getting you out of Jenny's way."

They're not trying to hurt me. I glance back, where Zamaya still has her bow leveled, and Gwen, their sharpshooter, is next to her, pistol clasped and finger nestled up against the trigger. Some of the most fearless people I know, and their hands are shaking.

They would never hurt me.

I thrash first, and when their grips tighten, cry out. Jenny turns back as I do, just in time to see Nolan and Seung hesitate, their holds slip. The warning leaves her mouth only after I wrestle free, and only after I activate the cryo gloves.

Jenny meets my gaze with a startling sadness I have not seen in a very, very long time.

"If you want to kill her"—I take a breath, steeling my glare—"you'll have to go through me."

"Do you think I won't?" she asks softly.

"You won't."

She raises her fist. A single tear drips down her cheek. "Then you are far too sympathetic for this line of work, Eris." She swallows hard. "But you were good. A good soldier. A good Gearbreaker. Nolan, Seung, get back."

I think it's when they scatter that I realize how real this all is, how insane I must seem, how insane I *am*, fighting for a *Pilot*, who stares back, eyes wide now, whose mouth is opening, gashed lips moving. She's saying—what is she saying?

The shriek of an arrow.

It hits the ice between me and Jenny, and the world dissolves in a blinding flash. I'm thrown from my stance, skin scraping against cold, clothes snagging against frost. I land on my side, breath torn out of my lungs.

Across the smoke, my sister rises to her feet and extends a finger toward Zamaya—who, looking bored as usual, notches another arrow.

"You are out of line, Z," Jenny snarls.

"I'm being nice, darling," she responds, shrugging. "That was a warning shot. We've been around your bickering enough as it is. Just kill the Bot and get it over with."

The haze clears. The blast blew Jenny backward, toward Sona, and I am too far away to do anything, too far away to stop Jen's fist from colliding with Glitch's cheekbone.

Jenny kicks Glitch onto her back and claims a wide stance, closed fists clenched above her head, the veins primed to burst.

"Any last words, Bot?" Jenny sneers.

Sona stares up, curls spread out beneath her like a pillow.

"Go ahead," she says, nudging her chin forward. Her face is softened, utterly without fear or hesitation. Her fingers lie relaxed against the ice.

Jenny sharpens her glare. "What did you say?"

"I cannot blame you for your mistrust. And I have long found that I do not care how I die, as long as it is not in a Windup and nowhere near Godolia's limits. I said go ahead, Gearbreaker."

Then, Sona tilts her head toward me, looking at me with a single doe eye. A small smile cracks her lips.

"Thank you, Eris," she says. "For everything."

"No . . . ," I whisper, then my voice leaps to a scream. "Jenny, don't!"

Jenny stares down at Sona, and in the stiffness of her shoulders and the trenches of her frown I see every single particle of hate embedded, everything that we have been taught from birth bubbling under the surface. She has a different voice in her head, belonging to whoever first uttered the words to her: *Go for the Pilot.* Her cheek dips as she bites the inside of her mouth.

"Did you save my sister?" Jenny asks. I don't think I've ever heard her voice dropped to a whisper before.

"We saved each other."

"You don't serve Godolia?"

"Everybody serves Godolia, in one way or another," Sona says, and then her fingers are dipping below the bandage, tugging it up past her curls. The red glow of her eye flickers into place as it blinks in the sudden light. "And because of this," she continues, "I will always serve its image, will always reinforce the fear it craves. The Academy made it so. And this is the reason why I begged Eris to help me escape."

She grins happily. The corners of Jenny's mouth twitch, fists still suspended in the air. It jars me a bit, seeing the tables suddenly turned like this: Jen fighting to keep her expression stoic, and Sona baring her teeth.

"I intend to make them pay for it. I *will* make them pay for it." She laughs, bright as wind chimes. I have the strange urge to run away. "That is, if you do decide not to kill me."

Jenny says, "Convince me."

Sona is silent for a moment. The corners of her smile flutter into something less brash, a little more sheepish. "So. I hope you have forgiven me for this. I dropped you in a river."

CHAPTER TWENTY-ONE

SONA

Jenny looks like Eris, down to the way she takes her steps—almost arrogantly, stomping proudly as she goes along, as if all Winterward is held under her reign. The difference is, when she looks at me, the obsidian is still hard in her eyes. She shoves me toward her truck, where the driver sits rigid in the front seat.

"You're being crazy, Jenny," he mutters half-heartedly, seeming to know that his efforts will be met with nothing but a sharp scoff.

"And you love it," Jenny responds, pushing me down into a corner of the truck bed. Eris promptly takes the place next to me, cracking her knuckles. Jenny takes the opposite side, mirroring her. "If anyone has something to say, say it so I can ignore it properly."

"She's corrupted, Jen," a Gearbreaker hisses as the truck hums to life. He drags his gloved fingers down his tawny face, cheekbone-to-jaw, fine, black eyes drawn down in morbidly pantomimed sadness. "Bummer."

Eris shoots him a poisonous glance. "Corrupted or not, Seung, I can still kick your teeth in."

"She still sounds like Eris, at least," remarks another boy. "Also a bummer."

The teasing seems more habit than humor. Fingers ghost quietly but not subtly over weapons.

"I trust you all with my life," Eris snaps, voice rising over the billowing of the wind. "The least you can do is trust my words."

A Gearbreaker with bright violet hair and tattoos on her copper-colored cheeks—the archer—chuckles. The sound is anything but light. "Babe, your words may be nothing but a programmed script."

"I'll kick your—"

"Stop," Jenny says, and the truck goes quiet. The gust even dies down a smidge. She tugs her goggles off, glancing at her reflection briefly. Then, without looking up, she says, "You. You're from the Badlands, supposedly. Where?"

"Silvertwin. It was—"

"No one survived the Silvertwin Massacre," Jenny says bluntly, and I hesitate for a moment. I have not heard my hometown's name on anyone else's tongue for as long as I can remember.

I shake my head. "They . . . they sent a Paladin first, to crush the tunnels. I managed to climb out, and . . . a Phantom was there to pick off the rest."

"So how are you alive?" Jenny demands. "How'd you get to Godolia?"

"A family friend found me," I say. "Went to get help. Got picked up. Got dropped."

Inside my pocket, my hand twists around my bandage, uncoils it, twists it again. Over and over and over, faster and faster and faster as my heartbeat rises. I swallow hard.

"I crawled toward the cargo train, fell into our coal quota. Lay there until it got to Godolia, crawled out, wandered around until the Academy services found me. They placed me in the Windup Program. They gave me food, shelter, clothing. A Windup. This eye, these wires, the—"

I do not realize how shrill I have become until Eris nudges her knee against mine. When I snap my gaze to her, her sight drops to her hands. Her goggles have cracked at some point today, my reflection thrown in pieces across them. My cheeks have been smeared bloody by the cuts I forgot I had.

"They saved my life," I murmur. "They also stole it from me. From everyone I cared about."

The wind picks up again. One of the Gearbreaker boys starts clapping slowly, pale skin scrubbed pink with the cold, but the rosy cheeks do nothing to dilute the viciousness that curls his mouth. I have a moment of complete clarity that he is imagining reducing me to a bloody pulp, to be deposited glistening into the snowbank.

"Does she know poetry, too?" he inquires drily, but his applauding abruptly ceases when Jenny raises a hand.

"Why did they send the Windups?" she asks, voice low. "You said that you fell into your coal quota. If Silvertwin had met it, why the massacre?"

"We met it," I say, hating how strained my tone is. After all these years. I feel my thumb flush purple within the confines of the bandage. "Something was wrong with the train's tech. No one knew how to fix it. The coal was never marked as having left town. They sent the Windups."

To my horror, a hot tear falls down my cheek. I wipe it away hurriedly.

"It wasn't our *fault*," I whisper.

"Nolan," Jenny snaps. "Clap again and you die."

"What? Come on, Jen, she's—"

"She's telling the truth," Jenny says flatly.

Next to me, Eris shifts slightly. "She is?"

"I thought you believed me, Frostbringer," I remark quietly.

"I . . . I do," she replies. "I just didn't think Jen would. Not so easily. She doesn't do easy."

"I was *there*," Jenny says. "Day after, once we had heard about what happened. We found no one left." She sticks up two of her fingers. "Footprints of a Phantom and a Paladin. The mining tunnel, collapsed. But we found the resource logs, and all the quotas were met for that month. We didn't know why the Windups were sent."

I meet her eyes. "There was no reason."

"Oh, come *on*," another Gearbreaker snaps. She leaps from her seat, one hand pressing against the edge of the truck as she leans across Eris, the other snatching my wrist. "*Look at it*. Eye closed like it doesn't love it, crying like it can feel remorse, like it can feel *anything*. I mean, you can't believe—"

Jenny's fist slams into the Gearbreaker's sternum, sending her careening backward. Nolan catches her before she teeters over the side of the car.

"Gwen, you were still learning how to cock a pistol when I was at Silvertwin. Those people in the mines were crushed so flat we couldn't separate them from one another. The blood—"

"Jenny," Eris says sharply, her shoulder against mine, rendering her painfully keen to my sudden flinch. As if her words are nothing I do not already know.

Jenny shakes her head, then points at me. I look at the ground as their eyes follow her gesture. "You think anyone true to Godolia, even a spy, would admit that their precious nation could ever be at fault?"

"Yes," everyone in the truck bed responds in unison.

Jenny bristles. "Fantastic that you believe this is a democracy. And any or all of you are, of course, welcome at any time to confront me about it."

"So just like that," Eris murmurs, "you believe her."

"Just an iota," Jenny quips, brushing her hands against her coat. Her grin is seeping back into place. "I believe in debts, Eris. She saved you. Now she's your problem."

Eris is quiet for a moment. I make my expression go blank as the snow, to hide how her hesitation jabs at me.

"Help me explain to Voxter," Eris states.

"For a price."

"And what would that be?"

"I get her," Jenny says, nodding at me. "All the questions I can ask. All the experiments I can do."

Eris's scowl returns, the delicate scar vanishing. "She's not mine to give away."

"I think it would be interesting," Jenny continues seamlessly. "All the Pilots we capture are all 'You can't do anything to me, I can't feel pain' this and 'I'll never talk' that. Starvation, extreme heat or cold—they take too long to break them, and when they do, they are still not quite as reliable as I'd like, and I have *so* many questions about their tech, about the Academy's Mods. But if she's not a prisoner—"

"She's not a guinea pig," Eris retorts.

"What would you like to know?" I respond at the same time.

Jenny's grin widens. "I think I'd like a look at that eye, for starters," she says.

I nod and reach for it, and Eris slaps my hand away.

"Gods, Sona, not here!"

"Oh," I say, retracting.

"And what if she *is* a spy?" Gwen asks tentatively, as if afraid that Jenny will hit her again. And by the look on Jenny's face, she is greatly considering it.

"Then I'll kill her," Jenny says smoothly, locking her gaze with mine, letting the threat ring clear. I barely pay attention to it, feeling Eris go rigid once again, jumping to be my protector for the billionth time today. The cold cracks a little at the thought, replaced by a different kind of chill. "And I'll kill her slow. Pain's not a factor, of course, but I can still cut off all her limbs and drop her like a stone to rest at the bottom of the lake, alongside all the other disagreeable Pilots."

"That is fair," I respond, just as seamlessly, and meaning it.

"So you don't trust her," Eris growls. "You just want her for your little tests."

"My dear sister," Jenny purrs. "We can't all go weak kneed at the sight of some girl with pretty curls and a pretty accent."

"I took out two Valkyries and a Phoenix in the span of a few days," she snaps. "I'd call that less than weak."

"And yet you couldn't escape Godolia by yourself," Jenny retorts harshly.

Eris's features go pink. "You want to talk about sympathetic?" she says, leaning forward to meet her sister's glower. "Fine. Let's do that, then. No Gearbreaker crew is *ever* assigned to take down a Valkyrie. And yet here you are, in Winterward, when I'm guessing that you didn't even have an assignment today. You knew it was a Valkyrie that snatched me up, so you forced your crew to come all the way here, all so that you could take your anger out on something that hurt your *dear sister*. I'm touched, Jen."

"You little—"

"Thing is, you were sloppy. They sent two Valkyries, and from the welt on Luca's forehead, the other one got *really* close to crushing all of you. Until Sona was kind enough to step in and help your pathetic asses."

Jenny's anger flares, bright against the frost. "Stop the car."

Her command is obeyed, and then she is standing, one hand around Eris's overall straps, hauling her up and then backward over the lip of the truck bed easily, like a cat carrying her kitten. Eris shrieks; Jenny grins, and calls, "Okay, you can go."

"Put me down!" Eris screams, clawing at Jenny's hands as the truck picks up speed. Her hair peels over to the right side of her head in a black slash, her shouts half terror, half glee. "Oh my Gods, please put me down!"

"It is so very good to have you home, you little bastard!" Jenny shouts down at her. Her eyes slide over to me, and somehow, inexplicably, this is the moment when I know—she is the greatest threat to Godolia. "Even if it was with a pet dogging at your heels."

They blindfold me, of course, when we make it out of Winterward. For a time there is just wind and sand across my cheeks, stripping their low chatter from my ears. The air is cold but the sun hovers bright and strong, a pinhole of light through the blindfold.

At one point, I tilt my face to warm my skin, and find that Jenny has, in fact, not dumped Eris over the side of the truck, when my cheek meets the slope of her shoulder. I sit straight with a fumbling apology. I know it's her because she does not shove me away; she leans closer, lips brushing my ear so I can hear her through the wind. "We're in for a lot of shit when we get home," she says.

After a few hours, we stop and someone tugs the blindfold away. I keep both eyes closed while I veil the Mod carefully with the fabric, and when I look, Luca is shutting off the engine, a hand slipping out the window to tap against the side of the truck. The ice that had clung to the metal is long melted, and his knuckles come away painted with mud.

"Nice knowing all of you," he says, and looks in my direction. "Because we're all about to be crucified."

"If any of you can't free yourselves after being drilled into a wooden pike, then I have failed as your captain," Jenny barks, gracefully leaping out of the truck. "Come on, then, Bot. We have a few dragons to slay before we can rest."

My boots land on a worn concrete path, Eris following after. Her stare is pasted against my cheek as I look upward, where a vivid array of oranges and yellows split the ashen sky into jagged slivers. I take a breath, smelling the rainfall and lush earth and pure air, not the sewage-laced and smog-choked stench that has clung to my skin for the past eight years.

The grounds are filled with a tattoo-blotted crowd, gone perfectly still at the sight of me. The Gearbreakers are not scared of me, not in this form. And they do not waste their breath on low whispers—they let their threats ring loudly, violent things slung from all sides.

I do not care. I cannot stop staring at these damn trees.

"Oh, shut up, the lot of you!" Jenny shouts back, voice barely overpowering theirs. "Make yourselves useful and wake up Voxter from whatever ditch he's sleeping in."

They continue their threats, and I list my gaze up to the sky again. Colors do not indicate the season in Godolia, so clouded with smog and smeared with gray that even the meager amount of snowfall looks like factory ash before it can ever find the ground.

"We call it the Hollows," Eris murmurs at my side. "It's strangely full of idiots today."

I run my hand across the bark of a tree as we walk by, fingertips brushing cold moss. "You were going to kill me not three hours ago."

"Oh," she says quietly. "I wasn't sure you caught that."

"You changed your mind."

"I did."

"Are you going to change it again?"

"Are you going to just sit there the next time Jenny hangs me out of a car?"

"Jenny and Eris Shindanai!" a voice booms, and in an instant the courtyard is rendered silent. "Where the hells have you two been?"

"Winterward," Jenny says.

"The Academy," Eris says.

A man emerges from a split in the crowd, the scowl pasted across his lips thoroughly crinkling the large discolored scar of his right cheek. He stops short in front of the truck, listing his weight against the silver-hooked cane clutched in his hand.

"Winterward? The Academy?" he sputters, gray eyes bulging at the sisters, who are not subtle in their smug looks. His sight flickers to me, my jacket, and his mouth falls open. "A Valkyrie."

I do not realize that his cane is en route to my temple until it is locked in Eris's grip midair. Meanwhile, Jenny sidles up next to me and throws a rough hand over my shoulders. I do not jump so much at the physical touch as the fact that she is not using it to throw me to the ground—though what really startles me is that when I look up, I realize Jenny looks a little like my mother, with the dark, dangerously delicate eyes and straight black hair, though Umma always tied it back in twin braids, and had freckles on her cheekbones where Jenny has only a beauty mark at the side of her mouth. I inherited my curls and my height from my father, alongside the sense of humor my mother always interpreted as "morbid," and leaned her small chin into her hand so we would not see her smile.

"Let me explain, Vox," Eris insists.

"You know your orders," he spits back. "Any Windup Pilot class Phantom or above is too loyal to Godolia to be interrogated. *Kill on sight.*"

"Oh, trust me, old man, you don't want to let this one wander out of here," Jenny purrs into my ear, her hand squeezing slightly. She is a tall, slim girl, her gaze dripping down from her vantage point to hungrily gloss over my bandaged Mod. Her fingertips twitch as if she is restraining herself from plucking it out of my skull this very instant, though I would vastly prefer doing it myself.

Jenny sets off at a brisk pace, hand sliding down to my sleeve and using it as a tether to tug me along. She heads directly for Voxter, and rather than stepping to the side, she shoves him out of her path. I twist my head back to see Eris release his cane to follow us, and he ends up being last in line.

Jenny reaches one of the taller buildings set in a large semicircular clearing outlined by oak trees, kicking open the entrance and marching inside. Silently, she pulls me up two flights of stairs and down a long hallway. Before a pair of large wooden doors, she promptly stops and shoves me down onto a bench. She points to the seat next to me once Eris catches up.

"Sit," she orders, and to my surprise, Eris does.

Voxter appears at the end of the hall a minute later, face a bit paler than when I last saw him. Jenny gestures wildly toward the doors, coaxing him along impatiently.

"You've corrupted my girls, haven't you, Bot?" he growls as she brushes past.

Jenny simply rolls her eyes and shoves him into the room.

"'Your girls.' You're going senile, old man," she barks, spinning back to point a finger at Eris. "We have a deal, remember."

"If you convince him," Eris says.

"Hmm. I still don't like hearing my attitude on your tongue. Try to cut if off by the time I'm done."

The door slams behind them, and suddenly everything is quiet. Eris pulls her goggles from around her neck and skims her fingers gingerly over their broken glass.

"I am sorry," I hear myself say. My voice echoes up the hall and back again. "When I was fighting Victoria . . . I should have been more careful. I must have nearly killed you."

Eris shakes her head, a slight gesture. For some reason, I cannot bring myself to look directly at her face, so I stare at her reflection, all fragmented and warbled in the glass.

"Getting 'nearly killed' is kind of my job," she says softly, and then she drops the goggles to her lap. I snap my sight up and find her watching me, a little bruised, brow scar glistening. "What you did was save me. Saved Jenny, too, even though she'll fling herself off a cliff before she admits it."

"You never told me that your sister is Starbreach."

"Of course not. Whenever I utter that name, her ego inflates exponentially, even if she's not in earshot."

The silence rings. I adjust the cloth around my eye.

"We have to find you a better system, Glitch," she says.

"May not live long enough to develop one, Gearbreaker."

"Why do you have to say shit like that?"

"Like what?" I ask nonchalantly, securing the knot.

"Like announcing you have a death wish."

I lift one shoulder. "I like to leave impressions."

"The things you say," she murmurs, peeling off her gloves. She folds them neatly and then feeds them through the strap of her goggles, forcing the small bundle into her jacket.

"Are you going to keep that?" I ask, eyeing the sliver of the Berserker insignia that peeks over her shoulder.

She shakes her head. "Too big for me. I'll give it to Milo; he'll get a kick out of it."

"Who's Milo?"

I note her smile before she can snuff it out, and it is different from any other microexpression I have seen her attempt to hide. It is nearly embarrassed, guiltily indulgent, the same look that flitted across Jole's face whenever he made Rose laugh, or she graced him with a cocky side-eye glance.

But all Eris says is, "You'll meet him."

"Will I?"

"And the rest of my crew. Xander, June, Nova, Theo, Arsen."

"And then what?"

"What do you mean, 'and then what?'"

"I mean . . ." I trail off, unsure of how it will sound, if what I have been imagining was nothing but a greedy, hopeful fantasy. "I . . . I am happy to help Jenny, whatever she needs. Questions,

193

experiments, anything. And it is not as if I am not grateful for all you have done for me, Eris, for whatever particle of trust you have relinquished into my care, but I—"

"Glitch, it's not like—"

"I have hurt people, Eris. I have been responsible for *so much death*, and it—I don't—I cannot carry it well." My fingers twist in my lap. "I want to be a Gearbreaker. So very much. But I feel this . . . this . . . terrible thing I have inside me. One I forced to grow because I needed that kind of control, that *anger*, to numb me. I do not know if I can ever stop myself from needing it, from craving it. I just . . . I am so scared that I am never going to be good."

A hand slides over mine, finds a hold. Squeezes hard, black, chipped paint scattering the nails. "You don't have to be good. You just have to be better than the bad you've done."

A beat of silence. I am acutely aware I am about to cry for the hundredth time today.

"What if I can't?" I whisper.

"Then that sucks. And it probably sucks for a lot of people, too." Suddenly she is on her feet, one hand pressed to her hip, the other shoving my shoulder into the back of the bench. I look up at her, startled. "But what if you *can?*"

Dark fire flicks around her eyes, the same flame that I would bet could singe Godolia's tallest skyscraper from the horizon.

"Are you going to change your mind?" I ask again.

Her hand moves from my shoulder to hover in front of me. Her head is still leaned over mine. It takes me a moment to drop my eye to her palm.

"How about this?" she says. "I don't kill you, and you join my crew. Deal?"

I hesitate.

"It's a handshake, Glitch, not a firecracker."

I knead the side of my cheek briefly between my teeth. "I look like a Bot, Eris."

"And you growl when you fight, and you fight like your opponent is already on their knees. My whole crew is full of kids like you. Loose cannons and wild cards and freaks. Glitches. And the thing about glitches is that they tend to be unpredictable. Which means they never see us coming."

She leans closer, and that is, of course, when the tears slip from my eyes. But there is not one ounce of ridicule across her face; she only continues in a fierce voice. "Hey. I won't tell you that we can burn Godolia to the ground. I won't even tell you that you won't be lying crushed flat by the end of your first mission. I won't promise you revenge; I can't. But I *can* promise you that every single takedown stabs another thorn in their side, and leaves you with more life in your lungs and more fire in your breath than should ever be humanly possible. So, what do you say, Sona? Wanna be an inconvenience with me?"

I manage the slightest dip of my chin, and suddenly, Eris is beaming with a smile that could crack the cruelest of storms apart.

Luckily, before I can open my mouth and say yet another rambling, imbecilic thing, the doors burst open and Jenny rushes out, bright grin pinching her features and speech like Berserker gunfire. Before the doors swing shut, I get a glimpse of Voxter with his elbows planted on an oak desk, rubbing small circles into his temples. It is a bit of an odd sight, because I was sure that *he* was the head of the Gearbreakers.

"Right, then!" Jenny chirps, and shoves a paper with a gold seal into Eris's hands. "That letter speaks on behalf of our Bot here and will be posted across the Gearbreaker campus by the end of the hour. So, that's my end of the bargain, now—"

"Not now," Eris says abruptly. She crumples the letter and shoves it into her pocket. "Glitch and I have had a very long day. And I have not had a bath in the better part of a week."

"We had a deal."

"And we still do. I'll bring her by your lab tomorrow."

"Don't walk away from—"

Jenny's fury is cut short when Eris turns on her heel and throws her arms around her sister's shoulders, the hug only lasting for a hummingbird's wing beat before she retracts. Eris smooths her hands down her jacket and forces them into her pockets.

"Thank you, Jenny," Eris says swiftly. "For coming for me."

For the first time, Jenny's eyes do not narrow when Eris speaks. But she does twist her lip into an unconvincing scowl, turning back toward the doors and flinging them open with both hands. Voxter is still slumped in the same position.

"Bright and early, you two," she calls as the doors slam shut behind her.

Afternoon light, softened down to its dregs, makes the silent air seem as tangible as fabric. Eris turns and offers me her hand again. This time, I take it.

She was wrong. This feels like a firecracker, like something dangerous. But it's also Eris. She is never going to feel like anything else.

We trail past the courtyard, and although the Gearbreakers stare again, this time none of them start screeching threats.

They do look like they want to when they first get a glimpse of me, but then they see the expression across Eris's face—a look that could suffocate a hurricane. Her steps carve a path, and anyone in her direct vicinity immediately scrambles to get out of her way lest they be trampled. And by the hardness in her eyes, she would not even register if they slipped beneath her boots.

We enter another building and climb a dust-streaked stairwell. On the fifth level, Eris chooses a door and punts it open.

A gray carpet runs up the single, long hallway, mussed and matted by countless feet. Walls, papered in pale blue, contain an array of photographs and drawings: a picture of a curly-haired boy viciously hugging a freckled one, a handful of crudely drawn stick figures shouting profanities, a photo of two girls dozing against each other on a love seat, a simple sketch of Eris's scowling profile leaned over a book.

Eris tugs off her boots and drops them haphazardly in the corner, where they land softly atop the heap already placed there. I start to follow her example. She does not wait until I have untied my laces before setting off again, practically sprinting to the last door on the right. Before she rounds its frame, her footsteps slow and she wavers, hand to the wall.

I come to a stop behind her, watching a silent inhale lift her shoulders. Around the curve of the doorjamb, voices spill into the hallway, sharp and clamorous.

"Are you all right?" I whisper, and she nods feverishly.

"Just can't wait to see the looks on their faces, is all," she murmurs.

Eris nods sharply, steeling her resolve, and smooths her palms against her jacket front. A small, giddy smile roots across her lips—happiness that this time she cannot smother before it glistens in her eyes. She rounds the corner, but I stay stuck at the threshold, noting how she clasps her twitching fingers in a hard ball behind her back.

Then she begins to scream.

"What the hells did I tell you idiots about getting candle wax on the table?!"

The room goes dead silent. Six heads turn in her direction, all blinking slowly, mouths opening and closing like goldfish.

A tiny girl with white-blond hair falls from her perch on the edge of the dark wood table, and slams flat against the floor. A groan, and then her head is lolling up, shockingly green eyes wide, a sizable red mark sprouting on her forehead.

"Holy shit," she breathes. "Juniper's séance worked!"

"You think my ghost would just come when called, like some sort of dog?" Eris scoffs, crossing her arms. "I'm insulted."

They all stay silent. Eris runs a hand through her hair, eyes skittering across her crew.

In a chair above the girl who fell is a boy with his legs tucked up underneath him, his raised brows hidden behind a curtain of pale bangs, an array of freckles spilled across his nose and cheeks. On a large couch listed at a careless diagonal from the back corner, a girl with bright green hair has snapped to attention, thoroughly jostling the boy who was asleep on her lap, something like soot smudged over the dark skin of his cheeks. He has propped himself onto his forearms now and stares with wide, saucerlike black eyes. Above them, sitting cross-legged on the back of the couch, gawks a boy with pixie-like features, drastically pale in contrast to his mop of dark curls.

It is clear that Eris's gaze snags a bit longer on the boy sitting alone in the love seat. His fair hair is brushed neatly back, revealing the twin lines of gear tattoos that emerge from his shirt collar and trickle up to his jawline. A worn paperback book rests clutched in hands riddled with scars as he stares back with such a vividness of blue in his eyes that it nearly seems artificial. Eris forces her gaze away.

"I said . . . ," she mumbles. "I said to not spill the candle wa—"

He is on his feet, book clattering softly against the ground. And then his arms are around her, so tightly that it forces something akin to a sob to fall from her lips, and tears spring to her eyes.

"Get off me," Eris growls half-heartedly as her hands wrap around his back. "I need a bath—get off me."

The rest of them peel away from their positions, crossing the room as silently as phantoms, enveloping Eris in their embrace until she is nothing but a small inkblot in the center of their limbs. I stand at the threshold, watching their tears flow hot, listening to their staggered sobs and frantic whispers, eyes pinned wide as if they believe that blinking will steal Eris away from them once more.

I wait for one of them to notice me, and when the blond girl does, her cries shut off like a faucet. In an instant, she has split from the embrace and flown over to the fireplace, an iron poker materializing in her hand. Then she is charging.

I sidestep, and she brushes clean through the door frame and promptly smashes into the opposite wall. She teeters back with one of her pearly cheeks stamped with a red mark.

"Nova!" Eris squeaks, batting away her crew's limbs and lunging toward me before the girl can shake off her stupor.

"Holy shit, is that a Pilot?" the freckled boy shouts, shredding the remnants of the peaceful air. Eris throws her arms across their path, taking a step backward.

"A Valkyrie," breathes the boy who I assume is Milo, eyes flicking over my jacket. "Eris—"

"Shut up for a Godsdamn second," she barks, and they do. She pats around in her pocket for a moment and then flings the letter at them. "Read this. The lot of you."

At once they all pounce for it, the letter zipping between their hands in a frenzy, fingernails ripping off the seal and tossing it to the side. One-second arguments spark and die out, until they resolve to gather around the paper in a semicircle, half in the hallway and half in the room, heads tucked against one another as Milo stretches the letter taut in the center of them. They read it once, then shake their heads, and read it again. And again.

"That was Voxter's seal, wasn't it?" Nova murmurs, dropping to her knees and tapping around the floor for the discarded wax. She finds it and immediately tosses it upward, directly into the freckled boy's waiting hands.

"No way," he breathes, thumbnail digging into the symbol.

The green-haired girl snaps her gaze at me, dark brown eyes locking on.

"I believe it," she says in a calm voice. "She doesn't give out that particularly evil air, does she?"

"What? Judging by how she hasn't started slaughtering us yet?" says the boy next to her in a slurred tone, as if sleep still clutches him.

The girl gives him a very long, stern look, and I get the strange sense that he wants to recoil, or even drop to his knees and start sputtering apologies.

"I don't believe it," Milo murmurs, listing his eyes toward Eris. "It got you out."

"*She* did," Eris replies.

"A Valkyrie not loyal to Godolia."

"Loyal to burning it to the ground."

"You are mocking me," I say softly.

"And I told you I'm not, Glitch."

"Oh no," the freckled boy groans. "She named it."

Eris's brow furrows, and she points rigidly back into the room.

"Inside, everyone, *now*," she snaps, and they oblige, scurrying to their places like field mice, save for Milo. He stares at me steadily for a few measured moments before following her command.

Eris gestures me inside, and then begins to pace back and forth, wringing her hands. We all watch her, silent. She stops a few times, brow furrowing deeper, and then continues her march. Only when Milo clears his throat does she come to a true halt, whirling around and slamming her palms against the tabletop.

"Listen up," she shouts. "In the span of a few days, I have taken out three Windups, escaped Godolia, and gone down in history as the only Gearbreaker to ever break out of Academy captivity. I am *tired*. I don't want to explain the situation for the billionth time today. You read the letter. Every word of it is true. And if you don't trust Voxter, trust me. And if you don't trust me, then I'll assume you'll want to be reassigned from this crew. *My crew*, I might add."

She points at me, and suddenly I am painfully aware of my jacket and my ripped face and my filthy, fraying bandage that hides the eye that still glows despite its restraints.

"Crew, meet Sona Steelcrest, our newest member. If I could trust her with my life in a place like Godolia, you sure as hells should trust her on Gearbreaker soil. And that is an order."

CHAPTER TWENTY-TWO

ERIS

"You think you can just march back in here, guns blazing, Bot in tow, and start shouting orders again?"

I open one of my eyes to peer at Nova, perched precariously on an edge as she always is, one hand spinning circles in the bathwater. Juniper sits next to her, jeans rolled halfway up her calves, feet submerged.

"I can," I say evenly. "And are you going to give me any privacy?"

"I have questions," Nova huffs, and then throws her thumb over her shoulder. In the corner, Sona is leaned over a small block of porcelain—our sorry excuse for a sink—dragging a damp rag over the cuts on her face. "And don't talk about wanting 'privacy' when you marched in here with *it* in tow."

"Don't be crass, Nova," Juniper says, wiggling her toes. She gives a slow smile to Glitch, who notes it for a moment before darting her eyes away. "Her name is Sona."

"I don't know why you're so on board with this, June."

"Just the other day you were up for my séance, in case Eris had died."

"Well, ghosts are real, *duh*, and I'm not talking about me."

"Well, Novs, think of this, then," Juniper says sweetly. "No Gearbreaker has ever escaped the Academy's captivity. In fact, all of them are presumed to have died very slow, meticulous, and unimaginably painful deaths. Escaping said captivity would have taken nothing short of a miracle, and I believe it is a miracle for a Bot to have any sort of feelings or remorse at all, and so there Sona sits."

Nova opens her mouth, closes it, then opens it again, crossing her arms. "And she's sitting in here with us because . . . ?"

"Eris feared for my life," Sona says nonchalantly, the first words she's spoken since we piled in here.

I go rigid. "I did not—"

"The others are not happy that I am a part of your crew," she continues smoothly, tucking a curl behind her ear to dab softly at the blood on her jawline. "No . . . I believe it was just Milo, and the boy who shares some of his features. Brothers? But the rest . . . Xander and Arsen, correct? They seemed more open to the idea of my being here."

Sona runs the rag under the tap, and the water flushes red once it reaches her hands. She turns her head to get to work on the other side of her face.

"You two seem nice as well," she murmurs. "Nova and Juniper. I like those names."

"I don't fear for your life," I say loudly, to distract from Juniper's blush and Nova's scoff.

"And here I was, enamored by your perceptiveness," Sona responds, setting down the rag.

"Ouch," Nova says.

"Glitch," I growl, kicking Nova's hand and sending it retreating from the water. "I'm your crew captain. I think I deserve a bit more respect."

A shadow of a smirk that vanishes just as quickly.

"It is hard to take your authoritative voice seriously when

you are sitting below me," Sona remarks, brushing her pinkie finger along her hairline. "Naked, I might add."

"Double ouch," Juniper whispers, as Nova shrieks with laughter.

I jump out of the bath and loop a towel under my arms, nearly slipping on the slick tile floor. Sona watches me steadily, holding my gaze until I reach her, before directing it back toward the mirror.

"No need for worry," she says, face stoic. "You have no reason to be self-conscious, from what I've seen."

Heat floods my face, and it's not from the bath steam.

"Are you going to yell at me for being observant?" Sona asks innocently, the smirk snaking across her lips again. "You are the one who dragged me in here, after all. For my safety."

"It wasn't for your safety!" I lie.

"Oh. Just to show off, then. I am flattered, Frostbringer."

My prepared screeching gets caught in my throat as Sona unwinds the bandage from around her head, revealing her closed eye with a perfect red circle burning underneath the lid. Behind me, Juniper's and Nova's laughter is stifled.

"I do not blame them," Sona says softly, folding the fabric neatly in her lap. "Theo and . . . Milo. That was his name, correct? I am surprised that I was not shot on sight the moment I entered the Hollows. That Jenny and Voxter did not go through with killing me. That . . . that you did not, once I was blind and defenseless in the Valkyrie. Despite every other voice in your head telling you to do otherwise."

At her words, I can suddenly place the look on her face: It's the same expression I used to wear constantly, in my young days of Gearbreaking, when the tremor of battle hadn't become familiar yet. It's the look you wear between hits, in the spaces between fights. And now Sona sits, gracefully cleaning her bloodied face, and waits for the inevitable point when her work will be undone. Be it by the hundred Gearbreakers who stared at her with disgust, or Theo, or Milo . . .

Or me.

She continues before my silence can fully take root. "I am surprised I ever got to see autumn trees again, or feel a breeze that did not emit from a blast of factory steam. And I'm surprised that I am still sitting upright, cleaning off my blood in a washroom that smells like jasmine tea, with three Gearbreakers who have not already buried their daggers in my back."

"We don't *all* carry daggers," Juniper says, looking pointedly at Nova.

"Because *look at me*, Eris," Sona murmurs. A finger goes up to tug back her left eyelid, and for a moment I see it again: the yearn to dig under, to rip out by the roots. "How much more luck do I have here? For how much longer should I expect people to be lenient with me, looking how I look, being what the Academy made me to be? Days? Hours?"

"Do you really think they're going to kill you?" I ask Sona gently. As if I didn't see the twin glints in Milo's and Theo's eyes as I left the common room, as if they didn't cause my hand to snap out and seize Sona's as I went past. As if both boys don't carry pistols in their belts and their trust in me can't be overcome by their fear of Godolia and the cruelty of their Pilots.

As if she wasn't right. As if I didn't fear for her life, because of people I would undoubtedly give mine for. And yeah, that thought kind of throbs a little.

"They can try," Sona responds, steel in her words. She

closes her eye again, turning on the faucet to soak the bandage through. "But I am here as long as you want me to be, Eris."

When I order Milo to give up his room for Sona, he shoots her a look with such a vicious gleam of hostility that my heart jumps to my throat.

For context: I was very relaxed from my bath, just at the point of recovery from Sona's sly remarks, Nova's and Juniper's snickering, and hells, let's also throw in there that I felt like the stress and terror of the past few days had started to peel away. And suddenly Milo is standing in front of me, breath twisted in a growl, tearing the slim illusion of peace to shreds.

And I get mad.

I bark for the rest of my crew to go to their rooms. Sona is the first to oblige.

Then I scream at Milo, and he screams back, and we scream from one end of the hallway to the other and back again. I scream about trust, and he screams about loyalty, until hot tears are flooding my eyes, trickling in two rivers that match his perfectly. We step into my bedroom, and he slams the door so hard that it makes the floor vibrate, and I flinch, and he notices, and suddenly there is silence.

I sit on the edge of my bed, and he sits next to me. I play with the fraying threads of my comforter. Someone, probably him, washed my sheets while I was gone.

The silence pulsates like a heartbeat, and it bursts when his hand flutters up to wipe the tears from my eyes.

"Did they hurt you?" he asks, voice scraped raw.

They hurt me, I think to myself, but I don't want to talk

because I don't want the yelling to start again. There's been too much anger and too much violence and too much noise. But I can't take a break, not now, not when I can still feel the threat on Sona's life in his tone. I'm in between hits, all for someone I met a mere few days ago, someone I was sure was going to deliver the next punch. A girl with hate strung between her features, a familiar fury—*my* fury—encased in a form that terrifies me.

In a form that saved me.

Milo tilts my chin with a single finger, and then brings his lips against mine. Moving slowly now. I can't. I slide a hand underneath his shirt. I'm too soft. Too weak. I kiss down his neck. Too in need of comfort. His palm presses against my back. Too desperate to scrub the fear from my skin, to expel every horrible fantasy of how they would have picked me apart. To forget how much they did.

When his fingers trace through my hair, when he holds me and murmurs, "You're home. You're okay now." I let him.

I'm too tired to say otherwise.

CHAPTER TWENTY-THREE

ERIS

Déjà vu.

Nova's outside my door again, screeching that the day started ages ago. My eyes fling open to the dust-filled dawn light and the cracks in the ceiling. Milo's toes and breath and heat against me under the blankets, his hand catching my wrist as I start to pull away.

"We're still fighting," I remind him.

He blinks a few times, trying to make me come into focus. "Are we?"

"Depends. How do you feel about the Bot?"

"Like Godolia's got her so twisted around in your head that you don't know which way is up."

I consider for a moment, then swing my leg around, punting him onto the floor. All the air leaves his lungs as he lands with a satisfying *oof*. I snatch the discarded Berserker jacket from the floor and chuck it over to him.

"I got this for you."

"This is a joke, right?"

"The joke is that you're still in here. Get out."

He mutters a vibrant string of profanity as he rises to his feet, stomping over to the door and shoving it open. Sona stands in the hallway, with horrendous bedhead, curls puffing around her ears and the curve of her bandage. Milo's so thrown off by her presence that he stops short.

"Nice jacket," Sona says, nodding at the bundle in his hands.

His shoulders stiffen, and suddenly he's leaning too close to her. My fingers curl into my mattress as I watch them, ready to pounce at a moment's notice. Sona, small compared to his height as everyone else is, stares up at him calmly.

"I can smell the copper on you," he growls.

"Milo!" I snap.

"And you smell like Eris," Sona replies, her sight slipping past him and into my room, gaze meeting mine. "We are supposed to meet Jenny, correct?"

"That's right," I say. Milo shoves past Sona and stalks up the hallway, the carpet useless in absorbing his heavy footsteps.

"Wonderful," she says evenly. "Do you think I can borrow a shirt?"

I lead Sona down the ten flights of stairs it takes to get to Jen's lab. The space is how it always is: a complete and utter mess. Large plastic spools of colorful wires, puffy sheaves of moth-eaten insulator foam, and cardboard boxes overflowing with miscellaneous junk sit piled high atop the two glass tables lining the left wall.

Jenny's face is buried between two of the spools, rummaging through the tools that I know hang on bolts behind the stacks. When she pulls back, a string of copper is entangled in her hair, and she uses the drill in her hand to gently yank it free.

She grins, hopping down from the small step stool that was wobbling fiercely under her weight. "There you are!" Her focus dips behind me. "And you brought the whole orphanage because . . . ?"

I turn around to see that my crew has silently slipped in behind us, Nova giving a smart salute as she closes the filthy glass door with her elbow.

"Nothing else to do," Arsen says.

"Though we will have a run at some point in the future, I think," Nova chirps. "So we gotta see if Jenny's going to leave enough of the Bot for her to join us."

Jenny marches across the room and tosses aside a stack of fabric that was covering a wooden chair, patting the seat enthusiastically.

"How many limbs do you need?" Jenny asks as Sona sits.

"I can spare a few," Sona replies.

"No way," I say, shaking my head, ignoring the snickering of my crew. Besides Milo, of course, who I can feel hovering behind me like a shadow. "Questions only."

"You want my eye, yes?" Sona says, tugging the bandage from her head.

"Yes, I believe I do," Jenny breathes.

I watch, at a loss for words, as Jenny flits over to the table and produces a pair of surgical gloves from one of the sagging boxes, while Sona carefully returns the fabric to her pocket.

"Is this really happening?" Theo asks, disgust clear in his tone. All their boots scuff softly against the tiles, wanting to recoil, but morbid interest keeps their gazes set. Little shits.

"Glitch, wait," I say, taking a step forward. "You don't have to—"

But then both of her eyes meet mine, the left festering like an infected cut, red throbbing, pulsating. The glow of Windups and the artificialness of Godolia bundled up neatly in a single socket. At the sight, just for a moment, I falter between my words. I try to collect my thoughts to continue before she can notice, but that expression is already on her face, laced with equal parts shame and sadness. She looks back to Jenny.

"Go ahead," she says to her.

Then, to my surprise, Jenny hesitates. Her eyes narrow sharply.

"Too easy . . . ," she mutters, unmoving. Her hand drops from the air and onto her hip. She leans closer to Sona. "What game are you playing, Bot?"

Sona smiles, prettily as she always does, but what makes my blood freeze is how her fingers begin to wander up her eye.

"An easy one, apparently," she says, and then there's a slick *pop*.

Behind me, Nova and Theo stifle a shriek, and I think Xander's breath stops altogether. I find myself staggering a step back, and Milo's chest meets my shoulder blades, impossibly still despite the scene in front of us.

Sona ignores our shock, delicately—*leisurely*—winding the copper trailing out of her socket around the tip of her forefinger. Her hand jolts forward, and another *pop* sounds, this time accompanied by the angry hiss of broken wire.

"Too easy," she murmurs, and then reaches for Jenny's wrist. "And too red and too vile and too . . ." She gently tips the eye, now flickered dull, into Jen's gloved palm. "Fragile. I would not close your hand too tightly. And unfortunately, that is the only Mod that is so simple to remove. The others are a tad more ingrained."

Sona tugs back the sleeves of her shirt, revealing the two rectangular ridges carved into her forearms. She trails a thumb over one of them, then presses. The panel springs open, revealing the silver dish inside.

"This wire here feeds into my radial artery," Sona says, shivering as she runs a finger down a cord that nestles comfortably beneath the cable openings. "From there, it splits into microscopic strands that coil next to my nerves. Did you know that there are approximately forty-six miles of nerves in a human body? If you count the ones they added, that number doubles to ninety-two miles. Ninety-two miles! All that tech, these lovely Mods—the true testament to how Godolia bests all others in brilliance and cleverness—and the Academy has so graciously entrusted them to me. All so that I could have the ability to feel pain while I do their killing and whatever else they require of me. Was that not so very kind of them?"

Her singular eye sweeps over the room, daring us to correct her.

"Did you know the eyes are connected?" Sona reaches back, gently brushing aside the hair at the nape of her neck. "At the base of the brain. The socket is just a receptacle that feeds into it. I can see through both eyes in a Windup with the sight Mod, because it isn't a superficial trinket." Her fingers lie lightly against the exposed skin. "It dives down."

No one really knows how to react to that, to her soft, faraway voice crawling from the dark smirk across her lips, and soon the only noise in the room is the slow start of Jenny's cackling.

"Eris calls you Glitch, doesn't she? That's a fitting nickname," she chuckles, shaking her head.

Jenny walks over to the circular stone countertop set in the center of the room, a space considerably less jumbled than the glass tables. Colorful liquids stand in neatly spaced rows, suspended in plastic stands, curling tape labels sporting Jenny's handwriting in blue marker. Beakers stacked by size live in a wooden box in the middle, also patterned at times by Jenny's scrawl, probably when she didn't have paper at hand. Large glass flasks gush spiral tubes, note cards shoved underneath them that read something along the lines of *You can't read this because you're not a genius.*

Jenny comfortably takes her place on a stool set in front of the small metal sink. I've seen her sit in that same exact spot for hours on end, nights bleeding into days and back again, making her concoctions and inventions and whatever else she believes Godolia will fear.

Jenny takes a small clean jar and gently places the eye inside, and then less gently, tips a vial of blue liquid into the opening. She secures the flask with a rubber stopper.

"A fitting nickname indeed, Glitch," Jenny murmurs, holding up the encased eye to the light. The blue fluid casts a rippling hue across the tiles. "Because you've definitely got a screw loose."

"Do you have a rag, by chance?" Sona asks, unfazed.

Jenny runs one under the tap and tosses it over her shoulder, along with a surgical patch and a tube of ointment produced from one of the drawers.

"Put that on," she orders, but as Sona moves to oblige, Jen suddenly springs forward and seizes her chin. She lifts Sona's face, tilting it from side to side, gaze slipping into the now-empty socket. A hum buzzes between her lips.

"Curious . . . ," she murmurs. "Titanium plating . . . no . . . would have to be something lighter . . . lithium, perhaps? But that could cause extraocular muscle abnormalities . . . which goes to ask . . . how deep does it root? Or not lithium at all, perhaps instead—"

"Jen," I warn.

"You're blushing," Jenny notes, leaning closer until they're nose to nose. "Why are you blushing, Glitch?"

"You are very pretty," Sona responds without hesitation. I roll my eyes, and she seems to see, one corner of her mouth lifting.

"Ah. I know." Her hand retracts, lifting the jar up to the light again. "Out, all of you," Jenny barks. "I need some time alone. And I would scurry along to the Junkyard, if I were you. See if you can find a glass eye lying around, or an orbital implant, or a suitable eye patch. Maybe even a weapon she'll fancy."

"You do not need me for anything else?" Sona asks.

Jenny's sight is still on Sona's eye, the one no longer in her skull.

"I'll be busy for quite a while with this," she purrs.

Sona hops down from her seat. "Thank you, Unnie."

Jenny glances away from the Mod to shoot me an absolute shit-eating grin—even though Dad wanted me to, I stopped calling my sister *Unnie* when she got fond of calling me *little bastard*—before saying, "Shut up and get out."

But she's pleased, I can tell, and I think Sona can tell, too, wandering over to us with light steps. My crew's wary gazes skip past my shoulder to land on her patch, and the bit of blood underneath her nails.

"You all right, Sona?" Arsen asks in a warbling voice.

"Just wonderful," she says, brushing her fingers innocently against the hem of her shirt. My shirt. I will not be asking for it back.

"That was hard-core," Theo murmurs as Sona begins to climb the stairwell. In the background, I'm vaguely aware of

Jenny still humming happily, and the slosh of the flask in her hand.

Nova pokes her head through the door to watch Sona climb. "Damn, why does she have to be so absolutely *gorgeous*?" she mutters, looking back. "Anyone else realize how she monologues like a supervillain?"

"She plucked out her own Godsdamn eye," Arsen gasps, smacking his lips together to imitate the sound. "Deserves some degree of respect, yeah?"

"Not like she could feel anything," Milo grumbles.

"And if you were hopped up on painkillers, you'd be perfectly fine with doing the same?" Juniper asks pleasantly, her hand between Xander's shoulders, rubbing small circles. Kid's still looking a little pale. "Are we going, Eris?"

I nod, running my hand through my hair, trying to listen for the remainder of Sona's footsteps. She smiled at me as she passed, a new flush in her cheeks, and the memory sparked again: *I hate red and I hate my heartbeat and I hate* being *this*.

If I didn't believe that string of statements then, I sure as hells do now.

CHAPTER TWENTY-FOUR

SONA

They chatter like birds to Eris, and she barks back at them as if she means to snap their wings. They pay her little mind. Milo has daggers falling from his gaze whenever he attempts to steal a quick glance in my direction. I do not mind much. Eris's leg is pressed against mine.

I look over the edge of the truck and watch the ground shed its shadows as we leave the Hollows' tree line in the dust. When the ground begins to dimple with large potholes and the truck takes to jumping over jagged shards of blasted concrete, I look away. I do not need to see the damaged landscape to know what it looks like or see their footprints to know they were here. The stench of their metal will always poison the air.

But the crew's laughter cuts it a little, along with their horrible singing when they try to accompany the music that Nova is blaring through her open windows. She seems to be intentionally driving over the potholes, just for the split second it flings us into the air.

"I like your music," I call to her, meaning it. I have not heard music in a very long time.

"Finally, someone with *taste*," she yells back over the wind. "I call it my Bot-killin' mix."

"Novs," Juniper hisses, stopping short when I begin to laugh.

"Your battle songs, then," I say, feeling the beat run up my spine.

Nova blinks at me in the rearview mirror, a stare brilliant as emeralds, hair nearly pale as fresh snow. She grins wildly.

"Hells yeah they are," she chirps, nodding decisively.

For perhaps the hundredth time since I took out the eye, I look over Eris's features again. Pale skin like porcelain embedded with two gleaming shards of obsidian, the careless nature of her raven hair. She is a black hole in the center of the midday world, an act of defiance without even trying. The inked tattoos across her collarbone glisten with the kiss of the uncloaked sun.

"Just a bit farther now," she says, snapping me out of my stupor.

"We are heading to the Junkyard, Jenny said?"

"Yeah. It's what it sounds like," she says, shrugging. "They had to put all the rubble and broken pieces somewhere, after all the fighting."

"And you really think we are just going to find a glass eye lying around?"

"Ah, Glitch," Eris sighs. "Have a little faith."

"It's the Junkyard," says Arsen wistfully.

"You can find anything if you look hard enough," Juniper adds. "An eye wouldn't be the oddest thing we've come across."

I hear the Junkyard before it comes into view. The wind plays cheerfully between its jagged edges, darting through the staggering piles of mismatched objects. I expected the entirety of it to be dull, items long forgotten and scraped of color by the elements. But when I step out of the car, my feet hit lush ground, the cool shadow of foliage shifting over my shoes.

"I was not expecting a forest," I murmur.

Awe has rooted my feet, and I move only when someone gently brushes past me as he slips out of the trunk. I apologize, looking down to find his sight already on me. His jacket droops limply from his form, shoulders and collarbone akin to a wire hanger. All he gives in return is a small tilt of his chin.

"No climbing. Except for Xander," says Eris, nodding at the shadow of a boy. "I don't need anything collapsing from your weight and someone getting buried under. I don't have an interest in carrying something as heavy as a corpse back to the truck."

"Always one for pep talks," Nova sings, already near one of the stacks, hand buried in the lavish coat of moss that has enveloped a rusted dishwasher.

Eris rolls her eyes and sets off, curling her fingers over her shoulder, beckoning for me to follow.

We walk and search without talking, Eris clattering around as she does, refusing to let her presence hold any degree of subtleness. At times, she climbs up about twenty feet onto one of the piles, ignoring her own advice, ripping away moss and vines and throwing aside whatever uninteresting thing she digs up.

Only when she disappears from my view—clambering over the peak of a garbled mound and dropping onto the other side, going after something that caught her curiosity—do I finally speak. But my words are not for her.

"Are you keeping an eye out for me, or her?" I say, leaning over to peer through a sizable crack of a paint-encrusted crate. All I see is darkness. "Or is that a poor choice of words?"

"You're funny," Milo responds, emerging from the shadow of a nearby tree.

I wrap my fingers around the crate's lid and tug. It breaks

apart instantly at its hinges, revealing nothing but a silver comb with half its bristles snapped at the base, and a necklace embedded with dust-muddled blue stones. I loop it around my finger and pull it into the light.

"At last, someone notices."

"Don't think you can just wander into the Hollows and be one of us, Bot. And don't think you have the rest of my crew fooled, either. They trust Eris, not you."

"But if they trust Eris, they trust her word, yes? But you do not, judging by the way you are clenching your hands."

"Of course I trust Eris," he spits. "I don't trust whatever voice you put inside her head while she was in Godolia. I see right through you."

I gently touch the surgical patch, trying not to imagine the hollow thud that would sound if I tapped with a bit more force.

"You think I am working for Godolia, leading a legion of Windups straight to the Hollows," I say. No use in phrasing it like a question.

"I know you are."

"Odd. Maybe I blinded myself more than I thought."

I drop the necklace—it is nothing but cheap costume jewelry.

"Milo, I looked up this morning and saw oak trees splitting the sky. And I woke up to see Juniper's lovely green hair, Theo's particularly erratic collection of freckles, and of course, Eris's eyes. Things seem more vibrant here, more alive. I quite like it."

"What's your point?" Milo snaps.

His sight skips to the junk mound that towers over us both, ears pricked for Eris's return. I reposition the broken lid gently onto the crate. He is the only one on the crew, including Eris, who has met my stare every single time. It's a gesture that reads *I am not afraid of you*, and a false one.

"Well, if what you said was true, that my loyalties lie with Godolia . . . ," I say, being the first one to break eye contact; he seems in need of small, trifling victories. "Then I would not have seen any orange trees, or green-dyed hair, or coal eyes. And that is assuming I would have woken at all, because overnight Godolia would have rained hellsfire over the Hollows while we slept and watched with utter boredom as we burned in our beds."

I cannot help but smile at his horrified expression, which only provokes his disgust to throb a bit more intensely. I have the faint, tired thought that I am not helping my case.

"Hey!" Eris shouts from above. "You guys playing nice down there?"

She hops down a path of precarious edges and questionable perches until her feet hit solid, safe ground. She opens her mouth to make another smart remark, but then her head snaps to the side.

Milo and I hear it, too, and then we are all sprinting.

The peaceful breeze has been shattered by a piercing shriek.

Milo extends an arm across both of our paths just before we make the clearing that holds the car, ushering us backward. We duck behind a junk pile where Xander, Juniper, and Arsen are already crouched, shoulders heaving.

"We saw it coming," Arsen whispers frantically. "June shouted a warning, but they couldn't get farther than the car."

Underneath the truck, Nova and Theo lie flat on their bellies with their palms clamped hard over their mouths. Above them, the Windup trails through the field leisurely, bending its head over the stacks and hovering for a moment before moving on to the next. When it straightens, the curves of its chain mail veil brush against the autumn foliage.

"An Argus," I murmur. In the Springtide War, they were used as nothing but scouts. But they were the quickest Windup in circulation before the Valkyries were created, attributed to the aerodynamic curves of their armor. The blades attached to their arms could cut through the thickest of tree trunks with the same ease as a razor through a moth's wings.

And skin and bone just as effortlessly, for that matter.

"What the hells is it doing in the middle of the forest?" whispers Juniper.

"Having a picnic, obviously," Arsen retorts.

"Darling, do shut up." Her fingers curl into the grass. "Damn it. It's so close to the Hollows, Eris."

"Milo," Eris hisses, eyes steadily trained on the mecha as it wanders, searching. "Where's the Berserker jacket?"

"Did you really think I would wear that thing?" he says angrily, but the tone wavers when he notices how much her color has plummeted.

"I'd hoped so," she responds. Her bare hands are in her lap, clasped against each other to keep from quivering. "Because I think I left my gloves in the pockets."

Milo swears vividly under his breath, then snaps to the three other Gearbreakers. "Quick. What have you guys got?"

Xander tosses a paper matchbook on the ground between us, shaking his head solemnly. Arsen throws out two small grenades, a cube of gray putty, and a handful of tiny barbed orbs from his pocket, as well as a flare stick from his boot. Juniper unhooks her chain necklace, dragging it from beneath her shirt collar and revealing a single plastic vial dangling off its end. She places the vial gently on the ground, murmuring something.

"Bless you," Milo says, and Juniper sighs.

"In layman's terms, it's acid. With my own spin. I made it in the bathtub."

"You didn't," Eris hisses.

"It's my baby. Should burn through the Argus if we get an even shot with it."

"Is there enough?" I ask, skeptical.

Juniper picks the bottle up again, bringing it to her eye level, looks at it dreamily. "If we spread it evenly in a single spot, should do the trick."

Arsen runs a hand through his curls. "And just how the hells are we supposed—"

He gets cut off as Nova's sharp swearing tears through the air. We all leap upright as the Argus effortlessly nudges the truck onto its side with the toe of its black metal boot. Theo is off the ground in the next moment, yanking Nova to her feet, though she seems more preoccupied with throwing obscene gestures at the Windup towering above than with her own safety. They just barely clear its next step, the force of it throwing them to hands and knees.

"Honeypot!" Eris screams, bending down and scooping the barbed orbs into her palm. "Milo, cover June and Arsen. Xander and Glitch, you're with me."

I follow the rest of the Gearbreakers' examples, as in I follow Eris's orders without question. She hurtles over the junk heap, her palm splaying open midair, sending the orbs flying toward the Windup. They burst with distinct *ping*s across its legs, and at once the clearing flushes gold, brilliant bright sparks zipping across the air. It lasts for only five seconds, but it creates a cloud that causes the Argus to hesitate its next footsteps and buys time for Nova and Theo to reach us. Eris catches both of their arms before they can slip back into the forest.

"Where do you think you're going?" she shouts. "We're the distractions!"

"Ah, shit, Honeypot," Theo grumbles, turning on his heel.

"Well," Nova says through gritted teeth, also turning back toward the mecha. "Guess it's a good thing they call me Four Knives Nova."

She considers a moment, then pats up her forearms.

"It's a good thing they call me Two Knives Nova," she decides.

"Eris," I say steadily, watching the cloud dissipate and the twin crimson eyes emerge into view again. "Can I ask a question?"

"Go ahead, Glitch."

"What is a Honeypot?"

"We make ourselves look . . . easily stomp-able."

"We *are* easily stomp-able."

"Your dark sense of humor never ceases to amaze me. See, we're distracting it so June and Arsen can come in with the honey."

"Jump!" Nova yelps, just before the Argus drops to its knees and swings its forearm low against the grass in an arc, palm flat against the ground.

We all leap into a junk heap sitting at the tree line, and the blade passes mere inches below our feet, slicing clean through the pile and sending us toppling toward the ground. Miraculously, none of us end up buried beneath a mountain of rusted steel.

The forearm stops short, and begins to spiral toward us.

"It's doubling back!" Theo warns.

"Peak climbers!" Eris barks, and knives materialize in Nova's hands. She tosses one into the air, where it is snatched by Xander. The forearm nears, but this time, Nova and Xander leap straight up, getting only the bare minimum air time to keep their ankles from being severed. They land hard on the Windup's hand, and the tips of their blades expertly wedge between the joints of the wrist.

The mecha bolts upright at a speed that should send them hurtling toward the earth, but they hold steady. The Argus lifts its forearm up to its eye level, peering at them. It barely gets a glance—in the next instant, Nova and Xander have bolted up its bladed edge and lunged onto its shoulder, knives instantly finding a new hook in the joint split there. A chill shoots up my back.

"How did you know that it would look?" I breathe, watching as the Windup's head swivels around, searching. "It could have easily just let the arm hang loose at its side."

Eris grins. "One thing you learn as a Gearbreaker, Glitch, is that arrogance runs through Pilots as much as their wires do. It can't help but steal a glance, remind itself how much it towers over us."

"Am I the same?"

"Didn't I say you fight like your opponent is already on their knees?"

Xander and Nova leap from the Argus's shoulder and cling to the edge of its chain mail veil, the large links providing more than ample hand- and footholds. At the same time, Milo, Arsen, and Juniper barrel from behind their heap, dashing into the clearing. Arsen has a grenade in his hand, its bulb-shaped base woven with the silver chain of Juniper's vial necklace. Jutting out from a space between the enwrapped chains is the putty cube.

"That's never going to work," Theo groans.

"Do your job," Eris calls. "Keep its back turned!"

"Step!" I shout, and we scatter.

Theo is the closest to the impact, the force sending him flying into the collapsed junk pile. He emerges with an angry gash across his collarbone and a fragmented glass bottle clutched tightly in his fingers. It explodes against the Windup's thigh, and his hand immediately sinks back into the heap for another thing to chuck.

Nova and Xander have dipped underneath the chain mail, pressing themselves up against the ledge of the Argus's eyes. I dodge the next footstep, leaping into the pile and following Theo and Eris's example, my shouts matching theirs in volume, keeping the Argus focused on us. As I reach back for more artillery, my hand finds something familiar, fingers automatically curling around the hilt.

I pull the sword free, into the light, my mouth unhinging slightly.

"Is this really the time, Glitch?" Eris shouts to my left.

"It's *so pretty*, Eris."

"Oh my Gods." She glances to me, and her next words are strung by a laugh. "Oh my *Gods*, the look on your face."

I stow the sword in my belt as Arsen and Juniper peel from their places. Arsen tosses the grenade to Juniper, and quick as a fox, she dashes behind the Windup and jumps to attach the grenade to its ankle. As she sprints away, a new piece of jewelry has replaced the one she gave up: the small silver pin of a grenade, encircling her right forefinger.

We take cover. The ensuing blast quakes across my chest and sends my teeth skipping against my tongue. I nearly forget myself: This is a different kind of exhilaration, different from what I felt in my alleyway fights, or sparring matches, or the first time I was wound.

"Theo, Glitch, we're up!" Eris shouts as she leaps down from the mound and into the clearing. The Argus has collapsed onto one knee, its ankle splayed behind its base with a sizable hole eating away at the heel.

I follow as she climbs up the calf and darts for the gap. Her hair streams behind her as she drops inside, and by the time I have slipped in after her, she has already reached the knee, where the ladder stretches up.

Once I climb into the hip, I find that she has rushed ahead again, attaching to a nearby support beam and hoisting herself toward the leg turbine. Here, with the danger as imminent as the adrenaline is fresh, and with hundreds of ripe gears churning in their sockets as if begging to be harvested, Eris is in her element.

There's a smile on her face, brash and wicked, and so vibrant that I do not see the shadow that peels back from the darkness.

It all happens too fast. The first bullet misses, pinging off into the void of the Windup, and the second buries itself in the meat of her shoulder. She screams, the chill bursting into spikes that thread down my spine, and hits the ground.

I am in front of her before the thought can fully form, my breath hot, fury bubbling beneath my snarl. The guard does not have a chance to readjust his crosshairs. The sword frees itself from my belt, slashing across his knuckles and drawing red against the air, knocking the firearm from his grasp. My blade presses underneath his chin, forcing him to my eye level.

"How many of you are there?" I murmur, nearly a whisper.

"Two!" he gasps instantly, eyes thrown wide, so very scared of me. With Eris bleeding at my feet, I cannot bring myself to care. "Two, including me!"

I nod my thanks. Then I twist the blade to the side, send its edge beneath the skin of his neck, and turn and drop close to Eris as his body crumples against the ground, slipping my hand beneath her back.

"Neat sword trick, Glitch," she groans as I haul her to sitting. Her left arm is limp in her lap.

"Ah, Eris," I sigh, helping her to her feet. There is the slightest twitch as she stands, a flutter of pain, but expelled so quickly I am not sure if I imagined it. "Are we meant to just keep saving each other?"

"Looks like it," she says through gritted teeth. "Where's Theo?"

I turn to find that Theo is not right behind me, as I had thought, and suddenly the hairs on my neck prickle.

"Heads up!" he calls from above, and Eris gently tugs on my sleeve, leading me a foot to the right.

The speed of the guard's plummet smears his uniform into a single gray blot, scream coiling around his failing limbs. A moment later we hear the sickening crack of gravity's embrace.

I list my gaze upward to see Theo peering back, grinning and crouched on a support beam high above. He must have slipped away as soon as the other guard gave up his comrade.

"The Pilot now?" he calls.

Eris nods. "Yeah, we'll come to you."

"No," I say sharply. "Theo, get Eris out of here. I will take out the Pilot."

Eris scoffs, but I still see the pain that spasms across her brow. My gut feels too tight, and my skin feels too hot, and somehow, inconceivably and impossibly, a tremor has set across my hands.

"Eris," I say before she can object. "Please. Let me do this."

She grits her teeth again. "*I'm* crew captain, Glitch."

"And I highly respect your authority as such."

Eris rolls her eyes. "Theo, get your ass down from there and help me out." She looks back to me, snarl still stitched into place. "What are you waiting for? A kiss goodbye?"

"Is that an offer?"

"Like hells." A beat. "Be careful."

By the time I locate the ladder, they have disappeared into the thigh. The Windup has begun to quake again, dipping its blade between the trees and the frail grass in its search for a bit of Gearbreaker flesh. It will not be successful. Not when the crew moves as one, not when their strengths are so interwoven and trust runs so thick between them that questions and hesitations do not have a chance to form.

I pull myself silently into the Argus's head, watching the Pilot swerve in front of me. His eyes are splayed wide, but they do not see me as I tread in front of him, just outside the outline of the glass mat. I wait for a moment of stillness, a slim pause in actions, and then step forward. My sword severs all his cords at once, in a single arc.

The Pilot blinks, mouth agape.

There is no rhyme or reason to my actions. No honor. The first jab would have been enough—through the stomach, a slight twist. As he falls, I find the sword dropping from my hands. I find my boot smashing into the wound. I find the glass meeting my knees, my fingers clenching around his shoulder, my knuckles bruising his cheekbone. He cannot feel it. I cannot feel it. There is no end to the dullness.

"Valkyrie," he chokes, blood on his lips, blood on my jacket sleeve.

He has curls and freckles like Rose. An eye that festers like hers once did.

"Yes," I breathe. "Godolia's shining hope. The Academy's greatest achievement."

I expect his features to draw wide with shock, but something I said makes him grin. Blood outlines each porcelain tooth; I can count them when he laughs.

"You're fucked," he rasps. "You're absolutely fucked."

His eyes flutter lightly. His smile is idle. A spike of unease, frigid and sudden, shoots through me.

My mind races. What is an Argus doing in the forest? What mission could it have here?

They blindfolded me, but we must have gone south—across the tops of the trees stands the bare line of snowcapped mountains, the Iolite Peaks. What city stands near the southern foothills? The Ore Cities cluster deeper into the mountains, but—

The Iolite Waypoint.

Where the Ore Cities funnel supplies from the Peaks to the Badlands to Godolia, a gaping mouth hewn straight through the mountainside. But Windup parts manufactured there are not usually escorted until the supply train makes it past the tree line; it is too complicated to have a mecha escort move through the forest.

That is . . . unless the cargo was deemed important enough.

"Are they building them?" I whisper, and I am shaking him, because his eyes are drooping, and I need him to say something else. "Are they building the Archangels?"

He seems sleepy, already cold under my touch, smile fixed there by the blatant panic lacing my tone. He's enjoying his last moments.

"You and your filthy Gearbreakers," he mumbles, euphoric. "You're all going to burn."

He goes limp. I rise, backing away, every nerve cold.

Eris and the crew are waiting outside. Besides Eris, they look unharmed. Happy, even, the fever of the fight still vibrant in their cheeks. When Eris looks at me, she is smiling.

Her expression freezes when I shake my head. The simple movement makes the world blur. I feel light-headed.

I cannot meet her eyes, so I drop them to the earth. The Pilot's blood speckles my boot, still warm, and such a lovely, deep red. I could start laughing, and just never stop. "There is something you all need to know."

CHAPTER TWENTY-FIVE

ERIS

Usually I'm downright excited whenever the Gearbreaker Council convenes. The captain of each crew holds one of its seats—besides me, but that'll change once I turn eighteen—plus Voxter at the forefront. Gathered around the curve of a semicircular table in the courtyard, they discuss any important matters regarding the life and welfare of the Gearbreakers as a collective, functional unit.

I'm kidding. They're all absolute hotheads.

Jenny threatens to throttle no less than five different people at every meeting, and consistently gets her hands on at least one of them. The vein in Voxter's forehead juts out a little farther each time someone speaks, and he's hoarse from yelling by the end. Depending on the situation, the other captains will either join in on the screaming match or simply try to survive it.

My crew loves it. We make a day of it, a picnic blanket spread on the grass to look between the legs of the other crews standing around, two bags of popcorn—one made by Nova (burned) and the other made by Theo (edible)—and Xander with his small chalkboard so he can make and display a score when necessary (insults about Voxter, Jenny's threats, verbal fights, physical fights).

But it's not as fun this time.

We watch as Sona approaches the semicircular table,

foliage-broken light smoothing over her curls, the perfectly held line of her shoulders, and we listen to her tell about the Archangels all over again. We already heard it once back in the Junkyard. Even though she was her typical collected self then, I still felt a bit ill by the end. Now, with all eyes on her, now that her voice is shaking just the slightest amount, I feel downright incurable.

When she's finished, there's silence. I don't remember the last time a Council meeting was silent. It draws out for ten seconds, twenty, and then bursts. People start screaming, not out of fear or panic, but at Sona—the Pilot, the sadistic enemy—as she wipes away the frustrated tears that sprouted during her speech.

She swallows hard, then raises her head. She looks as furious as the rest of them.

"They're going to have her head, Eris," Arsen murmurs, standing beside me.

"Good," Milo mutters.

I spin on him, eyes narrowing dangerously. "Are you really that dense, to think this was her doing? No, really, Milo, I want to know. When exactly did Sona mastermind this? You know, during the copious amount of free time she had between getting me out of the Academy living and breathing and dealing with your shit."

He opens his mouth to say something, but Theo puts a hand on his arm. "Walk away, Milo."

He's smart enough to heed his brother's warning, throwing me a disbelieving look before turning and disappearing into the crowd, steam practically rolling off his shoulders. I huff and brush the hair out of my eyes, glancing back at Sona. Another mini war has broken out among the captains.

"The Bot thinks . . ."

"Do we believe it . . ."

"Take care," Jenny juts in, grinning wickedly. "You insult the Bot, and you insult my judgment."

"Because your judgment is never skewed," groans Voxter, taking a sip from his thermos. I'm positive its contents don't just consist of coffee.

"Inklings party tonight," I tell the crew.

"Do you think that's a good idea?" Arsen asks skeptically.

Sona must feel me staring at her, because her eye flicks to me. I'm suddenly aware of the dull pain in my shoulder, nestled beneath two layers of stitches, salve, and bandages. Xander pried the bullet out of me after the Junkyard fight—the kid has a knack for that kind of stuff—and now, all I can think of is the memory of the snarl twisted into Sona's features as she slid her blade across the guard's neck.

She's saved me twice now. I'm falling behind.

"And champagne," I add. "We're having champagne, too."

I didn't realize Xander had brought his chalkboard today. Now he scribbles for a second and holds it up for us to read: *10/10*.

"Not for you," I snap, and he starts to write something foul before June gently removes the chalk from his skinny fingers.

Theo rubs the back of his neck. "Junha's crew has the liquor cellar key."

"So go steal it. We've done it before." I blink, an unexpected thought forming, then shake my head. "Go on, the lot of you," I hiss, gesturing vaguely, then push my way through the crowd.

I hesitate at its edge. We're not supposed to enter the semicircle unless the Council gives us permission. "Jenny—"

She doesn't glance at me. She's out of her seat, shouting

accompanied by a variety of hand movements, equally expressive and offensive. "Hey, shit-for-brains, stop talking to me like that or I'll—"

"Miss Shindanai—"

"Shove your judgments up your ass, Vox."

"Jen, hey!" I try again, louder.

She ignores me; they all ignore me, except Sona, head still tilted in my direction, so I skip past that idiotic invisible line we're not supposed to cross and stand beside her.

A glaze of tears clings to her right cheek, the bandage below her left brow darkening at its corner. My hand rises, and without thinking I brush the trail away with my thumb, one quick swipe up and across. The courtyard goes quiet once more; the Council is finally paying attention.

I dry my hands on my shirtfront, then say loudly, with much more confidence than I actually possess, "We should just destroy the pieces."

Low murmurs bubble across the courtyard.

Voxter clears his throat. "Absolutely not."

"We've sabotaged them before," I press. "Each one of our gears proves that. This is no different. We destroy the pieces, and—"

"And what, Shindanai? How long will it be until they build more?"

My cheeks burn. "What else are we supposed to do, Vox? Sit back and do nothing? This . . . this buys us time to come up with a plan, at least!"

"Yes," Sona says. "Before they release a new model of Windups, they are required to show a prototype to the Zeniths. They unveil it at the end of the year, on Heavensday. It is protocol. Tradition. It is holy to them to do so. That Argus was traveling to the Waypoint to escort the prototype pieces. They could leave as soon as tonight and be in the city by dawn."

One of the captains leans forward. "No Gearbreaker was with the Bot when this Pilot allegedly spoke of this threat, correct? This could all just be an elaborate trap to lead us right into a slaughter."

Gritting my teeth, I reach down and snatch Sona's wrist, yanking it up. Her palm is still bloody; she hasn't even had time to wash it.

"That's Pilot blood right there, from a Pilot *she* killed, from a takedown *she* assisted in," I growl. "Sona is a Gearbreaker, and her loyalties are to the Badlands. If Godolia intended to use her to find and slaughter us, they would've done it by now."

"Not quite what they want to hear, Frostbringer," Sona whispers low.

I toss her a jagged smirk. "I'm sure it's not what Milo wanted to hear, either."

She pulls her hand away, looking sheepish. "Ah. You heard our conversation today?"

"Yeah. I just can't put it as eloquently as you did."

Jenny smiles down at me. On all sides, people have erupted into argument again. "Vox says no, dear sister."

I frown. "Tell him to shove—"

"What's the alternative, Vox?" Jen says instead, sharp voice cutting through the chatter. "They build the Archangel. The Zeniths approve it. They make millions of them, and then Windups—too heavy to be transported on boats and planes now—can spill past the borders of the continent and over oceans. If Godolia hasn't overtaken the whole world by now, the Archangels seal that future."

Vox rubs his temples with weathered, calloused hands.

"Shindanai, you negotiated for this Bot's life, less than human as it is, and asked for its residence in our sanctuary. I have granted you this and will grant nothing more. I will not invest a single Gearbreaker life in a potential suicide mission off its word alone. This is the ruling. The Council is adjourned."

"You haven't voted," I snap. "What kind of government are you running here?"

He meets my glare evenly as he rises from his seat. He wavers a little once he's straight, and the thermos sloshes in his hand, held tight. "One I created, little girl."

Anger rises hot and fast in my throat, and beside me, Sona straightens. This time when she speaks, her voice is anything but wavering. "Your lack of self-preservation is remarkable."

Voxter bristles as I swallow my laugh. "Is that a threat, Bot?"

"I am being kind enough to provide you one, on Eris's behalf." Glitch looks at me out the side of her eye. "Otherwise, you would never see her coming."

Voxter's mouth falls open, and he snaps his head toward Jenny, who is barely restraining her laughter. Around us, the Hollows has dissolved into a murmured array of cackling amusement, even some hints of approval. If there's anything we can agree on, it's that getting under Vox's skin makes for good entertainment.

"... sounds like a Gearbreaker, at least."

"Well, if Jenny vouches for her ..."

"I heard she pulled her eye right out of her head this morning ..."

"... sole survivor of the Silvertwin Massacre, if that's even possible ..."

"I'm rescinding the agreement, Shindanai," Vox spits to

Jenny, then picks his head up, sweeping that storm-cloud-colored gaze across the crowd. "Grab the Bot. I want her at the bottom of the lake by nightfall."

Jenny's smile instantly widens, and in a voice equal parts thorns and rose petals, says, "Ah, yes, sure, go and toss her into the lake, all dismembered and whatnot. Then stop by my lab, where you'll be taking her place, and I'll pick you apart until I find something half as interesting as her."

I nudge Sona, jutting my chin toward a space in the crowd. We weave through the courtyard—luckily, no one tries to take a stab at her, besides with a few dirty looks—and into the dorm. She pauses after the first flight of stairs.

"What?" I ask, turning back.

She stares up at me from the landing, shifting her feet. "You believe me, right, Eris?"

Why wouldn't I? is the first thing that comes to mind, but the question has a million different answers. Plausible, logical answers that I wrestle with every time I look at her. I bite my lip at the thought. "About the Archangel?"

She laughs drily. "Sure. About the Archangel."

"Yeah, I believe you." Now I shift my feet. I'm two steps up above her, almost reaching her height. "I'm sorry they don't. You couldn't rescue *all* of them from the Academy, I guess."

"Yes. That would have made it easy."

"For them to trust you?"

"For them to see me." Her fingers flutter up, brushing against the edge of her eye bandage. "Past this. Past everything."

I lean up against the metal railing. "Why do you care if they see you?"

"Because no one ever sees *me*!" Glitch says, and her voice cracks. Shock spreads across her face—I don't think she expected it. Her cheeks flush pink, and she shakes her head. "I am sorry, never m—"

One step, two, landing. I've lost the higher ground. I look up at her. "No, not 'never mind.' Don't swallow your words. Out with it, Glitch."

"I did this to myself, Eris," Sona murmurs. "It's my fault that they see me like they do, so it is my fault if they do nothing about the Archangel. I thought that, if I became a Pilot, I could do what you do, could take them apart from the inside." She laughs again, mirthless, shaking her head. "I was my only possession, and I gave that up."

I frown, eyeing her up and down. "You look like you're all here to me. Right where you're supposed to be."

Sona doesn't answer, or crack a smile like I'd intended. In her silence, the air feels suddenly still. A window facing the courtyard trickles lazy, late-afternoon light into the stairwell, tree leaves shivering against the glass. Fidgeting, I pick a fraying seam in the front pocket of my overalls.

"Doesn't it feel like it, Sona?" I ask quietly, tugging at the loose string.

"I do not know," she says. Her eye, previously set to the concrete of the wall, drifts over to meet me, light crossing over her cheekbone to spark gold across the hazel ring. My fingers still, and go a little cold; maybe it's because all the heat goes to my face. "I feel better, though."

"Good—yeah, okay, good," I say stiffly, seemingly lacking any better words. I force myself to smooth my palm against my thigh; I've already had to beg Arsen too many times to stitch my pockets back together.

"What are we going to do about the Archangel, Eris?" Sona murmurs as we trace up the stairs again.

"Not nothing, that's for sure. I'd bet Jenny's coming up with something."

At that moment, a rumble of feet sounds from above. Nova's familiar shriek of glee pierces the air. A second later she whizzes by, a blond blur sliding down the steel railing, Theo and Arsen right behind her. Trailing them are a couple of boys from Junha's crew.

"Give it back!" one of them screeches before the front door slams shut.

Juniper and Xander are waiting at the entrance to our rooms. Xander holds up the liquor cellar key and hands it to me with a small smile.

"Honeypot?" Sona guesses.

"She's catching on fast," Juniper observes, and holds the door open.

CHAPTER TWENTY-SIX

SONA

"It's supposed to be a party, Glitch," Nova points out.

"I am aware."

"So have a little fun, maybe?"

She perches on the armrest of the love seat, legs folded to her chest, peering down as I work on cleaning my new blade. My feet are bare against the hardwood floor of the common room, warmed by the heat of the roaring fireplace beside me. The blood that caked my hands has been scrubbed off, leaving my palms untainted and soft.

I am at ease, I tell myself.

Like I do not hear that Pilot's voice underneath every comment, every laugh.

I focus on the sword in my hands, the reality of its weight, the security ingrained in its metal. Tiny laurel leaves detail the knuckle and loop guards. I rub the oil rag down the length of the blade, watching Nova's reflection emerge from beneath the grime. "What makes you think I am not having fun?"

The sword will need only a little sharpening, but otherwise, the condition is pristine. Another impossibility, the kind that seems to run rampant lately. It is a weapon equal parts indulgent and ridiculous in its degree of beauty.

Speaking of.

Eris lies flat on the common room's table, legs dangling

over the edge, head listed to the side, reading a worn paperback. Juniper hovers above, green hair cloaking her face as she works under the music trickling out through the wall speaker, the single needle dipping and retracting with an ease that only comes from repetition.

"I get four," Eris reminds Juniper, using her thumb to flip a page. Her sight touches on me for a moment, and I drop my focus back onto the sword. "One Phoenix, one Argus, and *two* fucking Valkyries."

"Don't let it get to your head or anything," Theo says, finger skimming over his new tattoo.

"Shut up. I deserve it."

Theo's sleeves are tucked back, gears pulled into full view, coiling in spirals down both wrists. He went first. Xander went second, adding to the neat row that spills down his spine. Then Nova, whose tattoos blot around her shoulder blades with the barest resemblance to wings. After her, Arsen, who added his new gear to the collection on the back of his right hand, and then Juniper, who added hers to her left. Then Milo, then Eris. I sat on the love seat, cleaning my blade.

Her gaze lands on me. The rest of theirs follow.

I fold the rag neatly in my lap. "Yes?"

Eris shoos Juniper away from her and sits upright, revealing the four new tattoos along her collarbone, black as night within the red marks. She dog-ears a page of the book and slaps it down on the table.

"Your turn, Glitch."

"Hells no," Milo says instantly.

"It was her takedown as much as the rest of us," Arsen says.

Nova frees the toffee pop from her lips and waves at him. "It's an Inklings party, Milo. People. Get. Inked."

"*Gearbreakers* get inked," he snaps, rising from his seat. Eris stays in her cross-legged position, watching with what would be perceived as disinterest if not for the fists in her lap.

"I may be blind," she muses, "but I could have sworn that Sona was the last one out of the Argus after it collapsed. Remind me, are we not counting a collapsed Windup and a killed Pilot as a takedown?"

"And those people who do the collapsing and killing are Gearbreakers, are they not?" Juniper adds.

Milo looks over all of them in disbelief. "So just like that, it's got you all fooled? It comes from Godolia, fresh out of the Academy, with some unbelievable, ludicrous story, and . . . don't you see it sitting there? For Gods' sakes, it's sharpening its *blade*—open your eyes! Are you really just going to wait until it kills us one by one in our sleep? After that stunt it tried to pull today with the Archangel, trying to lead us to a slaughter? Am I really the only one who sees what's going on here? Nova? Xander?"

Nova shoves the toffee pop back in her mouth and crosses her arms. Xander looks back toward the window.

"Milo . . . ," Theo says warningly, rising from his seat. "You didn't see her today. The guard was dead in an instant. She didn't even blink."

"You too?" Milo roars.

He starts for Theo, hands outstretched as if to throttle him. He changes his mind halfway, instead wheeling on me, shoving me into the plush back of the love seat.

"*Look at it*," he shouts. I feel the heat of his skin, his fury ringing in my ears. "No fear, no emotion, and it's still knotted up in your heads. What the hells is wrong with all of you?!"

"Fear would be wasted energy at this particular moment,

Milo," I say calmly, casting a meaningful glance down to my occupied hands. "If you are going to kill me, I would recommend doing it when I am defenseless."

"Twin hells, Sona," murmurs Nova. "You tryna provoke him?"

"He seems already provoked."

"Pilots like it have killed our people for decades! Have all of you forgotten that?"

Eris hops down from the table. "And have you forgotten that I am your crew captain?" she barks, and at the sharp tone everyone else besides Milo stops their fidgeting. "That we trust each other implicitly, that if I jump off a cliff you sure as hells would do it, too, because my actions would tell you that there was a net at the bottom? I put my trust in a person that we are raised to hate and kill, and I did it for *you*. I risked *everything* to come back to you, Milo! I staked my life, because I knew, I *knew* you would do the same for me. But if you can't even trust my word, maybe I've been wrong this entire time."

"Eris," Milo hisses, releasing me, his hand collapsing on Eris's wrist and constricting. Collectively, the entire room takes in a quick breath, and dark flame flashes hot across her eyes. *"It's not human."*

"*She's*," Eris growls, breaking the grip. "Yes, *she's* a Bot. Yes, *she's* a Pilot. And I don't give one shit about it. You know why? Because she's a Gearbreaker through and through, and any other Gearbreaker worth the tattoos they wear would value that fact above whatever is underneath her skin or whatever color her eyes are, or hells, how many she has left."

She shoves him backward, drilling a finger into his sternum before he can straighten.

"And if you *don't*," she snarls, "then I don't want you on my crew."

"You're really choosing her over me?" Milo yells.

"No. I'm choosing her life over your fear." Eris points toward the door. "Go cool off. I don't want to see you again tonight. Find somewhere else to sleep."

"I don't believe this," he mutters, and for a moment I believe he is going to raise his fist. But instead, he drops his gaze to me. "Wire-infested bitch."

"Eris is better at pet names," I say.

His footsteps echo up the hall, ending abruptly as the stairwell door crashes shut against its frame. Eris stays faced away from us.

Then she says, after the silence grows from a new thing into a cold thing, "Turn up that music, June."

A beat. Juniper touches two fingers to her brow and flicks them out. "Captain."

"Where do you want them, Sona?" Eris says breathlessly, whirling on me.

"Them?" I ask, bewildered, while she yanks a pair of disposable gloves from a box on the table, snaps them on with a flourish.

"A Valkyrie and an Argus!" Shouting, now, and I cannot help but smile at it, because even though she is hurting I can tell how much she loves this part, the good part, because she leans over me with her brow scar visible and brushed with the glow of the fireplace. The music bursts through the speakers, and the room roars to life again. Nova leaps from her spot to snatch Theo out of his stupor, twirling him around the dusty rug until he begins to dance on his own. Arsen hands Xander a chipped mug of champagne and taps their cups together, while June bubbles a laugh and plants a kiss on both their cheeks.

"Where?" she repeats, still hovering, and I am very aware this is why I forgot to answer.

I roll up my sleeves. "Here," I whisper, pressing on my right forearm panel. "I want them here."

Eris stares. "You just want to tell the Academy to bite you, huh, Glitch?"

My cheeks flush red. "Is that childish?"

The grin. The chill that trails after it. Eris tucks a hand under my arm, laying it gently against the armrest. "It's a good thing we're kids, then, isn't it?"

Her head bent close to mine as she sprays the antiseptic, she smells like hot tea and toffee and the sweet champagne being passed around. Nothing like Godolia and everything that I did not know I liked. Overalls scuffing softly against the rug, Eris kneels in front of me, a sterile needle balanced in her fingers, like a silver thread between the black of her nails.

"Ready?"

"Okay." *Okay.*

I do not feel it. I watch the ink bloom across my skin, guided by her careful hand, watch the little line form between her brows as she concentrates, and the others dancing around us, and the night leaned up against the window, and please remember it like this, just like this. The good part.

This part is so fucking good.

The paperback book Eris was reading sits abandoned, overturned on its pages, spine comfortably cracked. A line of tape borders the edge of the cover flap.

I look at her. "Did you paste over a different cover?"

Juniper flits by, arms in the air. "Eris likes us to pretend I'm the only one who reads the romance novels."

"You can laugh," Eris says, blushing. "But I'm holding the future of your skin hostage."

I crane my neck to peek at the book again. "Romantic."

"Dangerous."

"Dramatic."

"Glitch."

"Frostbringer."

"Done," Eris says, drawing the needle back. "Thoughts?"

Two gears. Petite and perfect . . . and something more. Flags marking reclaimed land. Skin that has become a little less theirs and a little more mine.

"I think you are a better insulter than you are an artist," I lie.

I wait for a scoff, for her to snap her grip away. But instead it tightens, and suddenly she leans in closer.

"And you are a better Gearbreaker than you are a Pilot," Eris says quietly. "And that is something I truly mean."

Something strange. An impossible, breathless feeling. I retract my arm from her touch before I forget myself. Before the want to move closer can throb any more intensely.

"I am a damn good Pilot," I say.

"I know," she says.

I have long learned to be cautious of pretty things.

But this. I did not account for this.

I am awake when he enters. I do not start. This is his room, after all. I do not question it. I know what he has come to do.

The only light is a small sliver of moon that has slipped through a space in the curtains. It falls in a slit down the right side of his face, igniting the pale eyes narrowed under the furrowed brow, the toss of fair hair, the bared teeth, and the black pistol held steadily. It lifts toward me. I drag the covers away and sit upright, spine pressing against the wood back of the bed. I will not die lying down.

"They will hear you after the first shot," I say. "Best make it count."

"I don't miss," Milo responds evenly. The gun stays leveled. I pull my knees to my chest.

"Eris will not—"

"You don't get to say her name!" Milo hisses, and suddenly he lunges forward. The gun drills into my temple, and I press a hand against the mattress to keep from falling sideways. "She may think you're her little pet, or whatever bullshit, but I'm not going to let her get hurt again!"

"She did not get hurt. *I* made sure of that."

"But all the other times, Bot," he says. "Years and years before you came along. Broken bones and split lips and bruises that never disappear, just get replaced. It's all because of you and the Academy and Godolia."

"You just want to protect her."

"From infestations like you."

I pause. "Ah. But it is not only that. *You* wanted to protect her."

"Wires in yours ears, Bot?" he growls.

I shake my head as best I can. "No. You do not hate me only because of what I am. It is because of what I did, for *her*. *You* wanted to be the one to save her from Godolia. *You* wanted to play the hero, for her to be grateful to you. And therein lies your selfishness. Your possessiveness."

The way in which his gun drives farther into my temple tells me all I need to know. I mean to smile, play coy with my observation. But, unexpectedly, my voice comes out in a snarl.

"You believe I stole that opportunity from you. That I stole *her* from you. But Eris is not an item that can be exchanged between hands, Milo. She is not something to be fought over. She is something to fight *for*."

Milo grins. "Don't pretend you give a damn about her. I know you can't feel. It's pitiful. This can be a mercy killing, if you'd like."

"Would that make you feel better? If I acted as if I did not know that your actions are driven by nothing but cold fear?"

"And *love*, Bot. You could never understand."

"Give it time," I say, words half snarl, half disbelieving laugh. "I'm beginning to."

CHAPTER TWENTY-SEVEN

ERIS

"Eris!"

I wake up knowing I shouldn't have gone to sleep. I should have stayed up, listening for his footsteps against the carpet, the low growl, the cocking of a gun. Something, anything.

But I did sleep with my gloves on.

They're raised before I even kick open the door, spilling the hallway light across Milo's startled features and Sona's strained expression. I get only fragments of the scene—one hand holding the pistol to her temple, the other wrapped around her mouth to silence her scream—before I dive for him.

I drive a hook into Milo's cheekbone that sends him smashing against the back of the bed. The instant his grip loosens, Sona snatches the barrel of the gun and digs her other fingers around his wrist, snapping the firearm upward. It goes off, plaster powder exploding from the ceiling. I wrap my fist around Milo's collar, hauling him off the mattress and dumping him at my feet.

"You idiot," I hiss. "What planet do you think we're on, that you can attack one of your crew members? Another Gear-breaker?"

"She's not—"

I twist the collar deeper, forcing him closer. The glove of

my free hand bursts to life. "Choose your words very carefully, Milo."

"You're really doing this?" he growls. "After everything we've been through together?"

I laugh drily. "Like I've said maybe a thousand times, if what we've been through meant jack shit to you, you would trust me."

"I trust you," Milo pleads. "I trust you with my life and everything else. But you're corrupted, Eris, you're—"

"The girl who's about to break your nose."

"Eris, please," he begs. "I just want to protect you."

"The fact that you think I need protection just shows how out of line you are," I say.

I pause to draw a quaking breath. I'm fully aware of the heat behind my eyes and the quiver to my voice. I hate it. I hate that I don't hate him.

"Get out," I say, voice so choked that the words sound like they've been twisted from my throat by pliers. "You're on suspension. Get the hells off my floor."

"Eris—"

"You heard me!" I say, voice leaping to a scream. I yank him up and shove him through the door. His back hits the opposite wall. "Get out while I'm being nice."

The stairwell blows cold air into the hallway as he leaves, spiking gooseflesh up my arms. For a few moments, everything is eerily silent.

Sona has skillfully disassembled the gun and is placing its pieces gently on the mattress. Her mouth is a tight line. Maybe the time of night has scraped away some of her guardedness.

"Your hair is a mess," she says, placing the clip down.

I can't help it. I start laughing.

Arsen and Juniper have their heads poked out of their rooms. Nova and Theo, still kicking around the common room at this ungodly hour, crowd its doorway. They saw the whole thing, but knew it was best to stay out of my way.

"Is Sona alive?" Nova asks.

I look back toward Glitch. "Well, speak up."

She trails a finger along the comforter. "I don't much fancy sleeping now."

I sigh, and gesture to her. She follows without another word, and we join Theo and Nova in the common room. Arsen and Juniper appear soon after, Juniper pausing a moment to pull a fraying quilt over Xander's unconscious form, slumped over the couch cushions. It's less likely that he slept through the gunshot than heard it, realized he literally couldn't care less, and went right back to sleep. We all take our seats silently.

Theo is the first to speak. "Sorry, Sona."

"That's pathetic," snaps Nova. Theo, rather than snap back, puts his head in his hands. Nova's growl immediately softens, and she nudges him with her shoulder. "Not your fault, you know."

"He's just being . . . I think he sees himself in you. Sees us in you."

"Oh?" murmurs Sona.

"We're not all born Gearbreakers," Nova chimes in, allowing him a moment to collect himself. She draws through the carpet with a fingertip, spewing a line of dust from the fibers. Her jade gaze flicks up, the look in her eyes so unlike the Nova we're used to. "Theo, Milo, and . . . and I aren't originally from the Hollows."

"We're like you," Theo continues, gaze unmoving from his toes. "Our towns destroyed by Windups for missed quotas, or rebellion, or . . . Gods!" He throws his hands up. "I don't know, take your pick. But we were lucky enough to get found by the Gearbreakers, and you, ending up in Godolia . . . I think Milo sees it like you made the choice to go there."

His gaze finally lifts, eyes landing on me, hesitant.

"It's not easy for any of us, Eris. Having the B—Having Sona here. But I . . . I'm not going to try to kill her or anything! Not unless you say."

Not unless I say. I steal another quick glance to Sona, who has reclaimed her stoic expression. She sits cross-legged near the fireplace, hands folded neatly in her lap, the soft light of the embers rippling over her curls. She meets my gaze, and suddenly I know that she knows I'm pretending. Pretending it's not hard for me, too, that every time I look at her there's not that same jolt, the same millisecond flash of anger, of fear. Like the thoughts don't still creep, that one night I'll wake to find her standing over me, grinning as her blade presses to my throat.

"Milo cares about you differently from the others," she says. "Loves you a bit differently from the rest of them, yes? And that type of love . . . it can make you do ridiculous things."

She pauses.

"Not that killing me is a ridiculous concept."

Nova huffs and leans forward. "You got some issues, don't you, Glitch?"

Sona's smile is almost wistful. "Acute ones."

I bite my thumb, considering, then stand. "All right. To bed, all of you. Theo, can you carry Xander back to his room?"

"Got it," Theo murmurs, picking the kid up with ease.

I stop him before he can make the hallway, brushing back Theo's bangs and planting a kiss on his forehead.

"Milo will come around," I tell him. "We'll all be back together soon."

"Night, Eris," Theo says, looking like he wants to say more. Nova closes the door on the way out.

I turn back and cross my arms, watching as Sona ignores me, her head tilted toward the fire as she sifts the dying cinders with the iron poker. A tiny circular indent is implanted in her right temple from the barrel of Milo's gun.

"How'd you learn to fight?" I ask. "Did you start before the Academy? Back in Silvertwin?"

She shakes her head, and for a moment, I think her knuckles flush white as she tightens her grip. "After Silvertwin and before the Academy, in Godolia's streets. It came from necessity. What about you?"

"By Jenny's wanting to knock me on my ass. To feed her ego."

"Oh?"

There's a pause. She stops fiddling with the cinders and glances over her shoulder at me, waiting for the other part of the story that she somehow, unnervingly, knows exists. I roll my neck around and sigh, suddenly exhausted, numb in the places where the anger has fizzled out. I sit on a nearby armrest and rub my temples.

"My dad," I hear myself say. "We're a Gearbreaker family, you know. Born to be fighters. He taught me how to shoot when I was seven, some basic hand-to-hand techniques not long after that. Apparently, I was a complete terror after my first few lessons, picking fights with everything that moved, thinking I could take on the world because I knew how to throw a left hook. Broke a few other kids' noses. Got my own broken at least once, for that matter."

"But he kept teaching you?"

"Yeah. I mean, I guess he thought at one point I'd grow out of looking for fights. Plus, he knew I'd have my hands full of giant robots at some point in the future, right, so I needed prep for that, too."

She smiles slightly. "Those poor children."

I shrug. "Exactly. Then, you know, he died, and I kept on looking for fights. I guess it was lucky that at that point, I could win them, too, since there was no one to pull me out. Gods know Jen liked to sit back and watch more than anything else. Said it was good for me."

I scratch at the back of my neck as the silence unfurls. We both know that we're dancing around the elephant in the room. His footprints pad the rug fibers. His fingerprints are on the sagging bookshelf and mark nearly every single page it holds.

"Milo will come around," I repeat.

"Am I . . . ," Sona murmurs, and one of the brittle logs snaps and spews orange, fireflylike sparks all over her clothes. She lays the poker down calmly and brushes them away. Now she turns, staring with her single doe eye. "I am more trouble than I'm worth."

"I prefer to run toward trouble," I say, quietly for some reason.

"Why's that, Eris?"

"Because it means something interesting's bound to happen."

Sona stands, dusting soot off her trousers. "You have issues."

"Absolutely rich, coming from you."

She stands there for a moment, backlit by the glow of the hearth, shoulders braced back in that ridiculous, perfect posture. Then they begin to shake.

I move, and she turns away, but my arms slip around her sides to clasp over her stomach. My cheek rests lightly against her spine; I can feel when she breathes.

"I think I have cried every day since I met you," Sona murmurs.

"I have that effect on people."

"I do not even know why."

"I'm kind of a bitch, honestly."

She pulls away and faces me, looking almost furious. "You are a riot with skin, Eris," she says hotly.

"Oh" is all I can bring myself to say. I like her words too much. I like how she chooses them and how she says them, even though I don't understand why she's angry now. But I do understand, with a rabid, desperate kick, that I want her to say more.

"And you . . . you are ridiculous, and chaotic, and arrogant, and a headache, and—and—" Her hands lift from her sides, unfurl helplessly. And then she's laughing. "You are going to kill me one day, Eris Shindanai. I have never been surer of anything."

I just stare at her. The fire crackles low in the hearth. Did I have anything to drink tonight? Why do I feel light-headed like I'm buzzed, lighthearted like I'm an idiot? Why do I say, "Do you want to dance?" and then hold my breath in the silence that spreads before her answer; why am I so viciously confident a *no* would kill me?

She answers. She doesn't say no.

The first song is a good one. So is the next, and the next. We start on the floor and end up on the tabletop, wrists bumping against hips and sides and ribs. She's never danced before, and I can tell; she looks ridiculous and it's so, so good, because

I do, too. She's grinning, and I don't know what time it is. She's just a kid but was never allowed to be, and I know how that can mess with you.

I tilt my head back as the room fills with long, hypnotic notes. "I love this song."

"It's softer than I would have pictured your taste."

"It picks up . . ."

She slips from the table and sticks out her hand. "I think I would like to dance."

I look at the palm and all the calluses that dot it. "We have been."

She rolls her eye. "Our flailing does not suit this."

"I thought we looked good."

"You do. Please show me how to do this."

Heartbeat in my throat, I join her on the carpet and take her by the wrists. I place her palms above my hips and intertwine my hands behind her neck, fingers dipping into her curls.

"So what now?" she asks.

"What do you mean, 'what now?'"

"Do we just sway?"

"I guess."

"Do you sway with Milo?"

"Milo doesn't like to dance." A beat. "Stop smiling. You know what—"

Before I can step away, her hands drop from my waist, one of them sliding up and catching my wrist. She gently tugs her grip upward, and then my feet are pivoting into the dusty carpet. As I catch myself, her fingers interlace behind my neck, pulling me closer.

"Did you just twirl me?" I'm stunned, and she looks all too pleased with herself.

"I like this position better," she murmurs, eye drawn low. "Is this okay?"

"Yeah. It's just . . . you sound tired."

"I am."

"Me too."

But we don't go to bed. We don't pull away. And I know she likes girls, have known for a while now that I do, too, but right now, this isn't something like that. We're just close. We're just leaning on each other.

"You were right," she says after a while. "It does pick up."

"What the hells are you two doing?"

I nearly yelp and jump back. Sona folds her hands neatly in front of her, gaze shifting toward the door.

"Good evening, Jenny."

"It's well past midnight, Bot. Good morning."

Jenny is wedged in the doorway, dulled gloves clutching the frame as if steadying herself. Her goggles are pushed past her forehead, giving us a clear view of the dark eyes and the even darker rings that encircle them. Her chest is heaving, giving the illusion that the tattoos inked along her collarbone are attempting to leap away.

I cross my arms as heat floods my face. "Funny, I don't remember giving you an invitation to come to my floor."

"And I don't remember you kicking Milo to the curb," Jenny responds seamlessly, tossing a pointed look at Sona. "Trouble in paradise?"

"What do you want, Jen?" I snap, then sigh. I already know. "We're going?"

"Why, yes, yes we are," she confirms with a wild grin. "Go wake the kids and meet my crew outside. And tell your driver to be quiet for once. That girl's shriek could knock Voxter out of whatever drunken blackout he's fallen into tonight. I expect everyone outside in ten. We're off to the Waypoint."

With that, Jenny turns on her heel and marches out.

"She looks unnervingly excited," Sona murmurs, then looks over at me. She sighs. "*You* look unnervingly excited."

I'm suddenly aware of the smile touching my lips. "What do you know about the Iolite Waypoint, Glitch?"

The Iolite Peaks is the mountain range that bubbles across most of the continent, and sitting at their dead center are the Ore Cities—a string of high-end resource towns from which Godolia gets its main imports of precious metal. They're also where the Academy receives most of the Windup materials from: manufactured in individual pieces, like limbs and digits, in the Peaks, and then sent to the Academy to be assembled into a full mecha.

Glitch says none of this, even though I'm sure she knows it as well as I do. Instead, she looks me dead in the eye and pinpoints the one thing I actually care about.

"There is a hells of a fight awaiting us there."

CHAPTER TWENTY-EIGHT

SONA

It is dawn when we reach the Waypoint, but just barely. The air stands cold and still, gray and dark sky stretched overhead; we can still see by the light of the stars.

While we wait for mechas to emerge from the ground, Jenny decides she wants to take a look under my skin.

"Is this yours?" she asks, tapping the panel where my new gears rest.

I fight the urge to pull away. "That is my skin, if that is what you are asking."

She hums, then slides her hand down my wrist, fingers poking the curve of bones in my forearm.

Jenny laughs lightly. "Quit scowling, Eris, I'm just sifting."

"You're just *what*?" she snaps.

"I'm kidding," Jenny sighs, flipping my palm in hers, pinching the base of each of my fingers. "You certainly didn't inherit a sense of humor."

"Please," Eris shoots back. "What would Dad find funny about this?"

"Not Appa." Her fingers tread up my arm and skip across my collarbone; I lift my chin toward the night sky. The oranges and reds of the tree leaves are the colors of bruises against the darkness. Jenny's voice drops to a murmur. "Mom always laughed at everything."

We hover in the shadows of a thickly wooded forest, just at the border of the Waypoint. Or rather, above the border. A massive underground complex sprawls below us, linked to a highway tunnel that runs throughout the Peaks and connects to each of the Ore Cities. About fifty feet to our left, the earth yawns open and spits an exit into the forest and the Badlands beyond.

"Yeah, well, she had a dark sense of humor."

"She didn't, actually." Jenny's touch treads up my neck, pressing lightly against my pulse. "She laughed at absurdity. Everything is absurd, so she laughed at everything. Your heartbeat is quite high, Glitch."

She can feel me swallow hard. "This seems quite personal. I should—"

"I think Dad would've liked her," Jenny interrupts. Her finger is under my chin, tilting from side to side. There is none of the hunger there was yesterday in her lab, as if now she is just going through the motions to keep her hands occupied.

I go still, cheeks burning. Eris is quiet for a moment, then says, "Why do you say that?"

"Because she saved you. Because he was trusting, like you. And Mom . . ." Jenny finally releases me, steps back. She looks over me once, head to toe, crosses her arms. Her smile is weary. "Mom would've torn her to pieces."

Eris flinches. I stay unmoving, the urge to recoil boiling over into the urge to run.

"Or she would've tried to. I think—" Jenny hesitates. I did not think she had the capacity to hesitate. She sighs again, tucks a loose strand of hair behind her ear. She has so many gear tattoos that they spill past her collarbone, dripping down into her shirt. "I think I would have stopped her."

Eris's scowl disappears for a second, then deepens. "You never can pass up a good guinea pig, after all."

Jenny sneers, pretty features sharpening. "I can never pass up a *weapon*. But I guess, if they were here, they wouldn't have to deal with Glitch at all, anyway."

"What's that supposed to mean?"

"If they hadn't gotten killed, you never would've been captured."

Eris's temper flares, and she pitches forward. "What, because I would've gotten more training? That's absolute bullsh—"

"Because if you had more than me waiting for you back home, maybe you would've thought twice about martyring yourself."

Eris pauses. She runs a nervous hand through her hair and shakes her head. "Ah, Jen. Don't say that. I was just trying to—"

"Buy time for your crew to get the hells out? That's what Mom and Dad did, too, don't you remember? It wasn't right, Eris. It wasn't right for you to go at it alone, when I wanted to stay and fight, and—"

Jenny stops abruptly, cheeks turning pink.

"Godsdamn it," she mutters. "I meant when 'your crew' wanted to stay and fight. You know that's what I meant."

Eris stares at her. "Uh, yeah, Jen. I know."

Jenny huffs and shoves her welding goggles into place, turning on her heel. "I'm doing a perimeter sweep. Do something useful and go check on the roadwork."

As we wander through the forest to the place where the path from the Waypoint meets the edge of the tree line, Eris is silent, scowl fixed. I knead the skin that Jenny poked at on my forearm, feeling for whatever she was looking for. *Mom would've torn her to pieces.* I open my mouth, close it. When I open it for a second time, still not knowing what to say, Eris speaks.

"My parents died on a run. Jenny was with them." She keeps her gaze pinned ahead. "In case you needed context."

I switch my touch to my collarbone. "I did not know you ended up at the Academy to save your crew. That was very brave of you, Eris."

"I was slow," she mutters. "I was trying to take out the guards first, didn't even notice that the Pilot had turned around. But I'll take brave, thanks."

"I'm sure Jenny thinks so, too."

"She's always been a little mad at them, I think. Our parents, I mean. For telling her to run. A little mad at herself for actually listening."

She slows her steps—the path out of the forest stretches before us, dotted with dark splotches of overturned earth. Buried beneath is a collection of explosives and magnetic disrupters, to ground the hoverbarge carrying the Archangel pieces. Arsen and Juniper toss us a little wave from their post by the road, faces streaked with dirt.

"They're probably all pissed at me," Eris murmurs, waving back. "I guess it's different for them, for Jenny. They're the ones who got left behind." She lowers her hand, clasping her fingers tightly together. "I just want to keep them alive, you know? Sometimes that's all I can think of, and so I don't think about the aftermath."

You got left behind, too, I want to say. But instead I say nothing, swallowing my words just like she told me not to. Because comforting people is new to me. I have grown thorns all over myself. Maybe that's what Jenny was feeling for. Suddenly, now, there are people around me that I do not want to hurt, and I do not know how to take my hard edges out, how to say the right things, how to comfort the girl who gave me living, breathing people to fight for.

"I'm not my mom, just so you know," Eris continues, interrupting my thoughts. She draws a line in the dirt with her boot.

I smile a little at that. "I am nothing like my parents. They would be so proud that I have the Mods." I tap each of my inked gears. "And appalled by what I have done with them. What I have done in general."

"That can't be true."

"It is."

"I'm sure—"

"You do not understand," I snap, my voice harsh, and she does not deserve it. But Eris does not match the flare of my anger, just waits quietly as I close my eyes against it and find that it's not even rage, not really. It's shame. "My parents were Mechvespers, Eris. They . . . we worshipped Godolia for bringing the Gods into the physical world."

A pause. I can feel the heat building in my cheeks, but she is not wearing the expression I expected when I look at her again, her head tilted up to mine as she speaks softly. "I know, Sona. I mean, I figured. Most of the villages up near the northern foothills are Mechvesper-heavy." She chooses her next words carefully. "Would they have wanted you to get revenge for them?"

"It is not just for them. I am doing this for me." I blink, surprised at myself, but Eris watches unflinchingly, and the thoughts bubble over and out. "My mother and father taught me that Godolia is good. Godolia is a merciful place. They might have died thinking so, and that . . . it isn't right. I am going to get revenge for them, revenge that they may not want but deserve nonetheless, but I am going to get revenge for me, too. Because I revered the same Gods that slaughtered them. Because I lived the first part of my life in awe, and now in anger, and throughout all of it, Godolia has owned me. That isn't right, either."

"You're fighting to own yourself." Her natural scowl drains a little when I nod, and she drums her fingertips against her own tattoos. "You're in the right place, Glitch—with the wrong kind of people, and the right kind of intentions. You're off to a good start."

"The explosives all set?" Jenny calls, emerging from the forest with the rest of the crew at her heels. "Good. Gather round, kids."

Arsen and Juniper trot over, followed by Zamaya and Seung, the other demolition and corrosives experts. Jenny sits down on a patch of forest moss and crosses her legs, chin rising like she is the reigning queen of the woods.

"If any of you damage the Archangel pieces," she says offhandedly, "I'll leave you as molten as the mechas."

The shocked silence weaves thick. Jenny takes it as a pass to continue.

"We have two goals: The first one is to take out the Windup escorts. The second is to protect Gwen."

"Me?" Gwen squeaks. "Why me? No, wait, I don't want to know, just let me die—"

"Because you are going to get onto the hoverbarge, get to its control tablet, disable the tracker, and reroute it."

The girl's cheeks pinked at her first mention, and now her whole face is sheet white. Her hands rise to rip at the ends of her short blonde hair. "Oh Gods. Reroute it to—"

"Home," Jenny says primly, unabashed about enjoying our confusion. "You turn it toward the Hollows."

"Holy hells," Nolan mutters, biting his thumbnail. "What are you planning?"

"In due time."

"No," Eris snaps. Jenny's gaze lolls to her, unamused. "I thought we were here to destroy the pieces."

"I never said that."

"What are you using them for, then?"

Jenny smiles slowly. "You talked about buying time with your plan. I don't do things to buy time. I do things to make history."

"And just how are you going to do that tonight?"

"Come now, where is your sense of dramatic anticipation?"

Eris growls. "Nonexistent when it involves throwing my crew into a fight I don't know the purpose of."

Jenny stands, dusting dirt off her pants. "I don't need your crew, actually. We can do this on our own."

"Then why did you even—"

"What kind of sister would I be if I let you miss out on a fight?"

"A sane one!"

"Can you imagine?" Zamaya mumbles.

"Fine. Sit this one out, then, if that's what you fancy," Jenny coos, head tilting toward the road. "We'll show you how it's done."

I do not know what caught her attention until I feel the footsteps and see the leaves above tremble. Then from within the gaping maw of the tunnel, we see the eyes—three pairs of red eclipses, set far above the earth. The hairs along my neck prickle, the static before a fight, and I know that it is our fight, too, due to the fiery expression already fixed on Eris's features. Jenny may be arrogant, but she is anything but ignorant.

"Like hells," Eris spits. Her cryo gloves burst to life, and she tugs her goggles down into place. "But you owe all of us an explanation."

Jenny simply touches her brow, miming the tipping of a hat, and sweeps her gaze over her crew. At the inaudible orders, they peel off from the group without a word, claiming their positions in the shadows.

Three Windups total. It should be four, but one of the Pilots lies dead twenty miles in the opposite direction. I still have his blood on my sleeve.

Three Windups total. I cock my head, brow furrowing as I listen. Two pairs of footsteps.

Eris goes rigid at my side at the exact moment it looms into view, and barely so, black metal skin nearly edgeless against the night, flanked by an Argus on each side. Its crimson gaze is the only splotch of color it holds.

"The Phantom is ours," Eris says softly, dangerously.

This time, from her place in the darkness, Jenny bows. When she comes up, she is meeting my eye, her smile wicked and sharp. Grinning at absurdity. Then she is gone, too, vanished into the tree line.

"All right!" Eris calls, and the crew snaps to attention. "Here's the plan . . ."

The static erupts into lightning, flowing into my breath. The Phantom nears, its footsteps soundless, but somehow, I hear it ticking, as if the gears' hum can break through layers and layers of iron, like a heartbeat. Like an invitation to rip it out.

I see you, I think to myself. *Tonight, you'll see me, too.*

"*Duck!*" Nova yells.

Theo and I rise carefully once the guard teeters over the edge of the platform, her and the knife in her neck swallowed by the darkness below. We did not hear her come up until the gun clicked in her hands, and Nova swung down from an upper support beam.

"Where the hells did you come from?" Theo shouts, gawking at the girl.

Nova frowns, her shoulders heaving from her efforts. She turns and stomps toward the platform supporting the hip mechanism. "I don't like your tone. Where's the *thank you, Novs, oh thank you so much for saving our sorry asses* I deserve?"

"Thank you, Nova," I offer as we follow, wiping the sweat on my brow away with my sleeve, forgetting that blood has drenched the fabric. Two guards down.

"That's all I wanted to hear," chirps Nova. Then, she buries another knife into the wall of gears feeding into the Phantom's hip mechanism.

The churning slows for a moment, but the blade flattens and breaks, and Nova yelps as the hilt pops off and pings past us.

She straightens quickly and looks at us, nose wrinkling. "Points for trying?"

Theo sighs. "Where's Xander?"

"And Eris?" I add.

"Xander's around here somewhere," Nova answers. "I thought Cap was with you."

"She must still be outside." I squint down into the leg where we entered, after Juniper and Arsen's explosives blasted a hole in the ankle. The moment the Phantom stumbled and fell on all fours, we weaved our way through the smoke and dust, slipping inside before it could stand again. "I could have sworn Eris was right behind me—"

"I am," she says, right behind me.

I spin around to find her clinging to the bolts of a vertical support beam, breathing labored. Her goggles reflect the darkness around us, sockets filled with void. "I got distracted. There's—"

The unmistakable screech of bullets tears the air, and instinctively, I flinch and duck my head. But after a distinct set of shots shriek without a ricochet to dodge, I realize that the barrage is not from inside.

"Berserkers," Nova curses. "How many?"

"Enough that we need all hands on deck. And Gods know how many more are following from the tunnel," Eris huffs. I realize that the gleam along the top of her goggles is not sweat, but blood. The gash along her hairline has reopened. "How many guards did you get?"

"Two," Theo says, tossing a sheepish glance to Nova. "There might be—"

A shot rings, vibrant and echoing, this time from within. We snap our heads upward, ready to scale, but all we see is a thin shadow peel from the darkness. It attaches to a curtain of wires and slips downward, landing neatly on a support beam ten feet away.

Xander props a crowbar on his shoulder, its end slick and glistening, and raises a single finger. The middle one.

"That should be all of them, then," Eris concludes, and points downward. "Theo, Nova, Xander, you're with me. It's chaos out there." Her smile is quick, then gone, and her glance toward me is solemn. "Do what you do here, Glitch."

My throat goes dry. They are already moving, Theo and Nova leaping to a lower platform, Xander vanishing altogether. Eris places both hands back on the support beam, but before she can slip away, too, I clamp a hand on her shoulder with a lurch of panic.

Eris cocks her head as the silence thickens. "Glitch? I kind of have somewhere to be."

"I . . . ," I start, voice wavering. "I can't do this."

She pushes her goggles up, brow furrowed. "What?"

I swallow hard. "Please do not make me do this."

"But you've done it before. Easily." She retracts her hand from the beam and places it on my wrist, squeezing slightly. There is concern across her features, and the guilt presses down hard. "I thought . . . I thought you knew this was part of the job description."

My eye widens. I reel from her touch, stepping back as far as the platform will allow. "You never said that! I . . . I can't do that again."

"Why not?"

Why not? Why do I never want to be wound again, to own a body greater than mine? Why would anyone pass up that opportunity? But all I say is, in a frustrated burst of breath, "I would not be able to Godsdamn see, for starters!"

Eris blinks once, then detaches from her hold and lands hard on the platform. Despite myself, I flinch as she nears, but she walks right past me, and the shadows recoil as her gloves flare to life.

She presses a hand against the gears of the hip mechanism. Where Nova's knife failed, the frost roots and ravages. Eris slams her fist against the ice, and the metal splits with a jagged, screeching complaint. Around us, the Windup shudders as the Phantom falters in its next step.

"Gods, Sona," Eris sighs, turning back, running a hand through her hair. "I wasn't sending you off to wind yourself. I wanted you to make sure the Pilot is out."

"Oh." I touch my blade, nestled at my side, finding the comfort ingrained in its metal. It only feels cold—the shock of panic draining from my veins. "Oh Gods, of course you were."

And now the heat floods in, into my cheeks, the base of my throat. I look away, locating the ladder to the neck.

"Go, Frostbringer" is all I manage, stepping off the platform and slipping from view, my heartbeat a cannon to accompany the mecha's faltering footsteps.

CHAPTER TWENTY-NINE

ERIS

I open my eyes when my body hits the ground, every nerve alive with energy, adrenaline chipping my breath thin. I bolt upright, fists clenched, head whipping around for the fight.

Theo yelps and falls back on his hands. Arsen stays upright but takes a step back, chuckling, palms up in defense. "Whoa, Cap. We just wanted to tell you we're almost home."

Oh. Right. I sigh and run a hand through my hair, then wince. Along the gash in my hairline crisscrosses a row of stitches, set by Xander's careful hands, and the whole area burns from the salve.

We survived, but every part of me is tense, coiled tight and ready to burst. Ready to bolt.

"Bad dream?" asks a voice from above.

I look up, where on the opposite side of the crate, Sona sits with her legs dangling, sword balanced across her knees. She's perched on a stack of metal pieces, each six feet long, sculpted into sharp points at their tips.

The Archangel's feathers. Some of them, anyway. Jenny thought it would be a smoother ride in the hoverbarge's crates rather than packing back into the trucks, but by the tightness in my stomach, I'm not sure that's the case.

Sona slips off the feathers, landing lightly, and takes a seat beside me. In my peripheral vision, she folds back the sleeve of her jacket, skimming over her tattoos.

"You get more now."

She doesn't respond. When I look over at her, there's a massive smile lifting her cheeks. I haven't seen her smile like that before. This isn't her just baring her teeth, and there's no coyness or wryness here—just a pure and bright kind of happiness.

It drains abruptly when she catches me staring, and she folds the arm close to her chest. "Why tattoos, Eris? Why not just keep a tally on a sheet of paper somewhere?"

I smirk. "You can do that instead, if you want."

"That is not what I said."

I reach up and lay my palm flat against my own gears. "People in the Badlands either worship Godolia or they fear it. Live their lives in awe or in terror. Gearbreakers refuse to do either." In the crook of my collarbone, my heartbeat thrums—*alive, alive, alive*—despite each drop of ink that screams I shouldn't be by now. "Where Godolia wants everyone to keep their dread close, we mark our strength. On the skin they think they own, we mark our freedom. They will see our defiance is infinite."

Sona sighs and rests her cheek on her hand. Her low whisper is to herself, but I still catch it: "I get more now." A slow, bittersweet joy fills my chest.

Soon, the hoverbarge slows, and my crew peels from their places and opens up our crate's entrance. Beyond is the Hollows' gate, and on the edge of the deck perches Jenny's crew—Jenny at the front, hands on her hips, everything about her pose telling me that a smirk is across her lips.

"I'm being nice," she calls down to the gate operator. "You let me in, or I'm going to make an entrance." She tosses her hair over her shoulder. "I always do."

"Voxter says you're on suspension," the operator yells back. Within, a crowd of Gearbreakers has gathered, faces pressed as close to the electrified gate as possible, whispers cackling and sharp. "That you're *all* on suspension."

"Hoorah." Jen yawns. "I need some sleep, anyway. Let us pass."

Eventually, after a few more rounds of shouting, a reluctant and exhausted groan sounds from below, and the gates unlock and creak open. My crew files out of the crate as the hoverbarge makes its way through the Hollows, coming to a dead stop at the courtyard, where it whirs off and lowers softly to the ground. Gearbreakers gather below, shuffling in anticipation.

Nova tenses as a stiff figure bats its way through the crowd. "Oh boy."

"We've done it now, haven't we?" Arsen murmurs.

"What in the names of the million Gods is this?" Voxter booms, cane rapping against the concrete path. Gwen presses a button, lowering the hoverbarge's ramp. Voxter clambers up it, listing on his cane. "Jenny Shindanai!"

"Yes, dear?" Jenny coos as Voxter nears. Her gloved hands hang relaxed at her sides.

Voxter sweeps his eyes over the deck, landing on one of the open crates, the sheaf of steel feathers glistening in the afternoon light.

"That's . . . You brought . . ." He straightens, collects himself, then begins to scream again. "You are *done* here, Shindanai! Disobeying the Council, bringing Archangel pieces here, putting us all in danger. You are banished, effective immediately."

"Ha. No thanks."

Voxter's vein pulsates in his temple. "No *thanks*? Who do you think you are?"

"The one who's going to end all of this, Vox," Jen says, voice rising proudly. The whispers of the crowd extinguish like a candle flame. "Godolia's always looking toward the ground for us, never once thinking to look above."

No one moves for a good ten seconds, letting her words ring. Then, Voxter steps forward and drives the end of his cane into Sona's shoulder. She falls, catches herself on the heels of her hands, crumples again when his boot meets her cheekbone.

"What delusions have you spread here, Bot?" he roars.

I shout and lunge at him, only to be caught by Jenny's iron grip. I expect her to hold me back, but instead, she forces me out of the way, snatching Voxter's cane. She snaps it up, smashing its end against the underside of his chin, tosses it to the deck as he stumbles back, swearing violently. It takes less time than my blink of surprise.

"We need her," she says simply. "Now, as I was saying . . . As everyone knows, I can take apart a Windup with my eyes closed. I can damn well put one back together again."

My mouth drops open. From the ground, Sona looks up, eye widening. She must hear it, too—Jenny's voice, casual and coy, *I can never pass up a weapon.*

My words come out sounding thin. "You want to *build* that thing?"

Startled murmurings burst across the courtyard, only

flaring for a few seconds before Vox slams his boot into the metal side of the hoverbarge, but my gaze is on Sona, on the new tremble to her shoulders. *Please do not make me do this.*

"You want to use a Windup to take out other Windups?" he grunts, blood dotting his lip as he snatches up his cane. "Don't be ludicrous."

Jenny chuckles. "Please. You're not thinking big enough. Why destroy a few pesky mechas when we could get them all in one go?"

"You want to hit the Academy," Sona gasps, rising shakily to her feet. "Use the Archangel to rain hellsfire over Godolia's streets."

"Hellsfire is the Gods' weaponry," Jenny responds, waving all primal ideas of the Gods away with a careless flick of her fingers. "I'm talking about those glorious missiles. I'm talking about using the very thing that Godolia calls its protection as its destruction."

"It won't work," Sona says. "You would need to kill the Zeniths, too, if you want to destroy their chances at recovery. And even then ... they are the puppet masters, but their subordinates can replace them just as easily. There are people groomed from birth to be Zeniths, dozens of them, backups upon backups. You cannot guarantee that they will all be at the Academy when you wish to strike."

"Same goes with the mechas," Voxter sneers. "The only time that a significant number of them would be gathered at the Academy would be—"

A beat of silence. Jenny waits, looking smug, drumming her fingers against her hips.

"Holy shit," I say.

"You want to attack the Heavensday Parade," Sona finishes.

"Ah, they finally catch up." Jen sighs. "The Heavens-day Parade, when the Zeniths and their subordinates and all the students and Pilots will be gathered in one place for the celebration. The streets around the Academy will be cleared and mechas from every unit will stand shoulder to shoulder to watch over the Zeniths' lavish party, held in that ridiculous gold courtyard. Unwound, of course, only serving as eye candy for the Academy's higher-ups as they eat their sweets and celebrate the new year, as well as a handsome reminder of Godolia's infinite strength for all those common folk milling about. They will serve as a perfect bull's-eye."

Another beat of silence.

Then Voxter starts to laugh.

"You would never get that thing in the air," he says.

"Watch me," Jen says, meeting his gaze with her own unflinching one. "We have more than enough mecha parts lying about."

"The end of the year is only a month and a half away, girl."

She shrugs. "So I'll lose a few nights' sleep. With everyone's help, we should pull through. And everyone *will* help, because no Gearbreaker would pass up an opportunity like this. No true Gearbreaker, anyway."

"I don't condone this," Voxter snarls. "And I am the final word around here, if you have forgotten that."

"I guess we know where you stand, then," remarks Jenny.

"You are undermining everything that the Gearbreakers stand for," Voxter presses. "Our *purpose* is to destroy Windups with nothing else except the talents we were born with, to show the Badlands people that humans still hold power in this Gods-infested world. Using a Windup to serve our cause *erases* our cause. I should damn well know that better than anyone, I'm—"

"The creator," Jenny finishes in a bored tone. "The great leader of the Gearbreakers, turning tail when there's some Gearbreaking to be done. As for your supposed 'purpose'—" She puts a hand up and twists her fingers in the air. The lanterns gleam over the orange glaze of her gloves, reflecting in her bared teeth. "Being human is highly overrated."

Vox sweeps his sight over the gathered crowd, sees the realization that each pair of eyes rests on Jen rather than himself. The creator. The great leader of the Gearbreakers. He swallows hard, steeling his glare.

"You are not to build the Archangel. That is a direct order, Jenny Shindanai."

Her grin is ravenous. "Ah, Vox. You always know what to say to motivate me."

Voxter's fingers tighten dangerously over the silver knob of the cane. Jen's eyes touch on his whitened knuckles before skipping up to his face, the dare embedded in her amused expression.

No one moves to claim it.

Jen crosses her arms, chuckling a bit. "Good, then. We have our engineer. We have our pieces."

I know what comes next. Glitch's eye flicks to me.

Please.

Jenny's sight slips down, onto Sona.

"Now," Jenny says, "we just need a Pilot."

I can't do this.

My hands rise toward the crates. The glow of the cryo gloves is harsh against the soft fall light. I barely recognize what I'm doing; I just know that my throat is tight, and Sona is part of my crew, and I protect my own.

But I hesitate nonetheless.

Because suddenly, in my glance over to her, I watch Godolia burn to the ground. A crater where it once sat. A burn mark on every single map where its blot used to taint the paper.

Because she could end this.

"Wait!"

To my surprise, the shout doesn't come from Jenny, but from Vox. The hook of his cane bites over my wrist, yanking. My crew yelps and scrambles out of the way, and I deactivate the gloves and shove him back.

"See, Vox?" Jenny croons. "You're already coming around."

He spits at the ground, smoothing a hand over his canvas jacket. "I just don't want a mess placed at the center of the compound."

I whirl on Jenny. "She didn't come here to do this!"

"She came here to get revenge," Jenny responds seamlessly. "I'm giving her the best chance any Gearbreaker has ever had to do just that."

"You can't make h—"

"Eris." Sona's voice silences me—something about how she says my name tells me she saw me pause. My cheeks burn when I turn to her, but her gaze is leveled at Jenny instead. "You believe this will work?"

"It'll work," Jen answers. "I'll even design a magma serum missile to ensure it. I have a brand to uphold, after all. So what do you say, Glitch?"

In response, Sona nods once, and smiles. Without happiness, pure or bright or otherwise, but with something akin to exhaustion, or resignation. I think, maybe, she's never had a difference between the two, and my heart tightens.

But I say nothing.

This isn't a hesitation.

This is a silence, because those images keep flashing behind my eyes, and I can't help but revel in them. All that glorious destruction at her fingertips.

CHAPTER THIRTY

SONA

For the next couple of weeks, I speak only when spoken to, one-word answers, sight set to the wall. Eris asks me if I am all right. I smile. I ease her conscience.

I wait in my own grave, and I let the cold fester.

They ask me if I am all right again and again. A dozen times. Fifty. Ninety-eight. Ninety-nine. Eris takes the hundredth. I am so full of lies and so ill from the false agreements that I feel as if my wires will snap if I voice another.

Rather than respond to her question, I say I need to wash up. I lock myself in the bathroom and scrub my skin with a nub of soap that smells like jasmine, rinse off, and step into the bath. My head slips under the water, and I listen to the hum that murmurs beneath my skin, so clear like this. I listen to my fear and my selfishness constrict around each other in an endless battle for dominance. There is no point. They both own me equally.

Nova's and Juniper's shrieks startle me, and I peer up at them from underneath the water's surface.

"Holy shit," Nova says as I sit up. "We thought you were dead."

"How long have you been down there?" Juniper asks.

I rouse myself, pulling my hands from the now-cold water to inspect. The skin is wrinkled like dead leaves. "Quite a while."

They stare, and I want to start screaming at them. It is nothing they deserve.

"Your eye is bleeding," Juniper tells me. "Your, uh . . . non-existent one?"

"Okay," I say, resisting the urge to peel back the patch. Jenny had installed an orbital implant a while ago, but without a prosthesis lying around, half of my stare has remained blank, absent a pupil. It still marked me, so I have hidden it. An eye patch is more ambiguous. I could say that I was injured in a takedown. Or saving one of my crew members. Spitting in Godolia's face. The list goes on.

Not that anyone has been foolish enough to ask. Patch or not, blank or glowing stare, they all know that I am just one of the Academy's products. The cloaking is for me more than anyone else.

"Uh . . . you coming out?" Nova asks.

"No."

Another hour passes. Someone will come along soon and ask if I am all right again. I will lie again. Over and over and over.

Being a Pilot has stolen from me. Flesh, breath, pain. But every time I'm wound, I get something back, too. A power that trickles in slow, fills me up fast. I do not own it, because no own should be able to own it, but I crave it nonetheless. I crave it like Eris craves adrenaline, and as soon as that last cord clicks into place, the hunger floods back in, all at once, an ocean of addiction, and under its surface, I do not care that I cannot breathe.

I am terrified of it. Terrified of what I could be, what I could have been if I was pinned to different loyalties from the start.

And when that damn eye is forced back inside, I will look in the mirror and see everything soaked through with red, and Victoria's reminder will scream beneath every false breath: *You will never not be theirs you will never not be theirs you will never—*

I climb out of the bath, hurriedly folding a towel under my arms and stopping short in front of the mirror. *Look at yourself, you coward.* Brown hair plastered against my forehead and a single brown eye. A pale pink bandage. Gears along my forearm—*my* gears, not theirs. Victoria is rotting in the twin hells at this very moment, and I am still letting her voice whip around in my head? I am still allowing Godolia's grip to seize around my neck?

One more time. I curl my fingers into the lip of the porcelain sink. One more Godsdamn time, and Godolia will be right where Victoria is.

I breathe. I can do this.

"Hey, Glitch!" Eris shouts from the hallway. "You good in there?"

I fling open the door, and she springs back, startled by my smile.

"I believe I told you I was all right, Frostbringer."

Eris throws her hands up and sets off down the hallway. "And here I was trying to be nice."

"Eris being nice," Theo scoffs from his doorway, shaking his head. "Glitch, I think you're a bad influence on her."

"You're all terrible influences on me," she barks back. "I would have thousands of tattoos by now if I wasn't weighed down by you lot."

"Yeah, but then who would you have to brag to?" Arsen asks.

Juniper emerges with Xander in tow from the common room, and she places a hand on her hip and straightens proudly.

"They're going to write the Frostbringer down in the history books for centuries, I tell you!" Juniper shouts proudly, fixing an Eris-esque scowl on her face and throwing a sheet of green hair over her shoulder. Xander gives a rigid salute and begins to clap. "Now, now, young man, I don't deserve your applause!"

"No!" Nova chirps, skipping from her bedroom, ducking underneath Eris's attempt to snatch her. "I, the Frostbringer, deserve much more! Mountains of gems and toffee pops and—"

"What you deserve is a broken limb!" Eris retorts.

"Like hells," everyone besides Xander chimes in unison.

She looks at me with strained desperation, and I stifle my laugh. "Want to help, Glitch?"

"Like hells," I say, just to get that delicious chilling stare, and then, "I believe they are suitable impressions."

"The wall's going to have their impressions if they keep speaking to me like this." Eris huffs again and heads for the stairwell. "Everyone better be in the truck in ten, or else I might fancy finding myself another crew!"

"As if anyone else could put up with her," Theo mutters once she is out of earshot, though an endearing hum runs underneath his tone.

The courtyard is in a frenzy, six other crews besides ours hauling into their vehicles, bustling around at Jenny's relentless shouting. She stands on the hood of her truck, gloved hands tying back her hair, eyes buried beneath her welding goggles. Yet the intensity of her stare is not lost on me. She waves wildly.

"Hey, Bot!" she calls. I look to the ground and pull myself into the truck. "I know you can hear me!"

I take a breath. "Good morning, Jenny."

She hops down from the hood and bats her way through the crowd, coming to rest her elbows on the filthy edge of the trunk. For a moment she stands there, watching. I do not know who her eyes are on.

"Need something?" Eris asks.

"A present," Jenny says suddenly, jumping back to dig through her pocket. She retrieves something and tosses it through the air, and my fingers slide against fabric. "That strip of cloth is horrendous. Thank me later."

Nova bursts into laughter as Jenny turns to leave. I flip the fabric in my palm, noting the graceful stitching over the curved material: thin strips of gold thread interweaving into the simple design of a gear.

"You're going to look like a pirate," Nova hoots, climbing into the driver's seat.

I gently peel back the bandage and hold the eye patch up before the blank socket can get a taste of the open light. I turn my head away from Eris.

"Mind tying?" I ask. There is a slight hesitation before her fingers take the threads, securing the knot nimbly. "Well, how do I look?"

"Jen's not one to give presents," she mutters low.

I turn and catch one of her hands before she can retract it, rotating the blue veins of her gloves into open view.

"Where did you say you got these again?"

"Grave robbing," she responds instantly.

"Whose?"

"What?"

"Whose grave?"

"Yours, if you don't let go of my hand."

"You robbed my future grave?"

She goes pink. The bright hue swirls in her cheeks like dye in water. "And I'd do it again."

"My, I'm thoroughly flattered." I take her chin between my fingers and tug gently downward.

"What are you doing?" she snaps, smacking my hand away.

"You did not answer me," I say, eyeing my reflection in the glass of her goggles.

"Didn't peg you as one for vanity, Glitch," says Arsen.

"On the contrary," I say, patting over the eye patch. "I believe I am the most concerned with my image out of all of you."

The ride to the Junkyard makes it seem like the Gearbreakers are trying to make their presence heard all the way back in Godolia. The crews yell from one truck to another in an attempt to best the rush of wind. It only amplifies once we reach the dead Argus, metal shining cheerfully on a bed of flattened field grass.

At Jenny's command they snap to work, stripping down its skin and harvesting innards of wires and gears and plates—anything that might be useful to the construction of the Archangel—piling it all into the trucks. Arsen and Theo strain to lift the Argus's chain mail veil, allowing the rest of us entrance. Eris presses her glove to the left pupil, ice flushing from beneath her palm. The blue glistens across her eyes, its light hopeless and dull against the darkness that churns there. She gives the glass a hard kick, and it snaps apart as easily as one would pluck a dandelion from the earth.

Eris doubles back and throws a hand over her mouth and nose. The rest follow her example. I consider mirroring them but choose instead to cease my breath. No point in trying to play pretend now, not when they are about to see what lies inside.

"Smells like death in there," Juniper gags.

The Argus's head is tilted slightly to the left, placing the Pilot's corpse near the ladder opening. He lies on his side, both arm panels sprung open to reveal the vicious glint of the silver dishes, the severed cords resting within curled around one another like worms. The absence of light has painted the blood over his shirtfront into a voidlike black.

But for a moment, there is none of this.

All I see when I look at the Pilot is the shape his mouth forms as I pluck the shocked cry from his lips, and all I feel is the sweet spark of power as the fear drowns his movements, as it presses them still.

And then I just feel sick.

"Glitch," Eris murmurs, her hand gripping onto my shoulder. I did not hear her enter. "Wipe the shame from your face. We don't live long enough for it."

Theo whistles low behind us, and I turn. "Man, if only Milo could see this."

"He's out there somewhere," Eris mutters bitterly. "Jenny needed all the muscle she could get today. Maybe go drag him in here, but after we're done. I want to get out of this stench as soon as possible."

I mull over their reactions silently as we commence our work: pulling up the glass mat and prying out the piston mechanism that allows it to shift fluidly under a Pilot's steps. My spine prickles as we labor—the corpse's blank stare pasted to the nape of my neck. I hope Milo never sees it; he already believes me to be destructive. It may be the only true thought he holds about me.

I steal a glance over at Eris, a split-second glimpse of the little line set between her brows, the slight ridge along her neck as she strains to tug at a bolt. *Wipe the shame from your face.*

But my shame is not such a superficial thing.

And she can still look at me like that. Look at me with such . . . care, and I cannot understand it, cannot hold it for myself, because it does not matter that the rage and the killing are so *easy* in the moment. I go cold alongside the corpses.

Once we have removed the bolts, Xander lowers himself into the crevice and works a strong rope around the mechanism, tying a hard knot around its base. Together, we haul the piston out of the space, dragging it out the broken eye and over the ledge, where it teeters for a moment before smashing onto the earth below.

"Hope that wasn't important," Juniper whispers, gaze flicking into the clearing, waiting for Jenny to materialize and begin screeching at us.

No such sound. But there are sudden screams.

"Berserkers!"

"Get down!" Eris yells instantly, and the prickly field grass is clinging to my cheeks.

The air shrieks to life with the whistle of bullets, ripping up dark plumes of dirt that smear our line of sight. A distinct series of *ping*s clang against the chain mail, causing it to ripple violently. I drop the rope and throw my arms over my head.

"How many?" Arsen shouts, and Juniper shimmies as close to the veil as she dares.

"Three," she reports. "Two in the entrance path, one in the tree line."

"Do you see Jen?" Eris asks.

"Middle of the clearing. Top of the Argus's hip."

She rolls her eyes. "Of course."

I curl my fingers into the grass, readying myself. "Which one are we going for?"

Eris grits her teeth, raising her hand toward the chain mail, glove primed. "Whichever one is about to step on you."

Cold air rushes across my skin as we enter the clearing, and my next breath exits in a cloud as Eris releases a shot onto the closest Berserker. The panels of its broad chest are peeled open, revealing a dozen gaping muzzles on a swiveling turret, and the shot lands home between the two leftmost cannons. The mecha teeters backward, a rush of white mist streaming across the clearing, and when it dissipates, the Berserker has a splitting chasm along its leg. I watch a handful of Gearbreakers sprint for it before something slams into me. My shoulder hits the ground, and a blue-veined glove smashes flat in front of me, inches from my nose.

"What the hells are you staring at?" Eris shouts, leaping off me. I gaze past her to see a sizable crater where I was just standing.

"Good shot," I murmur, a tad dazed, and very aware that she just saved my life, and that I liked it. "You, I mean, not the mecha. It missed, but you can see that—"

"Can you get up?" she snaps, and I do. Then I grab her overall strap and force us both to the ground again as more gunfire tears the air above us. We crawl toward one of the trucks and press our backs against its filthy metal. Its windows are shattered, each tire popped.

"This is just great," Eris murmurs, leaning back against me to peer into the car's side mirror.

"Are you not having fun?"

"Are you?"

"Quite a lot, actually. Seems like the other Gearbreakers are, too."

"Idiots and assholes, all of them."

The ground shakes, and a round of cheers sweeps across the Junkyard, just for a moment overpowering the sound of gunfire.

"Yes!" Eris hollers, eyes still trained on the mirror. "That's one down. Do you think you can make it to the tree line?"

"If you would like."

"I'd very much like that, Glitch. Go help them there, and I'll come as soon as I'm done with the other one here." A pause. "Don't die."

"Was not planning on it."

"I mean . . ." She runs a hand through her hair. "If you die now, it's my fault. Hells, if you die during any part of Jenny's plan, it's my fault."

I blink. "Why do you think that?"

"Because you're my problem."

"Thank you."

"No! I mean . . ." She takes a deep breath, eyes to the ground. "You're one of mine, Glitch. You're going to be wound again, and that must be something horrific. I'm . . . I'm letting it happen and it's shitty and I'm selfish and I should've destroyed the crates when I had the chance but I hesitated and—"

"I am getting what I wanted, Eris." I shake my head. "I cannot choose what I have been made into, but I *can* choose what I do next."

"It's still shitty."

"It is. And nothing new."

Her scar crinkles in her brow, there and gone in a flash. Eris shoves her goggles into place. "All right, then. Do me a favor and choose not to die."

Then she vanishes, leaping over the trunk of the car and onto the other side. I am gone as soon as the earth in front of me settles—signifying that the Berserker has moved on to another target—and sprint for the trees. The chaos has scattered the garbage out of its heaps and sprinkled its particulates throughout the forest, making for inconvenient obstacles and convenient covers, when I see the Berserker start to change direction. I dive for shelter three times, and the third I end up shoulder to shoulder with two Gearbreakers I recognize: Xander and Milo, who looks at me much less welcomingly than his companion.

"Good morning," I say to him as the bullets ping off the rusted object serving as our shield.

"Bot," he says evenly, teeth gritted.

He holds a pistol in his hands. My sword is in mine. But our sights are not on each other. Instead, they're on Xander, who clutches his forearm. Red blooms beneath his fingers.

"Xander," I start, reaching for him.

Milo slaps my wrist away. "Don't touch him!"

"What do you think I am going to do? Finish him off?"

"I bet you've done worse."

"Much worse. But never to my own crew," I say, specifically choosing the words that will make the vein in his neck pop a bit more.

"Your crew—!"

And then, to my astonishment, Xander *growls*. He rips off a strip of his shirt with his teeth and knots it above the wound—a graze, now that I can see it clearly. Then his black eyes snap to us, thin, sharp lips twisted in a snarl.

"If you two don't stop bickering," Xander mutters in a voice much gruffer than I had imagined, "the Berserker won't have a chance to finish you off. I'll do it myself."

I nearly burst out laughing.

"I did not know you could talk," I say.

"When he's injured, or angry," Milo says. "And then it's only threats."

"Because most of the time no one's worth my breath," Xander spits, and shakes out his arm with a nasty grin. "Gods-damn *hate* getting shot. Are we going to kill this thing?"

The sun disappears. We all look upward to see it replaced by two crimson eclipses, and the stench of smoke envelops us as the Windup bends, the row of muzzles in its chest like twelve perfect black holes.

"Scatter!" Milo shouts.

We manage to clear a few feet before the cannons become primed, but even so, the barrage sends all of us airborne. Somehow I manage to land on my feet, only to straighten and watch as the Berserker shifts its stance to turn toward me. For a moment it pauses, watching, and Eris's voice rings in my memory: *It can't help but steal a glance, remind itself how much it towers over us.*

Well, then. I clutch my blade until my knuckles scream white. *Take a good look.*

"What the hells are you doing, Bot?" Milo yells from my right.

Getting Xander out of range, but you can thank me, too.

I raise the sword. *En garde, Berserker.* A common, wasteful unit, and the epitome of Godolia's gluttony, stuffed full of bullets. No matter. They could never measure up to the cold grace of a Valkyrie.

A burst of heat suddenly washes over my skin, a sheen of sweat breaking across my forehead. The Berserker stumbles back, reaching an arm across its chest to grapple at its shoulder. I have seen this happen before—the metal armor bubbling from beneath the grip, liquefying before my eyes, an attack without a visible source. The Windup collapses onto one knee. Beneath it, the dainty thistles erupt into flame.

I turn to see Jenny in a firm stance on the peak of the Argus's knee, smirk so brilliant it slashes through the smoke. She gives the barest tilt of her chin.

"You're stealing my spotlight, Glitch," she calls. "Facing off a mecha like that. Best get going before it gets up. And do watch the molten bits."

I look toward Milo. "A little help, perhaps?"

I do not wait for a response. I begin to sprint, knowing—hoping—that a bit of Xander's sharp words got through. We can bicker all we like once we return to the safety of the Hollows.

As I reach the base of the Windup's knee, Milo appears with hands low and fingers intertwined. I jump into the foothold, and he springs upward, sending me flying toward the hole eating away at the mecha's thigh. I catch hold of a ladder rung before gravity has the chance to become greedy, and I begin to climb.

I do not give the guards a chance to raise their weapons. Giving them a flicker of hope would be cruel. These are quick killings, merciful ones, I tell myself.

Swallow hard. Swallow again, past the cold cracking my chest.

And then the Pilot, the poor, pitiful creature, not knowing that death is upon her even as I stand directly in front of her open, unseeing eyes. I wait for a hesitation in her steps, then sever the cords in a single swipe of my blade. The Windup shudders beneath me as the connection between its mind and body is ripped from existence, but remains upright.

I slide my palm against the Pilot's cheek as the focus returns to her gaze, see the fear there dance lively and wild. I relieve her of her terror, and I allow her rest. The body falls to my feet, and I bend to close her eye. *Her* eye, not theirs.

So easy. I think it's a prayer. I think I am begging. *This is so easy.*

CHAPTER THIRTY-ONE

SONA

My feet hit the singed grass, and my temple is met with the barrel of Milo's pistol. I throw him a sideways glance, finding his face carved into a scowl.

"You must be really afraid of Eris," I say, "the way you waver like this. You could have pulled the trigger ages ago and been done with it."

"How did they know?" he growls.

"This is getting a tad old, Milo."

"Vanguard! What the hells are you doing?" a familiar bark sounds, and then an orange-veined glove is clamping onto the pistol. Heat swells up the side of my face as I recoil, and Milo cries out, staggering a step back. Jenny's goggles are around her neck, giving full view of the venom in her gaze. She deactivates the magma gloves the barest moment before her finger jabs at Milo's sternum. "*We need her*, idiot!"

She drops the firearm to the ground. The imprint of her hand is pasted against the barrel, the magma serum collapsing the structure and leaving it as nothing but another broken item of the Junkyard.

"How did they know, Jenny?" Milo yells. "First an Argus, then *three* Berserkers! Twenty miles from the Hollows!"

He means to draw attention, turn the Gearbreakers against me. I am not worried. Jenny wants me alive, and as much as they may scream for my life, none of them will challenge her. And even if they did, she would knock them flat with a smirk and a clean punch. Same goes for Eris, minus the grin. The way she is stomping over to us now—breath hot despite the twin frosted Windups she leaves in her wake—makes me feel a bit sorry for Milo.

Eris stops short once she reaches us, staring down at the melted firearm.

"I'm surprised your head isn't like that by now," she spits at Milo, "with all that hot air bundled up inside."

"We are so close to the Hollows, Eris! They're looking for *it*, can't you *see* that?"

"And can't you see the work she's done? How she acts? How she hasn't slaughtered us in our beds yet? You know you're—"

"Can you just shut up, both of you?" Jenny interjects. "Gods, the bickering! I would throttle you all if grave digging wasn't so much effort. They've probably got mechas making rounds of the entire forest, looking for the Archangel pieces, looking for us, big whoop, what's new, now shut it."

Jenny turns to leave, then thinks better of it, clamping a hand onto Milo's shoulder. She matches his height, but he leans back when she leans in and towers magnificently. "I won't tell Vox about this little homicidal kick you seem to be on, but listen, kid, I need the Bot. And if you kill her, in whatever idiotic, oh-so-obviously-compensating-for-something act you fancy that day, that fact still won't change. And that means after I beat the living shit out of you, I'll harvest her parts and implant them inside *your* body. Because at the end of the day, I just need a Pilot, and I don't really care who it is. Feel free to take this threat very seriously. I happen to be so very smart."

I turn to Eris as Jenny marches off. "How was your fight, Frostbringer?"

"Wish I was still in it."

She crosses her arms and begins to chuckle low at the expression on Milo's face, which has visibly gone several shades paler. She waves a hand in front of his eyes, and he blinks hard.

"You're off suspension," she says, shaking her head, "now that I'm fairly positive Glitch is safe from you."

"You think I'm scared of Jenny?"

"I've found you're more of a coward than I thought you to be."

"And you are pathetically naive," he growls venomously, and suddenly his hand is around her wrist. For a moment, the flash of an image: my blade finding home across his neck, a choked cry dribbling from his lips. "Wake *up*, Eris! What did they do to you? What did they take? Your sight, your instinct? Your hate? And what did they replace it with? Trust and *weakness*. It's like I don't even know you anymore. I pity you."

For a moment, an expression of extreme hurt flickers across her features. It wavers there for a half instant, long enough to make fury throb inside my chest. My hand tightens around the sword. But then I see a new look burst in her eyes, a glare colder than any steel I could ever hope to wield. Milo drops his grip. Now the laugh that escapes her is akin to thunder, a storm's snarl.

"Maybe you're right. Maybe I am weak. I got sloppy. I got captured. But I also got *out*. I left bodies in my wake and the name of the Frostbringer embedded in both Gearbreaker history and the Academy's nightmares. *I did that.* So pity me all you want, Milo, but remember, fear is a waste of time. A waste of breath. I don't fear death and I don't fear Godolia and I sure as hells don't fear what you think of me."

Eris turns to leave, giving a slight nudge of her chin as indication to follow. She shoves her shoulder harshly against Milo's as she passes. "You know what I'm capable of. And I know you force yourself to pity me because you fear losing me. You're right to do so. We're done. And you can find yourself another crew as well. I don't fancy having any cowards in mine."

"Eris," I whisper as we peel away, leaving Milo lost in the tree line. To my surprise, her bottom lip quivers, just a bare moment before her teeth burrow into it. "Are you—?"

"Don't let me turn around, Sona."

"I won't."

"And if I do, slap me. Very hard."

I chuckle. "I do not think I can do that."

"It's an order from your commanding officer."

"You are not as scary as your sister. Her threats are a bit more effective."

"Don't I know it," she grumbles.

She shakes her head, scowl pinned to its usual spot, but I believe I see the corners of her mouth twitch. Just slightly.

"Glitch. Sona, hey—"

I wake up cold and with the taste of earth on my tongue. Her hand on my shoulder, Eris sighs and sits back on her heels.

I swallow hard to flush my dry throat. "Was I—"

"Third time this week," she says. "Got something on your mind?"

Everything . . . everything. Or there was, an instant ago. But now, the floor is quiet and I hear crickets outside Eris's window. The darkness wraps around us like thin sheets of silk. Eris is wearing a large T-shirt and looks moderately irritated. My heartbeat is slowing. I do not remember what I was dreaming.

"I told you I can sleep in Milo's room just fine," I respond, tilting my head toward her. My fingers find the eye patch underneath my pillow and tug it over my head.

"It's not Milo's room, not anymore," she retorts, scowling.

"So let me have it."

A slight pause. "Give it a cooldown period."

"In case he comes back? It's been a week already since he left." Silence. I pull my legs up and knead my cheek thoughtfully. "And if he comes looking for a fight, I can take him."

"May be a wild concept to you, Glitch, but I would prefer to have *both* of you living."

"The common room would suffice as well."

"It's filthy in there," Eris snaps.

"So is your floor," I say, freeing the loops of hair trapped beneath the strap of the eye patch.

"I said that there's enough room for both of us on the bed!"

"Intrusion."

"You've already intruded on my life, Glitch. And ruined it. Might as well go the whole nine miles."

"It is 'nine yards,' I think. Have I really ruined your life?"

"Absolutely. Especially my sleep schedule."

I sigh and sit upright, pulling back the quilt. "I will be in the common room, then."

"Like hells you will," she huffs, crossing her arms and leaning against the wood leg of her bed. "I want you here."

I pause my movements. Her eyes are closed, but I can tell that her ears are pricked for my threatened leaving. For a moment, I consider standing and making for the door, just to see what she would do.

"And why do you want me here?" I ask instead. She opens her mouth once, closes it. Does the same again. I get a glimpse of her brow scar before she shakes her head swiftly.

"I'm tired," she announces, and I wait for her to rise to her feet. Instead, she peels back my quilt and slips underneath, lying flat against the thin floor mattress.

"Get up," I say.

"Nope," she responds. "I'm rooted. Take the bed."

I sigh again and rise, stepping over her slumped form and pulling myself onto her sheets, twisted from her fitful sleep. Seems she fights in her dreams as well.

For maybe a half hour, all is quiet, but rest will not come. I stare up and try to locate the ceiling. The night has stolen it from above our heads.

I crawl back toward the end of the mattress, peering down over the footboard. Her back is to me, but I still see the way the quilt is puckered around her clenched fists.

"Stop watching me, Glitch," her voice sounds.

"You look like you are about to punch something."

"Yeah, you. Let me sleep."

"You cannot punch me from that distance."

The quilt flourishes, and suddenly she is on her knees, her nose inches from mine. In my peripheral vision, her fist is raised.

I sit back on my heels and wait. She drops her hand and clambers up onto the bed, collapsing atop the bundled sheets, throwing her arms over her head. "Go to sleep."

Before there's time to overthink it, I claim the space beside her, lying on my side. "You would have made a good Valkyrie, Eris."

She huffs and flips onto her side, too, facing me. Her shirt drapes over her form, outlining the delicate curve of her hip. "Good? I could've been at the top of your unit, easily."

"*I* was near the top of my unit. You think you could have bested me?"

"What is this 'could have'? I can beat you now."

"In what exactly, Frostbringer? Speed?"

"Sure."

"Swordsmanship?"

"If I put my mind to it."

"Escaping Godolia?"

A hesitation. "I could have done that on my own."

"Really."

"Really," she says, then shakes her head. "No, that's a lie. But I've thought about it, and you could've. Easily. Walked straight out of there in your Windup, hopped out wherever you pleased. So why didn't you, Glitch? Why did you stay?"

I smile slightly. "I needed somewhere to run to. Someone."

"So you're saying you needed me?"

She is teasing me, I know it, but I only look at her and say, "Without a doubt, Eris."

She rolls her eyes. "You want your entire existence to be a thorn in the Zeniths' sides, don't you, Glitch?"

"Or a blade."

"You just want to tell them to bite you."

"And bite them back."

"And spit on them at their funerals."

"Eris, if Jenny's plan works, there will be nothing left to spit on."

"That's dark," she muses, grinning broadly now. "Well, dance on their graves, then."

"I think I might need a few more lessons," I say.

She laughs, flipping onto her back. "That can be arranged." I stare at her profile for a silent five seconds before forcing myself to mirror her. She runs a hand through her hair. "So that's what you're always dreaming about? Godolia's death and whatever other destructive shit you're always saying so eloquently?"

"We both know I would not wake up screaming if I dreamed of Godolia's downfall."

She goes still next to me, ceasing the fiddling with her hair. I feel her smile dissipate, its warmth leached from the air, feel her eyes on my temple as she tilts her head toward me. I search for the ceiling again.

"So tell me about it," she says.

"About what?"

"Silvertwin, Sona," Eris says, voice dropped to a whisper now. She flips onto her side again, and before I can shift my head away, she wraps her finger in a coil of my hair and tugs sharply, forcing me to look in her direction. "You can talk to me."

"You know the story, Eris," I say evenly, resisting the urge to look away, to bolt.

"I don't know yours." Her fingers are still in my hair, her eyes off mine, drawn low, watching herself slowly wind the curl around her nail. "Come on."

"It hardly matters now," I say, though it does, much more than I want it to. "I'm not the same person."

"Isn't that *why* it matters?"

When I do not answer, she yanks my hair again. I let it happen, then look at her, deadpan.

"That hurt."

"Funny."

"They did not take away my sense of humor, at least."

Her eyes immediately darken. "Is that what you meant? When you said you're different now?"

"You did not think me human when we first met."

"Don't, Sona," she snaps, propping herself onto her forearm. I let her glare thread ice through me as her head leans over mine.

"You didn't."

"Can you blame me?"

I look past the shell of her ear, up to the black of the ceiling. My smile is idle and dry. "Precisely the point, Eris. I cannot."

"And what do I think of you now, then? Since you know everything."

"You think the same. But you are trying not to, Eris, and I . . . I did not think that anyone would ever try for me," I reply, ignoring the heat curling in my throat. My voice is rising. "But there are flaws in your attempts. You are trying to ignore all these *pieces* of me. Pieces Godolia put here, but they are still *me* now, and I just . . . I obsess over them. I try to pick them out, pluck them apart. I am literally so intertwined with them that their removal would kill me. I tried to convince myself I was not what I am when I woke after the Mods surgery. I looked in the mirror, covered my eye, and told myself over and over again that I was human. I do the same now. It is madness, and you making me feel that *I'm* . . . it only feeds it. I . . . I don't want you to get wrapped up in my delusion, too, Eris. It is not fair to you."

Eris opens her mouth, closes it just as quickly. Then she yanks on my hair again, much harder, forcing my head directly under hers. She looks down with a hard scowl.

"You're a Godsdamn hypocrite," she snaps, teeth bared. "It's not fair to *me*? How the hells do you know what's fair to me? What's good for me?"

"What did they do to you at the Academy?" I whisper. It is cruel and I know it, but it catches her off guard like I need it to. Her hand slips from my hair and she sits back, turns her weight away from me, the line of her shoulder blade slight under her shirt.

Regret claws at me as the silence grows, and I open my mouth to say something—I do not know what—when her fingers find the end of her shirt and lift.

The fabric hangs hooked in her knuckles, the shallow terrain of her ribs white even in the dull light. Briefly, I remember how she leaned her right side flush against the tiles of the bath, tucked away from the rest of us. I did not think much of it at the time.

The skin is not perfectly white. She peels away the edge of the bandage, just a bit, the small mouth of the first puncture wound ringed with a yellow bruise.

"Eris," I breathe.

"They knew what they were doing. They were really good, honestly," she says in a hoarse, horrible voice. The hand not lifting her shirt is hugged around her stomach. "Real smart with it, you know? They only hurt going in, but that wasn't the point. The tiny forest of needles sprouting from your side for hours is the point. You are so tense the entire time because you don't know what's going to happen if you move. Might sink into something important. Might hear something scrape. Might do absolutely nothing, too, that's the shitty thing. They know how to keep you balanced on the edge of your flinch. Joke's on them, right? Free acupuncture."

"Eris," I say again, because she is so far away, because I do not know what else to say.

"But I *won*, didn't I?" she says, but it's not to me. "I got out. I won."

Her fingers brush lightly over the bandage and hover there, and then she goes so perfectly still that it scares me. But my fear is gone in a moment, cracked apart by easy, simple rage. *This* I can understand. That they hurt me and I am going to destroy them for it. That they hurt her and I am going to kill them for it.

"Does it feel like you won?" I ask.

Silence. She shakes her head.

"All right. Let's keep going."

Her shirt falls back into place. Eris turns to me with such an unexpected, furious expression, I blink in surprise, and she reaches over to snatch my arm, thumb pressed to my gears. She is on her knees, hovering above me, my wrist in her grip.

"Do not *ever* deign to tell me what I see in you," she snarls. "Because I see it all, Glitch. The panels and the glow and the painlessness, and I keep looking, because that fury and that terrible sense of humor and the way that you stare at things as if you truly believe that they'll be stolen away in the next heartbeat . . . It's so much *more* than what they made you into.

How could you not know? I'm not ignoring the pieces they put inside you, Bellsona; I just can't focus on them when you're there, too." She bows her head over mine, a reaper plucking a soul from its mortal shell, and all I can think is, *Go ahead.* "Like hells I don't see you."

I take great care blinking over each feature: the stubborn lip, the furrowed brow, and those eyes, Gods, those damn eyes. Sometimes the darkness in them is too infinite. There is too much potential to drown me within a single look. *Bellsona.* And I wait for the recoil, the jump to my heart like an electric shock, the lurch of the desperate, familiar plea. *Say anything else.*

Say it again.

She drops my hand back to the bed and lies down beside it. "I feel ancient," she whispers, one arm draped over her eyes. "I don't think I'm supposed to."

"We are supposed to be children," I say.

She scoffs, teeth flashing. "Oh Gods, Sona. What a joke. This whole fucking world."

"So what do you want to do about it?"

"I don't know."

"Sleep it off?"

"Sleep what off?"

"The war. The era."

"Fine idea, Glitch," she whispers. "Just fine."

But she does not sleep. Neither do I. We stay up until the new hours of the day, and I whisper about sycamores and fleeting dawns and slight dusks and canaries with wings spread wide. By the end of it all, I am completely drained of both words and tears, and have spilled so much of the past onto the sheets between us that I do not have the strength to close my eye, and instead lie still, watching her profile.

And then, for the first time since I started the story, Eris moves. Her hand shifts against mine, our fingers threading together, palms clasping. She does not speak. There is nothing more to say.

CHAPTER THIRTY-TWO

ERIS

The snow on the ground never really seems to melt. The fire is fed constantly, and at night, we fight over the bit of heaven that is the length of rug next to the hearth. Sometimes the bedrooms get too cold and all of us pile into the common room, shoulder to shoulder, blankets layered together. I feed the mistletoe June hides around the apartment into the flames, as is our tradition.

Meanwhile, the construction of the Archangel renders Jenny more feral than usual.

As she stalks around the Hollows—whether it's toward the river, where the Archangel's head rests, or down toward the gates, where its feet lie in the slight ravine twisting through the east side of the forest—people who don't dive out of the way get trampled. She barely sleeps, and the circles under her eyes dig themselves deeper every time the sun rises to find her still milling around, shouting endlessly at no one but herself.

I instantly know what's happening when Xander bursts into the common room one morning, slams the door, and shoves a chair underneath the handle. If you're running from someone with that much fear on your face, you're running from Jenny.

He spins around, and his lips move, emitting no actual sound but mouthing two very distinct words: *Hide me.*

Juniper and Theo immediately leap off the couch and shove the bookshelf back, causing its sagging contents to spew dust, ushering Xander inside the crawl space hidden behind. Arsen heaves himself on top of the bookshelf once they've dragged it back into place, lying flat with his feet dangling over its edge, black eyes rolling closed.

A moment later, Jenny kicks open the door, sending the chair halfway across the room. Nova neatly springs back from her perch on the love seat to avoid her legs getting crushed by the flyaway furniture.

"Hi, Jen!" she chirps cheerfully, hopping onto the abused chair, pulling her feet underneath in a tidy crouch. She places her elbows on her knees and interlaces her fingers, grinning lazily. "What brings you to our humble abode this fine morning?"

"Where is he?" Jenny growls.

"Where is who?" Glitch asks from the couch, so nonchalant that I see Nova bite the inside of her cheek to keep from laughing.

Jenny huffs and pulls her hair back into a high ponytail, springing her crow's feet into full view. "You Godsdamn know who I'm talking about. Where's your twig boy?"

"Can you stop shouting?" Juniper asks sweetly, throwing a soft gesture toward Arsen. "He's sleeping."

Jen's sight flicks toward the bookshelf, and Juniper swallows hard.

Theo groans. "Subtle, June."

Arsen's eyes fly open when he hears Jenny's hard steps, pushing himself off the shelf a mere half second before she shoves it to the side, revealing the crawl space. Xander yelps and attempts to slip underneath her arm, but she sticks her foot out and sends him sprawling onto the rug. Dust takes the air again as Jen bends down and presses her palm tight against his shoulder.

"Jenny," I say steadily, choosing my words carefully. "Get the fuck out."

Jenny looms over Xander, her free palm curling open.

"Give it," she growls. "I'm not asking again, toothpick."

There's silence as we all wait, and then Xander slowly reaches into his pocket, retrieving something that Jenny snatches greedily. She springs to her feet and takes to pacing around my common room, keeping the item clutched in her palm.

"I leave my lab for five minutes, and I come back to find things moved around. One thing, one *key* thing, simply vanished. I turn around to see the mute scurrying up the steps."

"He's not mute," Juniper snaps, and Jenny lets out a dry laugh. She pauses her march to look at Xander, still on the floor.

"Let's hear the explanation, then, motor mouth," she says, opening her fingers for all to see. "Why in the twin hells would you take *this*?"

Sitting in her palm is a small jar of blue liquid. A single eye with a copper trail rests inside, its dulled pupil floating above the surface.

It's slight, but in my peripheral vision I see Sona shift, recoiling as much as she can without actually moving from her spot. By the time I get a good look at her, she's back to cleaning her blade. Gods, she does love that sword.

"Is there a specific reason you wanted that, Xander?" Glitch asks evenly. Her eye flicks toward the one in the jar.

I don't expect him to answer besides with an icy stare. But to my surprise, the kid's eyes are glazed with tears.

"You don't want it," he whispers. "You hate it. You want it destroyed."

"And you thought you would do that for me?"

Xander swallows hard and nods. Sona runs her tongue over her lips and stands, placing the oil rag gently on the table.

"Why would you do that for me?" she murmurs.

"You realize you could've ruined us?" Jenny spits. "You realize how *dead* I would've made you if—"

Xander motions at her to stop with a wave of his hand, and then grins, in a sick, dipshit kind of way that says blatantly, *I literally couldn't care less.*

Jenny lets out a short, disbelieving breath. The jar still in hand, she points rigidly at Sona.

"You have your test run this week. And if I catch any of you rats anywhere near my lab before then, I'll make sure the Council receives a hefty organ donation by dusk."

Everyone stays silent as she strides away, listening for the fading footsteps and the slamming of the stairwell door to signify safety. Nova begins to laugh.

"You're batshit, Xander," she crows. "Do you have a death wish or something?"

Xander ignores her, rising to his feet and tweaking his shirt collar, where Jenny's iron grip has left the fabric crimpled. His eyes go to rest on Sona's steadily held blade, the sure hand encased in the intricate silver knuckle guard. The glance is fleeting, but nonetheless, I know what he sees. It's the same image that's been throbbing inside my head for weeks now, burning like a fresh cut every time I look in Sona's direction: her form glistening in the forest's autumn shadow, blade steadfast in a tight fist, and an unflinching gaze leveled up at the Berserker. I saw the scene only for a split second before another Windup demanded my attention, but I saw her. A fight she couldn't possibly win, and yet her stance screamed otherwise.

Xander saw it, too. Just as I had against the Valkyrie, Sona had stood confidently not because she thought she would come out of the battle alive. She did it because the weapons were now turned toward her, and off her crew. *Our* crew.

Sona saved his life, and now he's trying to return the favor. He broke into Jenny's lab and stole the eye, hellsbent on saving her.

From winding?

No. A lump unearths at the base of my throat.

"You don't really want to kill all those people, do you?" Xander rasps.

The look on her face. The look on her face could shatter me, if it was turned toward me, but it's not; Xander holds steady under it, because he had the gall to do what I should have, what I can't. Her hair crowds her shoulders messily. I think that's what keeps me from seeing the hitch in her breath, but I know that her tell is in her hands, and I know that when they curl into themselves like they do now, she's bracing herself.

Massacre. That's what I'm putting on her shoulders; that's how we're finishing this. Because how could the end of war not be as barbaric as the rest of it? Why should we have hoped there was any other way?

Before I even register that she's placed the sword in her belt, Sona has stepped forward and wrapped her arms around Xander's thin frame. The embrace is quick, and Xander blinks in surprise as she straightens and places her palm lightly on his shoulder.

"Thank you," she says, smile and voice soft. "It was very kind of you to think of me."

Xander drops his gaze, hand treading up to hers. At first I think he's going to bat away her gesture, but instead he coils his fingers around her wrist and flips her palm toward the ceiling. Her gears come into full view, a meager amount now, but steadily blooming. Lightly, his fingertip taps against her forearm panel, on the first tattoo, the one I put there myself.

We make it a few more days before Jenny tries to kill one of us again. A midday run has the kids thrumming with restless energy, but because I'm ancient and dead tired, I'm grateful to find the common room empty after my bath, save for Sona comfortably cross-legged on the couch. She has one of my books in her hand, a blush staining each cheek.

"Oh Gods," I say.

Her sight touches on me and she holds it while she turns the page. "This is filthy," she says evenly.

"It is *not*."

Her finger traces the page. "*She watched her fiercely, and she was senseless for it, because she knew this was the turning point, the setting of the linchpin . . .*"

She swings over the back of the couch while I grapple for the book, up onto the window ledge, tall frame leaning against the glass. She hasn't stopped reading. Kneeling below on the cushions, I have to tilt my head all the way back to see her properly. "Rot, Glitch!"

"*She knew that her universe pulled taut around this girl, would eventually collapse around this girl, this force—*" Sona pauses. Her chin tilts toward the window, and then she says, "Chest."

"What?"

"Mecha chest."

I climb up the back of the couch and look out, where the Hollows' central courtyard has been overtaken by the Archangel. The crates from the Waypoint held only the defining details: a silver breastplate, greaves, arm guards, and an equal parts interesting and terrifying set of hands, each finger ending in a curved talon. A black metal halo rounds its crown. Half of the campus could cozily camp above its shoulders.

The thing is hideous. Whatever elegance the Archangel pieces hold is vastly overshadowed by Jenny's doctored parts—the Berserker's thighs, most of the Argus's torso, not to mention random bits and parts of the innards. It doesn't matter. The thing just has to fly.

On the Archangel's sternum, Theo sits on Arsen's shoulders, Nova on Juniper's. Xander is officiating the chicken fight. He got a whistle from somewhere, and its shriek claws at the glass.

"They're *dead*," I hiss.

"Jenny," Sona remarks. My sister has appeared on the mecha's hip with a look that would level the gates of the hells.

The effect is immediate. The kids fall off one another and ping off in different directions. Something flickers in Arsen's hand, and suddenly fog is rolling off the mecha in tendrils.

"Come on," I say, and we peel from the window. I lead her up the hallway and to the front door, flipping the lock three seconds before five pairs of fists begin whaling against it. Snickering, we sit back against the wood, heels scrubbing against the muddled carpet—we really need to clean—as they screech on the other side.

"Eris, *please*," Theo begs.

"Glitch! Glitch, let us in!" yelps Nova.

"I've decided to blow apart the door."

"Arsen, do *not*," I snap.

"Hold this, June. Thank you." Something hard smacks against the door. Sona, undisturbed beside me, untucks my book from under her arm and picks up where she left off. "You better back away."

"You will smear us against this carpet," Sona calls.

A round of shrieks. Then Jenny's grating voice, mere feet away. "There you are, you *little shits*, I am seriously about to—"

"Scatter!" Juniper shouts. The rush of panicked feet on the steps, Jen's growl winding out, and then it's quiet.

Sona's lips are parted slightly as she reads. One thumb rests lightly on a crease at the bottom of the page, where I dog-eared the paper the last time I read it.

"*Why are you watching me?*" she asks, and heat rushes to my cheeks before I realize she's reading aloud again. "*Because I cannot seem to stop. Because there is only meant to be you and everything else, and yet it is this: you as everything. But I say none of this—*"

I put my hands behind my head and my head between my legs. "Our door might blow up and us with it. This is not the last thing I want to hear."

"Is it not?" She glances at me. "These pages are worn to threads, Eris."

"It's not like we have the Academy's sprawling selection."

There is not one closed bedroom door in this hallway; I see the corner of Nova's pink comforter, June's bird nest collection teetering on her dresser, chess pieces scattered on Xander's floor. The unstuck corner of a poster depicting forest fungi species bows above Theo's bed; Arsen has his walls smudged with charcoal drawings. A stack of paperbacks teeter on the edge of my dresser. There's nothing in Sona's room, Milo's old room, save for some clothes on the wall hooks—once mine, now hers—and a neatly made bed; she hasn't slept in there since Milo tried to kill her. The first time.

Gray light trickles in from the window at the far end of the hallway, paling the blue wallpaper. Sona's toes dip into the rays, mine in the shadows, curling beside her shin. June insisted on painting her nails yesterday; Glitch wanted them black, like mine.

"Are you nervous about the test run tomorrow?" I ask.

I'm very aware that she's stopped reading, eye still trained on the page.

After a moment, Sona says quietly, "Yes."

"Why?" I ask, and then immediately feel like an ass.

Her long fingers twitch against the paperback. She leans her head back against the wood, eye sliding closed.

"I feel . . . big, during it," she murmurs, so soft I almost don't catch it, even inches away. "So big that my head may scrape the blue from the sky."

"And it's terrifying?"

"And it is glorious, Eris. Please—" She stops, voice breaking. I realize why her words come at a murmur. She's ashamed. "Please don't think less of me."

When I look at her for long enough, like I'm doing now, I'll see a crack splitting the passive features. And through it, there's the flicker of an expression that makes me go cold. It's the sudden, desperate urge to pop back the panels, to dig and rip and destroy.

Briefly, I imagine how her skin would feel against my mouth if I kissed her wrist to elbow, the need vicious, because she seems so sad and I hate it, and I feel so much and I hate it. We're at war and people die and I *care*, and that's going to hurt.

I swallow hard. "I'm only going to think less of you if you don't give me back my book."

Her shoulders seem to relax a little. She never stopped wearing her Valkyrie jacket, but it feels more like a taunt than anything else, sleeves rolled up so you can see her gears clearly. She opens her eye, drops it back to the page. "Worth it."

She puts her head on my shoulder and tucks her legs up. Nearest to us on the wall is one of Nova's scribbles, a plain stick figure next to blocky letters that simply read, TALK SHIT GET HIT. Seeing that just revs up the ridiculousness of the situation. I should really not be feeling this good. I'm meant to be a soldier with a stone heart. I'm meant to lose people because that's just what happens. I barely told Milo I loved him, and after everything, that seemed like the right thing to do. I should move away from Sona before I forget that, before I forget the state of this world just because her skin is against mine.

"Are you going to be okay?" I say instead.

Sona shakes her head. "I do not know." She turns the page. "But I feel okay right now."

Oh, I see what's happening to me, I think to myself, her curls against my jaw. *Oh, okay. Oh shit.*

CHAPTER THIRTY-THREE

ERIS

Her hands now empty, Jenny leans away from Sona. Glitch has already reset the eye patch. One of the glass tables was cleared for her to lie on, its contents scattered haphazardly around the room in Jenny's excited haste. Or maybe it's not excitement at all, but just the combination of a steady flow of caffeine in her veins and the jitters of a tired body begging for sleep.

"Come on, come on, come on!" she says, voice leaping to a shout in erratic intervals as she hops over the miscellaneous items on her way to the exit, gesturing wildly over her shoulder for Sona to follow. She promptly rams flat against the glass door, her brow knitting in confusion for a few moments as she pats against it, then wraps quivering fingers around the handle and flings it open. We watch silently as she stumbles up the stairwell.

"She's off her rocker, Eris," Juniper murmurs.

"She's always been like that," I say, watching as Sona steps gingerly over Jenny's junk. Xander politely starts punting boxes away as she nears. "People just feel safer admitting it now, since they think the accuracy of her punches solely relies on her not wobbling whenever she stands up straight."

"How ya feeling, Glitch?" Nova asks in an upbeat tone. "Ready to fly?"

Sona gives only a strained smile before following Jenny up the stairs.

We enter the courtyard to find that Arsen and Theo have claimed a comfortable perch atop the Archangel's ankle. Jenny is below them, screaming shrilly to remove themselves from her mecha, her threats utterly ineffective as she is faced toward the Windup's chest rather than its feet, and every other vowel is slurred.

At one point she must actually say something coherent, because Arsen chatters back a sly retort that makes Jen's fraying focus suddenly snap taut. Her hand is around Arsen's ankle before he can yelp an apology, and then he's facedown in the dirt.

Nova shrieks with laughter as Juniper disappears from my side and materializes above Arsen, her growl slashing through the morning air. Jen easily sidesteps her left jab and loops her boot behind Juniper's ankle, shoving her shoulder forward to send Juniper tumbling to the ground. Jen plants her feet between my fallen crew members' knees and stares down, squinting.

"Which ones are you again?" she asks.

"Nova," June chirps.

"Theo Vanguard," Arsen says smoothly. "Pleasure."

Jenny abruptly straightens and turns. Nova's laughter and Xander's quaking shoulders still as she throws them a death glare.

"We're good, we're good!" Nova cries.

Jenny growls and steps over June's body, advancing. Nova yelps and grips on to my jacket as she nears, but Jen stops before she reaches me, extending a wavering finger past us and back toward the dorm's entrance.

"I'm not after you," she growls.

I turn to see that a group of people has slunk into the courtyard after us, and when I tilt my gaze upward, I find an array of faces pressed against each available window. I can't not recognize every single one: They're Gearbreakers who I've fought alongside countless times, lived with, bickered with, beaten the hells out of in arguments or practices and gotten a sizable collection of bruises and fractures in return. And most of them have begun to tentatively accept Sona, especially after the triple takedown at the Junkyard, the story of her unflinching face-off with a Berserker spread in whispers throughout the Hollows. They're only here as onlookers, to see if Godolia's destruction could actually be possible with the combination of Jen's ludicrous plan, a handful of sleep-deprived renegades, and a rogue Pilot.

But the Gearbreakers near the front serve as the targets for Jenny's glare. I recognize them in a different light: people who display their crippling cowardice with vivid threats on Sona's life.

Standing at the center of their mass is Milo. His rifle is slung back casually, barrel rising over his shoulders. His stance is relaxed, but the furrow to his brow is a hard giveaway.

"You wanna go, too, Vanguard?" she asks.

Milo crosses his arms, and in my peripheral vision, Sona straightens the slightest amount, bracing for whatever comes next.

"That Pilot is not getting wound, Jenny," Milo says gruffly. There is a dangerous weight to the air. Jen ignores it completely, hand on her hip, yawn stretching her jaw.

"This again," she says. "Boring. Come on, Glitch, let's get you set up."

"It will kill all of us, Jenny!" Milo shouts at her back, and the crowd rumbles behind him. "The Hollows will burn if the Bot's wound!"

"Good," Jenny calls back. "This whole place needs a Gods-damn face-lift, with you lot milling around."

A bang rips the air.

A thin line of blood splatters the ground. Warmth spots on my neck.

Jenny somehow catches Sona in her arms as she stumbles, just long enough for me to see Glitch dazedly put one hand up to her temple, which is sticky with red. Realizing she's alive, Jen promptly shoves her away and moves so quickly that I don't even register it until the splintering crack of a broken nose bridge splits the air. Then Milo's blood is glistening over the black material of her right hand.

"You little bitch," Jenny breathes, and the crowd surges forward. Sona, from the ground, faintly nods her chin in their direction, and with a growl, I turn and send ice screaming against the ground.

"Are you okay?" I rasp to Sona, veins of the cryo gloves blistering blue.

"He missed."

"That's not an answer."

"It hurts so very much, Eris."

I roll my eyes. Jenny is batting her way through the crowd, and they let her, because they're terrified of her, and they're right to be. She has Milo's shirt bundled in one fist.

"I think you owe someone here an apology," she breathes, dropping him on the frostbitten ground. His hands come away flecked with shards of ice.

"I'm not apologizing to that thing," he seethes, shoulders

heaving. I think there are more lines on his face than there were the last time I saw him. More twisted anger. Or was it always there? He always told me I was the angry one, that he liked that about me. I thought it meant we balanced each other out, that his calm was something I needed. But maybe he wasn't calm, just coiled up.

"What?" Jenny glances back at Sona. "Glitch is fine. You apologize to *me*. I'm the one about to kick your ass."

"Do it," Milo spits. "We're all about to die, anyway."

"On a cosmic scale, absolutely." Jenny looms over him, one foot planted lightly on his fingers. "But your little head can't wrap itself around that, can you? So let me make it easy for you—we're not on a cosmic scale, we're on *my* scale, my clock, my timeline. You get to die when I say you get to die. The only reason I'm not going to kill you right now is because you truly believe Glitch is about to rain missiles on this entire hellscape, and I'm hoping the fear will make you piss yourself."

"Eris," Milo breathes. "This is insanity, and you know it."

I help Sona up from the ground. "Eat shit, Milo."

"Anyone else?" Jenny asks the crowd, throwing her hands wide, provoking a startled shuffling of feet, even though she doesn't have her gloves on. "No? Then can you all lighten up and let me end this war? Gods . . ."

She turns and grasps Sona's chin, eyeing the bullet graze. I watch warily as the crowd thins, some heading back into the dorms, others making their way into the forest, presumably to get out of the way for when Glitch goes to kill them all in a few minutes. Scared or not, Jenny's word means a lot around here, or at least her threats do. Most would probably rather die quick and easy by the missiles than however Starbreach personally decides to end them.

"You were paying attention," Jenny murmurs. "Just a graze. Get some cobwebs from that tree root, Eris. Now eat them. Just kidding, Gods, is everyone going to be so stiff today? Give them here."

She puts the cobwebs over the graze, patting over them lightly with her fingertip. Sona glances at me out of the corner of her eye.

"You look pale," she says.

Numbly, I touch the blood spots on my neck and smear them onto her jacket sleeve. "Please shut up."

"Put the entrance near the neck," Jenny says as we ascend onto the Archangel, the absence of a fight allowing her words to slur again. She waves her fingers at the mecha's skin. "Rest of the innards look like shit. Functional yes, but . . ." She trails off for a moment, forgetting herself. We reach a circular hatch set at the base of the neck, provided by the dead Argus, and she gestures weakly again. "Yes . . . looks like shit. Didn't want anyone else to see it. In you go."

"You aren't coming?" I ask.

"You think you are?"

I cross my arms. "Of course."

She mirrors me. "Why? She can damn well handle the cords and whatnot by herself."

"I know she can. What's the problem with me tagging along?"

A line forms between her brows as she fumbles for her thoughts, which I'm guessing have been stripped to mere filaments by her continuous refusal to sleep. She nods slowly, then triumphantly, plucking one out.

"If it ends up exploding, then my precious cryo gloves will be disintegrated."

I roll my eyes, vaguely aware of Sona stifling a dark laugh. "Gods, Jen, if it explodes, then the entirety of the Hollows will be disintegrated as well."

She looks at me blankly.

"Meaning that your *precious* gloves will get destroyed either way, so I might as well go."

"Ah, I got it," she murmurs, seeming like she doesn't quite get it. "Well, then . . . have fun, Glitch and little bastard. And if the thing flies, would you kindly mind resting my mecha in the Junkyard after the run? I don't need any other Gearbreakers rubbing their grubby hands all over it and breaking it before Heavensday. Especially your ex."

Jenny teeters toward the shoulder, falls off, and lands hard on the wing. She takes a few more wobbling steps and disappears over that edge, too, and I stare for a minute until she appears in view again, stalking away on solid ground with a miraculously unbroken skull.

"Is she going to be all right?" Sona asks.

"Yeah. Sure. If she can see straight long enough to get out of the way," I murmur, watching her ponytail bob as she goes. "Ready, then?"

Sona looks into the void and nods. The drop is about seven feet, and she lands steadily and shifts to allow me room. I wrap my fingers over the rim of the drop and slip inside, transferring my grip to the handle of the hatch as I lower myself, my weight allowing it to close. I land silently and in darkness. Sona's hand brushes against my shoulder, and without another word, we walk into the Archangel's head.

Since the Windup is laid flat, the glass mat takes up the wall behind us, while the one we face will become the ceiling once the mecha is upright. The connector cords trickle down from their holdings, copper nubs snaking across the floor. Which is the back of the Windup's head. Sona turns in a slow circle, looking around the room, then stops to stare up through the Archangel's eyes.

"I believe I am a bit disoriented," she murmurs.

I find that funny. She's used to seeing Windups upright. I'm more accustomed to them being anything but. I tap my boot against the floor.

"Lie down here," I instruct.

She obeys silently. I kneel and gather the left and right cords into neat bunches and place them beside her. I give a slight nod, and she pulls back her sleeves. I think she tries to suffocate the way her fingers hesitate over her tattoos before I can notice, popping open the right forearm panel swiftly, but a lump in my throat still bursts to life.

One by one, Sona attaches the cords, a small jolt rippling through her at each new addition. Before she reaches for the last one, her hand travels up to gently tug away the eye patch, revealing a closed lid with a perfect red circle glowing beneath the skin. It shifts toward me, mirroring her other iris, and she places the patch in my hands.

"Hold on to this for me, all right?" she whispers.

I close my fingers around it and smile wryly. "Ready to fly, Glitch?"

"A kiss would help my motivation."

"What about the fact that Jen's going to break in here in about five seconds if we don't get a move on?"

A sour look that makes me laugh crosses her face, and she considers it enough payment for her fingers to drift toward the last socket, clicking the cord into place.

My smile fractures.

Both of Sona's eyes spring wide open, and despite myself, despite *her*, I feel my blood cool. She lifts one of her hands, twisting her fingers in the air; does the same with the other. The red light spilling in from the Windup's eyes fragments as the Archangels' talons appear above, coiling and uncoiling in flawless correspondence to her movements.

Keeping her head lolled back, Sona rises to her feet, one palm flipping open. I clasp it as she slowly brings her face level, causing the room around us to tilt and the ground to angle. I lead her toward the glass wall as it shifts to become the floor, murmuring for her to step when the angle becomes steep. The Archangel shudders as she obliges, and the glass floor brightens beneath our weight. The blue light cascades over her features, wringing shadows from her eyelashes. I release her hand and step off the mat. Her fingers drop to her side.

Sona extends her neck a bit and rolls her shoulders. A small line appears between her brows, and she slowly repeats the process. Then she brings her hand around, tracing lightly down the ridge of her left shoulder blade as far as she can reach, a sigh escaping her.

"This . . . ," she murmurs. "This is strange."

"The wings?"

"Wings . . . yes."

I swallow hard as she tucks her shoulders back once more, adopting a proud stance. The armored wing tips could easily take out one of the Hollows' buildings. So could a step. Or a thought. The destruction is too effortless.

"Are you okay?" I manage. The words sound forced, trembling with uncertainty.

"Oh yes, I am perfectly all right, Frostbringer." Sona sighs. "In fact, I am feeling quite like myself again."

I go completely still. I don't pull my gaze from the smile settled against her features. My blood is frozen, threatening to crack.

But then Sona laughs, a bright, glittering sound that fills the space and overpowers the hum of electricity running through the Archangel wrapped around us.

"You should see the look on your face, Eris," she gasps.

I struggle for breath. "You can't see my face!"

"But I can feel it singeing my cheek. Are you really that terrified of me?"

"Oh, absolutely."

I mean it to sound like a joke, though I'm sure it isn't, but Sona's voice drops to a sudden hush.

"I am a bit afraid of you as well right now. If that makes you feel any safer."

Do I feel safer? Do I dare? I put those tattoos across her skin, marking her as one of our own. One of us. They don't just disappear because the flesh is peeled back. Even beneath the clash of the red light pouring from the Archangel's eyes and the glow of the floor, the ink still thrives.

"I'm not scared of you," I say, lying my ass off.

"Could you be?" she asks.

The words take a moment to settle, but then they hit me like a bat to the chest. Does she know what I'm thinking, that of course I'm scared of her, but the fear of seeing her in this form pales in comparison to the fear of seeing her every single day—the jump in my ribs when she smiles, the hook in my stomach when she moves closer. *Could you be?* Is she scared of me, too?

Do I want her to be?

Yes. "Yes."

Her expression softens. Sona takes a single, graceful step, shifting into a fighting stance. Her long fingers drop to her sides, twitching as her shoulders roll back once more. I don't realize what she's doing until her knees are bent, and I fumble for a bracing grip.

It's no use. The force of the Archangel's jump sends me to all fours, and beneath my palms, the floor takes in a rush of heat as the jets spark to life, their roar silencing my startled inhale. I rise—shakily—to my feet only out of necessity, to grab a hold as the floor begins to slant. The rubber of my boots securely rooting me, I look to see Sona's chin tilted toward her toes.

"Are you afraid of heights?" she murmurs.

"Are you kidding me?"

"Yes. Go toward the windows."

I oblige, pressing my hands against the red-dyed glass and peeking over the edge.

"Eris?"

"Yes?"

"Are you all right? You've gone quiet."

I'm glad she can't see me swallow hard. "Just taking in the nice view."

I do not have a fear of heights, but below us, past the tech mirage of bare, snowcapped branches Jenny has strung up, there is a single speck that represents the entirety of my home. And I imagine falling. The vast potentials of falling that the Gearbreakers have always utilized mean nothing to an Archangel. If the mecha were to drop from the sky, the only possible outcome would be calamity.

I see the same realization cross Sona's face, watch her knuckles go white, and hear the Archangel's talons screech into their golden palms.

"How does it feel?" I try, but she shakes her head.

"What is the *point*, Eris?" she murmurs. "I destroy the Academy; I burn the Zeniths and their subordinates and their students. And what then? How long will it take for them to rebuild? How much time will they allow for recovery before they start creating new Windups? Before models like this fill the skies, and what of their wrath afterward? Silvertwin . . . you know about Silvertwin. You are aware of how Godolia handles noncompliance in their resource towns. Kill one and the rest will be kept in line. It is simple. Efficient. Effective. And at no loss to them. They have thousands left over that will continue to provide their coal and iron and briskberries and whatever else to avoid meeting the same fate."

Even though her voice has gone shrill with anger that I know is not directed at me, her words still prick. We're hovering thirty thousand feet above the ground in a mecha that my sister worked tirelessly to create, and she's suggesting that it was all for nothing. Insinuating that the Gearbreakers' entire way of life, *my* entire way of life, is pinned to a futile cause.

And worst of all is the insufferable, excruciating idea that maybe she's right.

"Just what else are we supposed to do, then, Glitch?" I shout. "If we don't fight, it means Godolia owns us."

Sona makes her head even, straightening the floor, and grits her teeth. "Godolia will go into a frenzy looking for the Gearbreakers after Heavensday, on a scale that none of you have ever seen, once we exchange the thorn for a blade."

"I thought you intended to put that blade there yourself," I growl.

"I want to. I *will*, but . . . the Windup Program may still rise again."

"So we strike again!"

"And how many of us will be left, Eris, after the hellsfire? After their fury has scorched everything within a thousand miles of the Hollows?"

"So that's it, then, you're done? Godolia scares you that much? I wish you would've said *something* before Jenny almost killed herself making this damn thing!"

"I am scared!" Sona cries, and then flinches. But she recovers quickly. "Not of losing my life, or fighting, or the plan. I will be the cause of *everything* that comes afterward, Eris! It is . . . I . . . I cannot lose—"

Suddenly she stops, snapping her head to the side. I have to press my hand to the glass to keep from being flung to the left.

"What the hells, Glitch?" I groan.

"Helicopter," she breathes, and my blood freezes again.

Outside, a small dot works its way across the skyline. Maybe five miles out, and far, far too close. Close enough to see the *winged Windup* hovering in midair.

I bite the inside of my cheek hard, forcing my stupor to break.

"Sona—"

"I know," she says, brows knitted. "Are you braced?"

But she doesn't wait for an answer. The forest peels away, the slate stone of the ruined outskirts replacing the scraggly tangle of bare branches, and soon that's faded, too. The dot marking the helicopter contorts into a collection of edges: twin tails and four whirring circles that are the rotor blades. It's a large one, probably carrying no less than twenty people in its hold.

Because of this, and not for the first time, I find myself thankful for Sona's ruthlessness.

Her hand closes around the helicopter's base, nearly gently, and she goes still. Her shoulders are set back rigidly, allowing us to hover as she pinches one of the rotors between her forefinger and thumb. It yields under the pressure instantly.

"What the hells are you doing?"

"Stealing a look," she says, then pauses. "Kidding. About the sentiment, anyway. Do you think we should see if the missiles work?"

The blackened windows of the helicopter keep the chaos ensuing inside hidden from view. I don't have to answer her. We both know this will be a quicker death.

I watch the talons unfold, and the helicopter takes off like a clipped bird, the broken rotor sending it swiveling from side to side as it flies.

"Now?" I ask.

"Give me a second," she murmurs, and I watch the outline of her shoulder blades jut from her jacket before retracting. "How strange . . ."

"Do you even know what you're doing?"

Sona shakes her head, her smile breaking coyly.

The blue of the sky splits cleanly with a line of black smoke.

I don't see the point where the missile makes contact, but it'd be impossible to miss the aftermath: a bulb of flame twisting to life, screeching with joy as it tears apart the metal and flings charred shrapnel into open air. The wreckage drops from the sky, flaming tail as black and sure as the stroke of a paintbrush.

"I hit it," Sona says, and the shock in her tone makes a laugh rip free from my throat.

"You think?" There is a hitch in my chest I can recognize

only as giddiness. Face pressed close to the glass, I watch the tendrils of smoke coil below.

A short time later, after the wreckage has finished smoldering, Sona locates a gap in the Junkyard trees wide enough to hold the Windup. Naked branches scrape against the mecha's skin as we descend, and a breath of relief curls in my chest once the jolt of solid ground shudders beneath my feet. I guide Sona to a lying position again, minding the tilt of the floor, and she begins to pluck away the cords. The Archangel goes still around us.

Sona blinks once, blankness scattering from her expression. Both eyes, along with her skin and deep chestnut hair, are ignited with the red light pouring from above. The hue somehow softens the glow of the Mod.

"Are you going to let me up?" she says, snapping the eye shut.

I sit back on my heels, and she sits upright, opening her palm. A moment passes before I fumble for the eye patch and hand it over.

The air feels strangely heavy when we emerge from the mecha's neck. Making our way to the sternum, we wait for the small but strong crowd of voices to emerge from what looks like empty, junk-cluttered woods—my crew, bickering profusely, trailed by Jenny, walking backward with her chin arcing from the ground to the sky above. She keeps leaning back until she spots us, then straightens and wanders toward the Archangel's feet, one hand tracing the air to her left as she tests her mirage tech.

The crew clambers up onto the Windup, where Arsen sniffs the air and goes, "What exploded?"

"Helicopter," Sona says.

"Rot," June breathes.

"Is that bad?" Theo squeaks, eyes wide. "Hey, that seems bad, very *bad*—"

"Sona took care of it."

They hear it in my voice, something electric, and they stop their fidgeting to look at me. I hug my arms around myself as a grin splits my face.

Xander, standing as still and rigid as the branches above us, says, "Is this going to work?"

I turn to Sona. Her eye lifts to me, and the thrill of it freezes me, and the look in it shatters me. *I cannot carry it well.*

I am not good.

"This is going to work," Sona says.

My smile slips from my mouth, and she watches it fall.

CHAPTER THIRTY-FOUR

SONA

Godolia scares you that much?

Her voice sounded from all directions, horizon to horizon. I opened my mouth to tell her, fumbled with the thoughts. Too weak to align them, and too afraid of the weakness that would spill from doing so.

Mere months ago, I would have given anything for the opportunity to destroy the Academy. Damn the collateral. Damn the innocents. This was about me, about *my* town, *my* family. They never received proper burials. They died entangled in the limbs of others, last breaths inhaling a tonic of chaos and fear and earth. The least I can do for them is ensure that the Academy meets the same fate, no matter the cost.

Eris knows this about me, but she does not know how things have shifted. That *she* has shifted something, the detrimental, foundational need for vengeance. She sits in the place where its spire once stood, where I carved out all the violent fantasies that allowed me to sleep at night, where I built and nurtured my hate and awaited the day that Godolia would realize that all of it towered miles above their grandest skyscraper.

I do not know how to tell her that, despite it all, I would tear the spire from the skyline if she asked me to. That I would suffocate my hatred, that I would sit quietly if she fancied plucking out every unnatural wire. That even if Jenny's plan works, if the backlash that follows harms her in any way, I would consider none of it to be worth it.

Because she is more than all of it. The sum of my pain, my past, my hatred. The riot with skin, happiest with a deity kneeling before her.

Could she be happy with me?

I am not good. I am trying my best.

But I am about to kill so many people.

For the first time, I do not sleep at her side, where she can turn over in her sleep and have her cheek to my spine, hand under my ribs. I have my own room because I am one of them. I still feel I should offer an explanation, but I do not; I just come home and close the door behind me and crawl under the sheets. I feel small in the dark, inside my own chest.

It starts slow at first, tears leaking onto my cheeks.

By the end of the hour, I am writhing. Hands pressed over my mouth, sobs shuddering against my fingers, entire body shaking so hard it feels like it is about to splinter apart.

Godolia scares you that much?

I am not scared of Godolia.

I am scared of me.

"*No*," I gasp, coiled tight, limbs twitching. "*Nonononono-nono . . .*"

I miss my old, simple fear. I miss Jole and Lucindo and Rose and Victoria. Their sincere, effortless delusions, the bareness of their complete ease. I miss my old skin. I miss my parents.

My nails claw at the mattress. My cries carve the walls, but I cannot stop, I can only grapple blindly for nothing, nothing to hold on to, I am spinning, I have lost my footing, this will never stop, this is the last thing I am going to feel, I will carry this with me and nothing else nothing else nothing else—

"Sona." The sheets are pulled back; I can see it in the light the hallway sheds in yellow rays. Arms around mine, pulling me up—*no please no I don't want to go up*—but not all the way, eased into her lap. She is leaning against the headboard, hands smoothing my hair, head bent over mine. "Shhh, hey, love, it's okay, I got you, I'm here, hey—"

"I'm sorry." I am sobbing, scraping at her knees. "I'm sorry I'm sorry I'm sorry—"

"What do you need?" Her voice holds at a rare hush, soft as velvet. "Tell me what you need, Sona, please. I can help, I'll make it better."

I need not to be a killer, or to be all right with being one.

"Go," I choke. A small flourish of panic ripples in my chest when I feel her shift, because I did not mean her. But Eris knows, and she is helping me off the bed. She gets my jacket and hugs it around my shoulders, leans over to guide my fingers into a pair of gloves, because it is cold outside. Her arm gentle around mine, we make the hall. She ducks her head into the common room, still tethered to me.

Xander is curled up under the table, delicate features relaxed comfortably beneath the blanket of his black lashes. Nova and Theo lie on their backs on the tabletop. Nova's out cold, one small white hand limp off the edge of the table, but Theo's sight rolls toward Eris at her approach.

"We're going out," she says gruffly.

His kind, pale eyes touch on me before he nods toward Nova, hand dipping down to grace Xander's dark curls.

"Want me to wake them?"

"What, do they need me to tuck them in?"

"I, for one, would appreciate it."

She rolls her eyes. "This place better still be standing when we come back."

We shuffle out into the Hollows' courtyard, the winter air stinging my swollen face, heat and salt a tangible weight against my cheeks. She helps me into the front seat of the crew's pickup and slides into the driver's seat. The roar of the engine sounds alien in the hush of the night.

A near hush, at least. On our way toward the gates, we pass Jenny and Voxter, their bickering the only element distinguishing them from the shadows. Eris slows the car to a stop, leaning out the window to wave. We must be ten feet away, but they do not notice our presence: Jenny seems to still be living in her own distorted sleep-deprived world and Voxter's anger fixates his attention solely on her.

"Where is it?" he growls.

Jenny flips her hand over as if inspecting her nails, although her gloves cloak them. "Hmm. I'm trying to remember . . . but I don't seem to recall . . ."

"You built it on my campus, and you can't—"

Jenny waves her hand in the air dismissively. "I *can't*? I can do whatever I want, old man."

Her tone is light, joking, but Voxter's is tight with irritation.

"Jenny Shindanai, I am your commanding officer, and if you don't tell me where the Archangel is right *now*, I'll—"

She cuts him off again, this time with a low laugh. "Mind your words, Vox. You know I'll be running this place someday. That means I'll be the one who decides if you have a bed in which to wither away."

Suddenly Voxter leaps forward, grabbing Jenny by her shoulders.

"Where is the Archangel?" he screams, and she is so jarred by his tone that her grin wavers.

"Hey!" Eris shouts. From their perspective, she sits casually, but inside the car, her hand is wrapped around the door handle, ready to spring out. "You been drinking again, Voxter?"

For the barest moment, a whisper of a look shifts onto his face. Then he shoves his lip into a deep scowl, expelling it, and releases Jenny. He points his cane at Eris.

"I wish," he huffs, turning on his heel to totter toward the tree line. "But there isn't enough liquor in the world to stomach the both of you."

Jenny watches him go, a bewildered glint in her eye as if she did not quite grasp what just happened. Still, her smile sparks again as she lifts her gaze to us.

"Where you kids off to?" she says.

Eris copies Jenny's earlier dismissive wave and puts her foot to the gas. "Get some sleep, Jen."

I stay quiet after we leave the Hollows' limits, and still when we pass the Junkyard's grove of trees, bare branches creeping toward the open, bright sky, our weapons in the truck bed rattling beneath the rush of the wind. Eris asks if I want music, and I say yes, and then start sobbing again. She turns the volume up and puts an arm around my shoulders, holding me close, black-painted fingers braced on the bottom of the wheel. There is no road, only the dust and the cosmos and us.

"Do you want to go anywhere?" Eris murmurs, and it is a few moments before I say, "No." She keeps driving. There is no difference between going in circles and a straight, steady line.

My tears soak her shirtfront as I shudder under the crook of her arm. I watch the knees of her cotton sweatpants crease and relax as she presses the gas and lets it coast, short, lithe legs feeding into black boots. The Badlands are so blank—pressed to dust by war after damned pointless war—that she can take her sight off the road and look down at me.

Her hand slides up, fingers hooking the strap of my eye patch and tugging it free. The material hangs heavy with tears, skin underneath rubbed raw. I keep the eye closed, let it bleed salt and fuse shut.

I look up, and Eris tucks her head to place the softest kiss on the shut lid, there and gone, light as moths' wings.

Both my eyes open wide, and then she is red, and the glow pours over those features, that glorious, devastating face. "*Stop the car now,*" I say, and she does, and I am out in the Badlands, sand biting into my knees, emptying my stomach into the desert.

I sit back against the tire. Eris sits beside me. A star-freckled sky spans over us, listening close.

"You don't have to do this," Eris says, but she is lying, and we both know it. Because this is war and people are dying in droves, and it isn't right, so it does not matter that I am too young for this, that I will hurt so much for this.

It does not matter if I can survive it. What matters is if I can see it through.

We cannot be children, because we have to win.

"Yes, I do."

She is silent for a while. I have the incomprehensible knowing that we are facing the direction of Silvertwin. I wonder if my parents' photographs are still on their nightstand, their clothes still in their closet, twined with the scent of earth.

"This whole world can rot," Eris whispers. "Let's just sit here and watch it happen."

The cold blurs my edges, my leg against hers the only part of me that feels real.

"Do not let me die during Heavensday, Eris," I whisper. "I'm scared to die."

"You are not going to die," she says, her tone fierce. Her eyes are turned to where the sky meets the ground. "You're going to be okay, and you're going to come home."

My shoulders shudder, but I am all out of tears. Her fingers find mine in the sand.

"It's okay to be scared," she whispers.

"You are never scared."

"I'm scared all the time."

"Of what?"

She shakes her head, but I can see her fighting to bring the words forward. It takes a few moments, and she holds a breath and lets it go. "Of everything."

The night sighs and stretches out. I feel as if I have not slept for years, and when I drift off, my head in her lap, it is a sweet blankness. Quiet.

And quick. I am being shaken awake. I start, inhale on instinct, and choke on sand. Eris is on her feet. She is pulling me to mine.

"Sona," she says, pleading. There are stars reflected in her panicked eyes. "Sona, get up, I smell smoke."

CHAPTER THIRTY-FIVE

SONA

We pass the first Phoenix at the entrance to the ruins. Its limbs splay limp as a rag doll's, feet tucked into the decimated foundation of a home, thermal cannon propped a story up atop a concrete wall. The head lies in the center of the road, just before the mouth of the forest, neck curled back into the dirt. The Pilot is folded halfway out of the right eye, stomach sunken into the glass.

Eris does not shut off the engine before scrambling out, heaving herself over the Windup's black iron welding helmet and onto the chest. I tear my sword from the truck bed and race after her as she breaks for the tree line. She ignores the voices that call out her name, ignores the tendrils of flames that split the winter-bare forest. Her gloves are primed.

I can see nothing, and it feels as if it should be silent in the blank, heated gray. But everywhere there is screaming. Footsteps shake the ground and throw me off her path. From within the smoke someone lets out a screech that could cleave soul from bone, and another tremor sends me to all fours. The frost is gone, turned to mud that slicks my knees and palms, splatters up my jaw. And the steam shifts. *How many—*

Another Phoenix's boot falls inches before my finger-tips, and immediately, a puckering sensation ripples up my bare neck: my skin blistering at the heat sloughing from the metal. I recoil, hand to my collar, smearing earth there, and a hand curls around my forearm and yanks me to my feet. With a strangled growl, Eris presses her glove against the Phoenix and slams her boot to the metal. The mecha shudders, and every hair on my body stands to attention as the steam moves again, and then there are fingers, a massive hand descending from the heavens. Eris screams at me incomprehensibly and pulls us both into the jagged opening just before the Phoenix's fist hits the earth.

There is no time for a meticulous, clever hunt. We set a direct course for the Pilot. At times, Eris catches movement and disappears above me, a shrill scream following before she materializes back onto the ladder, snarl twisted tighter and tighter at each return. It takes shy of three seconds when we get to the head. One swipe of my sword severs the connecting cords, the next unstitches the flesh of his neck. We slide back to the legs and spill out onto scorched ground once again.

I lift my head to find the Phoenix has brought us to the Hollows' courtyard—what is left of it. The maple trees have been reduced to glistening, flickering steeples, flaming debris raining down on the concrete paths. Soot covers every surface; when Gearbreakers sprint by shouting, I can see black coating their molars.

Above us, the Phoenixes move as bloated silhouettes behind the veil of smoke, fingers or cannons or flashes of red gazes spitting flame. They have burned away the heavens themselves. They have dropped us like pebbles into the twin hells.

"Gwen!" Eris shouts, starting for two people sprinting for the tree line. They slow their steps, turning to reveal faces smeared in ash and sweat. "Seung! What the hells—what—"

Gwen is leaning hard against Seung, one of his arms looped under hers. Her leg is twisted at an unnatural angle.

"Oh shit, you're alive," Gwen gasps, reaching out a palm to cup Eris's chin. Her palms are singed, angry red flesh. Crying as she speaks, as she prays, "Thank deities. Oh, thank Gods—"

"We weren't here." Eris is gulping in air, voice scraped hoarse. "What happened, how did they find us—"

"All directions," Seung rasps. "We saw them first in the south, got those alarms going first, but the north, the dorms . . . I think we've taken out at least a dozen of them, but—"

"Jenny," Eris pleads, hands shaking at her sides. "Seung, where's Jenny?"

"Alive, last I saw her."

Eris shudders and doubles over. "Oh Gods," she says, over and over again, as our home disintegrates around us. She curls into me. "Oh Gods, oh Gods, oh Gods, Glitch, what do we do what do we do?"

"We need to move," I say, one hand on her shoulder, shaking her. The other squeezes hers tight. "Eris, we need to move!"

Her eyes lift and then stop, hanging on a point behind me with such rigid, palpable terror it spills into me. I turn, following her line of sight, and all noise siphons off into a single, shrieking note.

Across the courtyard, in front of what used to be the dormitory complex, two figures crouch low against the powdered earth. Their familiarity is not what makes my blood run cold; their presence screams the absence of the three other Gearbreakers who should be with them.

Eris's hand slips from mine, and we run. Theo's head is bent to the crook of Nova's neck, his tears glossing her collarbone, hers trickling over her chin and into his hair. Her fingers, intertwined behind his back, shake against his every stuttered breath.

"Where are they?" Eris screams, folding over them. Nova's head snaps up, dazed and bewildered, the two bleary green eyes piercing the black of the soot on her face. "*Where are they?*"

"Arsen and June went back for Xander," Nova sobs. Theo shudders again, and she tightens her grip. "We came down the stairs together, Eris, I *swear*. But we got outside and he was just gone!"

Eris turns on her heel, and I see the thought spark. She takes one step and I tackle her, both of us meeting scorched earth.

"Let go of me!" she screeches, rabid.

I press closer, keeping her pinned. Her fist meets my cheekbone with a shocking, distinct *pop*. I ignore her, gaze up to the fire-swollen complex, its heat scraping my skin even dozens of feet away. I let her punch me two, three, four more times, knee sinking to my stomach. It is only when she reaches for my eye patch that I look down, and as if I flipped a switch, Eris dissolves. She presses her palms to her eyes, mouth splitting in a croaking, inhuman wail. It is dematerializing. Tears well between the crevices of her fingers.

"June! Arsen!" Nova shouts, and at the shock of their names I lose my focus. Eris punts me to the side. She scrambles onto her feet, vaulting for the doors, skipping over my attempt to grab her heel.

Two figures emerge from the inferno: one with tightly wound curls and lips pressed together in a wire-taut line, and a girl with hazel skin and flagrant green hair whose lips are doing anything but, releasing round after round of blood-curdling shrieks. Arsen is holding tight around Juniper's middle, walking backward as she kicks and grabs at the open air in an attempt to return to the flames. Her elbow revs back into the bridge of Arsen's nose. He flinches violently and throws a wild, panicked glance over his shoulder.

"Help me!" he begs as Eris reaches him.

She catches Juniper's wrist in her next flail, and Juniper whirls around to reveal that the bangs framing her face have been singed away, leaving the strands looking sickly, pasted against salt-laced cheeks. Her shock lasts less than a second before her head whips back toward the doors.

"Xander!" Juniper screams, thrashing against Eris and Arsen. "Let me get him! Fucking let go of me! I will break your fucking nose, Arsen, I swear to all the rotted Gods, I will kill you! Let me *go*! *Xander! Xander!*"

Arsen's arms strain as he constricts around her, but if she is losing breath, it does not show in her cries.

"Please, June," he murmurs, again and again. "It's done, please—"

"No, no, *no*!"

"He's dead, June!" Arsen shouts, pressing his head to her hair. He falls to his knees. Juniper goes limp, eyes blank. "He's dead," Arsen sobs. "We were too late."

Nova presses a hand over her mouth. Theo lifts his head and blinks slowly at her. "Are you okay?" he asks, gaze water-logged and distant, so far away from all of this.

Nova simply doubles over into his lap. He traces the line between her shoulder blades absentmindedly, looking around. The kids are in their pajamas, barefoot, the pads of their feet painted black.

"Milo," Theo says, smiling. "You're alive."

I turn to find his hulking figure standing behind me. This time, there is no initial aggressive spark when he looks down and meets my eye, and it is not just because the smoke has blurred everything. I drop my head and step to the side, allowing him to pass, and he places an arm around his brother's shoulders.

"We need to go," Milo says, looking to Eris. "Eris, we need to go *now*."

She does not hear him. She stands straight and so incredibly, impossibly still while our home burns before her. All the pictures on the walls. All her books. The music tapes in the common room, the table where we danced, and the rug where we all slept on the colder nights, piled up like newborn kittens. Her littlest kid, blotted with ink. All fed to the flames.

Tears smearing my vision—I did have some left in me, after all—I reach for her. I have to peel the words from my tongue because I do not want to go, either. I do not want to leave the home I never thought I'd have to the inferno. "Eris, we have to—"

She wheels, and where I expected to find shock there is rage, and I know that beneath its veil she does not see me. She sees only the patch, the jacket, hears only the hum. In that moment, she sees Pilot Two-One-Zero-One-Nine.

I know it even before she raises her gloves.

I dive, the barest moment before the bolt bursts forth, streaking past my ear and angling into the branches flaming above us. It only takes a second to get back on my feet, and when I look, her expression has shifted.

"Sona," Eris gasps, guilt festering in the single word. "Wait, I didn't—"

She reaches for me, and I stumble back. I paste on a grin, the false one that I thought I left back at the Academy.

"It's all right," I say, backing away. I nod toward Milo. "Take care of your crew. I—I will help somewhere else."

"Wait, Glitch!" she tries, but I have already broken into a sprint.

How can I go so fast—the forest blurring, spines of trees chipped like teeth—when it feels like I have stones strung around my throat and bound to my feet?

Is it simply because I want to tear something apart? Is it easier to live in a world like this when you live with anger?

But everything around me is already broken, broiled down to cinders. I find a dead Phoenix, pick my way through the entrails, hoping to stumble across a guard with a bit of life still in their lungs. I come across only blank stares and slack bodies. Even the Pilot, tangled up in her array of colorful wires, does not flinch when I put my boot to her stomach. Pitiful and dull and infuriating.

I reach up and tug away my eye patch, letting it float down to the dead Pilot. When I make my way outside again, I find that the world has not much changed. Calamity only wears one color.

I bend over and spit the soot off my tongue. When I straighten, someone is wandering toward me. He has a large grappling gun strapped to his back that glints viciously among the glowing flames.

"You're still here," Voxter grunts, watching me wipe darkened spittle from my lip. In his hand, he grips the hook of his cane, but rather than sprouting its usual wooden spike, a blade is attached to its base.

"Looks like it." I breathe in, just to scrape my throat with the smoke. "They were looking for the Archangel."

"And they will keep looking," he spits. "Damn Shindanais. Mechas on my campus. *Pilots* wandering around free. This place has been burning for weeks."

He raises his blade, sends it down toward my neck. I twist easily out of his way—this, *this* I can do—and pull my sword from my side. Mud sucks against my boots as we trace a circle around each other.

"I do not want to fight."

"We're not fighting," Voxter says, cheerless grin on his face, strained, like his features do not know how to support it. "You died by your kin, crushed flat, burned alive—no, maybe you turned tail and ran back home."

"My *home* just burned to the ground."

"The Academy is still standing strong."

I lunge, and it is so simple to knock away his parry, to send him into the mud. I crush his wrist with my boot. "I am so much better than you at this," I murmur, tip of my sword over his neck, slick with the Phoenix Pilot's blood. "You may be a renegade, but I am a killer. You should count yourself lucky."

I move my hand; he flinches, and I nick a small tear in the collar of his canvas jacket. Mud sighs underfoot as I step off him. There is still soot on my tongue, between my teeth. I feel infected, veins winding slow, heavy with pollution. I could cry, but I have no more tears; I could mourn, but I do not know where to start.

"You will never be one of us!" Voxter roars after me, spine

stuck to the ground. His limbs churn the earth for purchase. "You will never be human!"

"We are at war, Voxter." I do not look back. The world is crumbling around us. "We do not need humanity. We need to win."

CHAPTER THIRTY-SIX

ERIS

"Eris?"

I don't know who's talking. It seems like a lot, figuring out whose voice is whose, and honestly, they feel too far away for it to matter much.

"Eris, you need to eat."

"Where is she?"

"Under the bed, Novs."

"Oh."

"Should we get Jenny?"

"Jenny's busy."

"What about—"

"Don't."

"Gods, Milo, can you just—"

"She doesn't want the Bot."

"Stop it."

"June, you saw what she—"

"I said *stop it*! You can fuck off! Who asked you to come back, anyway? Get *off* me, Arsen! You all can rot! You can sit in your hate and wither for it!"

"Juniper, wait—"

Footfalls. A door slamming shut against its threshold. The cobwebs flutter against the baseboard.

"Don't follow them, Milo."

"Someone needs to be crew captain around here."

Theo's laugh now, and it's dark. "Is that what you're trying to do?"

"Don't waste your breath. You have plenty of other villains to choose from. Can one of you get her to eat?"

The door closes lighter this time. Someone crawls onto the bed, wood frame sighing into my shoulder.

"Well. You wanna make out?"

"Get off the bed, Novs."

"She's not using it."

"We need to get Glitch."

"Ha! We don't need to do *anything*, Theo boy! We're already *so freaking screwed* that nothing we do even matters anymore!"

She starts crying. My hand folds over my mouth, and I curl into myself.

"Come on."

Her weight eases off the bed. I hear them pause before the door.

"Eris," Theo says, voice thick. "I love you, and Xander's not your fault. None of it is. But you need to get your shit together because we need you out here."

Get up.

They need you.

Get the hells on your feet.

There is an inch of the windowsill that slips under the bed, light reaching for me in a thin, gray box.

You need to move.

I need to move.

I watch the snow try to get in.

When it gets dark, someone comes into the room and sets a thermos down next to the bedpost. I haven't eaten in days because the act of swallowing is ridiculous. Fill your stomach sack so you won't die, Eris. Like I couldn't still burn to death after a full meal.

I say, "Not hungry," and Sona says, "Too bad."

I start, smacking my forehead on the underside of the bed frame, but she's already gone when I've rolled onto my other side.

Because I am miserable and so viciously in love with her, I eat the soup. I have the urge to stand and go show her the empty thermos. But this would require *standing* and *going*, and I have nothing better to say than *I finished my dinner and I'm sorry I tried to kill you*, so I stay put. This time I watch the door. Maybe she'll come back. Maybe I'll know what to say by then.

She doesn't come back.

Before dawn, I take a coat and a blanket and crawl over the bed to the window. Snow brushes the mattress as I open the window and slip onto the Winterward streets. The town is the Gearbreakers' long ally, our safe houses peppered along the rim of the lake. It's dead quiet, electric lanterns coated with snow so the streets are lit poorly.

I trace my way to the end of town, find a good, deep snowbank in the tree line, and lie down on my side. Already I can't feel the tip of my nose, my toes, my fingers. My hair goes stiff and frozen around my ears, lashes heavy with frost, but I close my eyes anyway. Distantly, I am aware I don't have long before I freeze to death, but I'm reaching for numbness, for sleep, and I'm too tired to think about the side effects.

It's not a lot to ask, and yet, a few minutes later, someone rams their foot into my thigh.

"You son of a—" I roar, leaping to my feet and sending the snow flurries billowing. Maybe a fight is just what I need—who needs a slow freeze when someone else can just knock me out cold, quick and easy—but once my vision clears, I stop short. Jenny cocks her head, white-speckled ponytail rippling.

"Don't insult Mom like that," she says, then offers the thermos in her hands. "Hot chocolate? They've got loads of it here. Very on-brand. Haven't seen any cows, though."

"Not thirsty."

"Suit yourself."

She takes a sip, leaning back against a briskwood tree. Her boots go over her knees, just high enough to best the snow.

"Ironic, isn't it?" she murmurs. "We go from broiling hot to a blizzard."

I don't say anything. Jenny looks down her nose at me, but where I expect amusement I find something . . . very un-Jenny-like.

"I'm sorry about the twig," she says softly. "Xander. He didn't deserve it."

I let my shoulders relax. "Neither did Luca."

"Or any of them," Jenny adds. "So what are we going to do about it, dear sister?"

"You have a plan."

"We already had one. The same one. Godolia got word of the Archangel, sent the Phoenixes to destroy it. So they believe it to be destroyed, yes? If we didn't have the element of surprise before, we certainly do now."

"Got word?" I repeat, my voice low.

She takes another sip of hot chocolate before turning away, starting the trek back toward the village. She gestures for me to follow.

"I think we have a mole in our midst, Eris," Jen says casually, and I nearly lose my footing.

"I thought it was because of the helicopter," I gasp. "That that's how they found us—"

"Perhaps. But I'm not risking it. Heavensday is in forty-eight hours. Tell only the ones you trust about the plan's commencement."

"I trust all the Gearbreakers."

Jenny throws me a sideways glance. "Haven't I always told you to be on the lookout for the next punch? And, Eris, everyone—*everyone*—here hits hard."

"I know. You also taught me to get back on my feet."

"And hit harder."

"And faster."

"And over and over and over again," she sings.

She pauses her march to put a hand on her hip, staring through the quiet streets curling before us. The snow nullifies everything, although it wouldn't be much louder if the ground were bare. We lost half of the Gearbreakers, half of ourselves. There isn't one crew that didn't suffer casualties, not one soul unsplintered by grief. Including Jen. Her eyes are rimmed red, pretty features puffy, lips split and dry. On her neck, the edge of a bandage peeks out from under her scarf. Morbidly I wonder if her tattoos are intact, if ink burns just the same as everything else.

"We leave before dawn day of. Go tell Glitch."

The hesitation before my nod is slight, but she still catches it.

"What?" she snaps. "What's the matter?"

"I . . . I think I messed up with Sona. I thought she . . . I raised my gloves and—"

"Holy shit, did you kill my Pilot?"

"Gods, Jen!"

"I swear, if you ruined our—"

"I didn't kill her! It's just . . . her and me . . ."

Jen gives me a long look. "So you fix it. Apologize."

I shake my head. "I feel like all I do is apologize to her."

"So make it stick this time," Jen says in a bored tone. "Honestly, as long as it doesn't affect her flight, I couldn't care less about your little lovers' quarrel."

"It's not—"

"Not what, Eris?" she interrupts coolly. "Not important? Not infuriating? Not painful? Tell me, is Miss Sona Steelcrest not important or infuriating or painful to you?"

I scowl as heat floods my cheeks, stupid warmth that dispels the numbness and lets in everything. "I was going to say it's not like that."

Jen grins. "Fine. Then you can kill her, but not till *after* she gets the job done. Bitch threw me in a river, anyway."

"I'm not going to kill her."

Something dark drops in her expression. Jen leans over me, fingertip drilling into my sternum.

"No? Then fix it," she growls. "Fix it because you need to, and because you need *her*."

"I—"

"Are you listening to me? Get. Yourself. Together. You

figure out who you need because they're the ones you're coming home to. They're the reason we still *have* a home." Her finger tucks under my chin. She looks exhausted, like she hasn't slept since I last saw her, crow's feet like claw marks under her dark gaze. "I know it's a lot. I know we've lost a lot."

Her eyes burn into mine. I realize that she isn't tired at all. She's furious.

"Are you listening to me, Eris Shindanai? We haven't lost, and we haven't lost everything, so we can keep going."

CHAPTER THIRTY-SEVEN

ERIS

Wrecked. That's the word that comes to mind after I finish talking over the Heavensday plan.

We're gathered in the attic of the safe house, soaking in air that smells like dust, puffy yellow sheets of insulation peeling from the ceiling above the mismatched furniture. I'm perched on a rolled-up rug, Sona at its opposite end. Her eyes are lifted, but not to me, same as the rest of the kids. I don't take it personally. Everyone finds it easier to look to the ceiling or floor, a slight hunch to their shoulders that doesn't suit any of them.

It makes me ache.

Arsen has salt lines on his cheeks he hasn't bothered to scrub away. Nova's fingernails are long bitten to the quick, and now she gnaws at the skin around them, fresh blood in her cuticles. Juniper and Theo would look better if it weren't so clear they hadn't slept in days, hadn't even thought to try.

And Sona. Sona just looks hollow. I've never, ever believed I could knock her over before. For some reason, that's the thought that rises—that I could push her over and it would be easy because she would let me, wouldn't even look at me.

Wrecked. The kids are so absolutely wrecked, and it's such a tangible measurement of exactly how much the world has fucked us over that it's *laughable*; and I would be laughing, if I weren't so completely aware I would immediately start crying instead.

"I am at a low," I hear myself say quietly, "just like the rest of you. It's dark down here and awful and we're going to be here for a while. No one is allowed to get used to it. I needed . . . I needed some time, but I'm up, okay? I'm on my feet, I'm here, and we have a next step. We'll figure out the rest as we go along, like we always do. We're not losing anyone else because I say so. How's that for a pep talk, Novs?"

Her chin lifts from the furrows of her sweater. "Middling."

I turn my head, watching Sona's profile. "It's your decision, Glitch."

Her eyes trace the floor. Her eye patch was lost in the chaos, and I haven't seen her attempt to hide the Mod some other way. The only time she closes it for longer than a blink is when she's sleeping, and even then it trails its red light across the curve of her cheek.

"They know where we are," Sona says, sureness embedded in her tone.

"They don't. They can't. We're still alive. Aren't we?" Arsen asks, picking off puffs from the insulation.

"Let them come," Nova says. "We'll destroy anything they send us, just like we did to their Phoenixes."

Now Sona picks up her head. She doesn't look as empty as I thought; it's worse than that—she looks so sad that my heart doesn't so much break as it twists and ruptures, and I press my palms to my eyes as heat breaks at their corners.

"And lose how many more Gearbreakers?" Sona says, voice warbled and rising. "Look at each other. If I *fail* . . . Who is going to be left, if I fail, if they find us again? Who else is going to be gone because of the retaliation I bring, just—*Gods*—who the fuck am I going to come home to?"

"It won't be an issue if you do your job right," Juniper murmurs.

"But if I—"

"If you fail, then don't come home."

I tense, hands slipping from my face, the venom off Juniper's tongue hanging in the air.

"*June,*" Theo snaps.

"Because you know what we're here to do?" Juniper's on her feet now, her hands on Sona's shoulders, ripping her two-toned gaze from the floor. "You know what we're here to do, Glitch? We are here to *die.*" Her dark eyes are ignited, angry tears serrating her cheeks. The gears on her hand stretch as she tightens her grip, her own shoulders trembling. "We are here to get killed, and then get up the next morning and do it all over again, so have some Godsdamn perspective. Come home, don't come home. Burn the city to the ground or kill us all. If you do this, fail or not, you're doing right by us, because you're giving us a chance. It's not for Xander. It's not for the dead. It's for *us,* Glitch. You do it for us and anyone else still suffocating under Godolia's thumb. Because if you give people that hope, we'll end up with more Gearbreakers than we'll know what to do with."

She waits for Sona to nod, and once she does, June releases her with a dry, cheerless laugh.

"Come on," Juniper says, and drags Arsen to his feet by his shirtsleeve. "Let's give them the room."

"But—" Nova protests, and June uses her other hand to pluck up the back of her sweater, Arsen still fastened in her other grip. Nova's tiny legs kick helplessly as she's lifted clean from the floor. "What—"

Theo rises and follows the procession down the attic stairs, the door at the bottom sighing shut.

Now Sona meets my eyes, and she meets them steadily, but her shoulders are braced. Like she's expecting me to flinch. Like she's making herself stone now so she doesn't crack when I recoil.

I move closer, and softly Sona says, "Eris."

It's a warning. It's clear in the way she holds my name, but still in the way I like that she does—with care, because she knows I'm something dangerous; she knows I'm something fragile, and she doesn't fault me for it. She can still see I'm made of sharp, sharp pieces.

There are marks against her neck where I tore at her. I tried to run into fire, and she stopped me, and I punished her for it.

Silently, I lower my brow to her shoulder. Am I praying? I haven't ever tried to speak to the Gods before—besides to scream at them, to damn them—and I don't know if praying is supposed to feel calm, but this doesn't, not when the only thought running through my head is *Please don't move away*.

She doesn't move away.

"How do I fix this?" I murmur, words traced into her shoulder.

"You don't. You do better."

"I almost killed you." There is a lump in my throat that hurts to dig around. "Gods, Glitch, what if I—"

"You are terrible at killing me. You will probably fail the next time, too."

"Stop it."

"I could stand very still and give you an easy shot—"

"*Stop it.*" I lean back, grasp her face in my hands and suspend them there, her expression knocking all words from my tongue—she's not laughing, she's miserable, and I'm the cause, or at least the catalyst. My fingertips shake against her jaw. "I'm sorry," I say, and it's not enough. "I'm so sorry, Sona."

Her hands find my wrists.

"I could hate you," she whispers, her words a live wire. "I could hate you, but it would kill me, and that is not how I am dying for you."

"I don't want you to die for me," I say fiercely. "Are you listening to me? *I don't want that.*"

"But you would do it for me. For everyone else. You do not get to be alone with that, Eris; you do not get to save people without them doing the same for you." Her gaze burns into mine; I try to look away, and her hands close against my jaw, forcing me still under the soft weight of her fingertips, and then she whispers, with a quiet, jagged kind of ache, "You do not get to love someone and think they won't feel it."

I'm crying. Of course I'm crying. I have a stone heart, but it shatters when it beats too fast, and I love to fight, but I hate these battles. It's not one war, but I have only one existence to give them, and they've molded it viciously. It's not who I want to be. I want to be soft, and I don't want to take shit from anyone. I want to be able to love someone I'm not afraid of, and I am so afraid all the time, because I love those kids *so damn much* it scares me, because it's so simple for them to be *gone*. I want quiet but not all the time, and I want good, teeth-rattling fights and a family that's alive and to stretch out on the rug with my books and to leave home knowing I'll be back soon.

"I—" I start, and stumble. I shake my head. "I'll outrun it, eventually."

She smiles a little, corners of her mouth tucking beneath my palms. "Outrun what, Eris?"

"All of it. Everything this world has done to us, to ruin us." This isn't a prayer. It's a declaration of war. "It's rotting me, but I'm not going to let it win."

CHAPTER THIRTY-EIGHT

SONA

We are not going to make it, I think to myself as the truck jolts again, nearly sending us all tipping into the desert. Jenny, frustration bubbling over, has attempted to grab the wheel again. Nova's thrumming music and their ceaseless bickering from the front seat complement each other perfectly, either sending the crew into a fit of laughter or a stunned silence at the severity of the threats.

"You're going the wrong way!" Jenny screeches.

"I am following the freaking *stars*, Jen! Are you literally going to tell me that the *sky* is conspiring to give us the wrong directions?" Nova spits back.

"I'm not blaming the sky, dumbass, I'm blaming *you*. You're too busy listening to your shitty music to figure out what direction you're going. I'm telling you, I should drive! At least I'd go faster than the pace of a brisk walk. And—and . . . hello? Earth to the ice princess?"

Nova has gone quiet, but her eyes are wild and grossly diverted from the path ahead. Then she jerks the wheel to the left, sending Jenny's head slamming into the curve of the car's roof.

"Don't insult my music taste," Nova says smoothly, tone glossy and sweet as Jenny curses violently.

Daybreak creeps over the horizon about an hour before the Junkyard peeks into view, and that is also the point where the smell of singed wood infiltrates the air, and another, unspeakable stench of burnt meat when any of us are careless enough to try to differentiate. Juniper pulls her shirt collar over her nose and buries her face into Arsen's shoulder. Nova, never one for quiet, chooses her most outrageous song and spins the volume knob until it threatens to pop away in her frantic fingers.

The Junkyard replaces the stench with the tang of rusted metal and the cold, fresh shock of snow. Nova maneuvers the car methodically through the maze of wreckage and tree trunks. We reach the Archangel's armored wing tip first, foliage over our heads one moment and metal the next as we pass through Jenny's mirage tech.

Once the engine is shut off, Jenny takes the lead, effortlessly leaping onto the wing and over its shoulder curve, despite the wicker basket pressed between her gloved hands.

We have breakfast atop the mecha's chest, the frigidness of the air kept at bay with a few thermoses of hot chocolate and thickly sliced milk bread slathered in a seed-speckled jam. I find myself enjoying the return of murmured conversations soon escalated to quick teasing, the comfort of a full stomach.

Eventually the bread has all been reduced to crumbs and the sun reaches a certain point in the sky. Jenny stands from her cross-legged position, brushing her palms against her jeans before shielding her eyes, chin tilting up.

"I was hoping for more coverage," she murmurs.

Eris shakes her head. "Doesn't matter. We'll be flying too high for anyone to see us. Well out of the wall cannons' range, too."

Jenny's eyes slowly drop to her sister. "So you're going with her, then," she says flatly.

Eris only gives a bare nod before leisurely licking the jam from her fingers. But when she stands and pulls her gloves from her pockets, it marks the end of the peace.

The crew rises along with her. An awkward silence ensues as everyone grasps for something to say—what could be said that has not already been said? I watch them grapple for any words that could add another layer of armor, another missile to the chamber, another particle of dumb luck.

I do not want any of that. I just want to hear their voices once more, reinforce the reminder that for once, after a fight, I have something worth returning to.

Nova swallows hard. "This is the boss battle, isn't it?"

Jenny snorts. "Let's hope not. A battle is not a part of the plan. Just a quick massacre, in and out. And they'll be back here before sunset. Mind stopping the solemn sentiments and getting the hells off my Windup?"

The crew obliges, but not before each giving Eris a lingering embrace, which she fails to pretend to accept begrudgingly. Jenny meets my eye over her shoulder and juts her chin, beckoning for me to follow. As I trail past, Juniper catches my hand and pulls me into a hug.

"You'll be fantastic," she says breathlessly, and the rest of them collapse on me, arms around my sides, kisses peppered on my cheeks until heat fills the skin.

"Wish I could see it," Arsen says. "But I'm sure we'll feel the tremors all the way back in Winterward."

Theo beams, freckles scrunching. "Give them hells, Sona."

"You're going to have more gears than all of us combined after this," Nova muses, rolling her shoulder blades back, where her own tattoos branch like wings beneath her coat. She cocks her head to the side. "As if you weren't already more mecha than the rest of us."

"Novs!" Theo hisses.

Nova snaps her hand out to yank one of my curls, laughing brightly. "Ah, come on. Glitch knows I'm joking."

"I will send the Zeniths your regards," I say, my smile effortless, muscle memory at last. Like it should be.

June gives me a last squeeze before leaning away. "We'll see you at home real soon, okay?"

I blink.

My Gods—holy *hells*—I actually have a home to come back to.

Complying with Jenny's impatient gesturing, I leave them to fawn over Eris for a bit longer, though her twitching expression is rather entertaining.

"Remember," Jenny grunts, leaning down and prying open the entrance hatch. "I put the magma serum missile last in the chamber. Should burn its way to the deepest level of the Academy, but you gotta give the foundation a fair divot for it to set right. We're not pulling our punches today. You use *everything*. Got that?"

"I understand."

"And Sona," Jenny says, her tone soft. She stands, and her hand clamps down on my shoulder, constricting harshly. "I want you to know that I do not care about you. At all. Live or die, just get the job done."

"Noted, Unnie."

"Shut that down immediately. As for Eris, I won't ask you to take care of her. She doesn't need anyone's protection. Just stay out of her way. But despite that—and believe me, I know this is terribly and hilariously ironic—if anything happens to her, I'm blaming you. And I know you can't feel pain or anything, but I'm sure I'll figure something out."

Eris's footsteps announce her approach, and Jen snaps her arm away. Her expression is still enraged, but for just an instant, I see a spark of doubt.

"Get going," Jenny barks once Eris is in earshot.

Eris rolls her eyes. "No 'good luck, hope you don't die'?"

"If you need luck, we're already screwed ten times over," Jenny says dismissively, turning away. But she pauses a moment. "You should know by now that you do not have my permission to die. Neither of you."

Then she is gone, vanished into the tree line along with the crew. For once, those words do not leave me feeling cold.

Eris huffs in exasperation. "This is just another Sunday morning to her, isn't it? What did she say to you?"

"Some threats."

"The full Starbreach treatment."

"Do I get anything from the Frostbringer, too?"

Eris grasps the door of the entrance hatch. "After you."

I drop my feet into the opening of the mecha. "And they say chivalry is dead."

"I'm not being polite." She drops in after me, jumping to close the hatch and seal us in darkness. "I'm trying to leave before Jenny comes back and insists on piloting this thing herself."

We glance at each other. Her color has drained a bit. I start laughing first, and she falls into it as we trace our way up the neck.

CHAPTER THIRTY-NINE

SONA

Heavensday

As much as I want to detest the thought, I cannot loathe flying.

I know, I *know* this is simply another conceited attempt of the Academy to replicate deities. This form, like all the others, is false, charged with narcissism. But for now, I have wings, and my fingers scrape the open sky.

"How far out are we?" Eris asks. I imagine her sitting cross-legged between my eyes, gaze purposely turned away from the windows, though she would be livid if she knew I had a slight suspicion of her acrophobia.

"Are you bored?" I ask, glancing over her question. Godolia has not yet broken the horizon, but the train tracks are becoming more frequent. It should be any moment now. From this height, they are reduced to threads that stitch the desert into pale red polygons.

"No." A pause. "That would be kind of . . . like—"

"Sadistic?"

I practically hear her scowl deepen. "I was going to say unsavory."

"You are an acquired taste."

"You little—" she starts, her jacket crinkling as she rises to her feet. I feel a slight vibration: her stepping onto the glass mat.

My wings stutter only for a moment, but Eris immediately

begins a vivid string of curses that overthrow the blaring of the jets, signifying her loss of footing.

"That's not fair!" she manages.

My lips twitch. "You are aware that I cannot see you, right?"

I look away from the tracks and toward the point where the sky meets the earth.

"Eris?"

"What, Glitch?"

"Why are you here? There is really no reason to be."

"Wow, okay," she huffs. Then, after a few moments, when she realizes that I am waiting for a viable reply, she sighs. "Did you think I would miss seeing this? I'm here for the best spot in the house."

I wiggle my toes as I absorb her words, reminding myself of the solidness that rests beneath me, rather than the weightless sensation of the soles of my feet dangling into the open air.

"Full circle," I murmur.

"What?"

"We escaped together. We return together. This is closing a cycle."

"We're not closing anything," she muses. "We're burning it to its roots."

The sun is pinned to the center of the sky, marking midday. The parade should be in full swing by now. Although Heavensday is the most celebrated event of the year—and the holiest, originally meant to give thanks to the Gods who allowed the world to complete another cosmic revolution—at the Academy, the students were still confined to their floor like every other day.

We were allowed our own party, though, with delicate lights strung above the simulations' wing, a degree of leniency from our set diets. I liked stealing sweets. Sugar-glazed fruit tarts, pink and yellow songpyeon with sweet sesame centers, fried rice cakes drizzled with honey, truffles with candied petals—all hauled back to my room to gorge on until I felt sick.

A bitter child then with a horrible sweet tooth. I am not much different now. The thought makes me smile.

Colonel Tether was always far below my feet, enjoying the warm glow of the gold oak tree statues in the courtyard. That was the main event of the students' party: watching the festivities below with wide, desirous eyes whenever the smog was kind enough to give a view, free of the instructors' cold supervision. Marveling over Windup after Windup that stood proudly on the bordering streets, and whispering excitingly that they, too, would one day be within an arm's length of the Zeniths. I imagined the same, alone in my room, licking the syrup from my sticky hands.

One day, I would be given the honor of attending the Heavensday Parade, and I would snap the neck of the first Zenith who was imbecilic enough to cross my path.

Oh, the peach tarts. Those were always my favorite.

"There," Eris murmurs, just as Godolia breaks the horizon. The black skyscrapers fragment the sky like tendrils of smoke. I shift the wings, soaring higher above the earth as giddiness clutches my chest.

I make sure to place myself far above the smog once it begins, pillowing over the factory district like a filthy quilt. I stop my breath altogether once I see the spires marking the walls, protruding outward like angular tombstones. Eris follows my example, ceasing the shuffling of her feet as the spires near. Their dark metal is puckered with darker openings, where the cannons will jut out like blisters when primed.

She mutters something under her breath, low and sharp, like a blade cutting smoke.

"What did you say?" I ask, expecting her to repeat something like a taunt on Godolia, or a prayer equal parts dark and sarcastic. Something to fuel the battle fervor.

"I said, there's that famed Godolia extravagance," she repeats, the barest ridiculing laugh trailing on her words. "Are there statues all the way around?"

"What statues?"

"Right up ahead."

"I do not—"

"Two o'clock. The one with wings. It's . . . it's massive."

And there it is—against the wall stretching between two of the spires, wings pinned wide and flat against the metal like a preserved moth. I can see why I missed it: The statue is pure black from its base to its head, blending against the barricade nearly seamlessly, save for the harsher way the light glints off its sculpted angles. In fact, it seems that there are no smooth curves to it whatsoever, each edge pointed, feathers and fingers slashed in peaks.

The humanoid form makes me think that it must be sculpted in the likeness of one of the infinite deities, and I almost laugh, picturing them pasted all along the outside of the city. As if they would condone the mass-produced imitations manufactured within, and past that, seek to protect them.

But of course there are no Gods here, good or bad, protective or vicious. There are only brutal people and their brutal toys, preying on those lacking in their own brutality.

Then there are no more thoughts of deities in my head, and only fear—cold and vivid and feral—pounding like gunfire in my ears, winding tight around my throat as I come to a dead stop.

Because in front of me, the statue's head has turned.

It meets my eyes.

Its red matches mine.

Eris sucks in a breath. "That's—"

"An Archangel."

I force power into the jets, soaring upward, higher and higher above the earth. The spires and the factories dotting the ground shrink to pinpricks, but the Archangel stays the same size, peeling off from its stasis and rising after me. It's quicker; a darker, perfect echo of Jenny's best efforts, mismatched parts nonexistent, and panic rises like an ocean in my chest.

"Sona—"

"Hang on to something."

I dart forward before the Archangel can reach my altitude, flying directly over the wall and into the city. The smog stretches below, expanding into the misted horizon, the tips of skyscrapers like fingers, reaching up, up, up.

"What are you doing?" Eris screams.

"We are doing this," I say through gritted teeth. "The Academy falls today."

The hairs on the back of my neck prickle, and below, pressed against the smog, are two winged silhouettes. There should only be mine.

It's right above me.

The shadow moves, clawed hands reaching down, down, down. It is reaching for my wing.

I tuck in my wings, and we plummet like a stone. My real

feet lose purchase, and a thud sounds from my left, followed by Eris's cry. We plunge into the smog. My vision goes dark.

The light pours in all at once, too fast, a flood of wicked glints. I realize what it is too late—the shimmering gloss of a skyscraper, and it is all I can do to throw my arms across my face before the impact. Pain, bright and shocking, immediately embeds itself in a hundred slashes across my body. My right eye is cracked, I can feel it, a rooting agony in the form of a spider's web.

I push it all away, and then push myself away from the building. Miraculously, it does not collapse, my shattered imprint thrown across a dozen stories of it, glass giving way to a cragged mess of concrete floors and iron support beams.

Amid the large fragments of glass, the Archangel lands in the street behind me, its wings untucking, relaxing.

Specks of people scatter on the street below, but the few blocks that separate us have been abandoned midfestivities. Street carts that I know sell everything from silk kimonos to paper masks to self-igniting sparklers stand abandoned. Hidden speakers must line the sidewalks, because the faintest bit of music trickles by weakly.

I face the Archangel and raise my chin. It stands still, regarding me evenly. *It can't help but steal a glance.* A dry laugh unfurls from my throat. Even now, when I am no longer small, when there is panic at my feet. They will always think I am insignificant, won't they?

Just another girl from the Badlands, from yet another massacred town. What a poor, pitiful barbarian, the girl who does not worship this place.

But I do not care that they do not see me. I already have people who matter who do.

They will burn blind, but burn nonetheless.

"Eris. Please tell me you're alive."

A groan. Relief breaks across my skin in a single, dizzying wave. I imagine the roll of her shoulders, shaking away this setback like all the rest.

"You going to fight that thing, Glitch?" she asks, breathing labored.

"I do not have much choice. But I need something from you."

"What?"

"Some help."

"Ha." A pause. "Oh. I really don't want to do that."

I look toward her voice, dropping my eyes to her height.

"I know you can't see me; stop staring. I hate it when you do that. How do you do that?" she mutters, her feet shuffling—her step is slightly off, I can tell. "Do—should I count down, or just go ahead?"

"Just—"

A striking pain, lively almost, and I cannot stop a cry from tearing free as cold roots and shatters the glass of my eye. It is all I can do not to fall to my knees. My right-side vision winks out instantly.

"Shit. You okay?"

I bite the inside of my cheek. "I'll get you in range."

I charge forward, my steps fluid and effortless—Jenny really did a fantastic job. But I am only a block away when I realize that the Archangel has not moved forward, or even taken up a guarding stance. And I realize why the barest moment before it is too late.

The missile goes soaring past my head, and I hear the instant it buries itself in the building behind me, glass and iron and concrete decimated in a shrieking flash of light. The fury rises fast, ravenous, eating away the choke of fear, of hesitation, and I barely think before my own missile screams across the air, traced by a dark slash of smoke. The Archangel twists out of its way, as expected, right into the path of my second missile, which catches it at the crook of its left wing.

Black vapor shrouds the street, but through it, I catch that glint of red eyes. They look unfazed. And then they are too close, boring into me, and a taloned fist is swinging out of the smoke, colliding with my side. I let it, let myself be forced into another building, let the destruction swell around me, and reach forward and grapple into the darkness. My claws find a hook, and I curl and pull, ripping the Archangel from its concealment.

We are face-to-face, brow-to-brow, and Eris is at my side, muttering, "Atta girl."

Cold flushes across my real skin, raw and clean and sharp. Light floods from my broken eye and swallows the sight of the other in a burst of white.

The first glimpse I get when I spiral back is of frost against metal, its delicate crystalline design raking across the perfectly sculpted brow of the Archangel.

The second is my fist cracking against it. The metal does not fracture. A growl of frustration vibrates my teeth. I raise my fist again.

The third is a neat row of black holes opening up, one by one, along the top of the Archangel's left wing. A flash of light within each void. One by one. And the rest seems to happen all at once.

I am on my back, looking up at a veiled sky, punctured by the fingers of skyscrapers. Pain grips my chest and spirals down my arms, the metal scorched and steaming from the impact of the rockets. I smell smoke, and somewhere close to me yet too, too distant, Eris is heaving, coughs scraping and violent. On instinct, I reach out in her direction, and the ugly, taloned hand rises to touch the clouds.

The Archangel descends. It does not use the missiles this time. It brings its boot directly down on my stomach, and the metal crumples, snapping inward. With the second kick, I am genuinely shocked that my real ribs do not break along with it. Black dots spark across my vision, the negative image of a sky filled with stars.

They are torn away in the next moment by another sudden, brilliant flash of light. The Archangel recoils back a step, frost clawing against a section of its left hip. When it tries to regain balance, another bolt flies free, injecting into the thigh, and the asphalt of the street cracks as the mecha collapses onto its knees.

Eris coughs once more, and then in a string of lovely, detrimentally rage-slurred words, snarls, "Send it back to the twin hells, Glitch."

I bury my hand directly into the building beside me, glass giving way to the concrete infrastructure instantly, a hold to heave myself up with. I flick my wrist, thoughts ignited with my intentions, and the foreign body obeys, dissecting the air with a stream of missiles. They make direct impact in the Archangel's thigh, shoulder, chest, three of them bursting apart across its arm sheath, thrown over its eyes at the last possible second.

I am on my feet, hand around its wrist, tearing the defense away. My other palm curls around the nape of its neck, and I bring my knee into its ribs, once, twice. This time, when the valves across its wing tips gape open, I am gone before the flashes of light, leaping straight up into the air. Flame and smoke explode across the building beneath me, and I do not hesitate before feeding it, sending another round of missiles into the hellsfire below.

"Is it dead?" Eris breathes, voice hoarse. "Please tell me that the motherf—"

A hand reaches out of the cloud of smoke, talons curling around the edge of a nearby building, and the Archangel hauls itself into our view. Its head swivels, searching the skies.

I do not give it a chance to spread its wings. I turn and force power to the jets, and the landscape smears beneath us.

"Damn it," I say through gritted teeth. There is some fault along my left wing now; I feel a stutter in its speed. I can only hope that we inflicted enough damage that the other Archangel falters, too.

"That's the Academy up ahead, right?" Eris asks. Her words sound labored.

"Are you all right? Is the air getting too thin?"

"I'll be all right when it's done," she snaps.

And there it is, outlined in gold, a gilded target. We are about ten blocks away, and up ahead, in their proud stances, tower the jewels of the Heavensday Parade: Windups upon Windups upon Windups, shoulder to shoulder in the streets touching the Academy, good soldiers set to march. Unwound, and laughably harmless. Like Jenny said, they are nothing but eye candy for the masses, the people standing outside the roped-off areas, gawking up with eyes wide, fantasizing that maybe someday they could hold that much power, too.

The Windups surround the Academy in a solid two-block radius around its campus. I reach their outer edge and slow to a stop.

I rip away these pitiful, worshipping fantasies, relieve the masses of their ignorance.

I save them all little by little, missile by missile released on the machines standing below, hellsfire by glorious hellsfire.

Godolia and the Windups are not invincible. They are not Godslike. They are not blameless of the pain and suffering they have spread across the world.

But I realize that I do not care if they do not realize this, that the people here today may tell the next generations that this was an unprovoked attack, that a Badlands girl so blessed by the Academy had no cause for such barbarity.

Because now I am in control.

Because people I have loved in the past have been hurt by this nation, and the people I love in the present have been hurt by it again, and because now I can do something to stop it.

Because you choose sides in war and I chose the one that makes me feel human, and this I will not apologize for.

I am violent. I am awful. But every vicious thing about me is mine in its entirety.

I will not die as theirs.

The Windups fall. The Academy nears, surrounded by an inferno of cracked metal and slain deities. The people are specks, and somewhere within them, the Zeniths are indistinct faces in the panic. They look for a way out past the flames. Past cracks of dark earth pressing in from above, the people around them too shocked to move.

I need to aim low, let the brilliance of Jenny's magma serum spread deep. I hover directly above the gold-foil trees, leaves glittering cheerfully in the rush of smoke swirling around the campus.

And all at once there is silence.

There are no more screams. There is no more hum. The pain and rage part ways for a veil of perfect calm.

Eris screams. All light becomes threaded with darkness.

I reach out—I do not know whether it is for her or because of the incredible pain that has sprouted along my left wing—and the sun comes into view as we are pulled above the smog. My form contorts as my wing tip snaps, a shriek barreling out of my throat. Without thinking, I throw my head back, vaguely aware of my real body losing purchase on the glass mat. A dull thump sounds to my left.

But I glimpse the Archangel, so black and jagged that against the sky, it simply looks like a part of the heavens has been torn away, and I meet its eyes.

I burn its sight with mine, then drop my gaze, and release the last missile directly downward.

Its descent seems almost lazy, cutting through the clouds. Anticlimactic. Quiet. *How many have I just killed?*

The Archangel's talons curl around the back of my neck, its heel on my spine. My hands search for metal and find only sky. Inside my head, someone is laughing and sobbing all at once. Eris is unconscious. It must be me.

Have we won? Is it over?

I am not good, and dear *Gods*—isn't it funny that it hardly matters?

A pressure, and then a pain like no other as the Archangel takes my wing away, and then lets me drop to the earth, into the city I set aflame.

CHAPTER FORTY

ERIS

Heavensday

Today is not as fun as I thought it was going to be.

"Come on," I mutter, picking my way through wires and glass, through the fog in my head, the slightly concerning pang in my ribs every time I draw a breath. "Come on, Sona, we have to go."

I kneel over her crumpled form. Cords tangle around her arms and neck, twisting the skin.

"Wake up," I murmur as I untangle her. "There isn't time for this."

I wipe my cheeks with the back of my hand, and curl over myself, forehead on her stomach.

"Come on," I mumble into her shirt. "Come on, you aren't doing this to me. You aren't leaving me here alone. Get up. We have to go home."

She's not moving. It doesn't make sense. Why isn't she moving?

"Wake up!" I scream. "Godsdamn it, wake up!"

Oh. I'm an idiot.

I wrap a hand around the cords and yank, popping them all out at once. Sona sits straight up, eyes springing wide. I lean forward and snatch her chin, tilting her face side to side to make sure she hasn't gone brain-dead.

"We are alive," she states.

"Seems like it."

"Oh. Shit."

"Yeah. Shit." I chuckle a bit. "Guess Nova was right, huh? There really was a boss battle."

"We lost."

I release her face. "Ha. Well, we—oh. You brought your sword."

"You knew this. Is that not a good thing? Since we are probably going to have to fight in about thirty seconds?"

"Uh-huh. But it's probably only going to be useful to us if you remove it from your *Godsdamn leg*."

The sword is slanted at an angle toward her body, the hilt resting on top of her thigh, several inches of the blade swallowed by her flesh, and the tip bursting free right before her hip. Sona sighs, inconvenienced, and pulls it free. She shrugs off her Valkyrie jacket and tears away the sleeves, tying them around the punctured skin.

She looks up at me. "You are injured."

"You just pulled a sword out of your leg. Please shut up."

She rises to her feet, far more gracefully than she should be able to. The smugness on her face makes me bark a laugh, and whatever is wrong with my ribs chuckles along with me.

Outside, there are sirens and running feet. Red light filters in from above through the one viable eye, and I realize that I definitely must be dreaming. Which is fantastic, because I really do need the sleep.

And then Sona asks calmly, "What do we do?" and the rigidness of that calm sets my teeth on edge. I'm awake. And there's virtually no way out of this.

"I'm going to take out as many of those bastards as I can," I hear myself say. "Go down screaming and kicking and everything in between. I may be going to hells, but I'm going to damn well bring some of it here first."

Her bottom lip trembles, the barest bit.

"I have a plan," I say.

"Oh?" she murmurs, laughing softly. "Oh no."

She laughs again when I finish explaining it.

"What?" I snap. "It's not terrible."

The corners of her mouth twitch before she turns away. "You do not have the face of a damsel in distress."

I scowl, which probably just amplifies her point. "You distress me plenty. Maybe that'll be good enough."

Sona gets to her spot in the shadows and looks over her shoulder, her smirk as piercing as it is slight.

I kneel in the base of the head, hands pressed to the floor. There are footsteps ringing across the metal, and then Godolia soldiers teem at the sockets above, maggots come to get their fill of a corpse. Ropes are unspooled, and bodies are dropping and shouting, and I'm shouting, too, "Please, don't shoot! I'm cooperating, I'm unarmed!"

I catch bits of images as they gather around: Godolia soldiers in black bodysuits, a few Pilots in the mix with harshly glinting eyes, and the glaze of a gun as it swings into the side of my head.

I give myself one generous moment to stop the world from tilting before raising my eyes again. A fractured chink in the side of the Archangel's head acts as a small porthole, a mouth of gray light. A food cart has toppled over and spilled its steaming contents onto the concrete. A shoe with gray laces lies on its side on top of a gutter grate. Paper banners have been torn from their holds and lie plastered against the asphalt by a thousand panicked footsteps.

And then the light splinters as Sona peels from her position. Her blade flashes in her hand, and at the point where a shriek and an arc of blood simultaneously split through the air, I coil my hand around the nearest ankle.

I rise as he falls, skin and bone eaten by frost.

A whisper of bullets cuts past my ear, and I twist, gathering my energy in my palm and releasing it in the direction of the gunfire. The blast hits the soldier square in the collarbone, her scream extinguishing almost as soon as it erupts. Sona ducks behind the upright corpse, and the bullets that follow her movement pucker the frozen flesh into particulates. I locate the shooter and dive for his base, smoothing a hand up his chest as we both fall. Once we hit the ground, I'm holding nothing but a body. A sensation equal parts revulsion and satisfaction rocks through me as I kick away.

The fight comes in sensations. Ricocheting bullets vibrate the floor beneath my toes. Cold air prickles gooseflesh across my skin. My hair glides against my cheeks as I go airborne; my breath hitches in my lungs as I descend, followed by the shock of my teeth biting down as I collapse onto another soldier. A warm slickness pastes my shirt to my stomach.

I am so damn good at this.

So very good at anger.

A back presses against my own, fingertip dragging across her blade. Her wrist flicks, speckling red across the floor.

She breathes something low, or maybe she laughs, dark and dangerous and lovely. Then she is gone, too.

When I turn to search for the next fight, a blistering spike of pain explodes against my side.

I manage to get one more shot off, somehow hitting the soldier despite seeing his movements only in my blurred peripheral vision, and then collapse onto all fours. I press a hand against my right ribs, vaguely noting that my palm comes away bloody.

"Hey, Glitch?" I call meekly, trying to focus on my breath. It hisses inside my chest like a broken wire.

No response, besides a few other screams and more empty husks colliding with the floor. Gunfire. The ping of bullets. A figure with hushed footsteps flickering all over the room, vanishing at each taken life and materializing in the wake of another, never hovering in one place for more than a half instant.

I must be losing it.

A sudden stillness, corrupted only by the stuttering of my chest.

The figure descends, a soft hand wrapping under my arms and gently tugging me back onto my heels. There's a slight pressure as her chin graces the top of my hair.

"Can you turn off the gloves for a moment?" Sona murmurs.

I grind my teeth and oblige, and she takes my arm and loops it behind her neck. Black spots surge across my vision as she hauls me to my feet, and we begin to make for the base of the Archangel's head.

"Where are we going?" I groan, pitifully mindful that she's carrying most of my weight.

She laughs. I feel it sing through my skin. "I have no idea."

Her feet slow, and I pick my head up. The light doesn't reach very far into the neck, but I can see that Jenny's modesty was well placed: the Archangel's innards really do look like shit. From the slim area that is visible, bundles of wires are tangled like cobwebs across the air, and the iron bars crisscross haphazardly between the spaces, the bolts sealing them mismatched in both size and color. And, since the Archangel has been thrown onto its back, the ladder stretches before us like a pathetic excuse for a bridge, splaying both into and over what seems like an infinite chasm.

"How the hells did Jenny get this thing to fly?" I mutter.

We both hear it at the same time: another round of shouting and the heart-thumping march of rubber-soled boots across the metal above. The next wave. I suppress my cringe as Sona releases me.

"Crawl," she orders, nodding at the ladder.

I place my knees on the side rails of the ladder and pull myself onto the next rung. We work our way toward the feet, toward the dark. My thoughts rabbit around in my skull. *Where are we going? Nowhere. We're not going anywhere. Ha. There's no way out. There is really no way out this time.*

I don't know if it's the panic that makes me glance back at her, but I'm glad I do. A soldier stands in the hollow of the neck, his firearm raised to the back of her head.

"Duck!" I yell, and the first bullet pings past us and into the abyss.

The agony of whatever ruptured inside my rib cage dulls, and adrenaline blurs both time and pain in a way I can only call *helpful*. Next thing I know, Sona and I have rolled away from the ladder and onto a support beam, across it, and under a curtain of wires. My back presses against the Archangel's side, and I make myself small, throwing my hands over my mouth to silence my labored breathing.

The beam is just wide enough to hold us both side by side, but Sona crouches in front of me, sword freed from her belt and one hand wrapped around a bolt for support. Her blade is positioned so that it'll sever the next person who dares emerge from the copper drapes, and maybe afterward she'll leap and manage to take out a second. And then . . .

And then she'll be peppered with bullet holes and list over the side, down, down, down.

This was not the plan. What *was* the plan?

Get out. Fight our way through, get her plugged into the first Windup we come across. Assuming any were spared. Shit. Glitch did a good job. She did a fantastic, devastating job, and the world severely owes her for it, but it has a fucked-up sense of humor, so instead it's just going to kill her.

Or . . . maybe not.

Because she's priceless.

Because she's got those Mods all wrapped up inside her flesh like a present, and that's worth something to them.

"Sona."

"Be quiet!"

"Just stop."

"What?"

"I said just stop!"

"How can you say that?" she hisses, whipping her head around. Her features are pinned in a snarl, the fire of her left eye carved down to a crescent. "Take out as many as we can; that is what *you* said. And that is what I am going to do."

"I said that's what *I'm* going to do. But you . . . you're their investment. You're valuable. They might take you alive."

Now she whirls on me. The light of her eye draws an arc through the air, and she slams her free hand directly next to my ear. The blow hums in the metal at my back, and she's so close and so damn pretty, and so furious. All I can think to myself, because she's scared off any semblance of eloquent thought in my head, is *This sucks.*

"How can you say that?" she screams, ignoring her own advice to keep quiet. "I am *not* theirs!"

There. My fury, my recklessness, stitched onto a different face. I had suffocated within my own fear, and I tried to remedy it with another punch, another battle cry, another violent thought. Not now. Now, I lift my gaze, and I draw a breath.

"No," I snap, with just as much ferocity. "But you're one of mine, and that damn well means something. It means everything."

"I belong to no one," she snarls. "I am not anyone's—"

"But doesn't it *feel* like it, Sona?" I reach up and place a bloody hand on her cheek. My vision is blurring. I'm spiraling. "It was unplanned, and maybe it was a mistake, but it *happened*, didn't it?" *We haven't lost everything. We can keep going.* "Doesn't it feel like we belong to each other?"

And then—silence.

I wait for it to collapse. I wait for it to splinter apart, to drown under the thud of my heartbeat, because stillness never liked me much, because there's always too much of the fight left for the good parts to hover.

But the moment doesn't recoil from me.

She holds the quiet in place, her hand on my ribs now. When she kisses me, she kisses me slow. Like we have all the time in the world. Like we're safe on the couch back in the common room, hearth breathing heat all over us, nothing to do but watch the sun bleed from the sky.

I need her for so much. To dance terribly. To read my books. To keep the ash in my mouth at bay, to keep me blushing and breathing and fighting. To come home.

I need her to live.

I am a Gearbreaker.

When my back's against a wall, I go *through* the wall.

My glove roars to life behind my back, forcing the serum into the metal supporting my spine. I bring my legs underneath me and shove my shoulders into the wall, and it shatters like glass.

The free fall lasts only a second, but I still get a clear view of the shock that breaks across Sona's features, and oh, it's stitched into place by an incredible, detrimental hurt.

Every strand of breath in my lungs rushes out in a single gasp the instant my back collides with the concrete below, and Sona miraculously catches herself before she can smash on top of me. Something warm and wet pastes my hair to the nape of my neck.

"You didn't," she screams down at me, miles away. "Eris, you *didn't!*"

But her attention does not stay on me for long. Dark figures emerge into my speckled peripheral vision, seizing her flailing form. Once, just once, she wrenches free, screeching incomprehensibly, and the stench of blood tinges the air again. More hands descend, tethering her limbs, tearing the sword from her grasp. I reach for it. They're not taking me alive.

A boot kicks it away, and I snap my sight up to find it was hers. She stares down with such a palpable fury twisting in her eyes that I flinch.

"You're not leaving me here," Sona shrieks. She rears her head back, curls flying, and breaks a soldier's nose with a harrowing crack. She kicks the blade farther away as more hands land on her. "You are not leaving me here alone!"

Frost bleeds from me, spills from my palms and devours asphalt and deity and flesh. Dripping serum, red slicking my neck and jaw, I make it onto my side, and then onto my arms, lifting my head.

"You'll win the next one," I rasp, her screams clawing at me. Ice scrapes the pavement, crystals rising up like closing teeth. "When you get out of here and find Jenny—you've really got it next time."

"Oh, you can *rot*," she spits as they haul her back, both eyes bright with rage. They got her; she knows it, and she's laughing, and it's terrible. "Wither, love, absolutely *wither*."

Planning on it, I think tiredly, because truly, I didn't get enough sleep last night. I have also lost a lot of blood. It's all adding up to something strange. I'm not on the asphalt, unspooling ice—

I'm home, and little. On the floor, angry as twin hells. I missed my stance, and Jenny shoved me down again. She bends over me, dark hair in my face, bouncing on the pads of her feet.

"You're good, you're good," she's chanting, grin wild. She offers her hand and I bat it away. "See? You're fine. Get up or they're going to get you. You've got ice in your veins, little Frostbringer—are you really just going to sit there and let yourself freeze? No? Good. Let's keep going."

CHAPTER FORTY-ONE

SONA

Did you kill her?

No. I . . . am not sure. I think she killed me.

Did you kill her?

Did she kill me?

It's dark.

She killed me.

I knew she would. She hit her mark this time. I stood still for her, too, just like I said I would—

"Did you kill her?" someone says. "Sona. *Wake the hells up.*"

I blink. There is a light, a cold table beneath me. We spent time here, before. We left, I am sure of it. I roll my eyes around the room. Shackles hold fast around my wrists. Someone stands over me, hands braced on the metal edge.

We left.

Did it even matter?

I murmur her name, but my throat is cotton and the word comes out as nothing.

"Answer me, Sona."

My sight finds a hold above.

Jole stares at me with the eyes that my weakness had allowed to become familiar. But the look in them is new, a bright, hardened fury festering within. I force myself to lift my chin.

"Do it," I rasp. "Whatever they sent you in here to do. Go ahead."

"Where is Rose, Sona?" Jole asks.

I do not answer.

"Did you kill her?"

My glare stutters, just for an instant, but he catches it. Suddenly he springs forward, a hand threading over my scalp and twisting through my hair. Another piece of him that I am familiar with, the hand that would squeeze my shoulders or pat my cheek affectionately. And now, the hand that slams my head onto the tabletop.

My sight smears. I feel sick. *Did it even matter?* It had to. Is that not an answer?

"Did you kill her?!" he shouts, though it does not sound like a question any longer. He tightens his grip. "Say it! Say you killed her!"

"I killed her," I say, watching the glaze of tears bubble onto his eyelashes. My voice is a whisper. "I killed her."

The barest flinch, and then, "Apologize."

"What?"

"Apologize!" Jole screams.

"To . . . Rose?"

"To Rose? To *Rose*?!" he gasps in disbelief. "To your Gods-damn friend, Sona! To the girl who showed you nothing but kindness, who defended you, who cared for you! Who would have killed for you!"

I am a Gearbreaker, I want to say. *Rose was loyal to Godolia. Rose deserved to die.*

But something burns inside my chest, and it constricts my breath and makes the room go hazy. Heat radiates off his cheeks and his tears and his words, and all I can find myself saying, in nothing but a mere croak, is, "I am not sorry."

And I know I should mean it. I know I should. But it was Rose. Rose, sweet as her name. Who was born entangled in the glory of a place I loathe.

Jole lifts my head, slams it back downward. The room tilts.

"Apologize!" he yells, tears dripping off his face and onto my cheeks. Gods, I hope that that is what is happening, at least, that the salt I taste does not come from my own eyes. "Tell her you're sorry!"

I bare my teeth, and I bite back the memories of her—her smile, her curls, her bell-like voice. She was never my Rose. She was Godolia's. They all are.

"I am not sorry that I cut her throat," I growl, refusing to look away at the shock that seeps across his features.

"Stop," Jole snaps, but it comes out in a sob. He tries to press a hand over my mouth, but I pull my chin away.

"One dead Pilot saves hundreds of Badlands lives, and so I will happily kill thousands more, starting with you if you do not take your *fucking hands off me*!"

"There is no reason to be profane, Miss Steelcrest."

There is someone standing in the doorway, someone I do not recognize.

I do not have to. Because on the lapel of his black suit, there is a tree. Its bare branches are woven tight, layered like intertwined fingers, and below, the roots spread thinly, entangled with the cosmos. A long time ago, the Aether Tree was the ceremonial symbol of the Gods, said to be inscribed on the gates of the heavens. But when Godolia came to rise, the Zeniths claimed it as their official emblem.

"*No*," I growl, anger and shock singeing my cheeks. "You are supposed to be dead. You are all supposed to be dead!"

"Mr. Westlin," the Zenith continues in a cool voice, ignoring me, "I believe you accomplished what you came here to do, yes? The Academy thanks you for your assistance."

Jole releases me immediately, but he leans in close, lips by my temple.

"It's all true, what they say," he whispers, so full of poison, so sure of his words. "You're monsters, every last one of you."

He stalks away. I close my eyes. I am exhausted, and there is no need to look.

"Where is the Frostbringer?" I snarl.

"Miss Steelcrest."

"Tell me where she is."

"Could we have a proper introduction? I was raised to shake hands, so this is awkward, but I could at least give you my name before we begin."

And I was raised to flinch in his presence. Forget the Windups, the Zeniths are Godolia's true deities. And unlike the mechas, their power is not false. Five of them in control at any given time. Five people who hold the world in their hands, be it their choice to nurture it, protect it, or, if they fancied hearing the sound of everything, *everything* splintering apart, simply tighten their grip.

But he cannot be much older than I am.

"So polite," I murmur. "You are just a child. You were not done being raised."

Just another kid. Just like me. It's laughable and heartbreaking, and it makes me ache for the end of this time, this age of children inheriting wars. *Could we just stop?* I want to ask.

Could you want to act your age and unmake this brutality within you? Could you know we are too young to feel so cruel?

"And yet, I have inherited my title forty years earlier than expected. You were . . ." A pause, a hitch of breath. Is he it? The last Zenith? "You were very thorough."

"There is only you left?"

"Yes."

"Apologies," I say. "I meant to kill you as well."

"You got close." I open my eyes to find his hand running along his wrist, pulling up his sleeve. A white bandage is wound up his arm, clean and soft, the visible skin so close in color that it makes him look sickly, veins shining through in dark rivers. His head tilts slightly as he regards the bindings, and I realize a medical patch has been set at the nape of his neck as well.

I burned him.

Was he conscious for all of it?

Did he watch them all crumble, just as I watched them all suffocate?

He cocks his head to the side. Black hair pulls back into a small knot at the back of his head; pretty, almost delicate features scattered between angular cheekbones. I have the excruciating realization that he looks a lot like how I would picture an older Xander. If Xander had ever gotten the chance to grow older.

"Why?" he asks.

"Why what?"

"Why the excess of it?"

I ignore the ridiculous question. "How many did I end up killing? Zeniths, subordinates, colonels? Bystanders? Might as well count the bystanders."

His mouth contorts. "We have not finished counting. You managed to collapse a few dozen stories with that last missile."

I cannot pinpoint what hits me first—the triumph, or the revulsion, or simply the exhaustion, the fight dribbling out of me, because what could be left after this? Maybe we did just fine, just enough, after all. One Zenith, and he is a teenager, alone. This nation has such vast weight. It is not a spectacular collapse, but a collapse nonetheless.

"Where is the Frostbringer?" I ask again.

"You two are an extraordinary case," the Zenith muses. "A Pilot and a Gearbreaker."

"*I* am a Gearbreaker," I snarl, and he laughs. The warmth of it is offset by the blankness of his eyes.

"You're a Gearbreaker," he repeats, a note of amusement in his tone. He is holding something in his hand, sends it slowly rolling through his fingertips. An ink pen. "Tell me, Bellsona: How could the renegades have possibly taken such a liking to you?"

"I have a lovely personality."

He laughs again. "No, no. I mean, Gearbreakers hate all Pilots. Zeniths. The Academy. Godolia. Everything about us. How exactly did you defy that? How did they, after everything they've been taught, accept the fact that you are simply not human?"

I lift my chin. "I am human."

The Zenith stops twirling his pen, takes a step forward, and drives the tip into my hand, straight through to the glass of the table. Blood ruptures from the wound and wets my hip. He does not flinch. And, of course, neither do I. Satisfied with the lack of a reaction, his smirk deepens.

"Martyrs are such a tricky business, aren't they, Miss Steelcrest?" he murmurs, inches away, and I wish he smelled of smoke, of singed flesh. But there's nothing besides the fresh tinge of salve on his wounds. He is already healing. "Badlands people . . . they feed on hope more than anything else. The Gearbreakers provided them that. As much as they were allowed, anyway."

I keep my features schooled, but my heartbeat kicks awake in my chest.

"The agreement was, simply, to tread lightly. Take those dime-a-dozen Windups—the Berserkers, the Arguses, the Phoenixes. Take some Pilots too dull to evolve into our more formidable deities, and give the people just enough hope to keep going. In their heads, they are rebels. Voxter was to leave our greater Gods alone to do their good work. No direct attack was to be made on Godolia, and his barbarians would be allowed their scraps of hope. In exchange, we would not slaughter every last Badlands soul in his army."

A bitter look flares across his features, but he stifles it quickly. The smirk twists into a smile, cold as tundra.

"And then, you. By some feat of heavens or hells, Voxter did not slaughter you as soon as he laid eyes on you, thought it would be a spectacle to have his Gearbreakers toy with an Archangel skeleton. Only when Jenny Shindanai *somehow* managed to get it to fly did he realize his mistake, realize that his Gearbreakers would be just another dust spot in the desert if it ever reached Godolia. He begged for the Zeniths to fix it, and they sent a few Phoenixes, deeming the problem solved. Except Voxter had blundered that as well. By the time he bothered to send word that Heavensday remained the target, well . . . the prototype Archangel wasn't ready until it was almost too late."

The pen rises from my hand, blood welling in a small pool. I could almost laugh. I realize I want to laugh, and so I do, and the sound spasms from me like it loathes being ripped free, but I keep pulling it out, like thread on a fraying sleeve. Jenny Shindanai is going to kill Voxter. She is going to kill him, and it will be horrifying and so precisely, brilliantly violent, and I am going to miss it.

He waits patiently for me to be done, and I roll my head back to him, smiling dizzily.

"My predecessors were fools, Miss Steelcrest," he says softly. This does get a reaction, surprise flitting across my features before I can stifle it. I never expected another Zenith to even consider the possibility, much less say it aloud. "Too merciful. Too empathetic about the whims of the people on the losing side, so blind to the fact that every single one of them, if given the opportunity, would let this nation crumble to ash. Like we are not the bridge to the heavens, the one pure strand of this mortal coil."

You fanatic, I think to myself, *you never even stood a chance, did you?*

"When will you kill me?"

The Zenith cocks his head to the side again, as if surprised by the question.

"My name is Enyo."

"I do not care."

"Miss Steelcrest, I am not going to kill you."

I look to the ceiling, let my vision drown under the light. My hate has carved furrows in me; it has cleaved a path up my throat where the words can follow effortlessly, but they come out tiredly, because I am tired of them, so exhausted of this anger without end.

"I would let this place crumble," I murmur. "I would let it all turn to ash."

I want it to be a burial ground, deep as hells; I want the soil to breathe and scream, and I want so much pain here. I want to take Eris's hand and to dance on this scorched earth until we are senseless, until we can forget we made this grave. Because the options were *run* or *fight*, *lose everything* or *win something*; there was little choice to begin with.

"It does not matter," Enyo says. "Because you are not one of them."

"This place . . ." I shake my head. "This place is so fucking delusional."

Enyo waves his hand dismissively. "To an extent. But with *you*, I have complete clarity. Natural skill, Bellsona . . . now, *that* is rare. We are not going to allow it to simply be thrown down the nearest incinerator or collect dust in a cell. As for that hatred and disgust . . . those are trivial feelings. They can be redirected." A pause. "Corrupted."

My stomach violently recoils at the word.

"The corruption process relies on pain," I manage. "It does not work on Pilots. It will not work on me."

The Zenith gives me a long look, and for a strange moment I get the sense that it is laced with something akin to disappointment.

"You are a Pilot, Bellsona," Enyo says. "Just like every machine, parts of you can be turned off and on. Your eyesight, your basic bodily functions, hells, even your taste buds. That includes your ability to feel pain. It takes a mere button press. And I, as a Zenith, happen to have every switch at my disposal."

I suffocate my burst of fear by forcing poison into my words. "I would think torture is beneath your status."

This time, the look that sparks in his eyes stays pinned. I was right. It was grief. Horrific, soul-wrenching grief. I cling to it like fingers do the shore after a shipwreck.

"Correct again, Miss Steelcrest. But I insisted. After all . . ." The coy smile disintegrates. "You did kill my family."

Enyo raises his hand and snaps his fingers once. A scream tears free from my throat as pain—real and viciously bright—fragments across my right hand, biting across the raw flesh of the open wound.

"All right." Enyo sighs, letting his pen come to rest between his fingers. With his other hand, he gently rolls back my sleeve, tucking it neatly above my elbow. "Let's see if we can get those pesky feelings out, shall we?"

Layer by layer, he carves my gears away. Eventually, my screams dwindle to meek whimpers, and then I hear him work all too clearly. By the last one, all I have the energy to give is a slight twitch, useless against the iron restraints.

"Where is the Frostbringer?" I murmur, when I can remember something else besides this pain. Sometimes I slip away but still forget to ask. Sometimes I am so far away from all of this, back home; sometimes I am in a place that looks like this but is not. I know because my ribs move differently, and I breathe not to pretend but to brace myself, because my pulse is fast in my fingertips and I do not know why. I have had a heart before, but never one like this. She rolls her eyes. *Please, Glitch. Does it look like I scare easy?*

It's okay to be scared.

Then I come back, and I am leaking red, but so is the rest of the world. Nothing new, nothing new.

"Where is she?" I say, again, because we save each other, and I need to be saved.

Enyo's hand smooths over my forehead, warmth smearing my brow.

"My dear Pilot, we are going to accomplish such great things together. There is no need to worry. Take comfort." He breathes his words like a prayer. "Godolia is a merciful place."

ACKNOWLEDGMENTS

This was supposed to be a book about mecha sword fights and angry kids, but it ended up being more along the lines of a love story, as these things usually turn out. A rom-com with robots, if you will. If you read the whole book before reading these words you might absolutely despise me for saying that, but I think it's a little funny, and besides, that would mean you *did* read the whole book, and so you can detest me all you'd like, I have so much love for you, thank you for everything.

I have so many people in my life I have such fierce adoration for, and I have the paper to attempt to convey it, so here it goes:

To Kiva, my darling, the strawberry to my shortcake. You spectacular entity. Thank you for telling me to breathe. I'll slay dragons with you, dear, when this reality permits it, our names scrawled on our apartment mailbox, the bathtub in the middle of the kitchen, the cat that owns us pacing the rugs we've strewn all over the floorboards.

To Titan. I'm older, but you seem ancient sometimes, and you've taught me a lot about the world without even intending to. You were right when you said it comes in waves.

To Dad. You're a rock, and you have a weird sense of humor. I can't help but think the world would've pummeled me beyond repair already if I hadn't adopted from you a healthy sheen of sarcasm and the ability to stand my ground, and when I can't, you have my back. I'm a tough kid because of you. I hope you liked the robots.

To Mom. You like to think I chose you, but I think I was just lucky. How fortunate I am to have the kind of relationship I do with you, how vividly I feel it when I treat myself harshly and you say no one can talk about your daughter like that, when you say I deserve the world. You have no idea how much weight it holds, how I carry it with me wherever I go because I cannot always feel that way about myself, and it saves me.

And to both of my parents: Yes, my characters are parentless, but please don't read too much into it. There's a lot of love in the story, and that's the element you both really inspired. I cannot thank you enough for it.

To the team at Feiwel & Friends. *Gearbreakers* could not have had a better home. Emily, you have my unstinting gratitude for saying what needs to be said, for your sharp insistences and your passion, and because of you, I can truly say I am proud of my work. I'm so excited to see what comes next.

To Taj Francis and Mike Burroughs, the artist and designer of the incredibly kick-ass cover, respectfully, with complete and constant stupefaction.

To Weronika, for finding my story in the slush pile and pushing me to make it unflinching. You're a fighter, and I am so grateful for it.

To Kerstin, for your overwhelming enthusiasm and for all the warmth you share—it's truly gotten me through the tough bits.

To Ally and Alex, and Alex's electrons.

To Tashie, my publishing wife, whose characters would make good Gearbreakers because they always have a lot of heart.

To the wonderful roundtable group, Nicki, Eric, Daniel, Spencer, Chance, and Avery. You all leave me in awe with your abilities, your strange, lovely words.

And, with so much affection, to the LGBTQ+ readers. Don't let anyone try to tell you that you don't deserve grand stories with love that is staggering. My Gal Palz club darlings, Ginger, Emiri, Fiona, Judas, Nikki, Maria, Rebecca, Olivia, Kat, Andy, Ryan, Stella, Jennifer, Leanne, Ames, Lindsay, and Haley—that's right, I'm listing—my Gods, I'm so happy to be able to give this sapphic cyberpunk story to you. Words cannot express the magnitude of the joy you all bring into my life. Darlings, with endless affection, thank you so much.

Thank you for reading this Feiwel & Friends book.
The friends who made

GEARBREAKERS

possible are:

Jean Feiwel, Publisher
Liz Szabla, Associate Publisher
Rich Deas, Senior Creative Director
Holly West, Senior Editor
Anna Roberto, Senior Editor
Kat Brzozowski, Senior Editor
Dawn Ryan, Senior Managing Editor
Celeste Cass, Assistant Production Manager
Emily Settle, Associate Editor
Erin Siu, Associate Editor
Rachel Diebel, Assistant Editor
Foyinsi Adegbonmire, Editorial Assistant
Michael Burroughs, Senior Designer
Ilana Worrell, Senior Production Editor

Follow us on Facebook or visit us online at fiercereads.com.
Our books are friends for life.